The Road to Tuam

by

Brian Fleming

DORRANCE PUBLISHING CO., INC.
PITTSBURGH, PENNSYLVANIA 15222

Dorrance Publishing Co., Inc.
701 Smithfield Street
Pittsburgh, PA 15222
Visit our website at *www.dorrancebookstore.com*

ISBN: 978-1-4349-1820-8
eISBN: 978-1-4349-1740-9

To Ruth, my wife who, at different times and in different ways, kept both this book and its author alive.

Chapter One

The Ford Poplar

The dark grey Ford Poplar that turned into Upper O'Connell Street in Dublin and merged with an almost solid stream of traffic was neither very old nor very new, was neither sparkling clean nor in need of a good wash, and was being driven neither aggressively nor over cautiously. It was the sort of vehicle that, if seen at a used car auction or on a garage forecourt waiting to be sold, would neither have stood out at the time of inspection, nor be easily remembered later. Its very number plate showed a registration number that would have been difficult to remember. Even someone used to working with mnemonics as an aid to memorising information would have found it difficult to re-arrange those letters and numbers into an order capable of being quickly and easily committed to memory. The little Ford had no obvious scratches or dents on its bodywork that would have easily individualised it. In fact, it was a virtually non-individual, nondescript, anonymous and ordinary car that several members of Dublin's Republican Active Service Community had more than once used in situations where it had been necessary to get a vehicle into and out of a location with little likelihood that it would be noticed at the time or remembered after the event. As the little car turned into O'Connell Street its humble exterior seemed to grant it almost immediate access into the almost solid queue of traffic where it was soon taking its place among the line of cars, buses, lorries and horse-drawn wagons.

With both driver and passenger sun-visors in the down position, leaving only a narrow strip of windscreen clear between the dashboard and the lower edge of the sun-visors, there was very little scope for a pedestrian or other car driver to see into the interior of the Ford or catch a glimpse of the occupants' faces.

On top of this, the street lighting in that part of O'Connell Street was less than a hundred per cent effective and, to add to the dullness of a grey and overcast early evening, a thin drizzle of rain was falling, making identification unlikely. The man in the front passenger seat was wearing a large flat cap or bonnet, making him look like one of those faded sepia portraits of men such as Big Bill Broonzy, Robert Johnson, and Blind Willie McTell, that would come to be so sought after by future generations of music historians, musicologists, and collectors. The car's driver was wearing a wide brimmed, brown felt hat, pulled well down over his face, making his features all but invisible. The two occupants of the car were the O'Brien brothers, Thomas Graham or T.G., later known as Two Gun, in the passenger seat, while his older brother, Kelly Joe, was driving. T.G. was a senior Republican quartermaster who, two years before, had accompanied his father, Captain Jamie O'Brien, a senior member of the Republican Council, on a lecturing/fundraising tour of the U.S.A., its Irish clubs, societies, and associations that had been successful beyond anyone's imaginings, resulting in donations of hundreds of thousands of dollars to fill the Irish Republicans' war chest. Being a skilled quartermaster, T.G. was able to purchase huge amounts of military equipment on that trip, which he had shipped to Dublin. One of his biggest coups being when he managed to purchase five hundred Thomson sub-machine guns at a very competitive price. Even the fact that these weapons were discovered by the C.I.A. when they boarded a Liverpool bound Irish freighter on the Hudson River and found that some of the crates, apparently containing tractor parts, actually held a much more deadly cargo; and although the Thomson sub-machine guns were impounded, that disaster did very little to dent the younger O'Brien brother's reputation as a whizz kid quartermaster. Towards the end of that American trip, Thomas Graham and his father visited the Manhattan gun shop of the man who was their main source of armaments in America. Over Irish coffees in the luxuriously appointed hunter's emporium, it was while in the middle of a general conversation on all things Irish that T.G.'s eye was caught by two vintage Colt Peacemaker revolvers well displayed in a glass-fronted cabinet.

"So, what are those two pistols in the glass case?" he asked Timothy O'Neil, the gun shop owner.

"Those are two original Colt Peacemakers from the 1880s. They are in beautiful condition, as you can probably see, and they work as well as they look.

"They are quite sought after and quite collectable and actually, they were out on loan to a Hollywood Film Studio until a few days ago and have only just come back into the store. Would you like to see them, young fellow?" O'Neil asked, answering a question and then asking one of his own.

"Looking won't hurt or cost me a fortune," T.G. replied. After a long moment searching for a key, the gun shop owner finally found it and unlocked the secure cabinet. Lifting the two heavy pistols out, he handed them to T.G., who began to examine them closely. All of the metal parts were profusely engraved and the polished bone mounted grips were carved with the likeness of a longhorn steer's head.

"Real cowboy weapons," O'Neil went on. "In fact, in their day, the Peacemakers were really popular weapons. Everybody used them, from cowboys out on the Western Plains, to the U.S. Army. One of the main reasons they were so popular is because they are virtually indestructible. Even if the rod-ejector was to bend or the lock to break, if the worst came to the worst, simply by holding it in one hand with the trigger depressed and by pulling back the hammer with the other hand and letting it fall, the Colt would fire. This became known as fanning the hammer and while not a very accurate way to use a handgun, it could save your life in a tight spot. But you know what they say about pistols anyway, gentlemen? That is if your target is not close enough to be capable of being hit with your pistol if you threw it at them, then don't bother using it in the first place."

Smiling to himself, T.G. continued to fondle and examine the weapons. "The real thing, for sure," O'Neil enthused. "Who knows where these beauties have been or what they have seen. They are the deluxe models. Do you like them, young fellow?"

"I've fallen in love with them," T.G. admitted. "Although that said, I'm not going to ask you the price of them."

At that, the elder O'Brien crossed the room to examine a hand-printed ticket still lying inside the glass-fronted display cabinet. Jamie O'Brien grimaced and shook his head as if in disbelief. "Do you want them, boy?" he asked, having already decided that if his son wanted the Colts, they were his.

"Sure do, Dad." T.G. replied. "Who wouldn't?"

"Then, if you want them, they're yours," his father continued. "We've had a great trip, successful beyond my wildest dreams and a lot of those big donations were only landed because of your input on the talks."

"Mr. O'Neil," he continued, turning to the gun shop owner, "would you just add them to our bill and send them in the usual way with our shipment?"

"I certainly will and, as always, it's been a real pleasure doing business with you. It was good to meet your son on this trip and give the Brits some hell from me when you get home, and hello to the Missus also. So, when do you think you will be back in New York again, Captain O'Brien?"

"The plan was to send me over every two years for a bit, but when the Council sees how well we have done this trip, it could become an annual thing or, who knows, even more regular than that." Jamie O'Brien smiled. "Maybe we should have an office over here, somewhere between a diplomatic mission and a supply office."

"Now, you're talkin'," O'Neill responded. "When I hear you speaking like that, I start to see the possibility of independence and an Irish state.

"We'll have to hurt them a bit more and cost them a lot more money before that happens but happen it surely will," the elder O'Brien replied. "But happen it will and when it does, it will be good to know that the American cousins helped, even if only with dollars. It seems there is a huge fundraising field for us over here. It would not surprise me if we have a potential in America far beyond what we have seen so far or even what we have imagined in our most optimistic moments," Jamie O'Brien added.

"See if you can get these pistols to us as fast as you can," T.G. added. "Just wait 'til the rest of the boys see these beauties. They're going to be green with envy. Not that they aren't green boys already."

"The only problem with these old weapons is getting ammunition for them," the gun shop owner went on. "I've got a customer who is a collector/enthusiast and he loads his own ammo. I can get it from him in small quantities. He even has a set of original .45 bullet moulds that he pours the lead into to make them the way they always used to be made. During the war between the States, there was an irregular Confederate cavalry outfit known as Quantrill's Raiders, sometimes known as Quantrill's Bushwhackers. Some of those boys were renowned pistol shots and pistol fighters and what those boys did to make these big pistols more accurate was to load their ammunition with only half the usual load of powder so, by reducing recoil, it made their pistol fire so much more accurate and that it is how the ammunition that I am going to send you will be made: less recoil but more than enough hitting power to get the job done. If I sent you say, two hundred rounds, would that do for a start?"

"That should be fine," T.G. replied. "If it comes to a real all-out war, I'll probably be using a Lee Enfield rifle like everybody else."

When the Ford Poplar was about halfway along O'Connell Street, T.G. leaned across and squeezed Kelly Joe's arm to catch his attention. "If you let me off just about here, I'll walk for a bit and meet you at Aunt Winnie's shop," T.G. said, fastening the buckle on the belt of the long raincoat he was wearing; a raincoat which hid the fact that beneath its folds were two British army webbing holsters with their button-down flaps cut off, each one securing a Colt Peacemaker.

Listening to his brother, Kelly Joe glanced into the back seat of the car to where a .303 Lee Enfield rifle was lying wrapped in an old overcoat. The Aunt Winnie that T.G. had mentioned was his mother's sister who, along with her husband, had a small farm not far from Dublin. Because the farm was little more than a smallholding, in an attempt to bring in some extra and much needed income, Winnie had opened a shop in Dublin a year or two before where she sold mostly cigarettes, tobacco and confectionary, plus some of the fruit, vegetables, and eggs that came from her farm. She had some apple trees on her land and, from her apple crop, she made the toffee apples that were so popular with the local children. Additionally, from her blackcurrant, gooseberry, and strawberry patch, she made her own jams and chutneys and sold these in the shop. She also sold milk and bread and, when she had time to make them, the scones and cakes that she baked at home. It was no secret in Dublin that she was related to several active Republicans, and that may have been a factor in the habit that a number of the British military intelligence community's Black and Tans had of visiting her shop, helping themselves to her stock and refusing to pay for it—no doubt trying to augment the ten shillings per day that they received from the British government as wages. Winnie had complained bitterly to her brother-in-law, Jamie O'Brien, when the week before, a truckload of Black and Tans had parked in the road outside her farm, climbed down from their vehicle with their rifles and, leaning their weapons on her farmyard gate, began to use her hens for target practice. Very soon, her birds were either dead or terrified out of their wits were hiding under the hen-house foundations so they could not be seen. At that point the Tans had turned their attention to Daisy, the farm's milk cow and, as much a pet as a real farm animal, and shot her dead. The elderly woman had been devastated by these incidents and so much so that she began to find it difficult to be at the farm on her own and had taken to spending more time at her shop where, at least, she had her customers for company. When it got to the point where she was afraid to be on her own, either at the farm or at the shop, she had asked Jamie O'Brien if something could not be done to help her. Jamie O'Brien, in turn, had asked the local Republican community to watch out for Winnie when they could and that was where T.G. and Kelly Joe were heading, just to keep an eye on the area around Winnie's Clontarf Way shop for a half hour or so, just quietly patrolling the streets of the neighbourhood.

"You sure you want to walk in this rain?" Kelly Joe asked. "Because I don't mind driving you."

"It's just that I feel a lot more secure, more in control when on foot, knowing these Dublin backstreets like I do."

"Well at least leave the pistols in the back beside my rifle. I'll drive them to the shop and you can get them there. There's no point going around armed when you don't have to," Kelly Joe argued.

"Thanks, bruv. I appreciate the concern but me and the Colts are going to walk. I'll just cut down to the river, cross over at the first bridge and then follow Bachelor's Walk to where it meets Clontarf Way and then get down to Aunt Winnie's for a toffee apple or a cake," T.G. explained.

"Well, I'll follow you slowly in the car and pick you up if the rain gets any worse or just be there as backup if you get into any trouble."

"Come on, Kelly Joe, we're not at school any more. Nowadays I can fight my own battles."

"It's still no bad thing to have somebody watching your back for you," Kelly Joe argued. "But if I can't talk sense into your thick head, get walking, bruv."

At that, T.G. turned his coat collar up against the wind and rain and, cutting through O'Connell Street's still heavy traffic until he was close to the river, he then turned onto a narrow flight of stone steps that led him down onto Bachelor's Walk, with the river Liffey out of sight somewhere to his left in the thick, feral darkness that hung heavy just beyond the watery haze of yellow artificial light tentatively thrown by the street lamps. At the foot of the stone stairway he walked on at a good pace until he came to a narrow bridge and immediately used it to cross to the far bank of the river. The grey buildings that reared up towering above him as he walked off the bridge were typical Dublin tenements with small shops at street level and apartments above. T.G. knew that several of those shops were little second-hand bookshops and, as he walked, he was looking to see if any of them were lit up and therefore still open. Slowing his pace outside of the first bookshop that he came to he paused in a pool of yellow light that spilled out beyond a dreary window display to show a table piled high with well-thumbed books protected from the rain by a sheet of clear plastic. Scanning the stacked, upward facing spines, a green volume with no title on its sun faded buckram binding caught his attention. Lifting the plastic cover back just far enough so that his hand could reach the book without letting any of the night's damp atmosphere reach the books, he slipped the volume free and opened it at its title page where he read, *A Search in Ireland* by H.V. Morton. Next, he opened the book so that he could read the pencilled price written on the front free end paper. For a moment, he hesitated whether he would pay that price or not; in the end, he decided he did not want to be carrying anything when he might need to have both hands free when he got to Winnie's shop. He had already decided that if he did manage to catch any of the old lady's tormentors, he was going to teach them a sharp lesson. So, slipping the book back into the space it had come out of, he realised the rain was getting heavier. Walking faster now, with the unseen river at his right side, his mind stayed with the H.V. Morton title. He knew that if he had found that same book in a Glasgow or London bookshop, the price would have been a fraction of what he had just seen. That this was just part of the price of living in Ireland, he mused to himself striding on and, secure in the knowledge that if anyone were following him, they would have no idea what his planned destination was. Just then, he reached the intersection of Bachelor's Walk and Clontarf Way and turned right into the narrow, badly lit street where his aunt's shop was situated. The wind was getting stronger but he had already given up hope of getting home either warm or dry, so he put the rain out of his mind and kept on walking. He looked relaxed and just like any other casual stroller, but he was keeping a close watch on intersections, tenement close entranceways and darkened shop doorways, making sure that the area was as deserted and silent as it should have been on such a cold, wet night. Behind him, at a walking pace, inside the Ford Poplar, Kelly Joe was relaxed but watchful and alert. Just short of the far end of the street, T.G. was able to make out the pool of light illuminating a little of the watery wet pavement which told him that Winnie's shop was open and that his aunt was at her post. When still some way off, he could make out the dull green paint of the shop's shabby frontage and the weathered gold gothic script that proclaimed WINNIE O'BRIEN TOBACCO AND CONFECTIONARY. At the top of the dusty plate glass window, a blue-lettered sign read "Senior Service Does Satisfy." At the bottom of the window, an orange sign read "Let Capstan Take The Strain." Pausing for a moment outside the shop's double doors that were closed but unlocked, T.G. pushed them away from himself with an energetic two-handed shove and quickly stepped into the dimly lit shop. At the far end of the narrow single shop unit, behind a rudimentary counter, a dumpy, grey haired woman of inscrutable demeanour and years was standing marking prices onto packets of cigars with a battered fountain pen.

"Good evening to you, Tommy," she said smiling, glancing in the direction of the doorway and the young man framed in it. "Are you on your own or is Kelly Joe with you?"

"He's outside parking the car. He'll be here in a second," T.G. said, looking around the shop with its slightly scruffy looking stock, until his gaze fell on the door on the wall behind his aunt, the door that led to the back shop store. Winnie recognised her nephew's unspoken question and smiled a warm reply.

"Yes, the kettle's on and just freshly boiled. Will I make you a cup of tea or would you rather make it for yourself, seeing that I'm busy here?... And hands off my toffee apples," T.G. heard his aunt say as he stepped into the high-stacked back storeroom. Unsealing one of several boxes of Smith's potato crisps standing on an ancient looking table, he opened a packet of crisps and rummaged through it for the twist of blue paper which held the salt that he was craving.

At his back, the door to the shop opened and Kelly Joe stepped into the storeroom. "Caught in the act!..." Kelly Joe laughed. "You're just as big a predator as the Tans and, talking of which, there were three of them hanging about outside when I was coming in."

"Then I had better go out and keep an eye on things," T.G. intimated.

"Okay, but be cool, bruv," Kelly Joe admonished. "And don't forget what Aunt Winnie said previously when she warned us that no packet of cigarettes or box of chocolates was worth anyone getting hurt over."

T.G. turned to the door into the shop and, putting his eye to the space where the edge of the door did not quite meet the doorframe, he found he could adequately observe most of the shop's interior. Standing there silently, he could see three figures dressed in the uniforms of Black and Tans. As he watched, the man on his left reached inside his rain dampened uniform jacket and produced a folded army kit bag and then, slowly walking round the shop's shelves, from time to time stopping to pick up a packet of cigarettes, a box of cigars, or a box of chocolates and pop them into his soon bulging bag.

A minute or two passed, by which time, his bag was beginning to look heavy. Then, he looked up and grinned in Winnie's direction with a cruel humourless smile. "Just doing a bit of early Christmas shopping, if that's all right with you, dear," he commented in an explanatory tone.

"I'm most definitely not your dear," Winnie responded. "I might just be your protector, but no, I'm not your dear. Paying customers are always welcome, whatever kind of shopping they're doing, early Christmas or whatever."

At that, T.G. pushed his right hand deeper into his coat pocket, searching for the opening he had made through the coat's lining, an opening that allowed him to reach a pistol without having to take his hand out of his pocket or unbuckle his coat. His hand settled around the smoothly polished butt of his Peacemaker and, in that moment, his adrenalin slowed down. He knew that the die was cast. Then, with both hands still in his coat pockets, he used his shoulder to push open the door and stepped through into the shop in the same moment that his aunt stepped past him to walk into the store. As the three men spun on their heels to stare at him, T.G. concluded that, as far as he could see, they were unarmed. Thinking to himself that it was unlikely that they would come into this particular shop unarmed, he spoke out.

"Christmas shopping is it lads?" he said tight-lipped and staring hard at the nearest man who had a corporal's stripes on his sleeves and was by now holding a half-full kitbag. As three pairs of eyes swivelled to lock down on him, T.G. pulled out his right hand Peacemaker and pointed it at the corporal's head. "This is or can turn to be a Christmas present from the Republic," T.G. hissed. "Listen very carefully lads because this is what I want you to do. Very slowly put the bag on the floor and, still moving very slowly, just take yourselves out of the door that you came in by and get yourselves out into the street. Do as you are told and you might just get home alive to your beds tonight. Any sudden or funny moves and the price to be paid is on your head, or maybe I should say *in* it."

The corporal laid his kitbag on the floor and led the way out onto the street, his companions falling into step behind him, T.G. following them until all four men were standing on the narrow pavement close to the parked Ford Poplar.

"Halt right there, lads!" T.G. ordered in a menacing tone. "Now, I know enough about British army uniforms to know that your battledress blouses have a concealed inner breast pocket and that's where you'll be keeping a hidden pistol if you're carrying one. I don't believe you three would come into this particular shop unarmed. I can't see any signs of weapons but I do believe that they're there. I wouldn't like to have to shoot you down in the way that a farmer would butcher a beast but I can if I have to. And you Tans sure having it coming."

The three men stood stock still and hesitated for a long moment, until the corporal's hand suddenly shot into his inside breast pocket to pull out what T.G. instantly recognised as being a .38 Webley service revolver. As the business end of the weapon swung in his direction, T.G. adopted his classic pistol shooter's stance and, with his legs apart and both feet braced for the big Colt's hefty recoil when it came, he held the Peacemaker in both hands, arms outstretched holding the weapon above his head, until, slowly, he let the weight of the pistol bring it steadily downward and then, with the gun levelled at the corporal's chest, he waited until the v-shaped notch of the rear sight was aligned with the foresight and gently squeezed the trigger. As the big Colt roared out its lethal greeting, T.G. swung the gun to the man on the corporal's right and fired again. The sound of the second shot was still reverberating in the damp night air when the Peacemaker fired for a third time.

Inside the storeroom of the shop, Kelly Joe was springing into action. Pulling back the side door's two bolts, he threw the door ajar and, leaping out into the darkened backyard, he was soon racing through the close that led out onto Clontarf Walk. Outside, he quickly took in the three crumpled figures lying on the ground and the fact that, despite the shooting, T.G. was still standing, apparently unscathed. Racing round the Ford Poplar, he hurriedly unlocked the car to snatch up the Lee Enfield rifle from its place on the back seat. Working the bolt action as he went, he walked towards the fallen corporal until, coming to a halt at the side of what looked like a large rag doll, he brought the muzzle of the rifle to within a few inches of the man's head and pulled the trigger. White-faced, T.G. looked on as his brother did the same with the other two fallen men. T.G. hesitated for a moment and then leapt back into the shop, his aunt looking on terrified as he grabbed her telephone and began to dial a number.

"Hello, this is wolf cub. We have an incident at Winnie's shop and need backup here. I want area security and the clean-up section and I want them here faster than fast."

"Okay, T.G.," a breathless voice on the other end of the telephone responded. "We have a training op on just around the corner from you so they will be with you in seconds."

T.G. dropped the telephone receiver back onto its cradle and turned his attention to Kelly Joe. "You stay here and talk to Aunt Winnie. I'm going to be outside waiting for the boys to arrive. Stress to her that our lives might depend on her saying and knowing nothing." So saying, T.G. left his brother and aunt in the shop and went back outside. As the shop door was closing behind him, Kelly Joe was speaking to his Aunt Winnie.

"Just remember, Auntie, and this is crucially important, that if anyone asks you, you must stick to the story that no Black and Tans came in here tonight, you did not see your nephews and you have no idea what went on outside your shop. If you stick to your story, all of us are okay.

"If you let them shake your story, your nephews are dead men."

Outside, T.G. looked on as a wine-coloured truck advertising McCullough's healthy bread pulled up at the kerbside. The moment the truck had stopped, the rear doors opened and six men jumped out. Three of them piled the bodies inside the vehicle while two others produced jerry cans full of water out of the truck's interior and began to sluice the bloodstains off the pavement slabs.

"How many shots were fired?" one of these two demanded.

"My used cases are still in my weapon because it's a non-ejector," T.G. explained.

"There will be three Lee Enfield cases around here somewhere but they should be easily spotted, being made of brass," Kelly Joe added.

"I've got two of them," one of the newcomers offered, bending down to pick something up from the gutter.

"If you can see any marks on the paving made by bullets, scuff mud into them so that nothing looks fresh or recently done," T.G. ordered.

"Got you!" one of the men replied, stooping down to retrieve the last cartridge case.

T.G. stood for a moment, looking at the bulk of the baker's truck and the signage on its side that read, THE WHITER THE BREAD - THE SOONER YOU'RE DEAD.

"Indeed!" he was muttering to himself as the vehicle began to pull away from the kerb. At that point, Kelly Joe was throwing his rifle into the back of his car and making sure that it was covered and out of view.

"Pleasant as this might be, bruv, this standing here taking the night air, still I suggest we get the hell out of it."

T.G. seemed to be in agreement because in the space of a moment, he had got himself into the little Ford's front passenger seat, Kelly Joe wasting no time to follow his brother's example, until they were soon shadowing the red tail lights of the baker's truck as it proceeded along Clontarf Way.

Chapter Two

The Chrysler Traveller

As the mud-splattered white Chrysler Traveller slid through the gates of Glasgow Airport's long stay car park, looking for all the world like a prop for an old Hollywood gangster movie, an onlooker would have to have been forgiven for half-expecting Faye Dunaway and Warren Beatty in their roles as Bonnie and Clyde to step out of the car. Big Pete Lafferty, the car's driver, realised that his companion had dozed off during their drive to the airport. So leaning across towards the passenger seat, he gripped his companion by the arm and gave him a friendly but vigorous shake.

"Wake up, Gordy O'Brien, champion sleepyhead! Come on, wake up, we're there!"

"But where's 'there'?" a sleepy voice responded and then went on. "Not only was I asleep but I was in the middle of a dream and you shook, shocked me right out of it." "What were you dreaming about?" Pete asked.

"Oh, nothing much," Gordon replied. "Just old O'Brien family history stuff. Stories I had heard as a kid and thought I had long since forgotten. But they were obviously still there, deep down in the memory banks."

"What, that old Republican stuff?" Pete asked.

"The same," Gordon replied. "I guess the fact that we are off to Galway to do a gig at the Galleon Acoustic Music Festival, and the fact that the venue at the University of Ireland at Galway is only a stone's throw from where my grandfather came from in 1912 has brought all of this Irish stuff bubbling up to the surface again."

"I don't mind," Pete interjected. "Just as long as you remember that my roots, when you go back far enough, are just as Irish as yours, even if mine are orange and not green."

"Have I told you about my experience with the Orange Walk in Glasgow a few days ago?" Gordon continued. "It was last weekend and I was in Glasgow city centre to buy some new guitar strings and a new harmonica, and, just as I was turning off Renfrew Street into Renfield Street, heading down to McCormicks in Bath Street, I heard this music, and realising it was flutes and drums, concluded it had to be the Orange Walk. A moment later, that street was a sea of wall-to-wall Orangemen and I knew I was either never going to get across the street or I was going to have to wait for a while for a gap in the procession. As you know, you break those ranks at your peril. Some folk even maintain that every fifth or sixth flute is made of solid lead so that it can be used as a weapon at need."

"That's just a Glasgow myth, a scurrilous rumour," Peter disagreed. "But leaving that aside, tell me about your Orange Walk, adventure man."

"Well, once I realised who they were," Gordon continued, "I decided that if you can't beat them, then joining them might be the answer and it kind of tickled my sense of humour that a Catholic brought-up son of a long line of Galway Micks might take a walk with the Orangemen and maybe even enjoy the colour, music and pageantry, and live to tell the tale."

"Which you clearly did," Pete laughed. "So tell on or we'll never get to the end of this tale."

"Well, I kept my eyes and ears open and my wits about me and at the first opportunity, I slipped into a space in the ranks, one near to the head of the column. There was this amazing little guy at the front, looking like a cross between your stereotypical Glaswegian and a less than handsome monkey. He seemed to be some sort of cheerleader, though with his long arms, bandy legs, and a face like a dog baboon, he was never picked for his good looks. He was right out front, a-leaping and a-dancing and urging the musicians on to ever more speed and volume. He was carrying some sort of ceremonial mace type thing and would throw it five, ten, fifteen feet into the air and, to the delight of the crowd, he always managed to catch it. He reminded me of Roger Daltrey of The Who at Woodstock, when he was throwing his singing mike into the air and catching it. I don't know if this little guy could sing or not, but on sheer energy and visual spectacle, he could have fronted any rock band."

"Okay, I've got the picture of this Glaswegian performing monkey," Pete interrupted, "but what next?"

"Well, we walked down Renfield Street a bit and then took a right into Bath Street, the mounted police controlling the crowd that had become enormous. It was just after we did our right turn when I remembered that at our gig of the night before Dirty Aggie, our one and only and long standing groupie, had handed me something in a little plastic envelope and told me that it was real good and that I should take it at the right time, maybe at a concert or with close friends. Well, there and then I fished it out of my pocket and had a look at it. It was just a single green tablet. In fact, it looked kind of innocuous, almost organic."

"Don't they always?" Pete said in a doubtful tone. "So, you took it?"

"Yes, I took it," Gordon replied. "Just like Alice in Wonderland with her Eat Me's and Drink Me's," Gordon continued. " Straight away, things began to change, colours became unusually vivid and every colour that I could see around me in the street had a musical note that accompanied it. This colour music at some points was just occasional, individual notes but, at other points, there were lots of them, sometimes combining to make amazing symphonies while, at other times, creating a hellish crescendo of ugly, discordant devil music." And then, it got really interesting and it was as if in the middle of this trip, I had some sort of vision or transcendental experience."

"Just keep the language simple." Pete protested. "Don't use big words that the audience don't understand."

"Then this huge, naked, black woman appeared and it was as if she was some sort of Earth Goddess figure. It wasn't that she was there in the street but more that she was manifesting in my mind."

"In your mind. It would have to be a naked Earth Goddess." Pete quipped. "Then the Earth Goddess woman began to sing," Gordon continued. "And in fact, she sang two songs. One song was an evocation of all of the pain, unhappiness, and grief that had ever happened on this planet, while the other song was evoking all the love, joy, hope, creativity, and friendship that the planet had ever seen. At a couple of points, I sang along with her," Gordon said, continuing his tale. "And when our voices merged, it was like trying to swim in a river with a hugely strong current. You know, like when you are swimming at full stretch and you still don't know if you are going to be swept away or not. More than once when we sang in harmony, the joy and pain were so intense, it felt as if my body and mind were in danger of exploding."

"But did you get her telephone number is what I want to know," Peter broke in.

"That's right, bring it down to mundanities," Gordon protested. "This was some sort of mystical/cosmic experience, or as near to one as I am likely to get., It wasn't something out of *Playboy* magazine," Gordon protested. "And what then, what happened next?" Pete asked in a conciliatory tone.

"And next came the fear," Gordon went on.

"What sort of fear?" Pete asked. "It started when they were singing 'The Sash," Gordon replied. "Well, there are alternative, Catholic words to that song and I was just singing '*It was green, white, and gold with Saint Patrick on the fold,*' when I saw this big guy glaring at me and I wondered for a second if he could lip read and I knew in that split second that if he could, then my proverbial goose was cooked. That was the start of the fear. But a few yards farther on, the little monkey man slowed his walk and, turning to face the front rank of banner carriers, began to chant, '*what do we want? what do we want and what are we going to do with it when we get it?*' Immediately, all of the people around him—the women in their flower print dresses and their white high-heeled shoes and the men in their sober suits and bowler hats—thundered back in response: "Blood! Blood! Up to our knees in fenian blood!" Right there and then, I felt the hatred, the centuries of hurt, torture, and murder and I knew in my heart like the gentle and peaceful Hindu/Buddhist that I am and like the Catholic/Christian that I was brought up to be (even if that was a club that I had never asked my parents to enrol me in) that I had nothing in common with those people, or with any other kind of bigot, or full of hate, negativity, and violence, person on the whole planet. At that point, and despite the fact that if for a second it was suspected who or what I was, I was going to be torn apart by bare hands and my blood splashed knee high. Right there and then I was walking in the middle of those massed Orange ranks, I remembered George Gurdjieff and what he had said and it made me laugh right out loud."

"So who is George Gurdjieff and what was it that he said that was so funny?" Pete asked. "Gurdjieff was a philosopher a mystic and a trickster and no doubt he said a whole lot of different things at different times and places but what had come to my mind just then was his comment *that most of the human race are just manure for the planet.*"

Gordon replied, "And I saw in a flash that all of those people, whether orange or green, the bigots and the gunmen and, to borrow a phrase from Bobby Dylan, *'those Masters of War are just shit to leaven our dark earth planet loam with.'* No more than that and just as inconsequential," Gordon continued. "But going back to my Earth Mother figure, do you remember the cover art for that Santana album, *Abraxas?*"

"Yes, I remember it well," Peter replied. "I can see it quite clearly in my mind's eye."

"So the black woman depicted on the album cover was like your vision woman?" Pete asked.

"They weren't exactly alike and I don't think that the Santana cover was any sort of source for my vision, or whatever you want to call it. When I thought about this mysterious black woman later, it put me in mind of the Fiona McLeod writings."

"Who she?" Pete asked.

"You'll be sorry you asked," "Gordon went on.

"Am I not always when I ask you a question?" Pete continued. "But just ignore that comment and go for it with your answer."

"I intend to," Gordon responded. "Well, you see, Pete, my black woman was obviously some sort of feminine wisdom archetype."

"As usual when travelling with you, I end up feeling that I should have brought my dictionary along, never mind spare guitar strings or extra finger-picks but a goddam dictionary."

"On this fine day and en route to Galway, the land of the forefathers, I am not going to rise to your redneck bait, Big Pete Lafferty; but, anyway, Fiona McLeod....

"In the early years of the twentieth century, a series of well-received and popular books were published, apparently written by some Scottish seeress or mystic wise woman who could spend twenty pages, perhaps ten thousand words, just describing the wind blowing through the grass. Like you couldn't say that these were novels or essays, or works of philosophy, or put them into any other well-known category but they did seem to be by some sort of wise woman author. While it was a well-kept and well-guarded secret, it turned out that these books were not written by an old Scottish seeress living in some rude stone cottage or black house in the Highlands but were written by a Scottish journalist living in London called William Sharp. It wasn't just a literary fraud like the *Lobsang Rampa* or *Grey Owl* books and, in fact, Emma Jung, the wife of C.G. Jung, the Swiss psychologist, said in her book, *Anima and Animus* (a fairly rare work published by the Analytical Psychology Club of New York in 1934) discussed Sharp/McLeod and appeared to take Wilfion seriously."

"And?" Pete interjected.

"Well," Gordon continued, "Emma Jung seemed to be saying that Sharp the journalist was not just using a convenient pen-name but had contacted some deep feminine part of his own psyche and that is where the Fiona books came from. W.B. Yeats once said that 'Fiona McLeod was one of the sweetest voices singing in the Celtic Renaissance and being the huge fan of W. B. Yeats that I am, his view of Sharp goes a long way with me. On top of that, William Sharp was not just your average hack journalist but he was also a member of the Hermetic Order of the Golden Dawn. So he was some sort of hermetic student also, and W.B. Yeats did write that well-known essay 'The Hermetic Students.' And all of this throws some sort of light on your Earth Goddess muse?" Pete asked in a doubtful tone.

"At the very least, I hope to get a song or a poem out of the experience Gordon replied. "Knowing me, that will happen after a while, you know, after it's gestated for a bit."

"That does seem to be the way that you work best and it's certainly how some of your best songs have come about. With me it's more instant, me being more of a strike-while-the-iron–is-hot sort of person and not at all like your mystical and mysterious self, Gordy O'Brien. Though, that said, that comment made, I wouldn't change you a single iota, even if I thought that I could." Pete went on, thinking out loud.

"If my Earth Mother person had come to me in a dream, or when awake and daydreaming, rather than as part of a drug inspired moment," Gordon went on, "I would be looking at this as some sort of important and inspirational moment, rather than as a reverie in an intoxicated, drug-fuelled mindscape. And bearing in mind that I am totally against drugs, still, man, we have to take our inspirations where we can get them."

"When Yeats mentioned Fiona McLeod as being one of the sweetest voices in the Celtic Renaissance, who would the other voices be?" Pete asked.

"There would have been a lot of them," Gordon replied. "Probably everyone that was around Yeats at the Abbey Theatre at that time as well as people like Florence Farr, his fellow Hermetic student and, of course, George Russell or A.E., the pioneer theosophist, writer, painter, land reform agitator, and mystic."

"I don't know him," Pete responded. "Did he write anything good?"

"When we get home, I'll give you a loan of my copy of his *The Candle of Vision,* which is an excellent way into his brand of mysticism."

"Right," Pete said, looking out of the windscreen of the car to where a family of magpies were ransacking one of the car park litterbins and throwing papers around with great crow abandon. "This sitting around talking is all well and good but pretty soon, we are going to have to start getting the show on the road and looking as if we are here to get ourselves and our bits and pieces onto a plane for Dublin."

"We can sit here for a minute yet because this car is more comfortable than those plastic airport seats in there," Gordon commented.

"You know, since you gave up your rare/antiquarian book business, you get to sound more and more like the occult bookseller that you used to be," Pete proffered, still thinking about what Gordon had been saying about Fiona McLeod.

"Well, that is what I was for a while. Though, as you know, I've always had a few other strings to my bow as well, the guitar and our Mavis Valley Ceilidh Band being one or two of them, depending on your point of view."

"How is your astrology, Tarot, and I Ching thing going from your little office in Edinburgh, or is it more of a witches' den than an office?" Pete asked.

"Well, I'm still offering those services, charts and readings, lectures and talks, the occasional workshop and seminar. People seem to want it. I've just given a talk on the I Ching as dowsing to the Scottish Association of Dowsers and it was fairly well received. That whole side of things is harder work than the books were and it pays less, but I find it interesting. The Tarot, astrology thing, in conjunction with the band and my solo gigs does keep the wolf from the door and the mixture makes for an interesting lifestyle."

Although Gordon and Pete were fairly well known around the Scottish folk and acoustic music scenes when they played together, they were equally well known in their independent roles as singer-songwriters and each had interests that they pursued separately from the other. Although Pete no longer boxed competitively, he had maintained an interest in and connection with the boxing world. Either together or alone, they sometimes played in other peoples' bands and did some freelance work as session players in one of Gordon's friend's recording studios. Being asked to play a festival as big or as far from home as the Galway Galleon Festival (named after the Spanish galleon believed to have sunk in Galway Bay at the time of the Spanish Armada) was unusual for them, though they were both keen to do it. Pete had even been asked to give a master class at the festival aside from their playing set. At first, he had thought this just ridiculous.

"What do I know about anything that I could impart to all of those academics at Galway University, the venue for the festival?" he had asked Gordon on several occasions.

"Just remember that you are the world expert on how you write your songs and how you sing and play your guitar. Nobody knows more about that than you so just relax. Do it and do it as well as you do everything else that you do and it will go well," Gordon had been reiterating ever since the master class invitation had arrived with Pete. "And while I remember and to keep the record straight," Gordon interjected, "I was never an occult book dealer, man. Occult, from the Latin *occultus*, is simply a Latin word that means 'hidden,' as in hidden traditions outside of mainstream Christianity. What always interested me and was reflected in my rare book business was the Eternal Verities and, before you ask me what the Eternal Verities are, in that put on hick farmer/dumb labourer voice that you like to pretend is you, the Eternal Verities are the age-old questions that every generation has asked since time beyond memory, like 'WHO AM I?' 'WHERE DID I COME FROM?' 'WHAT IS THE MEANING OF LIFE?' 'DO WE SURVIVE BODILY DEATH?' etc. Sure, some of my books were about the so-called occult, but only some."

At that, Gordon began to stretch in his seat and looked as if he were about to make a move of some sort.

"What I suggest we do is this," Pete began slipping the car keys out of the ignition and dropping them into his pocket. "I'll get the band trunk and my pack into the terminal building and get into the queue to check the trunk in for the Dublin flight and once that's done, I'll continue upstairs and get us a couple of seats in Starbucks. You just take your own rucksack and the two guitar cases and we can meet upstairs for coffee."

"Sounds like I've got the best of the deal because, from past experience, that trunk will weigh a ton."

"Well, it's got the two AER 120 acoustic cube amplifiers inside as well as the two mikes, the two folding mike stands and the one thousand and one other things that a two-piece band might need on the road, down to nine volt batteries and gaffer tape. So it's no wonder that it's heavy. I checked it yesterday and if anything important has been forgotten, it's not for lack of checking on my part. So it's no wonder that it's heavy and, before you start to offer to help me lift the thing out of the car, it's only weeks since you were seriously ill in hospital with that stroke type thing. In fact, this is your first festival and away from home gig since you did your stint in hospital, meaning that this is still recuperation time for you. So you have to be taking it easy. And just remember, it's Big Red inside my guitar case and not my Yamaha. So treat it gently." "It's just so typical of you, Pete," Gordon responded, "You've got a more than serviceable Yamaha gig guitar and you bring along a Gibson J200 pre-production model instrument, a rare and valuable piece of kit. You know there's only five or six of them in the world and you take it out on tour.," Gordon cajoled in a mock serious voice.

Next, Pete opened the door on his side of the car and stiffly eased his six feet, four-inch frame out of the cramped position in the little car's driving seat. And then, giving himself a good stretch, he pulled himself up to his full height and stood for a moment, breathing in the fresh air. His broad-shouldered frame spoke of a young life of physical effort and, if asked, either he or Gordon would have told the tale of his pretty physical past because, for a while, he had been a boxer, losing none of his fifteen professional fights, then becoming a bare-knuckle fighter for a time, when he got tired of making money for his manager and very little for himself. His powerful-looking frame reflected a story of countless gyms, weights and roadwork, as well as the hods he had carried as a building-site labourer and the countless lengths of tubular steel he had hefted as a scaffolder in the Scottish building industry. He was wearing a dark blue leather jerkin over a pair of faded jeans, at the bottom of which, a pair of blue and silver starred cowboy boots could just be seen. His hair was dark and shoulder length and he exuded strength and fitness. Opening the rear-door of the Chrysler, he stood for a moment, looking at the sturdy oak-built trunk that filled the boot space. Stencilled on to the side of it, in white letters, was the legend, The Mavis Valley Ceilidh Band, Mavis Valley being the long since abandoned mining village on the banks of the Forth & Clyde Canal, in the green and rolling countryside north of Glasgow, where Pete had grown up and where Pete's father, grandfather and many of his family had been miners. Thanks to his father's efforts, Pete had been steered away from a miner's life, though Pete was confident that he could have been a miner if his life had taken him in that direction. The area where he had grown up, although in the country, was heavily industrialised, full of mines and quarries, with much of the red and blonde sandstone used in building the city of Glasgow having been quarried close to Mavis Valley, as was so much of the sand used to mix the cement which held vast areas of that Clydeside City together.

Chapter Three
Dublin Bound

Peter only looked at the trunk for a moment before seizing the leather handles on the trunk's top, taking the weight, flexing his muscles and easily swinging the container out of the car, to be set on its metal castors on the car park's dark tarmacadam. As soon as the trunk was put down, the little car's passenger door opened and Gordon O'Brien stepped out. He was about five-foot-seven inches tall with collar-length fair hair and gold rim spectacles. He was slim and slightly built and had been told on, all too many occasions, that he was the double of John Denver.

"I'm a much better singer and a much better guitar player than that guy," he had been known to retort; that is, before the illness which Pete had mentioned, an illness which had weakened his singing voice and his good left guitar hand, as well as obliterating a large part of his performing repertoire, both songs that he had known and sung for most of his life and the ragtime influenced guitar playing style that had been his musical trademark. He was wearing a blue denim jacket, almost military looking in style with its epaulets and narrow belted waist. It looked as if it had been made from remnants of denim cloth because few of the segments were either the exact same colour or shape. Protruding from his breast pocket could be seen the small notebook and row of pens that this travelling singer-songwriter was never without. Just as Pete began to trundle the band trunk in the direction of the terminal building, he spun on his heel, fished the car keys out of his pocket, then, clapping his hands to attract Gordon's attention, he laid the car keys on the roof of the Chrysler, then pointed strongly at the keys so that Gordon knew to lock the car behind him. Gordon responded with a quick thumbs up and a nod of his head to show that he understood and then, as Pete continued on his way with the trunk, Gordon lifted first one guitar case and then the other out of the car. This was too much for the group of magpies, who took to the air with a loud, chattering protest. With his pack on his back and a guitar case in each hand, Gordon was soon inside the terminal building where he joined the Dublin bound queue to check in his pack and guitar. After which, and keeping Pete's guitar with him, he cut across the concourse to the elevators and up on to the next level where he found an empty table in the Starbucks café area, before getting himself a coffee from the counter, prior to making himself comfortable on a soft, sofa-like seat to wait for Pete's arrival. Then, just as Pete was approaching his table, the public address system clicked on and a female voice speaking in what Gordon thought of as being a Kelvinside accent, announced the Dublin flight. Within moments, a queue was forming and the boys joined it.

With the battered old green commando, military surplus rucksack that had accompanied him and Gordon on hitch-hiking trips all over Europe and once across the overland hippie trail to India on his back and the guitar case that he had just retrieved from Gordon in his huge right hand, Pete was impatient to be off and doing rather than waiting around. At the top of the boarding platform stairs and just inside the open door of the big Boeing, an airhostess was greeting embarking passengers one by one as they arrived in front of her. Pete took in, at a glance, the long blonde hair and long legs under a tartan uniform skirt, not failing to notice an ample bust. As Gordon stepped forward into the doorway, he scanned the airhostess's identity badge in his usual slightly short-sighted manner and was able to make our Mavis McIlreavy, Senior Flight Attendant.

"And good morning to you too Mavis," he said in response to the airhostess's greeting couched in cheerful Dublin tones. "My tall friend here is also a Mavis or, at least, he comes from Mavis Valley," Gordon quipped lightly in good natured banter.

"And good morning to you, Sir," the airhostess said dryly, "I assume that Mavis Valley is a place in Scotland?"

"It used to be," Pete replied. "Now it's either forgotten or it's just a name on old maps. Unless, like me, it just happens to be the place where you were born and brought up."

"If the name is anything to go by, it sounds as if it is or was a nice place," the airhostess observed and then looking at Pete's guitar case, she frowned. "Your guitar should really have gone into the cargo-hold, Sir."

"It's just that it's old, fragile, and quite valuable. So, if at all possible, I wanted to keep it with me," Pete explained. "I'm sure you will be able to find a safe place for it for me."

"If you feel that you can trust me with it, then I'll take it for you, keep it safe during the flight and when we land, I'll bring it to you," Mavis offered.

"Good," Pete responded. "But wherever you stow it just make sure it is not close to either water or heat."

"I know just the perfect safe place for it," Mavis continued and retreated inside the aircraft with her burden and then a few minutes after takeoff, she reappeared and, slipping into the empty seat between the two musicians, she turned to Pete."

"Could you tell me a little about your Mavis Valley?" she asked.

"Like any village or community," Pete replied, "its strength was the people who lived there. It was a small village made of two rows of miners' houses, with a single street between them.

"That was all that there was to it. Its strength being in its people, once those people moved away all you had left was a collection of empty, poor quality houses that were rapidly vandalised. Soon, everything that was capable of being stolen from the houses was gone, including the very stonework, which was looted for building until today. You have to know where to look to find any signs that a village ever stood on that spot. They had a bad pit disaster there in 1913 and not long after that, the mine closed and, once the pit was gone, it was only a matter of time before the people and the village also vanished. During World War II, part of the area was used as a vast military store. They used to bring tanks, artillery, and ammunition up the Clyde on ships, where the military supplies were transferred to barges to be ferried along the canal and stored well away from Glasgow and possible German air-raids. Again, you have to know where to look to find any signs that this ever took place. One night the German Luftwaffe did attack the area but missed their target, dropping a landmine close to Bishop Briggs, taking out some trees and blowing a huge hole in the ground that is probably still there."

"Did any of your family die in the mine disaster?" The airhostess asked.

"That was long before my time but, yes, a couple of my great uncles died in that one Pete replied. At that, the airhostess rose to her feet, glancing at her watch, "I have to get on because we are due to start our descent into Dublin soon." As she moved towards the front of the aircraft, the FASTEN SEAT BELTS sign came on and the tannoy system crackled into life.

"This is Captain Connor speaking. We will shortly be starting our descent into Dublin Airport. I would ask you to stay in your seats with your seat belts fastened until we are safely at rest on the ground. Also, as we may experience some turbulence between this point and landing, I would ask you to refrain from moving about in the cabin."

Gordon noticed that most of the people who had been milling about in the aisle went back to their seats and duly fastened their seat belts, all except for two men who had been sitting towards the front of the aircraft. They stood up and began to make their way towards the rear, probably heading towards the toilets. They both had neatly cut short hair and both looked as if their casual clothes were expensive and well thought out. Even their jeans were spotlessly clean and well pressed. Just as they were passing Pete's aisle seat the aircraft hit a patch of turbulence, throwing the pair off balance. The smaller of the two was catapulted into an empty seat on the far side of the aisle, while his companion landed heavily in Pete's lap. As he fell his elbow slammed into Pete's groin, completely winding him and leaving him in considerable pain. "I am awfully sorry. I do hope you are not hurt?" Pete heard a cultured and very polite upper crust Scottish accent saying to him as he fought not to vomit. "I'll live to tell the tale," Pete responded. "And going to Ireland, I'm going to be in the right country if the injury is worse than I imagine and I have to become a priest."

"Let's hope it does not come to that, Pete's attacker said in an embarrassed tone. "An elbow in the balls with my ten stone behind must have been damn sore."

"Compared with some of the boots in the balls and low punches that have come my way over the years, it was nothing," Pete said, shaking his head to clear it.

With a squeeze of Pete's arm and a conciliatory smile, the smaller of the pair led his companion back towards their seats.

"You were pretty good about that, Big Pete," Gordon said smiling when the pair had gone. "Not your usual testy self at all."

"He looked so sorry and embarrassed I would have felt like a creep and a bully if I had belted him one or chewed him out verbally," Pete commented.

"Getting mellow in your old age?" Gordon laughed. "You must be," Gordon continued, "especially when I hear you talking about belting somebody once. Your usual style is a flurry of fifteen or twenty punches and then you step back a bit so that the guy has room to collapse. You all right now?"

"Yes, I'm almost back to normal now. I can breathe again and I'm fairly sure I'm not going to vomit. So that's progress, clumsy git that he was!"

Just as Pete lapsed into silence, a great thump from beneath him testified to the fact that they were now on the ground. After a short taxi towards the terminal building, Gordon and Pete joined the queue forming in the aisle to disembark. Then, as they drew close to the open door of the aircraft, they saw Mavis standing waiting for them with Pete's guitar case.

"So how are you getting to Galway, boys?" she asked, handing the guitar to Pete.

"We've got a hire car booked," Pete explained. "We intend to see a little of the country between Dublin and Galway."

"How about you?" Gordon asked, "Is it another plane and another flight?" "No, I've got a week off and I'm going to visit my parents in Galway City."

"Come and see us at the Galleon Festival if you get a chance," Gordon suggested.

"I might just do that," Mavis responded.

"Thanks for a pleasant flight," Gordon said smiling as Pete stepped out on to the gangway.

Once they had reached the tarmac, a short walk took them into the terminal building where they were soon following the signs to the baggage reclaim. "You just get your guitar and I'll get the trunk," Pete said as they approached the carousel. At that, Pete spotted the MVCB trunk towering above most of the baggage that had just come off of the Glasgow flight. By the time that Pete had caught up with the trunk and swung in on to the ground, Gordon had spotted his guitar and was pursuing it round the carousel.

Retrieving his instrument, he returned to Pete to prise Big Red out of his hand so that Pete could concentrate on the heavy and, at times, unwieldy trunk. Pete spotted a sign and arrows pointing in the direction of the car hire area. Following a number of other arrows, they were soon approaching the car hire desk. Just as they were next to be served they spotted the two casually dressed men from the plane coming towards them.

"Why so glum looking, lads?" Pete hailed them, noticing their unhappy look.

"We had a car booked," the smaller of the two replied, "but they've no sign of the booking or any extra cars and we have to get to Galway University for a medical conference."

"Hope we fare better and time will surely tell," Pete responded, pushing the trunk towards Gordon so that he could approach the desk relatively unencumbered.

"Hi," Pete said, leaning his elbows on the paper-strewn hire desk. "The name's Lafferty and I booked a Ford Mondeo Estate to be collected today."

At that, the nearer of the two staff members consulted a computer screen and, shaking his head, said, "Sorry, Sir, I've got nothing here under that name. Our system is in an incredible mess today and I don't think there are any spare cars at all. But don't take that as final. Let me double check the computer for you. Sorry, there is still one car left in the compound but if you wanted a Mondeo, this one is probably of no use to you."

"So what is it?" Pete demanded in an irritable tone.

"It's a Renault People Carrier and, if you want it, you can have it for the same price as the Mondeo, though these are usually more expensive."

"It's not what I want or need," Pete continued, "but to make up for the inconvenience, if you can do a further discount, I'll think about the Renault."

"How about if we knock thirty Euros off the Mondeo price?" The clerk suggested.

"Thirty Euros and you've got a deal." Pete said, pulling out his wallet to look for his driving licence. Then as he put the licence down on the counter for inspection, the clerk placed thirty Euros, a set of car keys, and a plastic wallet full of paperwork at the side of the licence, which he picked up and begin to scrutinise.

"Make sure you check that everything is in working order before you drive the vehicle out of the compound, the clerk instructed.

"I sure intended to," Pete rejoined. "Having been a lorry driver once I know what my responsibilities are out there on the road."

Following Gordon where he was carrying the two guitar cases, Pete brought up the rear with the band trunk until they reached a wire- fenced compound where a solitary Renault People Carrier was sitting.

"It's as big as a house," Gordon observed.

"Better too big than too small," Pete disagreed as a clerk approached them from the open doorway of a grey portacabin. As the clerk was inspecting their paperwork, Pete waved Gordon over to him. "If you leave the guitars here, you can go and see if you can catch our two friends from the plane. We can give them a lift and get them to share the cost of gas," Pete suggested. "And while you're doing that, I'll check the vehicle over and get our bits and pieces on board. Leave your pack here as well."

"Sure will," Gordon responded, "and hopefully I'll see you back here in a couple of minutes."

Gordon had no sooner caught up with his two fellow travellers and explained the car hire situation to them than he spotted Mavis the airhostess, coming towards him, trundling her typical flight-crew little suitcase on wheels at her side. In the space of a moment, Gordon quickly repeated the story he had just told the two men. "So, young lady, can we offer you a lift to Galway?"

"And I am Don and this is my brother, Phil," the smaller of the two men said by way of introduction. "We are twins and, yes, we do believe that our mother was into the Everly Brothers around the time we were born. Back in Scotland, we are doctors and are travelling to a medical conference at Galway University."

"Yes, they have lots of those," Mavis put in. "Where we work they call it C.P.D. or continuing professional development," Don explained. "We have to do it but the government pays us for it so that every now and then we get some free travelling and a paid working holiday."

"What form does your conference take?" Gordon asked.

"Nothing too onerous," Don replied. "Not usually full day events that go on day after day but usually some half-day presentations with lots of time free for socialising and getting to meet people. For Phil here, it's usually an opportunity for him to develop his hobby at the same time, Phil being someone who likes meeting lady doctors."

"Watch it, young brother," Phil commented in good-natured tones. "That birth hour goes for a lot in family seniority."

Don ignored his twin's friendly ribbing and then with Gordon in the front passenger seat and Pete in the driving seat, he joined the others who were starting to get themselves and their luggage into the remaining space. Soon, they were ready for anything.

"At first, I thought this beast was enormous," Gordon mused, "but once you get five people and their luggage on board, it's not so big after all, or maybe its even a little on the small side."

"I've just noticed that it's an automatic," Gordon commented.

"Makes no difference to me, Pete responded. "Automatic or manual, four wheels or two. If it was built to be driven, I'll drive it and, by the way, does anyone know the way to Galway from here?"

"My sense of direction is notoriously bad," Mavis admitted. "And while I probably could be navigator, it's best that I decline. Does nobody have a map?"

"This band on tour never has a map," Pete explained. "It's a tradition with us. We navigate by osmosis and a sixth sense, which sometimes works and sometimes takes a day off. Anyway, I'd like to get the feel for Dublin streets and while driving to get that feel, no doubt we will pick up road signs, or we can ask a cabbie or a policeman."

So saying, Pete pushed his key into the ignition, started the engine and in a moment, they were leaving the hire car compound behind. Pete seemed to be driving aimlessly through a shabby semi-industrial area when he suddenly let out a whoop and pointed to a road sign that read, GALWAY AND THE WEST.

"Just when I was starting to enjoy my driving, someone throws a sign for Galway into the works and spoils it," Pete smilingly protested.

"Well, just pretend that you're lost, if that makes it easier for you," Gordon suggested.

"Or maybe I should hand the navigation over to Mavis and let her get us properly lost because I'm no good at this imaginary stuff," Pete protested.

"Do you think that tape machine might just be in working order?" Gordon said, pointing in the direction of the dashboard.

"Probably not, but it might just," Pete replied. "Why, do we have any tapes with us?"

Gordon went into his jacket pocket and fished out a cassette tape lacking a case. It looked as unlikely to work as the appearance of the tape player also suggested.

"Yea of little faith!" Gordon snorted as he slipped the cassette into the machine to find the Renault, a moment later, filled with the anguish-fuelled tones of Gram Parsons singing Hickory Wind. Time and roadway passed until, after a few moments, Pete fiddled with the track selector until they were being regaled by the Grievous Angel singing Love Hurts. Gordon was clapping his hands in some subtle and complex rhythm that somehow complemented that being laid down by Gram's backing group. "You know," he began thoughtfully, "for years, I thought that song was just a vapid piece of Tin Pan Alley disposable garbage of a song until I heard Gram sing it and then I heard its sheer power for the first time. Just then, Emmylou Harris's voice came in behind Gram Parsons and their poignant harmony filled the Renault." As Gordon clapped and sang along, Pete also began to sing and then Mavis added her tones to the mix.

Smiling to himself, Gordon switched off the tape machine and took Mavis by the arm. Looking very happy, "Girl," he began, "where on earth did you ever learn to sing like that?"

"Like what? I'm not any sort of a singer," Mavis responded.

"Have you ever been in a band, folk group, or choir?" Gordon asked.

"I used to be in the High School choir," Mavis admitted, "though I was never much good. Or on a good day I was kind of average. The music teacher could safely put me in the chorus but never any sort of lead part."

"Some of us get better as we get older," Gordon continued. "We get more life experience behind us and sometimes that comes out in the voice. Mind if I try something, Mavis?"

"No, I guess not," the airhostess replied.

At that, Gordon began to sing, "Love hurts, love scars," and just then, Pete came in with "Love wounds and mars. Any heart, not tough, not strong enough to take a lot of pain." After that, Gordon and Pete sang with Mavis following them, "Love is like a cloud, holds a lot of rain." And as their last notes faded away, Gordon was clapping enthusiastically, "Excellent, girlie, you could add a new dimension to our band and you could contribute a lot to our visual appeal." Pete added, "I don't suppose you ever learned to play a musical instrument on your journey through life?" "I learned a bit of piano as a kid," Mavis admitted.

"Did you?" Pete said with a huge grin. "We've got a Fender electric piano at home, though we've never had anyone in the band who wanted to play it or could play it."

Gordon could see that Pete was toying with the idea of having an extra vocalist in the band and one who could add some piano to their guitars. "Don't get carried away, guys," Gordon was already warning himself, "because although we do see these possibilities from time to time, usually they don't happen. Sadly, our band is probably fated to remain a duo on most of its gigs."

"My singing on most occasions is about as expert as my navigating skills," Mavis said, in a tone of voice that suggested she was fast losing interest in a musical career.

With Pete quietly at the wheel, the industrial looking units and warehouses that they had been passing began to thin out, until they were driving through an area which looked to be a mixture of industrial units and scattered detached houses. Most of the latter looked recently built and, in fact, they passed several building sites where bungalows were under construction. Soon, they were in an area that looked definitely suburban, with lots of greenery, established trees, and well kept gardens on neat, well-manicured streets. And in time as those suburbs were left behind the Renault and its passengers found themselves in an area of fields, hedgerows and dry stone dyke enclosed fields. "Well this has to be progress," Gordon chuckled enthusiastically. "That's what I like to see, the blacks and greys of the city giving way to country green. When you've seen even this little corner of the Irish countryside, you can see why people have been fighting over it for centuries."

"I guess we Scots have got a lot to answer for," Pete volunteered.

"Why the Scots?" Don asked.

"Well, you could argue that Robert the Bruce and, more particularly, his brother, Edward, were the start of Ireland's troubles back in the fourteenth century," Pete explained.

"W.B. Yeats wrote a play on that very subject," Gordon offered. "I think it was called *The Speaking of the Stones* or something of the sort. Do you think we might get to see Sligo this trip, Big Pete?" "If you want to see Sligo's Yeats' country, we'll do our best to fit it in," Pete replied. "What is the most important for you to see, Gordon, Sligo with its Yeats' connection or Tuam, where your folks came from?" Pete asked.

"I would like to see both," Gordon responded. "But if time only allows for one, then I guess it has to be Tuam. Sligo is an interest, but Tuam's in the blood."

"Look there, Gordon!" Pete said suddenly, pointing to a sign on the roadside.

Gordon looked where Pete was pointing and read out "Traveller's Rest Motel one kilometre."

Without even beginning to think about how much time they might lose through getting lost, Pete began, "I can see the possibility that by the time we get to Galway and find the university and our accommodation and get settled in, it might be quite late. So instead of having to be looking for somewhere to eat round bedtime, we should try and get a meal under our belts somewhere en route." "This might be as good a place as any to look for it," Gordon responded. "Guys, Don and Phil?" Pete said in a questioning tone, "what arrangements have you made for accommodation?"

"We've got two single rooms reserved," Don replied.

"Same as us," Pete volunteered. "I just hope your room arrangements turn out better than your car hire," Gordon smiled. "I'm sure they will but there's another sign," Gordon said, reading a road sign that declared, "Traveller's Rest Motel seven hundred and fifty metres on right."

No sooner had he said that when Pete spotted a third sign that announced, JOHN DELANEY'S TRAVELLER'S REST BAR & GRILL - NO FOOT-BALL COACHES.

Chapter Four

The Travellers' Rest Motel

Pete indicated for a right turn and turned across the carriageway into a conifer-lined red blaze driveway that opened out into a wide car park floored with the same material. Several cars were already parked in the car park, as was a battered coach. Opposite them at the far side of the parking area was a single story modern-looking building that appeared to be a shop/bar complex to the front with a row of weathered, chalet type buildings to either side.

"Do you think it's open?" Gordon asked. "It looks pretty lifeless to me."

"As long as the chef's on duty, it will do me," Pete responded. "I wonder if they need a band to liven things up?"

"What are you thinking, Big Pete. Is the band going to sing for its supper again?"

"That's not a bad idea, man. An extra practice session to help us get ready for our gig in Galway on Saturday would be no bad thing."

"Do you want me to check it out, turn my charm loose on the management, and see what sort of deal I can cut?" Gordon offered.

"No, you stay here with the others and I'll go see. Be right back."

With that, Pete was out of the Renault in a second and heading in the direction of what seemed to be the complex's main entrance.

Inside the dimly lit, modern building, Pete quickly came to the conclusion that the place looked typical of a type of heavy and over ornate steak house restaurant that can be found in almost every corner of Scotland or England. He took in at a glance, the cheap glossy prints in heavy gilt frames on the walls and the equally heavy gilt-framed mirrors amongst a profusion of imitation Tiffany lamps. Around the walls were dark oak tables and chairs, The chairs sporting pseudo rustic embroidery backs and cushion covers. Most of the tables and chairs were empty, except for three or four clustered close to the bar, which were occupied. The bar sported a huddle of fairly standard draught beer taps, with optics for spirits, mounted on the wall behind the bar. A chubby young waitress, with her blonde hair tied back in a ponytail, was standing at the bar with a gilt metal tray lying on the bar in front of her, on to which every now and then one of the two barmen working behind the bar would deposit a bottle or a glass. She leaned against the bar looking totally bored while she waited for the rest of her order to be made up. The two barmen hovering close to her were young, possibly students. Both were wearing white bar jackets with green collars and cuffs. Further along the bar, past the two barmen, an older man in a well-cut white evening jacket was lounging. Beneath the dinner jacket, he was wearing a white shirt and a black, almost string tie. He was taking occasional sips from a large brandy glass that was sitting at his elbow.

"That the manager, love?" Pete asked, appearing at the waitress's elbow.

"No, that's John Delaney, the owner," the girl replied.

"A word with you, boss?" Pete said, catching the owner's eye after a moment.

"Yes, young fellow, what can I do for you?" came the languid reply, a reply that was washed down with another sip of brandy.

"Pretty quiet in here tonight," Pete observed.

"Been that way for a while now, son," Delaney responded.

"Some live music would draw the punters in and liven the place up a bit," Pete commented.

"You a musician by any chance?" John Delaney asked.

"Yes, I'm Pete Lafferty from the MAVIS VALLEY BAND," Pete said, extending his hand. "Just en route from Glasgow to play at the Galleon Festival. Initially, we pulled in off the road looking to get something to eat but when I saw how quiet you were, I thought maybe we could do a set for you." "What do you usually get paid?" Delaney asked.

"Depends where our gig is," Pete replied.

"How about if I pay you ten Euros each and throw in dinner for everyone?"

"Today we have three in the band and two helpers," Pete responded. "So, five meals and thirty Euros and we'll play for an hour for you and your customers. We usually take a fifteen minute break halfway through." "Are you the Scottish band that's got the O'Brien boy in it?" Delaney asked.

"We sure are," Pete replied. "Gordy O'Brien, a Galway/Scottish O'Brien. But how is it that you know about Gordon and our band?"

"Well, this is Ireland and with our troubles, some of us have found that it pays to keep ourselves well informed. Over here, information can save your life or cost you it," the bar owner continued.

"Anyway, I'll go and tell the others what's happening and then we can get our instruments inside and get ourselves set up.," Pete said, drawing the conversation to a close.

Back at the hire car, Pete quickly explained to the others what was happening. "Don, Phil and Mavis, when we go in and are getting our equipment set up, you just get yourselves a drink and then sit back and watch us work for an hour and after our little set, we'll get us to Galway, in probably the last of the daylight and get us settled in for the night so that we are ready for whatever tomorrow brings our way. Gordon, when we go in, you take the guitars in with you and I'll bring the trunk. If you find out where they want us to perform, you can set up a couple of suitable seats for us and then get the instruments in tune. I'll set up the equipment on my own."

"Yet again, you're doing most of the work," Gordon commented.

"Well, at least when you tune the instruments for the start of a set, I can be confident that we are in tune and ready to go," Pete responded, "and that's important, man."

Gordon nodded his assent. next Pete, took the band trunk out of the car, trundled it off in the direction of the bar. Gordon picked up the two guitar cases and in moments, he was inside and setting up two stools just in front of the bar counter. He had just finished tuning his instrument when Pete and his trunk came in noisily from the car park. A moment later, Pete had become a one-man hive of activity.

First, he checked where the nearest electrical socket was, and then, pulling an extension cable with a multi-plug facility on its end out of the trunk, he ran it into the middle of the space where he and Gordon were going to perform and fixed it to the floor with gaffer tape. Next, came the two state-of-the-art AER one hundred and twenty watt, double channel amplifiers. The amps were small but with their high outputs and double channels they gave the band two channels for instruments and two for voices, all that this two-person band required on stage. While Gordon was tuning Big Red, Pete was placing the amplifiers where he thought they would be the most effective, plugging them in and setting the volume and tone controls. Next, he assembled the folding mike stands and then connected their leads to the amplifiers, before rigging the two mikes and foot operated on/off switches. Finally, he plugged the two guitar leads into the amplifiers, making sure that he left the business ends as close as possible to the places where he and Gordon would expect to find them when they were ready to start playing. By the time he had finished setting up and was just tidying some of his bits and pieces back into the trunk, Gordon was tuning the second guitar. Finishing that task to his eventual satisfaction, he placed both instruments back into their hardshell cases, knowing that they were ready for use.

Walking across to the table where Mavis was sitting with a bottle of coke in front of her, Gordon smiled. "I reckon Pete's just about ready," he began. "What I would like you to do tonight, Mavis, is stay close to where I am sitting and, if I sing any songs that you feel you know well, just join in on the chorus. Or, if you feel up to it, throw in a harmony."

"Maybe," Mavis responded in a hesitant tone. "I can't promise I'll do that."

"What to do is this," Gordon explained, "I'll be sitting on my stool; so stand just behind me and a little to my right. You won't be able to stand to my left because my guitar will be there but standing just behind me, if you get ready to join in, just lean over my shoulder until you are within range of the mike. Pretty soon you'll hear your voice coming from the amp, but don't let that throw you off your stride because sometimes it can if you're not used to it. The way Pete has set the amps up, the sound will come out of the speakers, hit the wall, and then be bounced back into the room. If we're lucky, that bounce will sound almost like a little bit of echo or reverb, which always helps. Don't worry at all about your singing, your voice will be fine and, anyway, Pete and I are looking at this gig as a practice session. So if the worst was to come to the worst and you were to hit the odd bum note, then - so what? From what I heard in the Renault, you'll be great."

"I'm really not sure about this, Gordon," Mavis said in a trembling voice. "Hopefully, I won't freeze or anything like that and, who knows, if I hear my voice and it sounds all right, that might give me confidence."

At that, Pete joined them. "I'm just going to get myself a pint for lubrication and then I'll be ready anytime that you are, Mr. O'Brien." So saying, he got himself a pint of stout and then choosing the stool that was closest to the bar, he took a long pull at his drink before sitting his glass on the bar's well-worn counter within easy arm reach of where he was going to be sitting

Retrieving his guitar, he plugged in his jack plug and, while holding down a G major chord with his left hand, he ran his right hand index finger across all six strings. Then, as a sweet sounding chord issued from his amplifier, he smiled with satisfaction until catching Gordon's eye, he gave his band partner an approving nod to let him know that his tuning efforts were appreciated. Still holding Gordon's gaze, he gave Gordon's stool a meaningful glance and Gordon realised he was being told to get a move on.

Understanding Pete's silent hint, he crossed the bar, took a drink from Pete's pint and then, retrieving his guitar, made his way to the empty stool and took his seat to quickly check his tuning one final time. He was aware that Mavis had crossed the room and taken up position just behind him. Giving her a welcoming smile, he stretched down to the foot switch on the floor, clicking his mike on and then, resisting the temptation to say something totally unoriginal like "Testing, one, two, three," he tapped the end of his mike three times with a fingernail and immediately the corresponding tones from his amp told him that his mike was live. Looking across to his side, he could see that Pete had pulled a thumbpick and two fingerpicks from his pocket and was busy slipping them on to his right hand fingers. Gordon himself did not use picks in his playing, neither the flatpick or fingerpick variety, but preferred the sound of flesh and nail driven music that he was able to push out of his instrument. He was well aware that this was an area of great controversy between some of the old classical guitar masters, some of them maintaining that flesh was wrong while nails were the way, others taking the opposite tack. By eschewing picks and choosing a combination of nails and flesh, he was sure that his choice was at least partly responsible for the distinctively mellow sound that his playing was known for. "What the Hell did Fernando Sor, know about it?" He had been known to say, "Different strokes for different folks. Simple as that."

A moment later after a slightly lingering silence which certainly drew the attention of the sprinkling of customers who were on the premises towards the band…Just as Pete and Gordon knew that it would.

Slipping his well-worn embroidered guitar strap over his head and shoulder and putting his instrument within easy and comfortable reach, he began to speak. "Good evening folks. My name is Gordon O'Brien, while this big guy at my side is Pete Lafferty. Collectively we are usually known as the Mavis Valley Ceilidh Band. We were on our way from Glasgow, our base to Galway, to perform at an acoustic music festival when we pulled in off the road to catch a bite to eat and have ended up with this impromptu gig, which we hope you are going to enjoy. Before we start I would like to tell you a little bit about our band. because our name is a bit of a misnomer as we don't play any traditional Scottish music, nor do we play for what our American cousins would call square dances. In fact, there is nothing square about us and, while we don't play electric guitars through walls of amplifiers, we see ourselves as being towards the funky end of folk/acoustic music. This is just to let you know that we will not be playing you music for a Dashing White Sergeant, a Witches Reel or a Strip the Willow. Big Pete and myself are both singer-song-writers in our own right and, while the band does perform a lot of its own ma-terial, we also include other peoples' songs in our sets, mostly from the area where folk music meets the like of Bob Dylan, Phil Ochs, Gram Parsons, Rambling Jack Elliot, Leadbelly, Mississippi John Hurt, Gary Davis, John Martyn and a whole lot of other influences and influencers. That said, we would like to start off by playing for you an old standard called Freight Train. Some of you will no doubt know it through Nancy Whiskey's cover version, while others will have heard it from the singing and influential guitar playing of the late, great Elizabeth Cotton. Elizabeth or Libby as she was generally known, was a bit like that other late greater Jimi Hendrix, both of whom being left-handers who played upside-down, right-handed guitars with a great deal of fire, fluidity, and creativity. Libby was amazing in that she was recording and performing well into her eighties, unlike Jimi who we lost at far too young an age."

That said, Gordon fingered a C major chord and, with his left hand pinkie dancing over the first and second strings of his guitar at the third fret, played a catchy two-bar introduction before beginning to sing:

Freight train, freight train, goin' so fast. Freight train, freight train goin' so fast
Please don't tell them which train I'm on so they won't know where I've gone;
When I die, please bury me deep down at the bottom of old Chestnut Street;
So I can hear ol' number nine as she goes rollin,' rollin' by."

Then, as he finished that line, Gordon turned his attention fully to his guitar to play a glittering solo that was part melody and partly rhythmic, chordal riffs and runs, many of them the standard building blocks of the trade that almost any blues, folk or ragtime guitarist would have known. Pete was also hunched over his instrument, throwing out a flurry of jazz tinged suspended chords to enhance Gordon's solo until, after a moment, their two part solo had fused into a harmonious single part offering.

Gordon began to play some bluesy sounding arpeggios, while Pete, holding his flat pick between the thumb and index fingers of his right hand at the same time as he was applying his second and third fingers of the same hand, delivered some ultra-slick hybrid picking that even a predominantly non guitar-playing audience could recognise as some fine acoustic musicianship and began to applaud enthusiastically.

"Thank you very kindly folks," Gordon responded warmly, "because, if you enjoy our performance then that adds so much to our enjoyment of this musical exchange and interchange." After that, Gordon concentrated fully on his guitar for a moment, going into an A major run that was an introduction to an old Willie Brown tune, Mississippi Blues. Then, as Pete recognised the piano-based guitar blues for what it was, he began to play a rolling boogie backing to Gordon's playing that was very similar to the boogie backing provided by Rory Block when she had provided back-up for Stefan Grossman on a well-known version of that tune. Finishing that number on a fairly standard blues turnaround that worked equally well as an ending, he then began to speak.

"For our next number we would like to do a song that I am sure many of you will know. While I think of it predominantly as being a Leadbelly song, some of you will know it as a top ten hit of some time back when it was recorded by an English pop group called The Four Pennies. Anyway, this is our version of a great little song that has had several different titles over the years. Some of you will know it as 'Black Girl or In The Pines,' or maybe as 'Little Girl.' There is a fabulous version done by Doc Watson and Dave Grisman, the mandolin player, and for anyone who is interested enough, check that one out because it is easily available on DVD. That said, enough talking and on with the music, because the band is itching to do "Black Girl" for you."

With that, Gordon played a quick introduction and as Pete fell into place behind him with his guitar, began to sing.

"Black girl, black girl, where did you sleep last night? In the pines, in the pines where the sun never shines. I shivered the whole night through;
Her husband was a railroad man, killed a mile and a half from here.
They found his body by the driving wheel but his head has never been found;
Black girl, black girl where did you sleep last night?
In the pines, in the pines, where the sun never shines;
I shivered the whole night through.

Pete then took up an extended version of Gordon's short introduction and ran it into a solo to play the song out, "No, he wasn't one of the Disappeared,"

Pete said, referring to those individuals who had simply vanished during the Irish troubles and had most likely been murdered by one group or another.

Shocked at his partner's clearly strongly held sentiment and lack of tact, Gordon caught Pete's eye and, glowering at him, silently willed him to say no more.

"While this might neither be the time nor the place for me to express my opinion," Pete went on, "what Gordon was singing there reminded me of the Disappeared which, in my opinion, is a cruel thing for families never to know for sure what happened to their loved ones and to be kept in the dark year after *painful* year for so long. I would have to implore anyone listening who has any information on this matter to do what you can to bring ease to those suffering families. Keeping all of these poor souls in the dark for so long is no Christian thing. So, if you can, do your bit to clear up this blot on the history of a very fine nation. Come on, guys, play the Whiteman or, maybe I should say, stop playing the Whiteman." Gordon caught Pete's eyes, held it for a long moment and then, with a single emphatic shake of his head, told his band partner to "shut up."

After that, Gordon fingered an A minor chord and launched into a fluid introductory run that he had lifted from John Renbourn's version of the American folk song, "Buffalo Skinners" and carried that into some flashy playing that he hoped would divert some attention away from Pete's comments. Next, Gordon became aware that Mavis had drawn close and was trying to speak into his ear.

"So why was it a pine wood in the song and not an oak or an elm plantation?" she was asking as he was switching off his mike so that their conversation was not reaching the audience. Mavis continued, "Bootleggers often work in the pines, getting juniper for their gin and gin is often used in abortion, so pure speculation as it may be, my guess is that this is a woman's song and that what we have in the song story is a woman in trouble trying to rid herself of an unwanted baby and not about a woman trying to break free of a man trying to own and control her sexuality as the song could suggest."

At that, Point Pete crossed over to join in the conversation.

"Sorry to interrupt," he apologised, "but we are here to do a set and time is passing." Leaning across, he clicked on Gordon's mike and began to speak.

"Thank you, good people, because we are going to take our short break now. If any of you want to grab another pint or visit the facilities, now's your opportunity."

Knowing only too well that their break would soon be over, Pete led the band and friends to a free table, where they all sat down. No sooner had they taken their seats than the motel owner came over to them.

"A good start, Gordon," he said, taking a sip of his brandy and giving the impression that he was speaking to Gordon alone and not the whole band. "Don't be in any way alarmed, Gordon, by what I am going to say, but the boys in the backroom would like to have a word with you."

"He goes nowhere without me with him," said Pete.

"It's all right, Big Pete," Gordon responded in a conciliatory tone. "I half expected something like this to happen somewhere along the line. It's okay and I don't mind. It's just a part of looking into the family roots. So where is your back room?" Gordon asked, already following Delaney, who led the way towards a small doorway just to the left of the main entranceway.

When they reached the small door, Delaney pushed it open and stood to the side to let Gordon walk forward on his own, a gesture that Pete did not like one little bit. Once inside the room, Gordon could see that it was a store full of crates and kegs. In the middle of the room, and taking up a large part of the available space, was a heavy old walnut table of a kind often to be seen in G.P. or dental waiting rooms. Scattered around the ponderous table was a collection of ill-assorted and mismatched chairs, three of them occupied by large, bearded men. The tallest of the three, who seemed to have been waiting for Gordon to enter, took a step forward as Gordon came in. Towering over Gordon, he was even taller than Pete, who had stepped forward to stand at Gordon's side.

"Hi there!" the tall stranger said in a convivial tone, extending a hand in Gordon's direction. "I've been curious and looking forward to meeting this descendant of Jamie O'Brien, excellent Galway Republican that he was. I'm Mike Smart and one of the meanings of 'smart' is 'intelligent' or 'intelligence'. What I do is keep an eye on things for the Republican lobby in an area that stretches from West Dublin to Galway and Cork, even if the Cork bastards didn't rise up when called. What I'm saying to you, young Gordon, I probably shouldn't but, because of who your family were, I'm sure it will be okay. Do you mind if I ask you a question, Gordon?"

"I don't mind at all," Gordon replied.

"What I want to ask you, lad, and it's just for personal reassurance, is what do you think of Irish Republicanism?"

"The question is too wide, too open," Gordon replied, taking the prof- fered hand and giving it a shake. "Could you narrow the question down a bit for me because being asked a question like that is like being asked what you think about life. Most people would want to know which aspects of life."

"I hear what you're saying, Gordon," Smart countered. "Just try and do your best with the question as it stands," Smart encouraged. "Just for fun."

"I have to admit that it's not something that I think about a lot," Gordon said, sure that whatever the question was about, it was not about fun. "Though, since I knew that I was going to be playing in Galway, I have been thinking about Ireland and my Irish roots more than usual. English bad treat- ment of the Irish goes back a long way and it's still going on." Mike Smart nodded emphatically in agreement.

"We got the Republic and, in time, we will get the six counties," Gordon continued. "But it will have to come through the ballot-box and not with bul- lets. Our northern brothers and sisters will have to come around to see that they will do better with the Republic and Strasbourg than they ever would with Westminster," Gordon explained, "and quickly thinking about your question, there have definitely been incidents during what you guys call the Armed Struggle that I would have wanted to distance myself from. Like everybody expects, a guerrilla force to go for the soft target options, nobody would expect such a force to take on a modern, well-equipped mechanised army in a head-to-head, set-piece battle, but blowing up the Household Cavalry was a cowardly and cruel disgrace. And I am not sure that the assassination of Mountbatten was much better. Certainly, Mountbatten had it coming, not least for the million Hindus and Moslems who died as a result of him botching Indian partition. That seems to be almost a post-Empire British tradition. Give a country its independence when you no longer have the resources to control it or exploit it any further and, when you do pull out, split it in two in such a way that you leave the population at loggerheads and weakened for generations to come. India and Ireland, in some ways, are not too different. It struck me, not so long ago, that there is a world of difference between seeing the Irish situation from the comfort, safety and security of your own armchair watching the television news, and seeing it over here. Last year, when I was on holiday in Ireland, I had come over on the ferry with the car and, at the same time as we were coming off the ship, a contingent of British troops and their vehicles were being disembarked. If what I saw had been a newsreel clip and I had been told that I was watching a port on the Mekong River during the Vietnam War, I would have had no problem believing that. Those young British soldiers were very clearly going on active service in a war zone."

Chapter Five

Paramilitary Encounter

"An interesting perspective," Mike Smart interjected, "but a point of view that few people in England would have come up with."

Gordon glanced down at the array of objects lying on the tabletop in front of Mike Smart. There was a black beret, a pair of black leather gloves, a set of car keys, and a dishtowel that had probably come in from the bar. Gordon had the suspicion that under the dishtowel, he could make out the shape of something that may have been a pistol.

"Considering how active your great grandfather had been on the Republican Army Council of the Civil War era," Mike Smart went on, "Could you ever imagine yourself involved in something like an armed struggle?"

"Growing up in Scotland, I was always aware that I was both Scottish and Irish," Gordon replied. "If I had grown up over here, who knows, I may have grown up closer to the Republican cause and its history than I did. Still, that didn't happen and the person that I am/became would never take up the gun. I can just about understand using violence to protect your family, colleagues or friends, but not taking to the gun as political expediency. When the Loyalist mob was burning down Catholic houses in Belfast, I can understand Martin Maginnis taking his rifle and a box of ammunition up into that church tower to break up the mob, or I can understand and just about condone Bernadette Devlin, when a Westminster M.P. throwing rocks to protect her friends when they were under attack, controversial as that was at the time. For me, though, it has to be the ballot-box and not the bullet. Or, at a pinch, self-defence, but no further than that."

"Sometimes self-defence can get a lot more complicated and a lot more violent than you might ever expect," Mike Smart commented.

"I could imagine that might be the case," Gordon admitted. "Over the years, I have become less and less of a Catholic/Christian and more and more of a Hindu/Buddhist and one of the foundational beliefs of both systems is Ahimsa or non-violence like I don't eat meat, fish or eggs. I won't buy or wear leather and I don't even kill moths or spiders. So, despite who or what my forebears were, I am no Fenian warrior and can't imagine myself helping with your armed struggle. I might just sneak in a hope that you win it rather than lose it in the end, if in these things there are ever any winners. Maybe we just get different kinds of losers."

At that point, Delaney put his head around the door.

"The natives are getting restless and clearly want the band on stage Delaney said in an apologetic tone, as if loath to intrude on the discussion.

"We won't be long," Mike Smart said, producing a notebook and a pen from the pocket of his leather jacket. He wrote a telephone number on to a page of his notebook, tore that page out and handed the page to Gordon. "Now, Gordon O'Brien," he began in a tongue-in-cheek lecturing tone, "If you should find yourself in any sort of trouble while over here in Ireland, ring me on that number for help at any time of the day or night. If anyone other than myself answers, I want you to assume that you are dealing with one of my senior boys and that he will be able to do anything that I can, or almost."

Just then, Pete, with an impatient look on his face, ignored Mike Smart by turning his back on him and motioned for Gordon to follow him back to the bar.

For a moment, Smart and Pete exchanged less than friendly looks as, inwardly, Pete was trying to assess if Smart was likely to be able to keep on his feet if he ever had to put a fist on his jaw. Feeling the antipathy and tension in the room, Gordon broke the mood by heading back towards the bar where he had soon regained his seat and instrument. Pete was also back in position and, for a moment, both of them were plugging in jack plugs and checking their tuning.

"Good to see you all back again, folks," Gordon said, smiling as he looked around the room, which seemed to have filled up somewhat while the band were meeting the Republicans.

Pete was scanning the faces of those members of the audience closest to him, trying to determine if the audience were happy with their set this far. He saw no obvious signs of boredom or dissatisfaction, though he had no doubt that his comments about the Disappeared would have done nothing for his popularity ratings in some quarters.

Just then, the main door opened and three couples came in to make their way to the bar where they ordered drinks. Soon, glasses in hand, they were making their way to the two tables closest to where Pete was sitting.

"This next song that we are going to do is one of our self-penned numbers or, more accurately, I should say, it is one of Gordon's self-penned numbers. This is what happens in a band where you have two songwriters. He starts to perform some of my songs and I take over some of his, which often means that I get the best of the bargain because Gordy is our ace songwriter.

"So this next song that we would like to do for you is one called 'Diamonds and Lace,'" Gordon explained, playing some fast arpeggios on his guitar while he was introducing the song. "It's a song that I wrote a few years ago now, though the events and the person that the song was written for and about, go a bit further back again. This song was written for one Maureen Dempsey, my first girlfriend at high school. This is a typical situation for a songwriter because we all remember our life experiences and use real life episodes for ideas to write about. If a song is based on real events and real experiences, it is much more likely to come from the heart and, in that way, be a statement, evocation that other people, i.e. yourselves as audience, can relate to. Conversely, a song written about a fictitious person, or fictional events, is unlikely to resonate with people. It's like the old joke, 'How do you define country music?' Answer, 'Three chords and honesty.'"

At that, Gordon fingered a G major chord and began to play a different arpeggio from the one he had been using while speaking. Finishing his introduction, he began to sing.

I only ever really loved the one woman, or maybe I should say, the one teenage girl. It was back down the years but I can still see her face, one minute hard as diamonds, next as soft as lace. You were always drawn to that wild side of life.

My friends all told me you'd never make a wife.

They liked to tell me how you were bad and all about the past they said you had, but to me you were always the best. You gave me what I wanted and I could leave the rest.

You could be as tough as your daddy's docks or as sweet as your mama's wind-up music box. You could be as gentle as a young man's dreams, all that poetry written for you in reams.

As he sang, Gordon would play his introductory arpeggio from time to time, using it to add colour and drama and hold the audience's attention in the space between verses. And then with Pete and Mavis singing along behind him, he did one more line as a chorus and a colourful ending.

One minute hard as diamonds, the next as soft as lace.

Then, when Gordon stopped singing, Pete began to speak.

"Anyone who knows us would tell you that the M.V.C.B. and myself like to do a lot of blues material in our sets and this next one is a blues. It's called Payday. Making it a working-class song and it's one that was written, performed, and recorded by that wonderful blues guitarist, Mississippi John Hurt. It's a song that has been reworked by a lot of people, ourselves included but nobody has bettered the original by the man from Avalon Mississippi. Although John is no longer with us, his music sure lives on. John Hurt was recorded in the late 1920s before vanishing off the radar for a lot of years, eventually resurfacing on the American folk song, coffee house circuit, after almost a lifetime spent doing just about every type of menial, manual work open to an American black man of his age and generation. Thankfully, through it all, John had kept up his singing and guitar playing and had lost little of his skills when it came his time to be rediscovered. The fact that several of his 1920s songs had been included on Harry Smith's famous and influential compilation of early American music had alerted some people to his existence and both they and other enthusiasts were there and ready to do the needful when John became available to stand in front of a milk or a camera. Sadly, John's second career did not last as long as it might have but this man who, until his elder years, had never lived in a house with either electricity or running water, did get to be properly recorded and, if any of you would like to know more about this wonderful musician, the recordings are out there and readily available.

Although this next number that we are going to do for you is a John Hurt number we are not going to try to duplicate all of John's style of finger-picking because it is just a little too complex for me."

That said, Gordon slipped a capo on to his fret board before settling into a rhythmic groove, which owed more to several Texas guitarists than it did to Mississippi stylists. Pete smiled to himself as he recognised a John Hurt run that Gordon had been working on for weeks, sneaking in at the corner of his aural perception. Gordon concentrated on his instrument and then, knowing well the point where Pete would begin his singing, started to play quieter so that his playing would not distract from Pete's vocal performance. Laying down a rhythm that perfectly complemented Pete's he threw in a swift run that was pure John Hurt, just as Pete began to sing. "*Payday, payday; Gonna take you back to your mama come payday;*

Tried so hard to get on with you; It's not your honey but the way you do;
Gonna take you back to your mama come payday."

Knowing that Pete had come to the end of a verse, Gordon was now playing as loud as he could, throwing in riffs and runs that were John Hurt to the note. Gordon's playing was now fast and fluid and, for any guitar players in the audience, it was somewhere between highly competent and dazzling. Then when Gordon brought the song to a conclusion on a run that had been used by generations of blues guitarists the audience seemed to recognise the calibre of what they were being given and applauded enthusiastically. At a high speed, Pete rattled off a Duck Baker run that both he and Gordon liked to use. He repeated it twice and used that to lead him into some Jorma Kaukenen lines built around fast changes from A minor to E major chords. Gordon recognised Pete's often used introduction to the traditional song, "Hesitation Blues, and began to lay down some hard driving lines as a background for Pete's vocal performance, who then began to sing;

Standing on a corner with a dollar in my hand;
Looking for a woman who's looking for a man.
Tell me how long do I have to wait?
Can I get you now, or must I hesitate?
Well pussy ain't nothin' but meat on the t

bone; You can take it, you can shake it
Or you can leave it alone."

As Pete finished that line, he went off into a long solo, which had the audience clapping and stamping their approval and encouragement. Then, just as Pete was playing a showy outro, one of the two young barmen appeared at his elbow.

"Message from the boss, guys." He hissed in Pete's ear. "When you finish your set, pack up your equipment as quick as you can, because we've been instructed to set up two tables just to the left of the doorway so that you can get your dinner. It was a great set, guys. I really enjoyed it."

"So did we," Pete responded. "A short set but I think a good one."

"I'll talk us to a close, Big Pete," Gordon interjected, "and while I'm doing that, you can be packing the gear into the trunk and getting the trunk ready to go to the car."

"Fine," Pete responded, "but keep it short. I don't want you getting into one of your long audience raps."

Ten minutes and three songs later, the set was finished. Gordon had said his thank-yous and good-byes to their audience. The band's. equipment was packed away and the trunk was in the Renault, Pete having worked hard and fast with his dismantling and stowing away. Soon, they were sitting down to their meal and, while the meal was an unhurried one, Pete was aware of the fact that he had a drive in front of him and was not keen for the meal to extend to a second coffee or an extended talk session.

"Anything that we can say here, we can say in the car," Commented Pete.

Nodding in agreement, Gordon pushed his empty plate away from him and, in the same moment, the motel owner appeared at his side and laid some Euros on the table. "Come and see me on your return journey and we can do it again," Delaney breezed, spun on his heel, and was gone in an instant. The motel owner paused in mid stride and continued his conversation almost as if as an afterthought. "Two of my regulars have commented that you guys really livened this place up and lightened it, too, and they say I should think about live music as a regular feature."

"Check with the Musicians' Union as they will know who's gigging in the area and they'll generally help you and keep you right," Pete suggested, "but in the meantime, This band needs to be moving along."

Out in the car park, they re-took their seats. "As I said earlier," Pete said, putting the key in the ignition and starting the Renault's engine, "there is still a good chunk of daylight left, so we can probably do most of the drive in the light and most likely reach Galway just before or just after dark." At that, Pete released his handbrake and, almost immediately, they were crossing the car park and heading for the red blaze driveway that would lead them back out onto the Galway road.

At first, there was some desultory conversation in the hire car but the combination of a solid meal and comfortable seats seemed to have brought a semi-sleepy atmosphere into the Renault. As Pete took the car and its occupants back on to the road and pointed it in the direction of Galway, Gordon was surveying the landscape on both sides of the road. Beyond the low, drystone dykes, that framed the road, some of the fields were under crops but many others were given over to cattle and sheep. Several were full of horses, suggesting that there might be a riding school or a racehorse breeding or/training establishment in the area. Mavis was the first to notice a small black cloud on the western horizon but it was Gordon who identified it as a great flock of crows. "By the looks of things, all we will have to do to reach our destination is to follow that little black cloud." Pete commented.

"It seems to be an enormous flight of rooks and jackdaws." Gordon observed.

"How do you know they are rooks and jackdaws?" Mavis asked.

"Well with rooks," Gordon began, "they have a big bald patch above their beaks which makes them pretty recognisable, while the grey heads of the jackdaws on top of that black body, make it pretty clear who they are and then there are the calls. The rooks are quite harsh and guttural, the jackdaws have a slightly more musical note to their crow talk."

"It's the biggest group of crows I've ever seen," Pete volunteered. "Can't say that I've ever seen a bigger one," Gordon agreed. "They must be heading for some well known and probably long established crow roosting site. It wouldn't surprise me if this is not a regular, maybe even a daily occurrence. What we are seeing up there probably accounts for most of the crows in west/central Ireland," Gordon continued.

Pete nodded in a relaxed, semi-contented way, having enjoyed his set, followed by his dinner, and now he was enjoying some relaxed travelling. "Remember that flat you had in Queens Crescent in Glasgow, man?" he asked.

Gordon nodded, remembering the Georgian crescent where he used to live. Because of the configuration of the buildings there, the ornamental gardens in the centre of the crescent were a great favourite with the Glasgow City centre starlings at roosting time. By late afternoon in winter, at first a thin trickle of the birds and, later, a great stream of them would begin to move north and away from George Square and the streets close around it and would begin to fill the sky to the north-west, where eventually a great spiral of birds would form up, going round and round, searching for just the right time and place to make a sudden swoop groundward, until all of the garden trees were crowded, black with starlings. Gordon had always been more impressed with the flocks' morning behaviour than what he was with their afternoon antics. In the morning, when he was just waking, he would be aware of the starlings' input into the dawn chorus and then, as he was getting more active himself and getting ready to go out, he would know by the increasing level of bird chatter that the flocks were almost ready to set off on a day's foraging. It was as if tension was rising in the flock with more and more nervous chattering going on as it got closer to flight time. On many occasions he had found himself wondering if the starlings' chattering was a language because, time after time, he had observed the same phenomena. The birds would get noisier and noisier until suddenly and all at once, the whole flock would make a co-ordinated leap skywards and, in that very instant, would take off. Gordon had no difficulty imagining a venerable old starling leader, suddenly giving the command that would catapult the flock into the air and get them aloft into a great swirling spiral that would soon break up into smaller groups as the different formations set off towards their preferred foraging grounds.

Pete was simultaneously watching the road ahead and the Galway bound flock of rooks and jackdaws and thinking about the Queens Crescent starlings as he steered the Renault into a long, gentle curving bend. Then, just as he was driving the hire car out of the curve and back into a long, straight stretch, a movement off to his left caught his eye and he realised than a man wearing matching camouflage jacket and trousers had stepped off the grass verge into the road, where he was now standing, signalling for the Renault to stop.

"What the Hell!" Pete muttered to himself. "Who is this joker and what does he want other than to be squashed like a bug in the road?" At first Pete did not notice the automatic weapon slung on a webbing sling which was hanging at the man's right side. "British Army," Mavis said in an explanatory tone, as Pete at first applied his brakes and then released them.

"He obviously doesn't know that Pete Lafferty hates to be told what to do and, while we do have plenty of time to get ourselves to Galway and get organised for our festival, we don't have time to waste. What do you think, folks? Should I just jink round him or should I stop?"

"For God's sake, Pete!" Mavis protested in a worried tone. "This is Ireland and there are people here who maintain that these guys have a shoot-to-kill policy."

"Meaning what, exactly?" Pete asked.

"Meaning that if a vehicle fails to heed an army command to stop, the squaddies will assume that it is paramilitary and open fire. And when they do start to shoot, it's not just to stop the vehicle but to make sure that the occupants are dead. No prisoners and no long and costly trials," Mavis replied.

"That right, love?" Pete asked.

"Nobody knows for sure," Mavis continued. "And if it is true, the authorities are sure not going to admit it. "Safest thing is to assume the worst and that it is true. Just remember, guys, that this is Ireland and different rules apply over here. The British Army is not your unarmed British bobby. Over here, we are dealing with Parachute Regiment, Marines, S.A.S., and who knows what else. And because of that, we tend to be cautious and just stop when ordered to."

At that, Pete pulled the Renault in close to the nearside grass verge and the soldier stepped round to his driver's side, motioning for Pete to open his window. Instead, Peter opened his door and stepped down onto the road.

"Good day, Sarge," Pete said breezily, looking at the stripes on the soldier's arm.

"I get the impression, young fellow, that you don't like to take orders. First, you were slow to obey my command to stop and, when I tell you to open the window, you open your door and step out. Where are you from? Where are you going? And do you have any I.D. on you?"

"We have come from Glasgow en route to Galway to play a concert with our band," Pete replied, noticing the soldier's Scottish accent. "On I.D. I can offer you passport or driving licence? Any preference?" As he asked that question, Pete took a half step forward so that he was close enough to reach the man if the need arose.

Recognising Pete's move for what it was, the soldier moved his position slightly so that his weapon was closer to Pete. "Let me see your passport. I get the feeling that I've seen you somewhere before, fellow. It makes me nervous when I think I recognise somebody but can't place them."

"That makes no difference to me," Pete said, fishing his passport out of his top pocket and holding it out for inspection.

"I got the feeling a minute ago that you were not going to stop for me, or that idea was running through your mind," the soldier commented. "I had no reason not to stop for you," Pete responded, "other than the fact that I hate to be told what to do."

"But you would have stopped," the soldier continued, smiling mirthlessly. "They would have stopped you." Pete looked back along the strip of grass verge to see who the soldier was referring to and just at that, a green and brown camouflage net was thrown aside to reveal two soldiers lying on the grass beside a machine gun set up on a tripod. One of the men was adjusting a belt of ammunition. "So, young fellow, if you had driven past me, you would have put yourself and your friends directly into their line of fire and that beauty is loaded with armour piercing; so you would have stopped, son." The soldier then glanced at Pete's passport before offering it back.

"I'm good with faces, too," Pete said, pushing his passport into one of the breast pockets on his leather jacket. "Hope to see you in Glasgow some day, Sarge, and if you have seen me before, it was either in connection with music, the boxing ring or maybe the building trade."

"Just remember one thing when you are over here, that there's a war going on in Ireland," the soldier said, moving away from the Renault, heading in the direction of the two other soldiers. He then waved in Pete's direction, motioning him to get the Renault moving.

Pete did not need to be told twice and, very soon, the MVCB. and friends were on the road again, proceeding towards Galway. As they drove, the sullen grey clouds that had been above them since leaving the motel began to break up and some very pleasant sunshine began to stream down through the gaps in the cloud cover, until they were heading west in a fine summery, early evening.

"I think we were lucky back there with that army patrol," "Mavis observed. "I wonder if they just happened to stop us as they did, or was there more to it than that?"

"Meaning, what?" Pete asked.

"Well, if some Republicans knew that Gordon is in Ireland, who else knows?" Mavis asked and continued. "If Gordon has friends over here, then he may also have enemies. There are people in Ireland with very long memories and not all of the scores that get settled are necessarily related to recent events."

"And what do we do with that thought?" Pete asked, irritation plain in his voice.

"What, indeed?" Mavis echoed. "I would say keep your heads down and your mouths shut other than for singing. Get to Galway, do your gig, and then get home as soon as possible. If anything happens that you don't like or need advice on, then ring Mike Smart."

By the time that the Renault was approaching the outskirts of Galway, the clouds had turned away to the north and vanished amidst signs of an imminent sunset.

"Any idea of the route to the University of Ireland, Mavis?" Pete asked.

"I have driven this road before but not for a long time," Mavis replied. "From what I can recall we come to a junction or maybe a roundabout that is signposted for the University campus."

"So it should be fairly straightforward," Pete mused. "Or should we ring Mike Smart for directions?"

"No, I don't think so," Gordon responded. "The IRA and the AA are not the same thing at all. Let's hope we never have to ring Mike Smart, because I suspect that his number is only for very serious emergencies and we can do without those. And, friendly as Mike Smart does seem to be on the surface, you can't help but get the feeling that, not too far beneath the surface, there's steel lurking. Not a man to cross unless you have a very good reason for going down that route." Just then, Gordon let out an enthusiastic whoop and pointed to a road sign that read 'Sligo and Tuam.' "Make a mental note of where this road junction is, Pete," Gordon said enthusiastically, "because, at some point on this trip, I will be visiting Tuam."

"Look there, Pete!" Mavis said, leaning forward to tap Pete on the shoulder. "I think those are further road signs up ahead."

Pete seemed to agree and, with the shadows lengthening and hints abounding that there was not a lot of daylight left, they drew abreast of a group of road signs, the third of which gave the second turn-off as the way to the University of Ireland at Galway. Just after they had taken that turn, Mavis pointed to a modern stonewall on their left and again tapped Pete on the shoulder.

"I believe I remember this wall from when I was doing a course to upgrade my first-aid certificate for my work here. Just a little further along, we should come to the entranceway."

No sooner had Mavis spoken than the unrelieved monotony of the modern wall with its faux old facing brick was broken by two gateposts of the same material. On the nearer of these, a heraldic style sign announced their destination. Pete quickly indicated for a left turn before steering the hire car between two open wrought-iron gates, on one of which hung a second sign declaring that they had reached Galway University. Soon they were driving past a large, modern looking building with lots of glass and concrete, which would probably have fitted most architects' assumptions on what a modern university main building should look like. Not sure where he should be heading or looking for, Pete slowed the Renault to walking pace and then brought the vehicle to a halt in front of what looked like another architectural feature. Either the original site had included a stream that ran through it and the planners had decided to put it between slate-lined banks, with lights here and there to show it off to full advantage, or someone had decided that the site would benefit from something that resembled an artificial millstream running through it. Certainly, it made a good visual barrier between the main building and the campus grounds and, with bridges spanning it here and there, it did seem to add something to the overall effect. Pete steered the Renault along the driveway that bordered the academic watercourse. Further on, and lying on both sides of the driveway, he could make out wide lawns with occasional areas of shrubbery. Beyond these, he could see one and two storied block-like buildings that he assumed must be student accommodation buildings.

"A pleasant enough looking place, Gordon. What do you think, man?" he asked in the direction of the front passenger seat.

"Reminds me of a few American university campuses I have seen," Gordon replied. "I don't see too many signs telling newly arrived performers where to go though."

"That would be just too much to expect," Pete responded in his usual, slightly cynical tone. Just then, he noticed that on one of the public park type benches that dotted the grounds here and there, two young men were sitting, one of whom was playing an acoustic guitar. "I'll just hop out, talk to these guys, and see what they know." At that, he quickly stopped the car, tucking it in close to the kerb at the edge of the lawn where it would cause the least obstruction and was unlikely to be struck by the wing-mirrors of passing vehicles. He switched off his ignition and leapt out of the car in the same moment.

"Hi, guys!" he hailed the two strangers. "An Echo Ranger. I used to have one of those. They seem to last forever and can take any amount of hard knocks and general abuse. In fact, the perfect gigging guitar."

"You here for the festival?" the guitarist answered.

"Yes," Pete replied. "We are the Mavis Valley Band here to play the festival and just this minute arrived on campus. Don't suppose you know where the performers are meant to check in, report for duty etc.?"

"Well, what I would do if I was you the guitarist volunteered, "is just follow this drive straight on. You'll notice that most of the accommodation blocks are in darkness but you'll come to one on your right that is lit up. A single storey building. It's just before you reach the café, which is probably still open. The single storey building with the lights on is the security office. I'm pretty sure those guys will know where you should be, or at least who to speak to."

"Thanks for that guys," Pete responded. "You fellows performers or just hanging out?"

"Performers in our dreams," the guitarist offered. "We're booked in for your concert tomorrow and for your masterclass on Sunday."

"Best of luck with that one," Pete laughed. "Keep up the guitar and performing will come when the time is right for you."

Back in the Renault, Pete reported his conversation with the two strangers and soon had the hire car moving again. At a very slow pace, he drove along the narrow driveway until, in the same second that he noticed a yellow and red café sign, he spotted a single storey building set back from the road a little with its lights on.

"That's probably the one we're looking for," he said, parking the Renault for a second time. "I'll go and check things out. Anybody else coming?"

Gordon, Don, Phil and Mavis quickly got out of the car and, with Pete to the fore, headed in the direction of the security office. Pete led the little group up a flagstone path across a verdant lawn to the open door of the security office. Inside the modern, fluorescent tube lit room they found themselves in a bright, modern office and one built for functional, even utilitarian purposes, rather than for any aesthetic considerations. Three of the office walls were hung with cork-tiled notice boards, each adorned with a profusion of posters, notices either telling students about things they were required to do, or else listing various prohibited activities. Along the wall opposite the entrance was a long pine counter, behind which two overweight, middle-aged men were lounging.

"Evening guys," Pete hailed them in a tone that was simultaneously friendly, convivial, and aggressive.

"And good evening to you," the taller of the two men responded, not sure how to react to this Glaswegian salutation.

"We are the MAVIS VALLEY BAND from Scotland and we have just arrived on campus. We are booked to play at the music festival and to take part in the masterclass programme, too, on Sunday and there should be some accommodation booked for us," Pete continued. The smaller of the two men reached for a clipboard lying closed on the counter in front of him. Opening it, he ran his finger down what, even upside down, looked like a list of names and came to a halt about halfway down his page.

"Yes, I've got you here. Pete Lafferty and Gordon O'Brien." That said, he closed his clipboard and pulled open a drawer that had been out of sight on his side of the counter and, rummaging through a pile of A4 size buff envelopes, he selected one and handed it to Pete. "There's everything in there that you'll need, from your performer I.D. cards, that you should wear at all times on campus, details of where you have to be and when included. We have two single rooms with a bathroom and kitchen booked for you. You are in block three, which is just up the slope from where you are parked, rooms one and two. Any questions guys?"

"No, I don't think so," Pete replied. "You say everything we need is in here; so we'll check out the accommodation first and then what's in your envelope. And, after that if we have any questions, then we know where you are."

As Pete, Gordon, and Mavis started towards the exit, Don and Phil came forward to instigate a conversation very similar to the one that had just taken place. A moment later, once security had identified the Medical Conference clipboard and found their names. Don and Phil were being given another buff envelope and directed towards accommodation block four, rooms one and two. Outside and back in the Renault, Pete was talking to the whole group.

"What I think we should do is this," he was saying. , "We can leave the band trunk here in the van but take our personal luggage with us and, of course, the guitars because the MVCB. always get paranoid when the instruments are not completely secure. And, after we've checked the rooms out, we can either hit the hay to meet up for Saturday adventures, or we can all head out for a coffee before bed."

"What's that we can hear?" Don asked, referring to sounds of music coming from further up the slope in front of them.

"Sounds as if someone is having an impromptu jam-session Gordon said, listening to a woman's voice singing a blues, at the same time as someone was playing a passable slide guitar accompaniment.

"They don't sound too bad," Pete commented, concentrating more on the voice than the guitar. "Mavis," he continued, "I suggest you come with Gordon and me. If me and Gordon can squeeze into the one room that will leave the other room free for you Mavis." Twenty minutes later, with the accommodation checked out and rooms allocated, Gordon and Peter with guitars cases in hands, were slipping in among the jamming musicians and finding seats.

Chapter Six

Galway University

"We're the Mavis Valley Band from Scotland" Pete said smiling in the direction of a girl with multi-coloured, short, cropped hair, wearing bright red lipstick and heavy black eye makeup. She was wearing a black leather shirt tucked into tight black leather trousers, with matching knee-length, high-heeled, black leather boots.

"Hi, heard of you and planned to catch your set tomorrow. I'm Sadie Sweet from Sadie and the Sugar Bowls. Why don't you come and sit in with us for a bit, it's early yet?" "We might just do that, but first, we'll go and check out our rooms," Pete replied. "Once we've done that, we can see you back here in about ten minutes," Pete continued.

"Is that a genuine vintage National guitar?" Gordon asked, staring at the chromium plated, metal instrument that Sadie was clutching.

"Sure is," Sadie responded. "Made in 1929 and takes strings that you could moor ships with."

"How did you get it?" Gordon asked in an admiring tone.

"I got it from this guy who lives just outside Glasgow who has a small business buying and selling vintage and collectable instruments. Seems like he bought it off some guy who had played in a well-known rock group where it had been one of their stage instruments. Apparently, when the rock band guy first got it, it still had some of the cloth covering that they had when they left the factory but he removed it and had it chromium plated. It looks fabulous on stage under house lights."

"I'm sure it does," Gordon said, smiling. "Read an interview with Son House in a guitar magazine once and he was asked why he played one of these. His reply was that he played in a lot of rough clubs and that he could knock a guy out cold with his National without even putting the guitar out of tune, never mind damaging the instrument."

"I can believe that," Sadie agreed. "In fact, if you wanted to destroy it for some reason, you would be hard put to do it."

"So the perfect gigging musician's instrument?" Gordon laughed smiling.

"What do you play yourself?" Sadie asked.

"A perfectly serviceable, inexpensive, and fairly ordinary Yamaha, which is my current gigging guitar. Unlike my rash friend here, Big Pete Lafferty, who has got a very similar Yamaha to mine at home but, being the rash sort of cat that he is, chooses to bring a fabulous early Gibson J200 on tour with him."

As Gordon spoke, Sadie's attention wandered away from him toward his fellow band. member. Gordon missed the looks that Sadie was throwing at Pete, but Mavis was well aware of them. *Eating him up with her eyes*, she was thinking to herself. If Pete himself was aware of them, he gave no sign and, after a moment, he turned away in the direction of their accommodation block, Mavis and Gordon following him.

"See you in a few minutes, people!" Gordon threw over his shoulder in the direction of Sadie and her friends.

Don and Phil, after catching sight of a conveniently placed, totem pole-like cluster of campus signs, turned off onto a paved path which led off on a tangent to the right of the security building looking for their accommodation. Pete, with Gordon and Mavis coming along in his wake, made his way directly uphill and past the impromptu jam session, until they were standing in front of the blue painted door of a two-storied student accommodation block that looked no different from so many others on campus.

Gazing up at the building's roughcast exterior, Gordon was singing to himself a snatch of lines from Pete Seeger's song "Little Boxes," which he knew were more than appropriate to the buildings all around them. Above them, all of the windows were in darkness, so that with the sunset that had overtaken their evening, Pete was struggling to find the keys in his envelope that would facilitate their ingress.

Finally finding the keys, he struggled for a moment to find one that would fit the lock. Eventually, the mechanism turned over and they were soon inside and exploring their university living space. On the ground floor were two closed and locked rooms that may or may not have been occupied. Then, following a narrow and steep flight of concrete stairs upwards, they found a door that let them into an apartment consisting of a kitchen, a toilet cum shower room and two tiny bedrooms that put Pete in mind of cells for monks. Looking into the first of these bedrooms, Pete observed a single bed, which was narrow and none too long against one wall, while on the other wall, there was an alcove, which held a rudimentary wardrobe, as well as an equally rudimentary desk sitting beneath a cluster of short shelves, no doubt intended for storing textbooks. Looking round the sparse facilities, Pete came to the conclusion that if you were not too tall a student, were serious about your studies, and with little interest in girlfriends or entertaining at home, it might just be possible to survive a term or two in such a place. As an afterthought, he concluded that having the Spartan mindset and personality of a monk, would certainly make long-term living there just about feasible. On the plus side, it was clean and freshly painted and, after all, it was only going to be a place to sleep in for a couple of nights. After a quick look round, Mavis commented that if there was any hot water, she was going to go off and have a shower.

Peter suggested that guitars could be kept in the kitchen during the course of their stay, to leave the tiny bedrooms as clutter free as possible. That said, he went on to suggest that Mavis choose whichever of the two rooms she preferred and he and Gordon would cram into the one that was left, one of them taking the bed while the other could be in a sleeping bag laid on the floor. No sooner had Pete made that suggestion than Mavis had put her bag into the room closest to the shower room and then, toilet bag in hand, she was off in search of hot water.

"So are we going to join the jam session outside?" Gordon asked.

"Might as well," Pete replied, "because, as the lady said, it's early yet and, on top of that, I kind of liked the look of her.

"Either see you later, Mavis, or we'll catch up with you for breakfast!" Pete shouted in the direction of the shower room door, and headed for the kitchen to retrieve his guitar.

"We'll come in quietly. Most likely, we won't see you until the morning," Gordon proffered, raising his voice to make himself heard above the sound of running shower water and then like Pete, went into the kitchen to pick up his guitar case.

Outside, they were soon approaching the little jam session. Dispensing with his guitar case, Gordon slipped into a space on one bench, sitting down between Sadie and one of her friends, while Pete found a seat on the facing bench.

After a moment, Sadie stood up, her body language suggesting that she preferred to play that way. Her gleaming chromium plated instrument was catching the bright light from an overhead electric light. Her instrument was hung on a wide black leather strap that matched the rest of her outfit.

"So what are we going to do?" Gordon asked, looking round the expectant circle of faces.

"Will we just jam or will we do a song each and see where that takes us?"

"This old guitar pretty much only likes to play blues," Sadie responded. "So, if nobody has any objection, I suggest we do just that."

And, so saying, she took off the gleaming metal bottleneck that she had on the pinkie of her left hand and slipped it into an open breast pocket, leaving it in such a way that she could get it back on quickly and easily if she required it. Next, she fingered a first position E major chord and began to play a rhythmic boogie figure, both hammering into her chord with her left hand index finger, while picking out the rest of the boogie notes with a very fast pinkie moving over her first and second strings. Gordon recognised what she was playing as a Brownie McGee technique that he was quite fond of himself, a technique that he used a lot. Although in deference to the young woman who was picking in front of him, he would leave this approach aside if he was playing with her.

"In our band," Sadie began by way of introduction, "I quite like the challenge of singing material that is usually seen as men's songs. It keeps the sisters guessing, you know. This next one is usually called 'Penicillin Blues' but the version that I learned it from was called 'Doctor Brownie's Famous Cure.'" Still playing her rhythmic figure and with Pete playing a high-powered, flat-picked boogie behind her that Chuck Berry or Status Quo would have been comfortable with, Sadie began to sing.

"You got your needle in me, baby, and I sure do feel all right;
Keep on kissin' me, baby, as well as holding me tight;
It's early yet, plenty of time before daylight."

Next, Sadie did what many blues singers do: taking a verse from another blues song and adding it into the performance, there being a huge pool of almost floating verses that can be mixed and matched, put in or left out according to the singer's knowledge of the genre And feeling at the moment of performance Sadie then went on to use a verse from a song that Pete often included in his sets, *Hesitation Blues.'*

"I've got the hesitation stockings and the hesitation shoes,
You know I've got those Hesitation blues,
know my dog anywhere I hear him bark
know that man when I feel him in the dark,
and pussy's just meat on the bone
I know you can take it, you can shake it, hope you can't leave it alone

Knowing where the verse was from, Pete was smiling to himself, enjoying the song but also aware that while she was singing it, Sadie was making strong and unmistakeable eye contact with him." *Later for you".* Pete was thinking to himself as, in his mind, he was singing to himself a phrase from the Rolling Stones song, "The Spider and The Fly."

Jump right ahead and you're dead!

His flat-picking was getting stronger as he dug deep into his strings. As soon as Sadie realised that her picking was not really required to keep up the momentum of the song she dropped her fingerpicking and, slipping her bottleneck back on to her finger, she began to play slide licks that Gordon recognised as coming both from Elmore James and Mississippi Fred MacDowall. The steely yet fiery tone of the National guitar sounded incredible. Even unamplified, Gordon realised that between himself, Pete and Sadie, they were making a lot of noise and decided that the jam session should not got on too late for fear of falling foul of security. Then, keeping in line with Sadie's ideas and to confuse everyone even more, he commented, "I would like to go on and sing a timeless Bessie Smith song and one that is a great example of a classy and classic blues. The words are probably as true now as they ever were." Gordon then fingered a G major chord in an F shape and began to play an arpeggio with a moving bass line and started to sing,

Once I lived the life of a millionaire, spending my money I didn't care;
Carried my friends out for a mighty fine time, buying bootleg liquor, cham-
pagne and wine; Then I began to fall so low, didn't have a nickel and no place to go;
If I ever get my hands on a dollar again, gonna hold on to it till them eagles
grin;
Nobody knows you when you're down and out;
In my pockets not one penny and my friends I haven't any;
But when I get back on my feet again, then I'll meet my long lost friends;
It's mighty strange without a doubt No lover can use you when you're down and
out.

At the conclusion of his singing Gordon went into a series of Micky Baker chords and played his offering out with a jazzy sounding ending. Then when he had finished, there was a sparse but enthusiastic burst of applause from his musicians audience. "A great song and a rendition which owes as much to Ramblin' Jack Elliot's version of it as it does to Bessie's fabulous original. It's a song that I always find to be poignant because, by the time that Bessie came to record it, she was beginning to live its story herself." Just then Gordon's phone began to ring in his pocket and he put it to his ear to hear a voice who declared himself to be Don and then continued.

"Well we found our rooms and got settled in and will probably hit the hay quite soon. That is, unless you guys are going to sing all night. We suggest that everybody gets to bed and Phil and I will be over in the morning when we can all go down to the campus café and hunt up some breakfast together."

"That was our friends telling us to shut up and get to bed and they will see us in the morning," Gordon explained. Sadie took another drink from her wine bottle and then passed it to Pete, inviting him to finish it while she put her guitar away. Pete did not need to be told twice and drained the remaining wine in two long drinks as, all around him, musicians were getting instruments back into cases.

When back upstairs, Gordon and Pete were as quiet as they could be, realising that Mavis, after a day's work and a longish drive on top of that, would probably be asleep already. No sooner was Pete in his narrow monk's bed than Gordon had his well travelled sleeping bag out of his equally well travelled pack and was into it and asleep.

Next morning, the two mainstays of the Mavis Valley Band wake–were wakened by what sounded like a bird tapping at their window. Pete heard it first and then, when lying back down to puzzle over whether he had imagined it or not, he heard it again and decided to investigate. Getting out of bed and opening the window so that he could look out, he was surprised to see Phil in the process of searching for another small stone to throw at his window.

"Gordon must have his mobile switched off. I didn't want to wake the whole building by pounding on the front door, so this seemed the best alternative!" Phil explained. "It's a beautiful day out here, so I'll just hang about until you guys are ready and then we can head down to the café," Phil went on.

Pete swivelled his head, first one way and then the other, to take in one hundred and eighty degrees of clear blue sky and had to agree about it being a beautiful day. When Gordon and Pete were showered and dressed, they found Mavis in the kitchen drinking a cup of coffee that she had been able to make from the meagre supplies found in the little kitchen. Looking radiant in jeans and a t-shirt, her hair still clearly wet from the shower, she was sitting astride Gordon's guitar case, its solid strength making it a perfect seat if you did not mind sitting on it astride the way you would sit on a horse or a bicycle.

"That's very much a musician's pose," Gordon smiled, looking at the guitar case between the girl's thighs.

"Or one for *Playboy* magazine," Pete interjected.

"Too many clothes on for that," Mavis disagreed.

"Don and Phil are waiting downstairs for us," Pete added, "so we should get going and we can all head down to the café for breakfast."

Outside, it was indeed a glorious morning with full bright sunshine and it was already hot. With Pete to the fore, they passed the site of the previous evening's jam session, headed down past the parked Renault and further down towards the security office, where they saw one of the two security men carrying some sort of loudhailer. Every few yards, he would put it to his mouth to repeatedly broadcast the message that, "Campers are reminded that fires are not allowed anywhere on the university," followed by, "All fires are prohibited, repeat, all fires are prohibited."

Looking around, them, they could see that here and there, tents had been set up, something they had failed to notice upon arrival the night before. Although it was still early, sunbathers were everywhere on the grass, as were small groups of people, some doing hatha yoga and tai chi, while others were cloistered around little circles playing guitars. Some people were throwing frisbees and, here and there, games of football were underway. As they approached the entrance to the café they could hear the sound of a banjo being played. Then they passed three children all playing luridly coloured ukuleles. Inside the café it was modern and bright with lots of plastic and neon, the décor suggesting that it was probably a franchise, its style suggestive of several well established high street coffee chains. They proceeded to order substantial breakfasts, Gordon trying to keep his full vegetarian breakfast as far as possible from the meaty fare favoured by the others.

"Why don't you move to another table and eat on your own," Pete suggested, seeing the less than enthusiastic look that Gordon was greeting the arrival of his plate with.

"I know I could do that," Gordon admitted, "but for the sake of the conversation and company, I will ignore what you're eating and meditate on blocking out its smell and appearance. Don't give it another thought folks, because I'm certainly not going to. What are we going to do today, guys? I think we should mostly hang out getting the feel of the campus and the crowd. There are sure to be people here that we know."

"According to this" Pete said, producing the envelope they had been given on arrival the night before, "As the guy said," Pete continued, holding the buff envelope from the security office, "everything that we need to know, where we have to be and when, sound check time, gig time and master class time, are indeed here and you better have this and start wearing it," Pete went on, handing Gordon his performer's identification and pass.

Gordon accepted the green and yellow piece of shiny cloth on a ribbon of the same hues and hung it round his neck, remembering that he was supposed to wear it at all times on campus.

"Right!" Pete said, as if having just come to some decision. Quickly, he drained his coffee cup and continued to speak. "I know we have to be in the main lecture theatre for the sound check, our gig tonight and my master class in the morning. So as well as going for a general wander around the place and getting a stretch into my legs, I'll find out where that is and report back to you all here. Don, would you mind if I borrowed your mobile phone for a bit? because, that way, I can keep in touch with Gordon and be able to make a start on rounding us back up should we get separated and, if any of you lot need me, then you can easily wind me back in."

"Absolutely. No problem, Pete," Don replied and passed his phone across.

Pete then got up from the table and, a moment later, he was out of the café and heading in the direction of the slate-sided stream. Following the stream uphill, he spotted a pair of double glass and wood doors that suggested a main entrance of some sort and, having crossed a narrow bridge to reach the doors, he was soon through them and into a corridor where a number of people were milling about, some standing talking in small groups with a larger group using the bottom steps of a flight of stairs that obviously led up to the next level or levels as seats. Almost immediately, he spotted a crudely lettered sign pointing in the direction of the first aid office, which was clearly off somewhere to his right. Beside that sign was a similar notice announcing the main lecture hall, which was apparently somewhere off to his left. Going in that direction, he came to a third sign pointing him up the stairs past a group of young women using the lowest steps as seats. As he pushed past them, they drew aside, leaving him just enough space to get by. Continuing on up the stairs, he found himself in another corridor and spotted a further sign for the lecture theatre. Just beside that sign, a languid looking young man with almost waist length hair was lounging or lounging/posing. Dressed in black leather, he looked like an aspiring rockstar and a perfect partner for Sadie, who also favoured head to toe black leather as her garb of choice. Around his waist, he was wearing an ornate silver and turquoise ornamented leather belt, which Pete recognised as being either Navajo work or a copy of the same.

"Are you looking for something?" asked the young man.

"Yes, I'm looking for the main lecture theatre and you looked as if you would know where that is."

"I do!" Joey Cassidy responded, "I'm in charge of sound for the festival. The lecture theatre is at the end of this corridor, double doors on the left."

"Great!" Pete responded. "We're due to do our sound check at five and I just wanted to know where we were meant to be."

"Five...." Joey mused. "Then you must be with the MAVIS VALLEY BAND?

"Right first time," Pete said, extending his hand, "Peter Lafferty."

"Good to meet you, man!" Joey said, taking the proffered hand. "See you and your guys fiveish and we'll get you set up to the best of our ability."

"Thanks and good to meet you. See you later," Pete said ready to get back to the others and breakfast. As the sound technician went on his way, Pete retraced his steps out of the building until he was following the driveway with the little stream at his right side. By now, the campus grounds were beginning to fill up. Lots of little knots of people were gathered around benches or sitting on the grass, the smell of marijuana heavy on the air. He could hear the sounds of the spontaneous jam sessions, that would fill the campus for days on end going on all around him. In one of them he spotted Sadie and her friends, her fiery slide playing unmistakeable. When she caught his eye, he responded with a breezy wave but kept on walking. Back at the café, he soon had his breakfast in front of him. The others were just starting on to their third coffee.

"So how did you get on?" Gordon asked immediately.

"No problems, man. I know where we have to be and I spoke to the sound tech. What would you like to do between now and sound check time?"

"Do you think we would have time to make it into Tuam and be back here for five?" Gordon asked.

"We could probably do it but it wouldn't give you much time in Tuam," Pete replied. "Probably better to do Tuam tomorrow after my master class workshop thing."

"But tomorrow's Sunday. Everything in Tuam will be closed," Gordon responded.

"Perhaps not," Mavis offered. "With a major festival on, two if you count the medical conference, a lot of places that would normally be closed on Sundays will very much be open for business, both in Galway and in a lot of smaller places round about."

As Pete slipped into his seat, a waitress put a mug of coffee in front of Gordon.

"When you were out on your reconnaissance, I was thinking about you, Big Pete," Gordon said.

"Positive and pleasant thoughts and not nasty stuff, I hope," Pete rejoined in a bantering tone.

"I was just thinking about that comment you passed earlier about how, when you are out on tour with me, you always end up wishing you had brought your dictionary along," Gordon smiled as if laughing to himself. "Not everyone here knows it but I know that that dumb labourer, stupid farmer persona that you like to put on, when you're pretending that you never went to school or read a book in your life, is just a front, a tough guy pose that's only half the story."

"Whether I went to school or not, I'm still a tough guy," Pete argued amiably. "And why would I try to kid you of all people about school when both of us know that you saw me every day at school for years on end and that was both at primary and high school."

"Not every day," Gordon disagreed. "I can remember seeing you at school on some days but, as often as not when I went looking for you, you were nowhere in evidence and, when I used to ask the other Mavis Valley kids who were bussed to school about you, they would tell me that you had been at the customary bus pick-up spot but, somewhere between getting off the bus outside of school and classes starting, you would have vanished."

"Well, as Ken Kesey used to say" Pete responded, "You're you're either on the bus or you're off the bus. In winter, I would mostly have been at school but in summer, I might have gone fishing, bird nesting, or just swimming in the Paradise sand quarry. I would get off the bus at the school gates and then cut down to the Cadder Bridge over the Forth and Clyde Canal, got myself on to the north bank to enjoy a quiet walk along the towpath, past the Possil Loch Bird Sanctuary, until I got beyond the Pike's Hole section and then I would decide where I was making for. Sometimes on my days away from school I would take one of my older girl cousins with me. A lot of guys will tell you just how dangerous older girl cousins can be and mine were not any different. Georgina I always felt sorry for because when our classmates said she was dirty and smelly, they were probably right. Unkind but right. Gina's dad was a miner killed in a roof cave-in and both her and her sister were brought up by her mother on her own. So she was just that little bit poorer and more neglected than the rest of us. Still, that was no excuse for the kids to be cruel to her. They used to call her Gym Shoe Gina in primary school. That was because we kids used to keep our gym shoes on the floor under our desks. With books in our desks there was never enough space for those shoes, hence them being kept on the floor. Some of the kids got into the habit that, as soon as the teacher would go out of the room, they would throw gym shoes at our Gina. In time, and to protect herself, she got into the habit of collecting up all those shoes and keeping them under her desk so that she knew exactly where they were and when the kids needed their shoes they would have to ask Gina for them and that is where the nickname came from. In that class, I beat up a few kids for Gina but you couldn't take on forty of the buggers. One of my other cousins, Doreen, was in that class with us and she was as tough as they came. Small and blonde with baby blue eyes, but she was made of high tensile steel. Pity help any of the boys who crossed Doreen because she would square up to them and slug it out with the best or the worst of them. Fist for fist and punch for punch. Eventually she became a good all round athlete and a keen competition cyclist. Her biggest problem was her own mouth because, being a bit precocious, she liked to boast that she had had sex in every bush between the school and Loch Lomond that being her favourite cycling route. In fact, a lot of the boys used to call her The Bike because everybody rode her. She was many a young lad's introduction into the world of sexuality, myself included. On some of those days away from school, particularly if I was feeling lazy, I would head up into the woods looking for Black Jake. I would scrounge a cup of wild herbs tea from him sitting at his fire. By then, I was close enough to my Valley home to be able to get back near enough to my normal time, making it look like I had come in off the bus with the other kids."

"Obviously, a well thought out scheme," Mavis said, looking at Pete over the rim of her coffee cup. "But what I would like to know," Mavis continued, "is who is Black Jake? From the name, he sounds pretty mysterious."

"Would you like to hear the tale of Black Jake Jarvis?" Pete asked. "Don't encourage him or we'll be here for the next month listening to tales of the old Mavis Valley, and there's thousands of them," Gordon cautioned in a mock serious tone.

"Well, I'm sure one tale won't take a month, so tell do Pete," Mavis smiled. "Well, according to some and according to your point of view," Pete began in a put on, mock melodramatic voice, "Jake Jarvis was a bad man, a practitioner of the evil eye, and someone reputed to have the second sight. His mother was from the Black Isle, where the Brahan Seer came from, and it was said that she was a witch, and not a white one, either. Some saw him as a teller of fortunes, others just as an eccentric, lonely old man who liked his own company and that of his own kind, the tramps, so-called down and outs and rough-sleepers. Most of our community would have described him as a useless old tramp and a work-shy beggar, even though he had been a miner in his youth. Apparently, he had worked in the Welsh pits where he had been in a mine explosion. Caught close to the epicentre of a blast in a coalmine, the shower of explosion driven particles of coal and coal dust that had assailed his face, hands and arms had virtually tattooed him, turning his normal pink skin into something darker and eventually gaining him the nickname Black Jake. Even years after the Welsh coalmine, little pieces of coal would still work their way up to the surface of his skin where he was able to worry them loose and finally be rid of them.

"As a kid, I always saw him as being a bit of a hermit, a rough and ready working class philosopher. Maybe the community was just never able to understand his unusual lifestyle and point of view." Pete suggested. "And you did?" Mavis responded.

"At least I tried," Pete went on, "but when it comes right down to it, do any of us ever really understand somebody else? Too many of us don't even understand our own inner person. Unless that is, you happen to be someone like our introspective sage here, Gordon O'Brien." "You have to at least try," Gordon responded, "because, as the inscription used to read, carved into the stones above the entrance to the Oracle at Delphi, 'Man know thyself.'"

"To me," Pete continued, "Jake was just one of the more interesting people who were around when I was growing up. I know that a lot of my neighbours, especially the women, saw something strange, even sinister, in him, I have to say that I never saw anything wicked or nasty in his nature. Looking at him through a kid's eyes, he was a friendly, kindly, and generous old man, who was one of the few adults around me who seemed able to understand that being locked in a classroom while they prepared me for wage-slave imprisonment might not be what I really wanted or needed. He probably would have found it easier to understand me when I was growing up than any of my own family with their strict work ethic and fundamental Christianity could have done. Like many of the tramps who habitually flocked into that area, he would have been attracted by the Cawder Woods with their plentiful supply of fuel and burns full of fresh water for drinking. Unlike most of them, he had been a miner, so he would have known many of the areas where miners and their families congregated. Also there was a large brickworks close by, the still warm kilns being a haven for homeless men trying to survive outdoors in winter and, remember, these islands were a lot colder then than they are now.

"Those kilns were dangerous sleeping places," Pete pointed out. "It would not have been the first rough sleeper falling asleep in a kiln, who would have failed to hear the arrival of the morning shift and be equally unaware that the nice, warm kiln of the night before, already stacked up with bricks for firing, was a dangerous potential death trap and would not have heard the entrance to his kiln being bricked up ready for firing and would come awake only long enough to realise that he was about to be roasted alive and that, for all his loud screams, nobody was coming to his aid. Eventually, a tramp's mortal remains would be found in the kiln, his fingers bloodied, nails broken and filled with brick dust where he had frantically tried to dig his way through bricks with his bare hands. Even a man who, in his youth, would have attacked solid rock with a pick if called to, could have done very little in his older years when needed to attack a brick wall with no more than flesh and nail at his disposal. While a sad and regrettable incident, what was one tramp more or less in the world, unless you just happened to be that tramp?"

"Can I say something at this point, boys, just before this tale gets too long?" Mavis asked.

"Sure you can, Mavis!" Pete replied, "Never let it be said that we boys hog all the conversation space. In these politically correct times, we are always careful to let the sisters speak." "It's taken us a long time to learn to drop our old chauvinistic ways, but we do our best," Gordon waited expectantly.

"Thanks for that one, Pete." Mavis commented, "I had the feeling that Black Jake would be an interesting one."

"Jake's been dead a lot of years now, but so have been many of my old neighbours," Pete observed. "Some of them are still alive but of those, few of them ever meet, or even keep in touch, though you get the odd exception like myself who still writes the occasional song about the place and sings them pretty much at any opportunity. With the disastrous fire of 1913, the writing was on the wall and, in fact, the seam was never really worked again. The Carron Company from Falkirk, who owned the mine, closed the place and soon the politicians, community leaders, and social workers were gathering like vultures to discuss the future or rather, the non future of the village. Before you knew it, strangers had made the decision that the village was no longer viable. One of the things that staggers me about the 1913 fire and the Carron Company was that they had to bring in a mine rescue team by road all the way from Alloa on that fateful night. Any company with any sort of concern for its men would have had a rescue unit closer than Alloa. No doubt, the Carron Company also had its say but soon it had been decided that Mavis Valley village was no longer viable and alternative housing was being offered to families. The majority of the people who had worked in the pit only knew that north side of the Clyde Valley, with its mines and quarries, the places where the men had been able to find work. When the politicians and bureaucrats began to offer housing with electricity and inside flush toilets, most of the people recognised that the village was finished. Tenement apartments were being offered in Springburn, Maryhill, on the Garscube Road, in Auchenairn and in Bishopbriggs. Some of the men got work in the Auchengeoch Colliery and a few of them were still there waiting for their retirement to come around when Auchengeoch exploded in a burning hell that is quite possibly still burning underground all of these years later. One by one the village families signed up to move, although families had been drifting away for a while. The local politicians and the press turned out in force to see the village abandoned and, on the final morning, a fleet of vehicles was waiting in and around the village to move the people and their belongings out. I've seen photographs of the great cavalcade that ferried us along the canal bank to the main road where the professional removal men with their trucks and lorries were waiting to make our move into the city. Some of our old neighbours rallied round to help out. A local farmer sent his tractor and trailer with two of his men, as did the green-keepers on the two golf courses that border the village. All of those men knew us well because we were renowned and incorrigible poachers. My dad used to pontificate regularly on how every man has a God-given right to take the occasional or not so occasional rabbit, pigeon, fish, or pheasant, or even a roe deer to feed his family regardless of who thought that he owned the land."

"As if land, air, or water can be owned by men and their little laws." Gordon interjected. We might live on the land, harvest our food from it and even raise our houses on it but how can men with their allotted three score years and ten think that by producing pieces of printed paper relating to it, they can own something as old as time itself?"

"Here goes." Pete said, smiling."It just goes to show that Gordon here can find a philosophical dimension in just about any conversation."

"Tell me this, Pete," Mavis interrupted, "who or what was the Carron Company you mentioned?"

"They were an East coast industrial concern. Big employers in their day. By 1814, they were the largest iron-founders in Europe, employing some two thousand men. In what used to be called heavy industry when Scotland still had one. Carron had interests in mines, foundries, quarries, and shipping and In what we would call the armaments industry.

"Probably through their shipbuilding interests, they developed weapons for warships. One well-known example being a small cannon called a Carronade, which would have been mounted on a swivel on a high part of a ship, so that it would dominate an enemy vessel in a sea fight. Once the long distance guns had had their say and the captains were ready to send out boarding parties and start the scramble for prize money, the two vessels would come alongside one another and in the embattled moments before the boarding parties went into action, the Carronades would be doing their deadly work."

"For someone who strikes me as being a fairly typical love and peace, hippy musician, you sound awfully knowledgeable about sea fights and cannons, Pete," Mavis observed.

"While I might be a fairly good example of your hippy musician, I do have other sides to my nature," Pete explained. "When I was a kid and most of my friends were going off to join the Boy Scouts or the Boys Brigade, I joined the Air Training Corp Cadets, where they used to take us over to the Royal Marines Reserves' headquarters at Eglinton Toll in Glasgow and there we used to get lectures and lessons on various weapons modern and not so modern and, while Gordon has Republican family tales about Lewis guns, I learned to use one, to field strip it and service it. They used to have us field strip and re-assemble the thing in a darkened room so that we could use one in the dark if we had to."

"Can you remember the exodus from the Valley?" Mavis asked.

"Yes and no," Pete replied. "When you have heard the same stories from your parents and other family members a hundred times over and even seen the newspaper clippings, it becomes difficult to know if you are dealing with your own memories or just memories of other people's memories. I can remember, or think I can remember, that I was allowed to ride on farmer Steel's tractor when he was moving a load of our furniture on his big trailer that day. It says a lot for the man that he did help us on the day because we had poached his land mercilessly and even helped ourselves to his winter stored potatoes when things were bad. I remember that I was in charge of Clyde, our dog, on that morning. He was running along at the side of the tractor, though I had his lead in my pocket for when we got to the main road where the removal men with their vehicles were meeting us to ferry us to Abbey Street in Lambhill where there was a tenement flat waiting for us. The Laffertys were going into exile in the city. I remember that the tractor that I was on had a double seat and I was sitting up front with one of the farmer's sons who were doing the driving. I sometimes wonder if I have mixed up this memory in some way because I have seen a lot of tractors since then and they all had a single seat, never a double. So I must be wrong on that one in some way."

"I don't know," Mavis disagreed.

"I'm sure that some of the older tractors that we had in Ireland had double seats. Tell me about the dog Clyde Big Pete."

"I would have come back to him anyway," Pete explained, "because eventually his story ties in with Jake's. He was Labrador in coat and colour but Alsatian in shape. He was a big, wise, gentle soul though his grizzled, grey muzzle, which began to turn white when he was still young, carried the scars of battles he had been in when little more than a puppy."

"I can tell you are still fond of him or still have fond memories of him," Mavis commented.

Hoping that the corners of his eyes would remain dry and not betray him, Pete shrugged, looking for an opportunity to change the subject. Gordon nodded understandingly, knowing that Pete, for all his height, broad shoulders, and tough guy exterior, still missed his old dog.

"Once we got to the bridge over the canal at the main road," Pete continued, "various cats and dogs plus humans of various ages with possessions were soon transferred to the removal vehicles for the drive through Springburn to Possilpark, where the cavalcade would turn north towards Lambhill, a village that had long been home to another mining community. Lambhill was not greatly bigger than where the Laffertys had just come from. With a busy road running through it, it was only a short walk to the cemetery where the miners killed in the 1913 disaster had been laid to rest in a communal grave, overlooked by an impressive mine-workers' monument. Men who had done hard and dangerous work deep underground, had been laid to rest in the working class solidarity that had been theirs, both in the pit and out of it. When I was a kid at school I wrote a poem called The Cadder Pit Disaster, a piece that coloured my relationship with that teacher ever after. Later I turned that poem into a song and sing it still. On our drive through Springburn that day we passed the gates of the Caledonian Locomotive works, where my father would eventually find work, helping to build the steam trains that travelled the length and breadth of the British Isles, as well as being exported all over the world. One of my school friends used to live in the street leading up to the gates of the Cally works, and from what he described, it was a cobbled street and when shifts changed at seven in the morning, with five hundred men coming off duty as the next shift was approaching, with the iron-shod boots of a thousand marching men striking sparks from the granite cobbles, the noise was like thunder. So much so that it was well known that on that street nobody ever slept on past seven o'clock. My dad was unemployed for a while after leaving the Valley but it was at the Cally he eventually found a berth. With the road to Milngavie and Strathblane running through its centre, Lambhill was close to the Forth and Clyde canal with a Co-operative Society grocery store, a post office, a chip shop/café and St. Agnes's chapel, a red sandstone Roman Catholic church that had been built by the local mining community. A walk of a few hundred metres out of the village, would either have taken a stroller into the rolling Greenfield countryside bordering the Balmore Road, or in the direction of the area's two pubs, Malan's Bar and The Glen Douglas, the former being green, the latter blue and the two clienteles knew full well which was which. The free spirits in the community would drink in either or shun both because of their sectarianism. The Lafferty' new flat was a well worn room and kitchen, meaning that it consisted of two rooms, one being the bedroom where everyone slept, the other being a combined living/cooking/dining-room. With the help of the farmer's two sons and a sprinkling of new neighbours, some of whom were also pitmen, the Lafferty's furniture, such as it was, was soon up the close stairs, past the stair head communal toilets and into the battered apartment where it was deposited in a rudimentary order, beds into the bedroom, the three-piece suite into the living-room and boxes anywhere they could be deposited or stacked up. No sooner was the furniture inside than my father realised that the front door was lying open and the dog appeared to have vanished.

"Probably gone to mark out his territory and make his presence known to the local dogs," Pete had commented.

"But that's a busy road down there with the traffic and all. And Clyde's a country dog," Pete's mother had pointed out.

Picking up his jacket and the dog's lead, Pete volunteered to go and look for the animal. Soon outside and down a flight of stone steps worn smooth by generations of hurrying feet, Pete passed the stair head toilet, too, facilities that were at best basic but were better than the lean-to shed in the garden that he had grown up with in the village. It did not take Pete long to realise that the dog was not around and, slipping the short, plaited leather lead into his jacket pocket, he began to wonder if it was possible that the dog knew its way back to Mavis Valley. Watching the busy traffic in the street outside, he could remember at least two occasions when he had walked the dog from his previous home to Lambhill, tying the dog to the railings outside of Hannah's fish and chip shop, before going in to buy a fish supper to be enjoyed and shared with the dog on the way home. Coming to the conclusion that he knew exactly where the dog was going, he headed down towards the canal and its lifting road bridge and, crossing over to the north bank, he settled down to a brisk walk along the towpath, a walk he had taken so often when he was meant to be at school.

Chapter Seven
Mavis Valley Tales

Concentrating on keeping up a good pace, though one commensurate with enjoying his surroundings, he stopped for a moment to watch a family of magpies outside of a huge nest in a row of hawthorns close to a shabby redbrick garage, he was sure had been there when he had collected magpie eggs on one of his jaunts away from school. "Shows you they are just as attached to their nests as we are to ours." He mused. Not sure if he had seen a flash of dog-coloured movement ahead of him on the towpath or not, he felt he had no time to be hanging around daydreaming with crows and began to push on at a faster pace. As he grew closer to the silent and deserted village, he grew more sure that was where he was going to find the dog. "Cross that bridge when you get to it," he admonished himself, though aware that on more than one occasion, Clyde had gone off looking for Jake up in the woods. Pete was looking ahead to where normally he would have been seeing welcoming lights in windows and felt a wrench in his stomach on realising that he would never see welcoming lights in Mavis Valley ever again. "Only in my memory, head, and heart." He spoke inwardly as he remembered his old friends and neighbours in their new city houses, where they would no longer have to rely on their oil lamps. Then, remembering old western films he had seen and their stories about ghost towns with tumbleweeds blowing down streets that did not look a whit more desolate than the Valley street in front of him. "Hi, Clyde, you there boy?" He heard the echo of his voice as he looked around at the darkened windows of houses where he could have listed the names of all the people who had once lived there, not just their names but a vast amount of information on each and every one of them—their likes and dislikes, characters, strengths and weaknesses, the ones who liked the bottle, the ones who liked their neighbours' wives, the good cooks and keen gardeners, the football players and brass band men. "Come on, Clyde," he shouted again. "Don't want to lose you too, boy. Are you there?" At that, Clyde appeared at Pete's side and pushed his head against Pete's hand to get his ears fondled. Pete was not sure if it was his mind playing tricks or not but he had the strong feeling that the dog needed to be reassured. "Don't you look so worried, Clyde." He had spoken out loud. "Your human friends always looked out for you in the past and we won't stop just because we've moved to Lambhill. We'll come back here from time to time and, who knows, someday we may be able to move home and stay." Pete was aware that he was having a long conversation with an animal that could not understand a word of what he was saying but mentally. He wrote that off as just being part of humans' ways with dogs.

"Should we be starting to think about the sound check and be getting ready for that?" Gordon put in. "Because we have been sitting here for a while and time is passing."

"What I think we should do is this," Pete began, "We can slowly wander back in the direction of the rooms, see if we can spot where Don and Phil have wandered off to, and let them know the arrangements for later and that way, they can make the start of the gig at seven. You and I can get the instruments into the van and then I'll drive the van, with the trunk in it, as close to the main hall as possible. If you get the guitars inside, I can be getting our trunk to the main stage area and see if Joey, the sound tech, wants to use any of it. He has a pretty good-looking P.A. up there on stage already, so probably he won't need any of our gear."

"As long as I've got a seat to sit on, an open mike in front of me, and my guitar lead close to hand when I want to plug in, I'll be happy," Gordon commented.

"We doing our usual set list?"

"Pretty much," Pete replied. "I'll open with my mining material and see how it develops from there. From what I've seen of the crowd here this far, our self-penned material should go down well enough. If we need to lighten it out a bit, we can throw in a few standards, Jackson Brown, The Eagles, America, etc."

"Am I expected to be singing tonight?" Mavis asked, picking up a till slip that a waitress had just deposited on the table as she walked past.

"I'll get that," Gordon said, taking the slip from her. "Just be in your usual place when we start and see how you feel. If the spirit moves you to sing, then just go for it but, if it feels more appropriate to go for a coffee, then just do that. My guess is that if you are on stage with us, you will sing and, not only that, you'll do it well and enjoy it, too."

It was just a few minutes after five when Pete rolled the MVCB. trunk through the double swing doors of the lecture theatre and stood for a moment, looking round the steeply tiered room. Taking a moment to get his bearings, he could see that already, most of the seats were taken, with very few empty seats visible. *What are this lot doing in here at sound check time?* Pete was thinking to himself, noting that Gordon and Mavis, with Don and Phil, were sitting in the front row of the audience. Immediately as Joey Cassidy came forward to greet him, Pete could see that Gordon already had two chairs set up close to the front of the stage, their acoustic guitars sitting in stands close to the two seats and probably already tuned.

"Sorry about the audience being in here before us,," Joey began. "I was a few minutes late getting here and the audience were pretty quick at grabbing their seats. I guess I could have chucked them out but only at the risk of starting a riot. It may help the sound check anyway because this place empty can have too much of an echo to it. At least it's not raining outside and they are not coming in with wet jackets and coats because wet clothes really dampen things down and mute the treble side of guitars as you will know."

"So it's all for the best," Pete smiled.

"Indeed," Joey responded.

"What do you guys have in your trunk?" Pete, quickly going on to list the trunk's contents.

"Want to use any of it?"

"I'll use the two A.E.R. amps and your singing mikes. I'll run your amps into the P.A. and place them to be your playback monitors. That way, you'll get to hear yourselves the way you are used to; that is, through your own gear," Joey explained.

"Of course, the P.A. will bleed into what you will hear, as you would expect, but not too much. Anything else that the sound crew can do for you?"

"A little echo on the voice mikes if possible," Pete replied. "Like John Lennon, I don't like to hear my own voice without some echo on it."

"Consider it done," Joey responded and headed up on to the stage.

Gordon and Pete followed him, Joey going off to the left where his sound desk was sited, Gordon and Pete taking their seats to double check their tuning. Joey, sitting at his desk, waved his two assistants over and quickly told them what changes he wanted made to the stage setup. Then, turning his attention to his sound desk in front of him, he was soon hitting switches and slider controls with an ease that suggested he knew exactly what he was doing.

After a moment, he caught Gordon's eye and extended his hand, palm up, as if inviting the duo to play. Not needing to be told twice, Gordon smiled a greeting to Mavis as she arrived at his side to take up position just behind him. Next, he fingered an E major chord and then, hammering into and pulling off notes with his pinkie, he played a jazzy introduction where he was both laying down a solid acoustic rock rhythm and moving backwards and forwards between E major and E7th chords, and then began to sing:

See her standin' there in her faded jeans;
She's a hard-lovin' woman got me feelin' mean;
Sundown you better beware if I find you been sneakin' round my backstairs.

Then, when he reached the chorus of that fine Gordon Lightfoot song, Pete was right on the beat for a harmony chorus, Mavis coming in a fraction of a second later:

See her standin' there in her satin dress;In a room where you do what you don't confess; Sundown you better beware if I find you been sneakin' round my backstairs."

Pete then picked up the chorus again at the same time as laying down a fine single string solo that, while not as impressive as the slow, stunningly funky, solo played by Gordon Lightfoot's electric guitarist, Red Shea, on the original hit record, was a dazzling solo none the less. Gordon played a short outro next and, as the last notes of that were fading way, Joey scanned his meters and made some quick notes onto a pad that was lying in front of him. "Thank you " he said into the mike on the gooseneck stand attached to his console. "I've got my levels and, if the sound is as clear during the concert, we'll do well." That said, Joey shut down his console and made his way across the stage to where Pete and Gordon were putting instruments into cases.

"Just a quick word with you guys." Joey began. "The set order of performers has got a bit mixed up over the course of the day. So would you mind if we put you on at nine rather than seven? By then we'll be back on schedule with all of the gremlins ironed out of the system."

"I don't see that it will make much difference to us." Pete replied. "Everything on track for my master class thing in the morning?" "Yes!" Joey said, glancing at a clipboard he was carrying under his arm.

"What now?" Gordon asked, as Pete began to wander off in the direction of the others. "I'm just going to let the guys know about the schedule changes. What are you going to do, man?"

"I'm going to have a wander round, just to get a feel for the type of audience that's here and, at the same time, I'll see if there are any performers hanging round that I know." So saying, Gordon went back out through the double doors they had come in earlier and into the corridor beyond. Every now and then he would nod to a familiar face or stop to speak to someone he knew.

When Mavis saw Gordon leaving the hall, she followed him but, where he had turned left beyond the double doors, she had turned right and then, like Gordon, she had also decided to just wander. She was nodding in the direction of familiar faces and occasionally stopping to speak to old acquaintances. Ten minutes later, as she was retracing her steps, she was just approaching the entrance to the lecture theatre when she spotted Gordon coming towards her. Immediately, she realised that Gordon was looking pale and shaken.

"You all right, Gordon?" she said, catching him by the arm. "You look like you've just seen a ghost?" She added in a concerned tone.

"Something like that, Mavis," Gordon replied.

"Though it was more like not seeing a ghost where a ghost should have been, you are shaking like a leaf and look as if you've had a real shock," Mavis continued.

"I've just bumped into Donegal Donna whom I haven't seen in years and, yes, that was a shock."

"So who is this Donegal Donna?" Mavis asked, her tone somewhere between concerned and worried.

"At one time she was my long-standing girlfriend and then she was my wife for a while. We've been divorced for years and up until tonight, I hadn't seen her or even heard anything about her for a long, long time. That was part of the problem and the fact that I didn't know her at first. It was only when she spoke and I heard her voice that I knew who it was. People can and do change as the years pass, but it was a huge shock to realise that I had just met somebody I used to be close to and not even known her. Somehow, when you leave someone, you kind of assume that the old life you used to be part of is still going on in a reduced way, even if you are off and doing different things in a circle of different people. When I realised I had no recognition for Donna, I knew with one hundred per cent certainty that I had really lost that old, one time lover and it's like a kick in the balls to realise that it's gone, lost forever. Except in your memory, that person no longer exists. You know that they are still alive, still walking God's good green earth, but the woman of your memory does not even look like that any more. If any part of you had ever thought about going back to that person to try and make a go of it again, then you can't because you cannot live with and love, a figment of your imagination, a mere memory. After the initial shock, when I was forced to come to terms with the finality of it all, I took some moments to find a quiet corner where I was able to sit and explore it, think it through and ponder its implications and realised that I had suddenly been thrown into a deep and completely unexpected grief and what was dead was my youth. When something like that happens to you, it gives you a glimpse into your own mortality and how one day, my life as Gordon O'Brien, will stop in its tracks and, like it or not, and fully believing in metempsychosis or reincarnation as I do, all of what I hold to be important and dear as Gordon O'Brien will have to be relinquished. All of the friends, relationships, possessions such as they are, and even the projects will have to be let go. While I do expect to continue as someone or something else, I do not expect any recollection of this Gordon O'Brien life to remain. No doubt I will be a bit like the wave that continues as a wave-forming force, even although the water of the previous wave is left behind or, as Socrates famously said. *I am confident that there truly is such a thing as living again, that the living spring from the dead and that the souls of the dead are in existence.*'"

"Let us not get too morbid," Mavis protested. "Right now I am more concerned about the living flesh and blood Gordon O'Brien, who still looks to me to be in a state of shock. Do you happen to know where Pete parked the car? I left a cake of chocolate by my seat and I think some of that would help ground you."

"From what Pete said he had done, the car is parked outside and, for once, I've got the keys in my pocket."

"Let's go then," Mavis responded and, catching Gordon by the hand, began pulling him in the direction of the nearest exit that led to the campus grounds

Outside, they could see the Renault, parked in deep shadow beneath a stand of elm trees. It was about forty metres away and, as soon as they had reached the hire car and Gordon had unlocked it, Mavis climbed into the rear seat area where she normally sat and, sitting in the left seat, she fumbled around the right seat trying to find the chocolate bar by touch alone. Finally finding it, she told Gordon to come in and sit down; just as he took the high step up and inside, his foot slipped and he landed heavily in Mavis's lap. In the moment that he slipped and Mavis reached out to catch him, she held him for a moment before beginning to speak.

"I've been wanting to do that since first seeing you coming up the steps on to the aircraft."

As Mavis continued to hold him and worry about his pallor, Gordon reached up and pulled her head lower and closer to him. In a moment, their lips met and suddenly each was hungrily searching for the other. Then glued lips to lips and tongue to tongue, Gordon's hand found the area where her t-shirt met the waistband of her jeans and he slipped it in, running his hand up the naked flesh of her back. When his exploratory hand brushed her bra, he acknowledged to himself the fact that she was wearing one and that it needed to be removed. He let his hand slide down a little, intending to bring it round to her front, knowing at that point that either she would protest by pinning his arm to her side with her elbow, or else she would acquiesce and let him reach his objective. As Gordon's hand cupped itself over that delightful, muscle-free part of the female anatomy and began to fondle it, he could feel the nipple becoming erect. A moment later he had unhooked the scrap of black lacy material that was being a cursed nuisance and was generally getting in his way, he was squeezing both of her breasts, one in each hand. Then, moments later, as he was pushing the car door closed with his foot and pushing down the button that locked the door, Mavis was unzipping her trousers and wriggling her way out of them. Continuing to hold her in a deep, kissing embrace, he slipped his hand inside her knickers, down past the bush of pubic hair until his fingers were between her legs and the abundant moisture was telling him that she was more than ready for him.

"You on the pill or do I need a condom?" he asked as he struggled to get out of his jeans.

"Yes to the pill question and, despite all of the good advice that is around on safe sex, I'm going to take a chance on you and skip the condom because you don't strike me as being either an intravenous drug user, or into gay sex."

Soon, they had come together in energetic, rapturously breathless lovemaking that both rocked the Renault and steamed up its windows. A little later, when Gordon's urgency had peaked and then receded, Mavis kissed his closed eyelids.

"Thank you, Gordon, that was marvellous. How did you get to be so good at that?"

"It's a bit like guitar," Gordon replied. "You have to practice all the time."

"When we get back to the room after tonight's gig, you can forget sleeping on Pete's floor because you will be with me."

"Suits me just fine, but what I suggest we do now," Gordon smiled, "is get ourselves straightened up so that we can have a little walk in the fresh air of the grounds and then we can slowly wander back in the direction of the hall."

"Sounds good to me," Mavis said, hooking up her underwear and then getting back into her jeans and shoes.

Outside, they locked up the Renault and hand in hand, began to follow the little stream further down through the campus grounds, munching on Mavis' chocolate bar as they walked. It was five minutes before nine when they walked into the lecture theatre, just in time to see the previous band leaving the stage. Then, as the last of that band's members was walking off backstage, still hand in hand, Gordon led Mavis to the side of the stage where a handful of steps allowed them to ascend on to the scarred and battered platform. Pete looked at them hand in hand, smiled, but said nothing. Then, catching Gordon's eye, his huge grin said all that one man can say to another in a situation of that sort. It was a look which both said, *Well done,* and *You lucky devil.*

Gordon sat down in his seat and checked his tuning while Mavis took up her position behind him. At his right hand, Pete retrieved his instrument and also checked his tuning. For a moment, Pete hesitated, looking out at the audience, while he decided what to say to start the gig off.

"Hiya, Galway and your amazing Galleon Festival," he began. "I hope you're all having as much fun as we are. My name is Pete Lafferty and I'm part of the Mavis Valley Band. I'm very aware that tonight is not the first set that we have played since leaving Glasgow and getting to Ireland. So it's just possible that, what I'm going to say next by way of introduction, some of you may have heard already. However, we always like to clarify the fact that, despite our band name, we do not play music for traditional Scottish dancing. So, that said, sit back, relax and we will do our best to entertain you. There will be no interval during this set but if anybody needs to slip out to get another pint of stout at any point, then do just that. And here is a message from the organisers that when we finish our set, today's session is over. All of the performances that were due to take place today but couldn't be fitted in because of delays and gremlins in the system will be slotted in tomorrow. Check the notice boards for details and, if any of you are booked in for my master class thing, I'll look forward to seeing you here about eleven. So, folks, that is the last of the housekeeping stuff, next comes the music.

"Because I hail from a mining community village in Scotland and many of my family were and are miners, I often start off an set with a selection of my favourite miners' songs. The first one that I would like to do is an old Bob Dylan song and it is one of his that you might not know, ; because of it being one of his early songs and not one of his real famous tunes, it's almost a bit obscure. As you probably all know, Mr Dylan grew up in Minnesota's Iron Range country. So I guess he, too knows his miners and mining towns.

"So, here goes with North Country Blues,' a great mining song and a great Bob Dylan song."

Pete then slid into a D minor chord and, while holding it down, with his peripatetic pinkie, he played a catchy riff on his first string as an introduction, then quickly settled into a steady singer's groove:

Come gather round, Friends and I'll tell you a tale of when the red iron
pits ran plenty;
But the cardboard filled windows and old men on the benches
tell you now that the whole town is empty;
In the north end of town, my own children are grown
but I was raised on the other;
In the wee hours of youth, my mother took sick
and I was brought up by my brother;
The iron-ore poured as the years passed the door,
the drag-lines and shovels was a hummin'
Til one day my brother failed to come home
The same as my father before him'
Well a long winter's wait from the window I watched,my friends,
they couldn't have been kinder
And my schooling was cut as I quit in the spring to marry John Thomas, a miner;
Oh, the years passed again and the givin' was good,
with the lunch buckets filled every season;
What with three babies born the work was cut down
to half a day's shift with no reason;
Then the shaft was soon shut and more work was cut;
And the fire in the air it felt frozen, 'till a man come to speak;
And he said in one week that number eleven was closin;
They complained in the East they are paying too high;
They say that your ore ain't worth diggin';'
That it's much cheaper down in the South American towns;
Where the miners work almost for nothin;'
So the mining gates locked and the red iron rotted;
And the room smelled heavy from drinking;
Where the sad silent song made the hour twice as long;
As I waited for the sun to go sinking;
I lived by the window as he talked to himself;
This silence of tongues it was building;
Then one morning's wake, the bed it was bare
and I's left alone with three children;
The summer is gone, the ground's turning cold,
the store's one by one they're a foldin;'
My children will go as soon as they grow;
Well there ain't nothin' here now to hold them;

As Pete finished this last line, he repeated the introductory phrase on his guitar, that led into a short instrumental that he finished with his best showman's flourish. His song drew a huge round of applause and he stood quickly to acknowledge it.

"The applause, folks, should be for Bob Dylan and a wonderfully evocative piece of song-writing. I was just the delivery boy in that performance. I would like to continue with 'The Days of Forty-Nine,' a slightly more cheerful miner's song and one that is about gold rather than iron." So saying, Pete caught hold of an A minor chord and played a fast introduction, built around a cluster of hammered-on notes, and began to sing:

I'm old Tom Moore, a relic of former times;
They call me a bummer and a gin-sot too but what cares I for praise?
For my heart is filled with the days of yore and oft do I repine;
For the days of old when we dug up the gold;
Those were the days of forty-nine;
I'd comrades then who loved me well, a jolly, sassy crew;
A few hard cases I do recall, though they were both brave and true;
Whatever the pinch they never would flinch, never would fret or whine;
Like good old bricks they stood the kicks in the days of forty-nine;
There was New York Jake, the butcher's boy, who was always getting tight;
And every time that he got booked, he was spoilin' for a fight;
Till Jake rampaged against a knife in the hand of old Bob Syne;
And over Jake we held a wake in the days of forty-nine;
There was Poker Bill, one of the boys, who was always in a game;
And whether he lost or whether he won, to Bill it was all the same;
He would ante up and draw his cards and would you go a hatful blind?;
In a game with death Bill lost his breath in the days of forty-nine;
Then there was Rackensack Jim from Idaho, whom I never will forget;
He'd roar all day and he'd roar all night and I guess he's roarin' yet;
One night he fell in a prospect hole of a roarin' bad design;
And in that hole he roared out his soul in the days of forty-nine;
Of all the comrades I had then, not one remains to toast;
And I'm left alone in my misery, like some poor wandrin' ghost;
And as I go from place to placePeople saying 'Here's Tom Moore,' a bummer sure
from the days of forty-nine.

Pete stood up and bowed as, once again, the audience greeted his song with enthusiastic applause. "A wonderful piece of folk poetry and a great guitar story but after that I'm going to rest my vocal chords for a bit and let my band partner, Gordon O'Brien, take the vocal lead for a bit." For a moment, Gordon was engrossed in adjusting his capo before realising that the audience was waiting for him. "Well, we have just started our set in the way that the M.V.C.B. often does. That is with a selection of mining songs from Big Pete Lafferty, a miner's son from the Mavis Valley country. So to continue, although neither my dad nor myself or any of my family were ever cowboys, I would like to sing you some of my favourite cowboy songs and we'll intersperse those with what Pete still has to come for you."

Just then, a man with a camera stepped forward towards the stage, ready to snap a photograph of the band and, in that instant, Gordon realised that Mike Smart was sitting in the front row of the audience. Quick as the photographer was in coming forward, Mike Smart was even faster, throwing himself between the man and the stage, where he seemed to be saying, "No photography!" "It's alright, really alright." Gordon said, looking down from the stage while two other men appeared at Smart's side and were soon hustling the would-be photographer out of the room. At that, Gordon leaned his guitar against his seat and went forward to talk to the Republican. "It's all right, we don't mind, it's just part of being a performer."

"It's better for you, young Gordon, that every Tom, Dick, and Harry in Ireland doesn't have your picture in front of them. Trust me, Gordon, this is Ireland and I know my job and my own turf," Smart said.

With that, Gordon retraced his steps to his seat and, retrieving his instrument, began to quickly retune. After playing a two-bar introduction, he announced. , "This next song is one from the very able pen of Woodrow Wilson Guthrie, better known to us all as Woody Guthrie, 'The Ballad of Pretty Boy Floyd.' Then, repeating his instrumental introduction, he began to sing:

> *Come gather round me people and a story I will tell;*
> *About Pretty Boy Floyd the outlaw Oklahoma knew him well;*
> *It was in the town of Shawnee on a Saturday afternoon;*
> *With his wife in his wagon beside him as into town they rode;*
> *A deputy sheriff approached them in a manner rather rude;*
> *Using vulgar words and language and his wife she overheard;*
> *Pretty Boy grabbed a log chain and that deputy grabbed his gun;*
> *And in the fight that followed, he laid that deputy down;*
> *He fled to the hills and woodlands to live a life of shame;*
> *Half the crimes in Oklahoma were added to his name;*
> *Now many a struggling farmer this same story told;*
> *How an outlaw paid his mortgage and saved his farm and home;*
> *Others tell of a stranger who came to beg a meal;*
> *And underneath his napkin left a thousand dollar bill;*
> *It was in Oklahoma City, it was on Christmas Day,*
> *came a whole carload of groceries;*
> *And a letter did say; Oh, you say that I'm an outlaw, you say that I'm a thief;*
> *Well, here's a Christmas dinner for the Families on Relief;*
> *Now as through this life I've rambled I've met a lot funny men;*
> *Some would rob you with a six-gun, some with a fountain pen;*
> *But as through this life I've rambled and as through this life I've roamed;*
> *Never known an outlaw drive a family from their home.*

Then as the song ended, Gordon fingered a C major chord and played Pretty Boy Floyd out with a little instrumental that started with a bass run before moving into paired octave notes that made his instrument sound like a twelve-string guitar. Finally, after a moment's pause that allowed him to flex and then relax his fingers, while he got his breath back, he spoke on.

"This next song is called 'Turn, Turn, Turn,' and it owes a bit to bit Pete here, a bit to Pete Seeger, a bit to the Byrds and a tad to the Book of Ecclesiastes. If you know it and are in the mood, you can sing along." Next, Gordon moved into an E minor chord and some flashy runs he had taken both from the Rev. Gary Davis and from Jorma Kaukenen's slant on Gary Davis. From there, he took up a strummed rhythm and began to sing:-

To everything, turn, turn, turn, there is a season, turn, turn, turn;
And a time for every purpose under heaven;
A time to be born, a time to die;
A time to plant, a time to reap;
A time to kill, a time to heal;
A time to laugh, a time to weep;
To everything, turn, turn, turn;
And a time for everything under heaven.

Then, as his voice trailed off and a trickle of applause rippled round the audience, he went back to his Blind Gary licks to end with a fast flourish. "Although that song tells us that there is a time to kill and I have just been singing that sentiment to you, I have to let you know that personally I don't sign up for that one. And that said, there is a great line from Bob Dylan where he said, '*Don't hate nothing at all 'cept hatred.*' And to that one, I can and do sign up to and offer it to you as a counterbalance to the Book of Ecclesiastes." Gordon's comment drew at least as much applause as his song had done and, bowing in reaction to that applause, he stayed with his key of C and played some bluesy sounding lines.

"This next tune that I would like to do is a cowboy song called 'Diamond Joe' and, although I think it was part of Bob Dylan's repertoire at one time, it first really came to my attention when I heard James Taylor do it at a marvellous concert that James gave at Edinburgh Castle some time back." Playing one of his favourite picking patterns, Gordon began to sing.:-

There's a man you'll hear about most anywhere you go;
His holdings are in Texas and his name is Diamond Joe;
He carries all his money in a diamond-studded jar;
And he never took much trouble for the process of the law;
I hired out to Diamond Joe boys,d offeerd him my hand;
He gave me a string of horses so old they could hardly stand;
And I nearly starved to death, boys;
He did mistreat me so and I never saved a dollar in the pay of Diamond Joe;
Now his bread it was corn-dodger and his meat you couldn't chaw;
Nearly drove me crazy with the waggin' of his jaw;
By telling of this story, it's just to let you know;
There never was a rounder could lie like Diamond Joe;

> *I tried three times to quit him but he did argue so;*
> *And I'm still punchin' cattle in the pay of Diamond Joe;*
> *And when I'm called up yonder and it's my time to go;*
> *Give my blankets to my buddies, give the fleas to Diamond Joe.*

As Gordon finished singing Pete was plying his flat pick, playing the melody of the song as an ending. Then as the audience applauded the M.V.C.B. effort, Pete was staring hard at Gordon and thinking to himself, *"Seems to be in a talkative mood today, ever the storyteller.* "As I was coming towards the end of that turn, turn, turn, song, folks, I was thinking about the line that I wasn't comfortable with and thinking about the words to Pretty Boy Floyd, and it strikes me that we've probably all had bosses a bit like Diamond Joe and met foul-mouthed cops like the one Pretty Boy Floyd had to chastise Gordon commented. "Still, thinking about cowboy songs, I used to do The Eagles' 'Desperado' at this point in my set but during a time when Big Pete wasn't doing so much with the band I had another singer/guitarist with me for a while. His name was Ronnie Mair and he was really great at that song, Sadly, Ronnie died not so long ago and, for that reason, I don't do 'Desperado' any more. However, at this point in my set, I often send up a thought for Ronnie. I wrote a song for Ronnie which is simply called 'Ronnie's Song' and if it's all right out there in the body of the kirk, I would like to do it for you. A quick word of explanation before I start: I don't know about in Ireland but in Scotland the word *'sair'* means sore or painful." Next, Gordon played some introductory lines based on E and F major chords that he had culled from a Flamenco piece he had been working on with his guitar teacher back in Scotland and began to sing:-

> *Oh, Ronnie sair, do you think that it was fair for you to just go and be leavin'?*
> *When you slipped away in that hour before day, did you think of us here grievin'?'*
> *So who will hold sweet Carol's hand when she walks along the sand;*
> *And will you be her lover foR ever?*
> *Where will you be when she's gazing out to sea and when she lingers by the river?*
> *So where are you now and can you tell me how, or are you gone forever?*
> *Is it just like you said, or are you forever dead, or are you waiting at the river?*
> *Leavin' fast, leavin' slow, did you really have to go?;*
> *Or could not not just have been here a-staying?*
> *Leavin' fast, leavin' slow, did I hear you say Jericho;*
> *Or was it something about Canaan?*

"Ronnie, as the words of this song might suggest, was one of my practising Christian friends, and that is how Jericho and Canaan found their way in there." As Gordon took the capo off his guitar and slipped it into his pocket, he was looking around for his guitar case looking like the short-sighted owl he often appeared to be. Pete swapped his finger- picks for his flat pick and, as he got ready to ply it, he began to talk to the crowd, who were applauding enthusiastically for Gordon's song.

"Thank you, folks. Although Fleetwood Mac gave the game away when they used that line, *'Players only love you when they're playing,'* Gordon and myself, as well as Mavis and Sadie, would like to thank you for being such a warm and appreciative audience, although you would expect nothing less in Ireland. I would like to do a couple of further mining songs for you, if that is all right?" A ripple of applause suggested that it was. "This next one is a self-penned number and, although I wrote it and am going to be singing it for you, the person telling the story could have been my late father or any of a number of miner uncles." With that said, Pete fingered a G major chord and, while laying down a heavy and bluesy rhythm, began to sing. Dropping his rhythmic figure every few beats so that he could inject some lead lines at the dramatic points in the song, he could see Sadie dropping her guitar strap over her shoulder and slipping her slide on to the little finger of her left hand. With the coloured stage lights bouncing off the highly polished metal of her instrument, she was playing high octane lead lines behind both Pete and Gordon's guitars:-

No son of mine will ever go down that deep dark mine," Pete sang,
"Nor cough his lungs up for overtime;
And no daughter of mine will ever a miner marry;
To wait the long wait and see him brought home broken on a carry;
Oh a miner I've been and worked a three foot seam;
With only my helmet lamp against the dark and the damp."

"You're very generous." Pete responded as the audience's applause for his song came at him in a wave.

"This next song that I am going to do is not, strictly speaking, a mining song but because it touches on mining, is a song written by Woody Guthrie and is a song that I enjoy performing, gives me three good reasons for including it in this set." And then, digging in deep with his flat pick and in a voice somewhere between aggressive and threatening, Pete began to sing:-

"I've been doin' some hard travelling, I thought you knowed;
I've been doin' some hard travelling, way down the road;
I've been doin' some hard rock mining, I thought you knowed;
I've been doin' some hard rock mining way down the road;
I've been doin' some hard ramblin' hard gamblin' I thought you knowed;
I've been out with Tom Joad way down the road.

At the end of each sung line Sadie's slide guitar shrieked, squealed and shimmered as the audience clapped and stamped along. At the same time Gordon was concentrating on throwing energetic bass and treble string runs into the mix and, before long, some of the audience had taken to dancing in the aisles and in front of the stage. Mavis crossed the stage to take up position close to Sadie and the two women danced along adding a strong visual element that was new to the M.V.C.B.'s performance. Pete was beginning to think that the M.V.C.B. was starting to sound more like a rock band in full flight than an acoustic band playing at an acoustic festival, when he caught Joey's eye at his mixing console and began vigorously pointing at the floor with an index finger signifying that he wanted the sound volume lowered. Joey duly obliged but, when the audience came close to drowning out the band, he slid it up again. Pete then slipped his guitar strap off over his head, following that with a low bow to the audience to let them know that that section of their set was finished. Gordon breezed a wave to the packed rows of seats. then, falling into step behind Pete, headed for the back of the stage where he walked on past a wall of Marshall amplifiers and speaker cabinets to reach a little backwater out of sight of the audience. Sadie, Mavis and Pete were there already, along with Joey Cassidy and Mike Smart. Behind them and from around the hall, the audience was getting louder and louder, and from the rhythmic clapping and stamping, were clearly demanding their return to the stage. What could we do for an encore?" Pete asked.

"Beats me," Gordon replied. "How about something Irish?" Mike Smart suggested, ever the patriot. I've got something I could do and it's probably Irish enough." Gordon went on. "I would go for something in the middle," Mike Smart suggested, "neither too green nor too blue." "What was all that about the photographer earlier?" Gordon asked. "In Scotland, you have the Great Glen dividing the country north from south Mike Smart replied. In Ireland we have no Great Glen but the divide is there nonetheless, just as deep and just as wide. On both sides of the Irish divide, you get guys like me who look and listen and gather information. We also gather photographs and keep them on file. Me and my guys spend a lot of time looking at old photographs because, some day, we will be faced by somebody that we would like to be able to recognise. Seeing that face, unless you have an exceptional memory, will not lead to triggering the memory of a name or file information. But what we hope to do is recognise that here is somebody that I need to be careful around. On the door tonight I had young Seamus O'Brady, a very bright lad. He came to me to tell me about a man who had just come into the gig, "A wrong 'un'" as young Seamus put it. Seamus asked me to look at the face in question and, although I didn't know who he was, I knew that I knew him." "What happened to him is what I want to know," Gordon demanded.

"Well, my young brother Martin, who is here tonight, has this Triumph Bonneville motorcycle that he loves to drive fast and far and, even as we speak, our doubtful stranger is on the pillion of that Triumph, two of Martin's friends shadowing them on a second bike, all on their way to our photographer's home in Belfast. Considering that he was only wearing jeans and a T-shirt he'll be frozen when he gets there. But knowing Martin's ways, he'll drop him off somewhere and let him walk the last ten or fifteen miles home and that should thaw him out." "Just as long as I know that he's getting home safely," Gordon continued. "I would hate to think that somebody got hurt through coming to one of my gigs." That said, Gordon broke off from conversation and, guitar in hand and Pete following him, the band went forward to retake their seats. So thank you for bringing us back again, we are at that point where we are feeling the need to do something Irish for you and this song that we are going to do next was written by Christy Moore in 1983 for the memory of the many Irishmen who fought in Spain during the Spanish Civil War. My own great great grandfather, Jamie O'Brien, a staunch Galway Republican, was one of the men who went out from Dublin to Spain with Frank Ryan and his boys. By choosing this Christy Moore song and taking up the subject of the Spanish Civil War, I am not trying to promote Ireland or the Irish beyond or above other countries or nations because, although our boys did their bit in Spain against the Fascists, there was another side to that coin there were Irishmen who fought for Hitler, some even serving in the Waffen SS and there were Irishmen who did propaganda broadcasts for the Nazis. Back in an era when people commonly signed their letters with *Yours Truly*, Woody Guthrie, our illustrious forebear/mentor and still influential singer/songwriter, commonly signed his letters *Yours, True as the average, Woody,* and by singing this Christy Moore for you, this is the band's way of recognising that those stalwart Irishmen who fought in Spain, were at least as true as the average and certainly did their Irish bit to help contain the forces of fascism in the 1930s. This song is called 'Viva la Quince Brigade' and I know that many of you will know it well." At that, Gordon fingered a third fret C7 chord, slid it from the third to the first position and began to play an introduction built around various D7 and C7 chords, played up and down his fingerboard. Then, as the last notes of his introduction and the applause which that followed it began to fade away, Gordon began to sing:

> *Ten years before I saw the light of morning;*
> *A comradeship of heroes was laid;*
> *From every corner of the world came sailing;*
> *The Fifteenth International Brigade;*
> *They came to stand beside the Spanish people;*
> *To stem the rising fascist tide;*
> *Even the olives were bleeding;*
> *As the battle of Madrid thundered on;*
> *Truth and love against the forces of evil;*
> *Viva la Quince Brigade;*
> *And let us remember them tonight, our brotherhood of man."*

Next, Gordon replayed his introduction, thanked the audience and, with Pete at his side, headed off backstage.

"A brilliant choice of song," Mike Smart enthused and the audience clearly agreed.

"I didn't want to do something obvious like an Irish rebel song," Gordon explained. "I wanted something a bit ecumenical, something to bridge and unite rather than polarise and separate."

"A man after my own heart." Mike Smart responded. "If you ever chose to move to Ireland, I get the feeling that I could work with you. As musicians you would do well over here."

With this conversation almost being drowned out by a wildly vociferous audience, Pete signed that they should go back out front. Leaving their guitars behind, where Sadie began returning them to their protective cases, Gordon and Pete retook their seats. Pete pretended to put his fingers in his ears to block out the din coming from the audience as Gordon began to talk to the crowd. "Big Pete Lafferty!" Gordon began, pointing at Pete and clapping along with the audience. "And like so many Peter's foundational stuff, the bedrock that the M.V.C.B. is built on."

"And Gordon O'Brien, Galway's own Pete continued, pointing at Gordon and clapping vigorously. "One of the best travelling companions that a bandman could hope for and I should know, because we've travelled a lot of miles together, sung a lot of songs and played a lot of guitar. You've been a great audience and, if any of you are booked in for my masterclass tomorrow, I'll see you in the morning."

With Pete's words reverberating round the packed hall, they left the stage.

Chapter Eight

Masterclass Programme and On

It was just after ten in the morning when Gordon and Pete returned to the stage that had been the scene of their triumph of the evening before. Leaving Mavis to sleep on, Gordon had followed Pete back to the main stage because, knowing Pete's reluctance to say much to audiences, he was concerned that Pete might dry up and run out of things to say during his workshop. So just in case that happened, the other half of the band was back on stage ready to speak or play guitar if needed.

"Just a word of thanks for Joey Cassidy and his crew who did the sound for us last night and are back with us again this morning," Pete smiled. "A big Scottish thanks to you, guys. You know, people," Pete continued, "I was talking to this guy in the bar of the Student's Union just a few hours ago. He was one of those academic, folklorist/musicologist sort of guys and he was telling me how you and me can't write folksongs and how they have to be around for generations, if not for centuries, and even cross the Atlantic a few times before they become folksongs. You know, he was one of those purist type folk singers who sing with one finger in their ear, the kind of guys who booed Bob Dylan when he appeared on stage with an electric guitar." Pete began looking out at the thirty-five or forty people clustered in the front rows of seats. Although he was feeling nervous in a way that he would never have felt in front of an audience with a guitar in his hands, he was determined that nobody else would know how he was feeling. "Now you don't have to take notes here this morning, unlike with other mornings here but you can if you like." Pete said, laughing. "My first reaction at being invited to give this so-called masterclass was to howl with laughter, because I am just like any other rough and ready street guy. There is nothing special about me. I have no academic background at all and have got nothing in any way scholarly to offer to you. However, as my good friend, Gordon O'Brien, here has pointed out to me on more than one occasion, I am the world authority on how I play guitar and how I write my songs and perform them. With songs, whether my own or with other people's songs, what I look for is a good and interesting story that it clearly told from the heart. It's like that old joke, *'How do you define country music?'* Answer: *'Three chords and honesty.'* If you mess around with guitars enough and have something to say, something that you want to have your say on, before you know it, a song will pop out and you'll be a singer-songwriter. It's not easy but, equally, it's sure not rocket science. People will have their opinions and points of view on what you write and how you perform it, but that isn't something that we can afford to get in the way of our creative process. Write the songs and sing them and let the critics do what they do. The only thing you have to know about them is the fact that damn few of them write songs, play guitars, or sing. As the old adage goes, *'Hew to the line and let the chips fall where they will!'* According to my Mr. PhD, some subjects are more likely to be accepted as folksongs than others when you and me write them. For example, if you are writing about your experiences of deep sea fishing, coal mining, or drilling for oil, because it is sweat and toil work, that seems to be more acceptable to the academic folklorists than if you or I decide to write about the girl next door or, say, football. Some of you probably heard my mining songs here last night and I feel that my self-penned one is a folksong and, who knows, it may appear in folksong collections years or generations from now. But having done a lot of sweaty, poorly paid, manual labour type work in my time, I know that there is nothing romantic about it, or any level that could make it more appropriate for becoming a folksong than any other aspect of the human condition. I would like to sing you one of my songs right now that I feel is a folksong, probably because of its subject matter. This one is called Flodden Field and it's about a great battle fought between the Scots and your old friends, the English, one that we lost and, through poor tactics, one where we got slaughtered. Some of you will know the poem, 'Floors of the Forest,' also about Flodden and that one is usually accepted as a folk poem. Mine is going to have to be around for a long time yet before my academic friend will accept it as a folksong." Slipping his capo on to his guitar and settling for the People's key of D, Pete picked out a single string introduction and began to sing;

Flodden was a bugger. Aye it was that and more;
When we came down off the high ground, to do our bloody chore;
With imprecations and full force;
We greet everyone who ever stood against us;
And with broadsword and targe to the fore;
We formed up for the charge to see our men;
Go down score upon score;
And then with amen to those who would never turn for home again;
We turned to that long, cold, dark, defeated and deadly road home;

Long miles and damn few smiles;
Flodden was a bugger. Aye it was that and more;
When we came down off the high ground to do our bloody chore."

"So what do you think people, a folksong or not?" Pete asked the audience. Their burst of applause seemed to say, 'Yes. 'Thank you for that,'" Pete said, removing his capo and slipping it into the breast pocket of his jacket. "Who knows, maybe that one and the 'Floors of the Forest will appear side by side in the anthologies of a thousand years from now. Though, as we all know, that's just academic." Glancing around the rows of seats in front of him, Pete had a slightly self-satisfied look on his face, as if he were already getting the feeling that the session was going to be a good one. "With our band.," he went on, "we have quite a wide repertoire. One of the tricks that we use to make it manageable is to split it into sections, I have my mining songs and Gordon likes to do his cowboy material. From time to time, as we find new songs, we add to these two sections so that they are not static. But we also have one of our largest sections, our self-penned stuff. This can be either material which that we have produced together, or it can be songs that just one of us has written. The one rule that we both try to stick to with our song writing is that our songs should come out of our life experience and, in that way, we can usually come up with strong songs that both the performer and an audience can relate to. Only occasionally do we write songs about topical events or personalities. Though, recently, Gordon wrote a song that does fit into that category. It's a song that I like a lot and one that also fits into Gordon's cowboy song section. So, without saying any more about it, I'm going to ask Gordon to tell you about it and if he will, also sing it for you."

"The song that Pete is talking about is called 'Booger Red' and it came to me after I had been reading about a famous American cowboy, horseman, and horse trainer. When Red, real name, Thomas Privett, was just a boy, he was playing around with gunpowder and matches when he caused an explosion, which left him disfigured for life, so much so, that in his lifetime, there was a popular jingle which went *'Booger Red, Booger Red, ugliest man living or dead.'"* Next, Gordon fingered an A major chord and began to play a slide-led motif that picked out the melody of his song and led him into singing:

Booger Red, Booger Red, ugliest man living or dead;
A veteran of the Wildwest Show, bronco cowboy from the rodeo;
A single horse or a longhorn herd, he'd see them roped, branded, watered, and fed;
Just five–foot–four inches tall, nobody ever called Booger small."

Next, Gordon went back to his melodic guitar slides and used them as a lead into an instrumental where he was playing the melody and a chord accompaniment in a polished piece of showcase finger picking. He played that solo through twice and then went into a slick ending, and looked up in expectation of the applause, which came at him as if on cue. "While I know nothing about horses or cowboys folks, there was just something there which caught my imagination enough to be able to use it in a song. Wherever these things come from, songwriters rely on these little inspirations finding their way to us and through us." Next, Gordon adjusted the tuning on his guitar and, even the snatch of Haydn melody that he played to convince himself that his instrument was well in tune brought a fresh burst of applause from what had been a particularly appreciative, intimate and enthusiastic audience. Next, Pete began to speak.

"This thing that we're doing this morning being called a masterclass. Although I don't consider myself a master, whatever that is, I would like to talk to you about the guitar for a bit—or more like what I do with the guitar. The very fact that we are all here at an acoustic music festival is a testament to the fact that, recently, there has been a huge resurgence of interest in acoustic music. For a lot of years, electric guitars seemed to rule the roost and the stage but recently, the humble acoustic has been coming back into its own. I would like to tell you a bit about my approach to acoustic guitar.

"At one time, a lot of guitarists would simply play chords with their left hand while strumming a rhythm with their right hand at the same time as they sang. Nowadays, people and audiences are more sophisticated and more knowledgeable musically. So that earlier approach is no longer really acceptable. That point or opinion brings me to something that Gordon's guitar teacher once said, which is that the left hand is the labourer while the right hand is the artist. With my right hand, what I mostly do is called pattern picking. , an approach that some people will tell you is boring and repetitive, though that doesn't have to be the case. I will sometimes use one pattern, also called a roll or arpeggio, for an introduction, another for an ending and a couple of others, one for the verses, and one for the chorus, when doing a song. On top of that, if you can use treble and bass runs to lead you into and out of your chords, plus using the kinds of ornaments that you get through the use of hammer-ons, pull-offs and slides by mixing and matching all of this, you can develop your own style of playing and one that is far from being boring or repetitive. To become a competent guitarist usually takes a few years and a lot of hard work, as does getting a good university degree. Now I know that Gordon has written a new song since we arrived here on campus and, while he might not agree, I am going to ask him to do it for you *And* look out for all of the guitar playing stuff that I was telling you about because, what Gordon does with his playing is not too different from my own. Also, listen to the words because they tell the story and, with a guitar in his hands, Gordon is a great storyteller."

Gordon then played a minor key introduction and, in an intense, emotion packed voice, began to sing:-
> *How could such a thing ever have come to pass,*
> *that I could lose my little Donegal lass?*

Pete added his applause to that of their small but clearly focussed audience as Gordon played a melodic phrase on his guitar that he knew would add interest between sung lines. At the same time, he scanned the seats and faces in front of him, clearly looking for someone: in the audience.

> *How could we ever have fallen out of love,*
> *who used to fit together like hand and glove?"*
> *Can I really have lost my Donegal lass?*
> *Can the years have passed that fast, my Donegal lass?*
> *Is it all in the past? Donegal lass?*

Next, Gordon played a series of chords married to some Travis picking before starting to speak. "Actually, folks, I've written two new songs since coming here to the land of inspiration and, while I don't usually air material this new, or this rough in front of an audience, with this being a workshop situation, if it's all right with you, I'd like to do this other new song for you." Changing his key, but sticking with his Travis picking, Gordon began to sing:

> *Close your eyes, honey, but try to stay awake;*
> *There's still some loving with you that I need to make;*
> *Close your eyes, honey, but please don't fall asleep;*
> *Although this love is new, I know that I'm in deep;*
> *Close your eyes, darling, but try to stay awake;*
> *There's still some loving that we need to make.*

Pete was clapping along with the audience for a long moment before he began to talk. "Trust the O'Brien to keep the best for last. If I know anything about songs, that last one could be a hit for somebody. So, for what it's worth, people, that's most of what I had intended to present to you during this session. Hopefully, I've given you one or two things to think about and I hope I haven't been shoving my opinions down your throats too much. Anyone who knows me would tell you that I'm not renowned for my tact and diplomacy. What you see is pretty much what you get. One other thing that I do feel the need to talk to you about is guitars. For most singer-songwriters and, for folk or traditional music, an acoustic guitar is the instrument of choice. If you want to play in a blues or a rock band, or in an Irish showband, you will need an electric guitar but, in any case, it's best to learn on an acoustic because it really is a band in a box and it's easier to learn on an acoustic and switch to electric later than what it is to do it the other way round. Avoid nylon strung guitars unless you are an aspiring classical guitarist or are looking for a new sound for your next album. Always buy the best guitar you can afford because guitar playing is difficult enough without trying to do it on something that is impossible to play in the first place. And every time that you take it up to play, always tune because even the best guitar in the world will sound awful when out of tune. If you look at my friend Gordon, here, what he is playing is an inexpensive Yamaha guitar,. a good enough professional standard instrument that gets the job done. Not too many frills but it deliver the goods. This sunburst finish instrument that I'm playing is an old friend that I like to call Big Red. It's a Gibson J200 but, more than that, it is a Gibson J200 prototype model. Which means that when some of the big guitar manufacturing companies are developing a new model, they will build maybe five or six experimental examples before the newcomer goes into full production line building. Those prototype models are then usually shown to a selection of good and, sometimes, very well know players, so that their suggestions for improvements can be incorporated into the new design. There are never many of these prototypes, and because they are usually just that little bit different from what will eventually come off the production line, they are usually sought after and correspondingly expensive."

"Very true," Gordon commented, and then went on. "Back in Glasgow, Pete and I often play in some rough clubs in rough parts of the city and that often means that Pete and Big Red are out there alone in the wee small hours of the morning while Pete gets gear back to the car or hunts down a taxi. I've often been concerned for the safety of Pete and Big Red because even if you are a tough, one-time boxing man like Pete is, what chance do you have of holding on to your instrument if five or six guys jump you?"

"They would have to go some to get my guitar," Pete said in a tone which contained nothing of bravado, boasting or machismo, speaking in a tone of voice suggesting that while he might be unhappy or even saddened by being put into such a situation but having just to accept where he found himself, he would give one hundred per cent to the task of defending himself and Big Red.

Looking round the tiered auditorium, Pete's attention was caught by the clock on the wall to his left and in the same moment, he noticed one or two people in front of him looking at their watches,; it seemed to be just about the right moment to draw his class to a close.

"I don't know what your plans are for the rest of the day folks but whether you are going to be catching further musical events here on campus or just getting out into our fine sunshine, as the saying goes, '*Take it easy, but be sure to take it.*' Thank you."

A ripple of applause greeted Pete's words and, while Pete had brought the masterclass to a close, there was no scramble for the exits, the audience looking at Pete as if to say that they could take more if Pete wanted to give it. "And in our song-writing," he said, smiling, "if we haven't found exactly the right line to end our song on, repeating the second last line often works, or it suffices until we can come up with a better one later. So often with words, the first and last ones are crucial as they lead us into and out of whatever scenario we are having our say on or about. A generation or two ago, a workshop like this one would have probably concentrated more on piano than guitar but lots of things have changed in the world. Like you can't hitchhike with a piano. One thing that I meant to say to you earlier is that, myself, like most guitarists I know, am largely self-taught. We borrow a lot from other guitarists, some of whom are people we meet along the way, others we know through the vast amount of recordings that are available. Nowadays, for acoustic music, there are instructional videos and DVDs by the hundred. Actually, we are living in the middle of a huge renaissance in acoustic guitar building, and teaching. So there has never been a better time for acquiring a really good acoustic guitar, learning to play and even embarking on the performing and song-writing journey. Guys, like Happy Traum and Stefan Grossman, as well as being fine players themselves, have rescued, recorded, and made available a vast amount of acoustic music, often by the earlier masters. So check those two guys out if you don't know them already." As their audience began to drift away, both Gordon and Pete were happy with how the master-class had gone. Pete was just glad that it was behind him and that it had turned out to be less problematic than he had feared. Considering that neither gigs nor boxing bouts had ever worried him at all over the years he had been less than confident about giving a workshop on his approach to music and performing but, as he moved off backstage towards the little area that was out of sight to

An audience, he was just glad that the event was over. At the rear of the stage, they found Mavis, Sadie, and Joey Cassidy already there and sat down beside them.

"Message from Don and Phil," Sadie quickly threw in. "They have to go and check the venue and time for some medical presentation they have to attend but say they will catch up with you later, either to go into Tuam with you or to see what is happening tonight."

As Gordon and Pete were getting comfortable sitting on their amplifier seats, Mike Smart appeared carrying a tray of paper cups of tea and a plate of chocolate biscuits. "Compliments of the management," he said, laying the tray on top of an ancient speaker cabinet.

I wonder which management: university, festival, or paramilitary? Pete was thinking to himself, as he reached for both tea and biscuits, less than comfortable with the idea of accepting Republican hospitality."*My old dad would turn in his grave at the very idea* He was thinking to himself. "And much appreciated," Gordon smiled, helping himself to two handfuls from the tray. "A very West of Scotland thing," Gordon continued. "That is, not enjoying a drink of tea unless we have something to munch with it."

"It's the same here in Ireland," Mike Smart responded. "But I'm sure there are any number of similarities between the two countries. When I was talking previously about the Great Glen and the blue and green divide here in Ireland, did you experience that growing up in Scotland or were you well out of it?"

"Sure, it's just as bad there," Gordon replied.

"It reminds me of my very first day at primary school, primary one, aged five. The first morning under Miss Butler's tender mercy was traumatic enough but at midday, when I was ready for the walk home to my gran's house where I lived with my mum and dad, the two grandparents, an uncle and aunt or two and one of my cousins, I was just about to start off for home when one of the boys in my class came up to me and that was the point where the poison got poured. 'Make sure that you fill up your pockets with stones as soon as you are outside of the school gates,' he advised. 'Why?' I asked. 'Because the Protestant boys might attack you on the way home and you'll need some ammunition to fight back with.' So, I duly filled my pockets with stones to be got rid of before going into our house. And that was the pattern for all of the time

I was at that school, though I don't remember the Prods ever attacking us. No doubt they filled their pockets in the same way in expectation of attacks from us. My little friend, David, who lived next door to us and who my gran described as being a very, very bad boy, was reported to have gone to the Protestant school with some of his thuggish friends and attacked the children there with sticks and flung stones. So those things did happen. My feeling and memory tell me the whole Catholic/Protestant thing had been dying out, fading away into a natural and timely oblivion. That is until the troubles flared up in Ireland again." "With your concert and master-class behind you, is that the M.V.C.B. thinking about the road home?" Mike Smart asked.

"No, not for a bit yet," Pete replied.

"It's about a week to our next scheduled gig in Edinburgh. So we thought we would just hang out over here for a bit, have a few days holiday, especially with this good weather that you are having," Gordon replied and then went on. "This is a question for you, Joey, you being a local man and a musician: If this band was going to do some street busking in these parts, where would be the best place to do it?"

"It would have to be in Galway because that's where the people are Joey replied. "There is an area down around the quay side that has been smartened up a lot in recent years. At one time, it was a good area to avoid, especially at night, but now that it has been redeveloped, I think it would be a good area for you. It is quite touristy now with some car-parking areas and some almost park-like seating areas. There are good bars and restaurants there now and some of the old buildings have been converted into smart flats. There is a place there called Sean O'Riordan's Café/Bar. Outside in the street there would probably be a good spot for you. Sean is a good old boy and, if you asked him nicely, I'm sure he would plug a lead in for you and let you power your amps."

"If you do speak to Sean," Mike Smart put in, "be sure to mention my name because I went to school with Sean and really know him well. Just tell him you are friends of mine and that should smooth things out for you. And for you, Gordon, Kenny's bookshop is down that way; and you would probably enjoy a look at it."

"It's quite a famous bookshop," Gordon responded, then went on questioningly. "But you seem very interested in our plans?"

"Well it's just that you're on my patch, so I have to be thinking about you or I wouldn't be doing my job," Mike Smart explained. "Last night when I was lying in bed I got to thinking about that photographer and started to ask myself, was he just an acoustic music enthusiast who came along to a gig and brought his camera along so that he could snap some of the performers, or was he something else completely? Here and in and around the university we can keep an eye on you but out there around Galway, or over in Tuam, it's less easy. When you get to Tuam, you'll probably be thinking about the old O'Brien place and wondering where the farm is. I would like you to look out for Terry O'Farrell, the Estate Agent's office. If anybody can tell you about the O'Brien place, it's him. His office is in the main street, if you can call anything in Tuam a main street, you'll soon find out that there isn't much to Tuam, just a typical small Irish town, or an overgrown village, depending on your point of view. It's better that you talk to Terry than just stopping strangers and asking them because, sure as fate, somebody is going to ask you who wants to know and why, and I don't want you coming to the attention of the wrong people., though I've got a feeling that they know you are here already. What I would really like to see, young Gordon, is you and the band. safely on your way home. It's a couple of days yet to your flight, isn't it?"

"You're dead right," Pete replied. "Two days to relax and enjoy this good weather that you're getting."

"You know, you don't have to go home by plane., " Mike Smart went on. "What would you say if I could have you dropped off on the Broomielaw with two black taxis waiting at the kerbside to take you and your gear right home to your front doors?" "How could you do that?" Gordon asked.

"Well I've got access to this fishing boat that's sitting on the quayside in Galway as we speak and the owners owe me a favour or two. It's Chinese owned but that's something in its favour because some of these Irish Chinese are good boys. Tough boys but good. Do you have the Triads in Scotland, Gordon?"

"How would I know? I don't move in those sorts of circles," Gordon replied. "Are they active in Ireland?"

"They are and we kind of turn a blind eye to some of their activities because they cooperate with us in certain areas," Mike Smart replied. "They own this hotel down in Wicklow and they do a lot of their people smuggling from there. A lot of the illegal immigrants who work in the U.K.'s Chinese restaurants start off from Ireland. This was one of my big intelligence coups of a couple of years ago, when I stumbled on the fact that there was a connection between certain Belfast Freemasons and a number of Chinese secret societies," Mike Smart continued. "It seems that this was the key to where much of the loyalist weaponry that was reaching Ireland was coming from. In the short term, we were able to disrupt that supply route and, later, we were able to utilise it for our own purposes."

"Of course, the connection between the Triads and Freemasonry is no new thing," Gordon commented. "Back in the 1930s, a John Ward wrote a three-volume study of just that, exploring the similarities between their rituals and symbolism in some detail. When I was running my rare book business, I used to come across sets of it from time to time. One of the strange things that I noticed about most of those sets that passed through my hands was that, not only did they look unread, but they looked as if they had been printed and bound the day before. So much so that I began to wonder if some book dealer had come across a supply of them in printer's sheets and, every now and then, was having a set bound up to sell on. If that was the case then it could only have been one set at a time or, every now and then, otherwise, a rash of them on the market would have been noticed and the value and price correspondingly pushed down."

"Should you ever come across another set of those, I would like to buy it from you," Mike Smart put in.

"Leave it until I get home, then I will have a look around and see what I can do for you," Gordon offered.

"Excellent!" Mike Smart responded. "So what is it next, guys? Is it my boat trip home or into Tuam for a look about?"

"I guess it has to be the latter," Gordon replied. "As Pete put it earlier, I've got Tuam in the blood and, as everybody knows, blood will out."

"In Ireland, that certainly seems to be the case," Mike Smart said with a smile, which conveyed neither warmth or humour. "Just as long as it's the next guy's blood and not my own." Just then, Mike Smart's mobile phone rang in his pocket and, pulling it out, he walked further off towards the rear of the stage, past the wall of Marshall speakers, to where he was able to take his call out of earshot of the others. "That photographer guy," Smart said, partly speaking in Pete's direction and partly including the rest of the group. "I was wondering about him not turning up for your masterclass when he had bought and paid for his ticket weeks ago."

"Maybe he didn't like your taxi service," Pete quipped.

"That was Terry O'Farrell, the estate agent, on the 'phone to me. Mike Smart continued

It seems that somebody has just shot our photographer friend on the Ardoyne."

"But that's terrible." Gordon said with feeling.

"Saves me the trouble," Mike Smart said with a shrug of his shoulders. "Terry O'Farrell will be looking out for you if you want to pop into his office and say hello," Smart continued.

"Thanks for that introduction," Gordon said, picking up his guitar case with one hand while he passed Pete's to Mavis with the other.

Just then, Joey let out a shrill whistle and waved over a skinny roadie whose bare arms were completely covered in green and red tattoos. "Yes boss," the roadie said, hurrying over. "Need something done?"

"The MVCB gear Matt, strip it out of the stage setup and into the black trunk at the back of the stage that's got the band's name on it. And, if Pete here will give you his keys, you can stow it in his vehicle for him."

"Consider it done, boss," The tattooed roadie said, taking the keys from Pete's outstretched hand.

"It's the Renault People Carrier parked under the trees close to the little stream," Pete explained.

The roadie only hesitated long enough to round up Joey's other assistant before starting to separate the equipment and pack it away. In what seemed to be almost no time at all, the two assistant sound techs were back and the keys were being returned to Pete.

"What I think we should do," Sadie suggested, "is take the instruments back to the rooms and leave them there and then we can meet up for our jaunt into wherever it is that we're going. to."

"Okay, so if you three want to be off with the guitars, I'll reclaim the Renault and we can meet up outside the security office where we parked previously," Pete suggested, jangling the car keys in his pocket.

With Gordon and Pete leading, and Sadie and Mavis bringing up the rear, the M.V.C.B. were soon out of the stuffy atmosphere of the performance space and into the fresh air of the sun-drenched campus. In a matter of just a few minutes, Pete had gotten to the Renault and was soon parking it at the designated rendezvous spot. With the engine switched off, he was sitting in a totally relaxed state with his window fully open. He had just settled back to have a semi-drowsy wait until the others arrived when the mobile phone in his pocket began to ring. Almost grudgingly, he pulled his attention away from the group of attractive young women who were practising Tai Chi and Chi Gung on the grass in front of him until, finally, and with very little in the way of enthusiasm, he turned his attention towards his phone and his caller. Thinking to himself, he was just internally reinforcing his long held opinion that Tai Chi was more of a dance or a meditation than a serious fighting art and remembering his youth when he had had a flirtation with Tai Chi, before giving it up in favour of Tae Kwon Do, Aikido, and Tai Boxing, all of which he had studied for years, while keeping up his involvement with conventional boxing. "Right now, Don," he spoke into his phone while trying to keep the irritation he was feeling out of his voice, "I'm sitting in the car outside of the security place. Gordon, Mavis, and Sadie are due to meet me here for a drive into Tuam. So if you or you and Phil fancy getting yourselves on down here, we can all go in together."

"I'll just report back to my brother Pete and guess that we'll be with you shortly. If there are any problems at our end, I'll let you know."

"But failing that, see you!"

When Gordon and Mavis arrived, Gordon announced that just in case a good busking opportunity arose around Tuam he had changed his mind and decided to bring the guitars along. That said, he got the two instruments loaded into the luggage compartment and went on to explain that Sadie was just a short way behind them and would be along shortly. Then, just as they were all getting into their seats, Sadie appeared and, pushing her multi-hued head in through Pete's open window and almost into his face, she had soon retreated to go and get her guitar stowed in the back.

"So, do you remember your way to that Sligo and Tuam road sign by the roundabout that I pointed out to you on our way here?" Gordon asked as Sadie was getting herself on board.

"Of course I do," Pete replied as the Renault started to roll until, in a surprisingly short time, they were across campus and were sliding out through the metal gates that had first welcomed them to the University of Ireland.

"I just hope that your visit to Tuam turns out to be all that you would hope for, Gordon," Mavis said, leaning forward until she was almost breathing her words into Gordon's ear. "You know, Gordon," she continued, "I've never known my real parents, having been adopted. And while searching out my biological parents was always an option, it was a route I chose not to go down."

"Why was that?" Gordon asked.

"Well, basically, I am happy with my adoptive parents whom I love dearly. So searching out my biological parents could have been a betrayal of the only parents I have ever known. I doubt that my adoptive parents could have loved me anymore or done any better by me if they had been my true parents. And on top of that, my biological parents were an unknown quantity and who knows what bringing them into my life might have resulted in. so for all these and for several other reasons, I decided to leave well alone. With all that said, Gordon, I just hope and pray that your visit to Tuam only brings good and positive things to you!"

"My going there is little more than curiosity, almost idle curiosity, simply wanting to see where my folks came from. I am not expecting anything wonderful or life changing to come from this jaunt," Gordon explained.

That said, Pete quickly had car and occupants driving through green and rolling countryside that, in turn, gave way to the outskirts of Tuam. Gordon, who, if truth be told, had been dozing in the front seat sunshine, had completely missed the first part of Tuam that the Renault traversed and only opened his eyes to find himself looking out at a narrow street running between tall red brick buildings with an industrial feel to them. That put him in mind of Speirs Wharf in the Port Dundas area of Glasgow. Looking around him, he got the impression that the buildings they were passing may have been built as stables at street level and perhaps for grain and hay storage above. Certainly, those upper parts which still had the remains of old lifting tackle in place, looked as if they had been haylofts in the past. Just then, on his left side, he spotted a sign for parking and drew it to Pete's attention who, a moment later, was executing a left turn and was off in search of the designated parking area. Picking up and following two further parking signs, it was not long before they had come to a halt on the edge of a flat expanse of concrete, which gave the impression it had been left behind when the building that had been above it was demolished and the site cleared. There were only two vehicles on the car park, a grey Fordson Major tractor with studded iron wheels and a Mercedes estate car with EU plates. Pete drove the Renault into the space between the tractor and the Mercedes, and was still in the process of switching off his engine and pulling on his handbrake when Gordon was getting out, eager to make his acquaintance with Tuam.

"What I suggest we do, at least at first," he proffered, "is not to look for the Estate Agent's office or ask for directions but just go for a gentle walk so that I can get the feel of the place."

The others seemed to agree with him, or, at least, were not disagreeing, as he set off at a pace, that suggested he knew where he was going even when he did not. In a straggling line the others followed him until, after two or three haphazard turns, they came to a sloping street which led them downhill until they came to an area where a scruffy-looking pond sat surrounded by straggly bushes and two park-type benches. The feel of the patch of greenery and water was like a deliberately created wildlife area of the kind often seen surrounded by urban sprawls. If it had been better maintained, it could have suggested a village or town green reverting back to nature through neglect. As they all struggled to fit themselves on to the nearest bench, there was a great eruption of squawking and bird protests from the handful of ducks and geese resting on the pond's weedy surface. as the birds settled down into a watchful silence, a cyclist appeared on the far side of the pond. Stepping off of his old Raleigh bicycle, he leaned it against the trunk of a handy silver birch tree. Pulling a penny whistle from the waistband of his trousers as he walked, he approached close to the water's edge and, ignoring the Mavis Valley Band., put the whistle to his lips and proceeded to play first one and then several other Irish airs. Eventually, he stopped and, slipping his whistle into his belt, he approached where Gordon and the others were sitting. The newcomer, with his great shaggy beard and well worn clothes, looked like a farm worker or perhaps a particularly ragged street musician.

"There is something in there after my ducks, probably a mink," he said as Gordon extended a hand to invite the stranger to sit on the bench at his side.

"Really enjoyed your playing there," Gordon commented. "It was wonderful."

"You a musician yourself?" the whistler asked, ignoring Gordon's invitation to sit. "Singer and guitarist," Gordon replied. "I don't play any wind instruments, unless you count a little blues harmonica."

"Some of them old bluesmen were great fife and reed flute players, though that's probably a tradition that's dying out, all of the youngsters trying to emulate Jimmy Reed or B.B. King. You from around here or just passing through?"

"Passing through. Though my folks were from these parts," Gordon replied. "Do you know where the O'Farrell Estate Agent office is?"

"I believe I do," the whistler replied. "Continue on past where my bike is parked, follow that street, take a right, followed by a left and when you come to a long straight street crossing the slope at an angle, follow that street downhill and you can't miss it."

"Thank you, friend," Gordon responded.

Bypassing the bicycle as directed, they began to follow the whistler's route until, in a few minutes, they had arrived outside of a two-windowed, double shop unit, where both windows were full of photographs of houses, shops and plots of land. Gordon stood in front of first one window, and then the other, scanning the displays for as long as it took to get a sense of the sort of properties that were currently up for sale in the area. After a moment, Mavis appeared at his elbow.

"Any idea where your folks' farm was or its name?" she asked.

"Where it was I have no idea," he replied, "but its name was Colonel's Fallow."

"An unusual name," Mavis commented. "How did it come to be called that?"

"Well, about two hundred and fifty years ago, there was an English colonel of dragoons called Naismith active in the area. Seemingly, he came to own four or five farms round about." Gordon explained. "He must have known something about crop rotation because apparently, he would leave one whole farm at a time free of crops, and the one that became my family's place, lay untouched longer than any, earning itself a nickname that stuck and one that continued to be used long after Naismith had gone. I am just going to wander inside," Gordon said to nobody in particular. "Anyone who likes can come in with me."

"So how many are we going to buy?" Pete asked dryly.

Taking that question as being rhetorical or just Pete's way of telling him to get a move on, Gordon pushed the glass door open and stepped into the office, Mavis at his side. Inside, the well lit and modern-looking office was painted stark white. The combination of the white paint and the enlarged photographs of a selection of some of the choicer properties currently for sale in the area hanging on the walls reminded Gordon of a modern art gallery in Glasgow's West Regent Street that he liked to visit, Gordon knowing as many artists in Scotland as he did musicians. In the estate Agent's shop behind a long, modern partner desk, two people were sitting, each with a computer terminal on the desk in front of them. On the left was a middle-aged looking man in a flamboyant, double-breasted, blue striped suit that made him look not unlike George Melly. He stood up to greet them and then while his companion, a younger-looking, blonde-haired woman in a sober business suit looked on, the man leapt into action, quickly seizing various chairs that were standing here and there around the office, until he had them in a row in front of his desk.

"Good day to you folks," he began breezily. "Terence O'Farrell at your service. Please do have a seat and what can I do for you this fine day?"

"Good day to you Mr. O'Farrell," Gordon said, taking a seat as bidden. "Please call me Terry," the estate agent went on, "because if you insist on calling me mister I will start to feel that I am like my dad and that would never do, I can tell you. Can I sell you a house or perhaps some land?"

"Just some information would suffice at this stage." Gordon continued. "What I would like to know is, have you ever dealt with, or know of a house in these parts known as Colonel's Fallow?"

At the mention of the house name, much of the estate agent's easy affability seemed to vanish and his face took on a more serious cast. "And how is it that you know of that particular property?" the estate agent asked, a little suspiciously it seemed.

"It's just that at one time, my family used to own that farm," Gordon explained.

"And are you, by any chance, Gordon O'Brien?" O'Farrell asked.

"I am, but how is it that you know that?" Gordon countered.

"Julie, my dear," O'Farrell said, turning to his colleague, "would you do two things for me? First, reverse the sign on the door so that it read 'CLOSED' rather than 'OPEN' and then deal with any calls that might come in for me, as I would rather not be disturbed."

As the blonde-haired woman reversed the sign on the door and began to press buttons on the telephone sitting close to her computer terminal, the estate agent turned his attention back to Gordon. "To answer your question, Mr. O'Brien: This morning, I received a telephone call from Mike Smart, who I believe you know. He told me a little about you and the fact that you were travelling in the area and how he thought you might turn up here eventually. I am honoured and pleased to meet you." At that, he extended a podgy hand to Gordon, who accepted it and gave it a friendly squeeze. Looking across to check that the door sign had been reversed, he leaned closer to Gordon."In my youth, I was a fairly active Republican. In fact, I was an activist but as the years passed and I became older and more cautious, my involvement diminished. Mike Smart was my commander way back then and even when I became almost inactive, we always kept in touch. In the years when my business was going through its boom time, I became little more than a financial contributor and then when the property market went into decline and I was no longer able to keep up my financial commitment, I would try to contribute in kind."

"How did that work?" Gordon asked, also keeping his voice low so that it was only the estate agent who could hear what he was saying.

"Well in this line of work you can get properties which are empty for a very long time. So when my funds were scarce, I would make some of those properties available for Mike and his men to use, either for storage purposes or as safe houses," O'Farrell continued. "Anyway, last year, Julie here and myself took on the huge task of transferring all of this firm's old hard-copy files on to computer discs. Because of the sheer size of the task, we employed three I.T. students to help us but the long and the short of it is that we now have an excellent and easily accessible record of almost all of the properties that this firm has ever dealt with. My dad was a bit of a local historian and an amateur folklorist. Some of his files contained considerably more information on properties and families than you would expect. After Mike Smart's call, I checked the computer for Colonel's Fallow just to refresh my memory. It seems there were O'Briens on that land at least as far back as famine times. One of them was a bonesetter, what nowadays would be called a chiropractor or an osteopath, with some interest in and knowledge of herbal medicine and it seems that all of those years ago, the family were active in the community, demonstrating a social conscience and a concern for their fellow man, to the extent that the O'Brien farm was a place where poor people could go for medical help in extremity. The Galway O'Briens always had a reputation for being a wild lot, not a bad lot but definitely wild. As far back as the fourteenth century, they were in the thick of it, falling foul of Edward I, the notorious Longshanks. Thomas De Clare, one of Edward's main men in Ireland at that time, personally executed Brian O'Brien at Dunratty in 1282. At your great, great grandmother's death, your family property was deeded to her sister, Winnie, Colonel's Fallow having been Winnie's home for some time by then, that fact probably being a factor in her coming to inherit. Eventually Winnie remarried and in time the farm passed to her second husband and later to one of his relatives who just about ruined the place, the local Cassidys always being a shiftless bunch. one thing you have to realise, Gordon is that Colonel's Fallow has been a Republican house for a long time and, on a practical level, still is one. From what I can see, the last time that this firm dealt with the property was six or seven years ago when it was purchased by a show-jumper from Essex and an Arab shipping magnate from Dubai. They were both great equestrians and went into partnership intending to use the farm for horse breeding and racehorse training. The Arab chap poured capital into the venture and that is when the house was upgraded and modernised. Though, that said, Nan O'Brien, who is probably a distant relative of yours and lives close by, assures me that there are still bits and pieces in the house that go back to Captain Jamie's time. With the equestrians, both the house and the land were greatly improved at that time and, as far as I could see, the horse breeding was successful enough, even though the racing wins the partners were looking for were to prove more elusive. I believe that that business is in abeyance rather than terminated because, a couple of years ago, the Arab chap went back to Dubai, though he did deposit some funds with me so that the place could be adequately maintained, a responsibility that I have seen to with great care. Mike Smart employs the nearest neighbour, this Nan O'Brien, to look after the interior of the house and see that it is spick and span for visitors and for his meetings. And at the same time, he employs Murdo MacDonnel, the shepherd on the Quinn farm, to keep the gardens tidy and generally deal with any outside maintenance that needs to be done. So, all in all, the old O'Brien place is probably kept at its best. When I spoke to Mike Smart he wanted me to find out, if possible, what your plans are. I get the impression, Gordon, that Mike Smart has taken a liking to you because he said that, if you did turn up here, I can either take you out there and let you see the house or, failing that, I can give you the keys and let you take a look around for yourself. In fact, he said to tell you that if you do go out there and want to stop over, then you can have the house for a day or two as long as you are gone by Saturday, when Mike has an important meeting scheduled." At that, the estate agent opened a desk drawer and pulled out a wallet file, what looked like a prospectus and a set of keys, and then, putting the prospectus and the keys into the folder, passed the package across to Gordon. "If you do go out to the house, Mike usually keeps the place quite well stocked up. So he said to tell you just to use up any food that you find there and simply enjoy some Republican hospitality. And don't be surprised if Nan or Murdo, or even Mike himself, pops in to see you. And, Gordon, if you can get the keys back to me before you head home, that will be appreciated."

"You can be sure that I will," Gordon responded.

"I fully expect that you will because if Mike was not pretty sure that you were a decent, respectable, and responsible group of people, he would never have offered you the use of the house. As far as I can tell, we are not expecting any visitors who might need to use the house in a hurry but, if that should change, we will let you know. It's not our only safe house in the area. If Mike Smart says you can have the house until Saturday, Mike being the kind of man that he is, you can take it that that's a good as a contract. Mike has always been a stubborn man of his word, a good friend, and a bad enemy. So if you want to be getting out there while there is still some daylight left, best to be going soon."

"Thank you for your hospitality, Terry," Gordon said, reaching for the folder as he stood up. "It was kind of you to spend so much time with us and give us the benefit of your immense local knowledge."

"It was a pleasure," the estate agent responded. "It was great to meet the current generation of O'Briens and to be able to know, even if only for a short time, that there is an O'Brien back in the old house. Julie, my dear, could you just unlock the front door and show our friends out."

As they followed the woman to the door the estate agent brought up the rear.

"What now?" Pete said once they were all outside standing on the pavement and the estate agent had gone back inside.

"A gentle walk through Tuam and back to the car park and probably by a different route from the one which brought us here," Gordon replied, noticing that the sign on the door behind them now read "OPEN". Then, leading the way, he was more intent on steering the group in the general direction of the car park, rather than trying to retrace their earlier steps. Ten minutes later and, without passing the duck pond, they were back in the hire car and back in their seats.

"Does that brochure give travel directions?" Pete asked as Gordon pulled the prospectus out of his folder and ran his eye down it until he got to the Travel Directions' section. "Looks simple enough," Pete said, lifting the prospectus out of Gordon's hands and skimming the contents. "Strikes me, Gordon, that thus far our Irish trip is going pretty well." he mused. "Don't you think?"

"Seems fine to me," Gordon replied. As Pete finished his reversing manoeuvre and began to concentrate on putting the Mercedes and the tractor behind them and the hire car on to a course that would take it away from the streets of Tuam and back on to the Sligo road. "So what were the directions once we were back on this Yeatsian road?" he asked a little later, trying unsuccessfully to drive and read the estate agent's printed instructions at the same time. "We continue on our bardic highway for five kilometres," Gordon said, taking the prospectus away from Pete and reading from it. "After the five kilometres, we will come to a Shell garage on our right and, after that, I will give you further directions as and when needed." In what seemed to be only moments, as Pete was squinting into the glaringly bright Irish distance while trying to position himself behind his sun visor, he became aware of a largish building on the horizon but, because of the distance and the fierce glare of the sun in his eyes, he was at first unable to make out what it was. Then, as they proceeded, he began to think that he could make out bands of red and yellow, tantalisingly reminiscent of other Shell garages he had seen in the past. As they continued, although he could not make out the letters on a huge advertising hoarding, he began to be sure that they were in fact approaching a Shell garage. "What do we look for after the garage?" he asked in Gordon's direction. "I was just going to tell you that," Gordon responded. "After the garage, we continue for a further two kilometres and then we should come to a conifer copse on our right. Just as we reach the farther side of that plantation, the house should be nestling close to the trees. There is a second clump of conifers close to the first with a second house close to them. But we are warned not to confuse the two because it is definitely the first house that we are looking for."

Pete nodded, watching the Shell garage slipping behind them in his rear view mirror. "Conifers coming up," he murmured a moment later, pointing them out to Gordon, who had already spotted them and come to the conclusion that he was drawing close to the place where his forebears had lived and died and put their unique stamp on the land, their community, and environment. Pete was watching the conifers and as the trees began to thin out, and both he and Gordon were becoming convinced that they had to be close to the house, Pete noticed a modern looking fence on his right. It was seven or eight feet high, looked to be constructed of green, plastic covered metal links, supported on lengths of galvanised angle iron and probably set into concrete imbedded in the ground. The fence ran for forty or fifty feet with white painted wrought iron double gates set into it about halfway along its length. In a lozenge shaped section of one of the gates, small pieces of metal had been welded into the gate's design, forming a sign that read Colonel's Fallow.

Pete switched on his indicator and pulled the Renault on to the middle of the carriageway, well positioned for a turn into the space between the edge of the road and the white gates. As he was pulling on his handbrake and killing his engine, Gordon was getting his passenger-side door open and was clearly ready to approach the gates for a better look at the house, which they could now make out beyond the fence. One of the first things that Gordon noticed, when his feet kicked into the soil at the edge of the road's tarmacadam, was just how dark, rich, and fertile it looked where it had spattered his trainers. Breathing in the fresh Colonel's Fallow air, he was both savouring its freshness and taking looks all around him as he approached the double gates. Reaching the gates, which looked to have been recently painted, he leaned his forearms on the top rung of the left hand gate and looked over into a large rectangular garden with a medium sized house at its far end. Almost anywhere in the British Isles, it would have been recognised as a fairly typical farmhouse building of the late nineteenth/early twentieth century period. It looked substantial without being in any way ostentatious. Built on two levels, its white painted stonewalls, even at a distance, looked strong and thick. The traditional slate roof had two dormers facing the road, which were white painted, as were the soffits above them. With a modern looking white door, the whole house exuded order and a well- maintained calm. In front of the entrance door was a low porch overhung by a slated lean-to style canopy, its grey slates matching those on the roof above. In Scotland, they would most likely have come from the famous slate quarries of Balachulish on Loch Levenside. While pleasantly enjoying a long and leisurely study of the property in front of him, Gordon was musing on the fact that he was now gazing on a house that he had both seen depicted in photographs and heard described by his father on numerous occasions and how the house looked pretty much as he had expected. Banishing these stored memories, he focused on what was in front of him, taking in what seemed to be a well tended garden with a T-shaped driveway of gold-coloured pebbles, that ran from the gates and the road, the crossbar part of the driveway providing two car parking spaces, one in front of each of the ground floor, road facing windows. The space in front of the doorway and on the longer part of the driveway gave space for further vehicles to park if necessary. To the left of the driveway, a large and apparently recently hoed flowerbed was taken up by an enormous fuchsia bush. It was a good fifteen feet high and about twenty-five feet long, enormous branches heavy with bunches of flame red blossom. The sheer size of the plant suggested that it had been there for a long time. On the opposite side of the driveway were several rhododendron bushes and, while not in bloom, the thick carpet of discoloured pink and blue blossom around their bases was testament to how magnificent they must have been earlier in the growing season. The whole area of the house and garden exuded a sense of well-ordered and well-maintained peacefulness. Drinking in and savouring the serenity of the scene, Gordon pulled the heavy bunch of keys that the estate agent had given him out of his jacket pocket and, selecting one of the three larger keys on the ring, he inserted it into the gate's lock. Then, applying minimal pressure, he was almost surprised when the lock's mechanism turned over with a well-oiled click. He slipped his hand through two of the gate's iron bars, to catch hold of the gate's long retaining bolt and, lifting the bolt out of its socket in the ground, he turned the handle to the side and pushed both gates well back until they were up against the grey coping stones that separated the driveway from the garden beds. As he motioned for Pete to bring the Renault in off the road, he realised that Mavis had got out her side of the vehicle and was now standing at his side.

"Come on, girlie," he said as Mavis took his arm, "let's go and take a look at the house." As Mavis nodded her agreement and gave his arm a meaningful squeeze, he retrieved the keys from the white gates to drop them into his pocket again

Then, with their feet crunching on the pebbles, they walked up the driveway where generations of O'Briens had walked before them. Taking the one step that let him mount onto the long wooden porch that framed the front door, Gordon stood in front of the door for a moment in thoughtful silence. Seeing that her companion was deep in thought and not wanting to disturb him, Mavis dipped her hand into his jacket pocket to seize the house keys. Running her eye over the door in front of her, Mavis selected first, one of the larger keys and then, one of the smaller keys. Both keys turned over easily and, in a moment, they found themselves looking into a shadowy hall. Gordon ran his hand down the wall to his left just inside the house door and, by feel alone, found the light switch where he had expected it to be. A moment later, he clicked it on to see that they were facing a small, almost square vestibule. To their left was a dark wood dresser, clearly meant to store coats, boots and umbrellas. Two umbrellas and a rustic shepherd's crook-type walking stick were in the umbrella stand section of the dresser but, otherwise, it was empty. To their right was a doorway, suggesting a further room beyond. Directly in front of them stood a grandfather clock with a decidedly antique cast. to its appearance Its cabinet was constructed of a mottled yellowish timber which Gordon, with his knowledge of the timber preferences of musical instrument makers, believed to be maple. Through the little glass window in the front of the clock case, he could see the clock mechanism and, quickly checking the cheap, modern watch on his wrist, realised that this clock, which was possibly from an earlier era of O'Briens, was still keeping good time. And then, thinking back to the many occasions when his father had told him that his grandfather had been want wont to say, "You never know the minute when you might want a good gun close to hand!" and, for that reason, kept the souvenir Luger pistol that his great great grandfather had brought back from the Spanish Civil War inside the cabinet of his grandfather clock. Peering at the clock in front of him, Gordon spotted the little brass key that was protruding from the clock's cabinet and, with a single step forward, unlocked the door and slipping a Questioning hand down past the clock's weights to reach a space large enough to hold a handgun. He was not really surprised that there was nothing there but, having checked out the Luger pistol, he now turned his attention to the hall beyond the vestibule which, with the light now on, he could see quite clearly. He gazed at dark varnished door facings and skirtings and a William Morris style wallpaper which had clearly graced the hall for some time and would not have been out of place in his grandparents' era. Pushing the front door behind him shut with a gentle push of his heel, he opened the door to his right and, with Mavis following him, stepped into a room which, in the past, must have been the front parlour. Around the window area was sitting a solid looking brown leather three-piece suite which, with its scuffed corners and edges, suggested that it would be as comfortable as a pair of familiar slippers. Against the wall facing the doorway where Gordon and Mavis stood framed was a traditional wooden fireplace surrounding an open fire, already laid and set, as if just waiting to be lit. The whole centre of the room was taken up by a huge walnut table which looked as if it should have been gracing the dining room of some castle or be the centre of attraction in a boardroom somewhere. The table appeared to be set for a meeting. It had eight chairs and eight placemats set in position, each place having a blank notepad, two pens and a pencil. Also at each place was an empty cut-glass decanter and a cut-glass whiskey glass, carefully turned upside down to keep it dust free, while in the centre of the table was an ornate silver tray holding two bottles of malt whiskey, as well as bottles of water and bottles of diluting orange and lime juice. Gordon smiled to himself at the sight of the orange and green bottles sitting in close and, apparently, peaceful proximity. A whiteboard and pens, set up on an easel close to the couch, just finished off the meeting space, the whole room suggesting that a careful and methodical hand had set it up.

"Whoever's meeting here sure won't go thirsty," Gordon commented. "Nor will they be cold." Mavis said glancing to where two large wicker baskets placed one on either side of the fire and both stacked up with cut logs, were sitting.

"Well, I've seen enough of this room. Shall we explore further?" Gordon suggested and, so saying, retraced his steps back to the vestibule, Mavis following him to where they passed a gilt-framed colour print of Jesus as the Sacred Heart, which gave the impression that it may have been in the hall as long as the wallpaper. "It wouldn't surprise me if that print does not go all the way back to the O'Briens." Gordon ventured.

"Well, in Ireland, it's the kind of thing that few would think of binning, so it could have hung there for a long time Mavis commented.

At that, Gordon quickly slipped the picture off its hanging hook, and in the moment between pulling the print down and slipping it up again, it was clear that the wallpaper was faded with age, so the print had hung there for some considerable time.

And then, just beyond the Sacred Heart print, they stopped to examine a second gilt and glass frame.

"What's this about?" Mavis asked, pointing at what appeared to be an age-yellowed newspaper clipping preserved under glass. The photograph in the centre of the newspaper article showed a group of clergymen in their church vestments, looking as if they were caught in the act of waving for the camera.

"I think that article is in Spanish," Gordon began. "And, in fact, I think I've seen that sinister photograph before. I saw it used in a book on the songs of Christy Moore. Those clergymen were supporters of Franco and Mussolini and, while they look as if they are waving for the camera, they are actually giving the nazi/fascist salute. Hope they all got their comeuppance a long time ago."

"I wonder why it was kept and framed?" Mavis pondered, following Gordon along the hall until an open door on their right let them look into a large square room that appeared to be both a kitchen and a dining room. *With the front parlour for more formal dining*, Mavis was thinking to herself, as she paused in the doorway of the room.

"Maybe it was kept there as a reminder that the Sacred Heart is only one facet of the Church of Rome and that there is a harder and darker side to it," Gordon mused, still looking at the photograph of the clergymen. "It reminds me of that infamous newsreel clip from the 1930s where the Pontiff is seen blessing Italian warplanes caught in the act of taking off to attack with 1930s state of the art military technology, Abyssinian tribesmen armed only with spears and bows and arrows. Perhaps it's a salutary reminder that fascism needs to be fought wherever it rears its ugly head. There's an Irish folksong that says, *'We fought the fascists in Germany and Spain. We'll fight them in Belfast, Dublin, or Kilgrain,'* or words to that effect. We have to remember that Captain O'Brien was with the International Brigades in Spain and that was where he acquired his military skills. Because of his prowess as a sniper, he was nicknamed 'The Lone Wolf.'"

"Gordon O'Brien," Mavis began in a gently chiding tone, "your head seems to hold an almost endless store of bits of songs and poems, quotes from philosophers and Indian sages, all mixed up with a generous seasoning of O'Brien family myth and history. Let's just try and stay in the here and now with you and me and, while simply agreeing to ignore these probably long dead priests and bishops, we can continue to take a look at the rest of the house." So saying, she stepped through the open doorway where they had halted, Gordon following her into what turned out to be a large room, perhaps twenty-five feet long by the same wide, and very clearly the main kitchen. At Mavis's right hand, there was a long rosewood patterned formica worktop which, against the wall running the full width of the room, connected with the wall at the opposite side of the room, which had a matching worktop built around a cooker and a sink. Above and below these two worktops, which were like a frame to the whole room, was a series of cupboards and storage units. Pulling open the nearest of the cupboard doors, Mavis was surprised to find that it hid a fairly well-stocked, large, modern-looking refrigerator. Largely ignoring the kitchen's specifics, Gordon strode across the room, past the cooker that, even from the doorway, Mavis had identified as having both gas and electricity. On the wall just beyond the cooker and the sink there was a large double window and a modern door, the latter made of the same white UPVC as the door that had led them off the porch. Gordon stood for a long moment trying to reconcile what he was seeing with a lifetime of family stories and descriptions of the old O'Brien farm and farmhouse. Gordon's father probably had not read Karen Blixen's book, *'Out of Africa,'* so would not have known how the authoress, from time to time, would repeat the line *'I had a farm once in Africa,'* or known how similar that was to his own oft repeated, *'When we had the Galway farm,'* but Gordon had recollections of countless descriptions of that farm and was having difficulty making the material farm fit the memory farm. Mavis seemed to have some inkling of what he was doing because, although she came up behind him and slipped a comradely arm around his waist, at first she did not speak. Looking out the window, Gordon to his left, could see a red sandstone wall about as tall as a man. It ran parallel to the Galway end of the house and came to connect with a second, similar wall running parallel to the rear of the house. In the area framed by these two walls was a tidy and clearly, currently unused, cobbled farmyard. In the corner of which, and over to Gordon's left, was a substantial stone-built barn that, with its white painted exterior and its slated, pitched roof, made it a perfect working partner to the domestic part of the farm. "Penny for your thoughts.," Mavis said finally, shattering Gordon's introspective moment. It's just not right," he replied, pointing to the modern door where it stood beyond the end of the window and the modern-looking open-plan stairs that no doubt led to the bedrooms above.

"If you have never been here before, you can't know what's right and what's not," Mavis pointed out.

"I was here as a child and, while I've no recollections of those early visits, I've heard so many stories about this place that I've had pictures of it in my mind's eye for as long as I can remember and when I spot something that is out of kilter with aural history, it does jar."

Gordon was glaring at the one piece, modern white kitchen door and thinking of how, on many occasions, he had been told how Captain, the family plough-horse in his grandfather's time, seemed to know just how long the men took for their midday meal and how the horse would appear after exactly thirty minutes, push his great Clydesdale head in through the open top half of the split rustic door, and snuffle around for the dish of apples that were often kept close by at that time. Gordon frowned, thinking to himself that whoever had replaced the old kitchen door with this modern monstrosity had paid scant attention to neither the style or the history of the old farmhouse.

"So how much is there to Colonel's Fallow?" Mavis asked.

"It was bigger at one time," Gordon replied. "As the family fortunes dwindled, parts of the land were sold off and every now and then a son would marry and a parcel of land would go off with son and bride. By my grandfather's time, the family had apparently decided that the old place should not be diminished any further, otherwise it would have become too small to be able to support a family. That is why my grandfather, the youngest son at the time, was asked to take himself off and, if not exactly seek his fortune, at least seek to support himself separate from the farm. There is not much beyond what we can see from this window, Mavis," Gordon continued. "There is the house and barn and I believe that what is now the front garden previously would have been the kitchen garden. Beyond the wall in front of us is a large field, always known as the Home Pasture. Within the Home Pasture, there is a small walled-in area, usually called the Nursery Pasture, because any newborn or sickly animals could be kept there where they were within view from the house. Beyond the Home Pasture there is the High Pasture, while beyond the High Pasture and, affording it some shelter, is the Grocery Wood, so-called because according, to legend, any time an O'Brien walked that way with a shotgun, or even the tools of the archer's trade, he was almost guaranteed to return with a pair of rabbits or pigeons for the table. Beyond the Grocery Wood is the Quinn Farm. The original farmer Quinn was an O'Brien tenant. But it seems that, as the years passed and the O'Brien farm dwindled, the Quinn place grew at a corresponding rate. The two families were always close and it was common for Quinns and O'Briens to marry. They would borrow one another's horses and wagons and, of course, help with each other's harvests. Even after my grandfather was well settled in Scotland, he would time his annual holiday from his work so that he could be back here to help with the harvest. His two sons, that is my father and my uncle, Jimmy, were also often gathered here at harvest time. So that, Mavis, is a quick thumbnail sketch of Colonel's Fallow, its fields and its O'Brien custodians. If I put my mind to it, you would probably find that just about every part of the place has a story or stories attached to it." "In detail and right down to the name of the plough horse." Mavis commented.

"There were two of those, and not just one," Gordon responded. "There was obviously Captain, the lead horse, and the family tractor of his day, but there was also Bess. Captain lived to a great age, eventually to be buried under the barn, where his stall had been. But Bess died in her prime and her story is much sadder than Captain's. So much so that I really don't want to tell it to you."

"Go on," Mavis encouraged. "Here we, are, a band of friends, brothers and sisters, gathered on this fine day with, as the estate agent put it, an O'Brien back in Colonel's Fallow again. So, even a sad story can be told in such a time and place."

"I'm sure" The Bess story...," Gordon began in an exaggerated tone of voice, the kind of slightly melodramatic and affected tone that he might have used if reading something he had written to his Southside Writers' Circle back in Glasgow. "It was harvest time and the High Pasture was under wheat and, remember, that this was at a time before the proliferation of the combine harvester. So, the crop being ready to be brought in, my grandfather, that is, the man who had moved to Scotland, was back at the farm to help with the harvest. Anyway, he had assembled in the High Pasture various relatives, friends and neighbours, plus a sprinkling of hired hands. They were preparing to harvest the wheat in the old way—that is, with scythes. There was one hand who my grandfather had hired before and therefore knew well. His name was Edward McTurk and he liked to call himself a full-blood gypsy, though to the Galway farmers, he was always known as Tinker Ed. Knowing this man's habits of old, my grandfather had spent longer than usual that morning sharpening the scythe that the Tinker would use, not wanting to give this particular hand the opportunity to claim that his scythe was blunt because that would have given the man the chance to be doing nothing, smoking a cigarette while he sharpened his scythe with a whetstone, it being considerably easier to sharpen a scythe than swing one against a crop. So, spending longer than he normally would have done at his task, my grandfather got to the point where that scythe was as sharp as a razor. Then when the men, in an extended line, had passed along the length of the pasture, scything, binding, and stacking the crop as they went. my grandfather had sent McTurk to bring up the farm wagon, pulled by the faithful Bess It seems that McTurk had brought the wagon up, approaching from the Grocery Wood side, driven in into the High Pasture and parking the wagon close to the wall dividing that field from the Home Pasture. As my grandfather came up riding Captain and also approaching from the Wood side, a sudden movement in the Home Pasture caught his eye and, in the very same moment, he heard the scream of a horse in pain and realised instantly that McTurk had released Bess into the same field as Benny, the farm's prize bull. The movement that my grandfather had spotted, he was told later, was a flick of the huge bull's never dehorned head, which had sent a long horn deep into the horse's flank. Urging his plough horse into as much of a run as the Clydesdale was capable of, my grandfather was soon in the Home Pasture, where Bess was down in the field in a widening pool of blood. When Captain refused to approach any closer than within twenty feet of the stricken mare, my grandfather rode him to the side of the field and tethered him there. Sprinting back across the Home Pasture, he threw open the gate to the Nursery Field's walled enclosure. Then, taking off his jacket and using it almost like a weapon, he drove the bull into the walled-off area and closed the gate on him. At that point, he noticed McTurk's scythe lying close by. Snatching it up, he quickly undid the two bolts and butterfly nuts which kept the gleaming blade attached to the scythe's wooden handle, driven to even greater speed by the frantic cries of the downed horse. Running to the side of Bess, he thanked providence that the blade was so unusually sharp and drew the glinting steel across the horse's throat. Immediately, the blade cup deep into the jugular vein, sending a great welter of blood gushing out to mingle with that already splattering the field. That heart-breaking task done and as the great beast's life was slipping away, my grandfather held the horse's head in both of his arms, holding her close to his chest and speaking to her gently as she gave up her breath and her life. By the time it was all over, one of the neighbours had untethered Captain and led him away from the scene of such a shocking incident until he could be returned to his stall in the barn where the companion of most of his life would never again be stabled beside him. McTurk was quickly paid off and told to go harvest the fields of Hell for his next job. And, certainly, when word of his carelessness and what that carelessness had wrought spread, there was little work for McTurk to be found in Galway. Well, was that a sad enough tale for you, Mavis?" Gordon asked, having reached the end of his telling.

"It certainly was," Mavis replied, listening to something she could almost hear in the background. "I think there might be someone knocking on the front door. I'll just go and check." At that, she slipped out of the kitchen and back down the hall to where the knocking was growing more insistent. A moment later, she returned, walking over to the kitchen window where Gordon was standing as if entranced, far away in his thoughts.

"Was there someone at the door?" he eventually asked.

"There certainly was," Mavis answered. "An old lady who wanted to know if the young master was home and when I asked her who that was, she asked for you by name."

"Young master indeed!" Gordon snorted. "So what did you tell her or do with her?"

"I put her in the front parlour and said you would be with her shortly," Mavis answered.

"Then I had better do just that," Gordon responded, already heading for the hall.

As soon as Gordon pushed open the door to the front parlour, he saw the little old lady sitting on the sofa, her short but stocky person framed in the light coming through the window from the front garden. Her small but broad stature suggested a life of hard work. Her hair was between grey and white and, as soon as she saw Gordon, she made as if to stand.

"No, don't get up," Gordon protested, noticing that although the elderly woman's face was wrinkled and suggested full years, her vivid blue eyes were clear and bright with a certain subdued fierceness to her gaze.

Allowing Gordon to protest at her attempt to rise to greet him, she sank back into her seat while scrutinising the young man in front of her. "I would have known you for an O'Brien anywhere," she said with a smile. "You are very like your grandfather and, although I was only a girl when I met Captain O'Brien, I have several photographs of him and I can see him in you, too."

"How did you know I was here?" Gordon asked.

"I suppose I had better tell you who I am first before I start answering questions and filling your head with family history. I'm Nan O'Brien, Colonel Fallows' closest neighbour and I am your great aunt Winnie's niece. I guess that makes me some sort of distant relative to you. You can call me auntie if you like?"

"I would sure like to," Gordon responded warmly. "Because it's not every day that you meet an aunt you never even knew you had."

"To answer your question, lad, I had two telephone calls about you. One from Mr. Terence, the estate agent and one from Mr. Smart, and after that, two of Smart's boys popped in to see me earlier today and they thought that you were here. That reminds me, I'm supposed to pass on a message from Mr. Smart for you, and it's to let you know that he has one of his secret meetings on in here at the weekend. So he will need the house by Saturday morning. He will try to drop in and see you at some point. He also told me to warn you that there are some suspicious people about the area and how, because of that, you should be on your guard. He had seemingly been talking to old Murdo McGregor, who is the shepherd on the Quinn place, the farm beyond the Grocery Wood. It seems that an army helicopter landed in one of the fields up there last week and, ever since, Murdo has been seeing new tracks in the wood but with no sign of whoever is making them. He has also been finding snares set around the place and of a kind he does not recognise and so not set by any of our local wild harvesters. Smart thinks that there might be some sort of British Army group active in the area. Them fellas are like foxes. They dig a hole in the ground and then live in it as quiet as mice, looking and listening and snooping about. Smart doesn't like it at all because of it being so close to his meeting. He told me to tell you that his brother, Martin, and two of his boys will be camping up in the Grocery Wood tonight and for the next couple of nights, just as a precaution, but that you probably won't see or hear them. Young Martin is a nice lad and quite different from his brother. But enough of the bandits. I am pretty sure that that was one of the reasons for your grandfather moving to Glasgow all those years ago. Everybody knew that he would take over the farm here one day but some thought that he would have to take over some of his dad's other roles, and he was maybe a farmer and a bit of a dreamer and philosopher, but he was never going to become any sort of gunman. So, he was well out of that one. Tell me this though, is your grandfather still alive?"

"No, he's been dead these twenty years," Gordon replied. "He had a stroke of some sort and then was in a nursing home for a bit. If I put my mind to it, I can just about remember his funeral. I can remember it being a fine bright, sunny day, though not much more."

"Over the years I have often wondered if Jimmy was still alive or not but then, as the years passed, and they do, his being still alive grew less and less likely," Nan continued. "I often wondered if he had got drawn into the war. So many of our lads who left Ireland and were looking for no more than an opportunity to earn a wage across the water, ended up in the British forces and lost their lives that way. Of course there was a time when stupid women were going around handing men white feathers if they were not in a uniform of some sort."

"I know he was an air raid warden for some time because, as a child, I used to play with his steel helmet and gas mask. Both of his sons were in the war and survived it, though neither of them is with us now," Gordon said.

"I can remember your grandfather with his suitcase, waiting for the bus to Dublin, when he was leaving to go to Glasgow," Nan continued. "Even after he was well settled in Scotland, every summer when he got his holiday from his work, he used to come back over, help his dad with the harvest, and generally help around the farm. I can remember when he brought his Scots lass over with him. I think she suspected that I was more than just a neighbour's daughter. Then, in time, there were the two boys. I can fair remember the noise of them playing cowboys and Indians up in the High Pasture. I guess one of them would have been your dad?"

"I guess so," Gordon responded. "My dad and Uncle Jimmy, both of them gone now."

"How time and people pass," Nan said thoughtfully. "So what did Jimmy do with his life in Scotland?"

"From what I can remember," Gordon replied, "he was always good with horses and later with tractors. He worked as a carter when he first got to Glasgow. He drove a four-horse team delivering sugar in two hundred weight bags at a time when a man was expected to carry one of those on his own. Grandpa used to say that it was more about knack than strength and how it all depended on how a man broke the sack across his shoulder, allowing half of the load to hang down his back, while the other half was over the chest.

Chapter Nine

At the Old O'Brien Farm

Of course, they wore broad leather belts around their middles, buckled up tight so that their stomach muscles had some protection. I know that he had a hard life at that time. Up at four in the morning, down at the stable to start cleaning it out by five. Then there was all of the curry-combing of the horses, maintaining their harness and out on the road with the first of the day's loads while it was still dark. He used to tell me about the two hydraulic lifts, one on either side of the River Clyde and how they were connected by a tunnel under the river. The carter would drive his team and load on to one lift, which was then lowered and then, when the wagon had gone down and traversed the tunnel, they would drive on to the lowered lift on the far side to be brought up to street level. I can remember grandpa saying how it took a good team and a good driver to get a heavily laden wagon off the lift and up the ramp to the street level. He used to say that to do it at all, the horses had to hit that ramp at a gallop."

Nan nodded her head thoughtfully as if envisaging the scene, imagining her old boyfriend at his reins, just as she had often seen him in the past. "And did he prosper in Scotland, son?" Nan asked.

"I believe that he did," Gordon replied. "Or as much as any working man can be said to have prospered at that time. I know that by the years between the wars he had bought his own house in a nice city suburb and not many working-class people were buying houses in those days. He saw both of his boys grown up, in good jobs and married by the time that his health began to fail him. He worked hard and was out in all weather doing it, too. There were no Goretex jackets in those days. He would have been out on his wagon hail, rain or shine and with no more than an old grain sack across his shoulders for protection, It's a wonder that he lived as long as he did because that was only the first of a whole string of hard jobs he took on. He was always good to me, slipping me a half-crown every time I saw him. I can still picture him in my mind's eye, sitting in his working clothes, with a glass of beer and his pipe loaded with Thick Black. He was a keen gardener, with legendary rosebushes. He loved anything that was clockwork and his garden shed was full of the tick of clocks belonging to neighbours or friends that he was fixing or servicing and always for free. In that shed he even had a barograph that he had salvaged, repaired, and put back into working order, it's weekly cycle competing to be heard amongst all of the ticking and hour chiming timepieces that filled every inch of that old cabin Usually, you could hardly breathe for the fumes of his pipe, both it and its owner being banned from the house by my gran once the thing was lit up. Eventually, he did get back to working on the land, which was no doubt what he knew best and what suited him best, and he was doing that almost right up to the end when he had the stroke that finally incapacitated him. It seems to get to that stage with families that eventually they are just a list of names in somebody's memory, like snow off the dyke, as the old saying goes." "And even the dykes collapse and disappear in time." Nan responded. "I've seen that happen before now. The weather gets into a dyke over winter, it starts to crumble and in the Spring, somebody is pinching the rocks to build something of his own and before you know it, there's very little sign that a dyke was even there."

"Just like people." Gordon continued. "Few of us leave much sign of our passing behind us. Still, if we have done our bit and our best, something worthwhile should remain, even if it is only a spark in the mind of one of those people in the list of names that we were talking about, Auntie Nan, or a twinkle in someone's eye."

"Aye," Nan said, looking at her feet, where, unnoticed by Gordon and Mavis, a small milk pail was sitting beside a wickerwork basket, whose contents was covered by a tea towel. Nan noticed that Gordon's gaze had followed hers. "Yes, that's another reason for me coming up here to see you. I've brought you some milk from this morning's milking, as well as some fresh eggs and a loaf and some fruit scones I baked earlier."

"You're spoiling us." Gordon responded.

"Just glad of the opportunity to do so." Nan smiled."In fact, it makes my day and your whole visit is like an answer to my prayers. It brings back to me a lot of good old times and good people. It's just great to know that one of Jamie and Jimmy's descendants is walking the Lord's good green earth and that, even if it is only for a short time, he has been brought back to Tuam and the old place."

Gordon looked at the galvanised milk pail and the wicker basket for a moment and began to rummage in his pocket for money.

"Don't you dare, boy!" Nan shot back in a mock angry tone. "Keep your good O'Brien money because I have enough and I am never out of pocket for anything that I put into Colonel's Fallow. Mike Smart pays me well for keeping the house in good order for his secret meetings and occasional visitors, just as he pays Murdo, the shepherd, to keep an eye on the outside of the house, keeping the garden tidy and doing any maintenance that he sees needs to be done. This has been a Republican house for a long time and looks like being one for a while yet. Nowadays, I think it's what they call a Safe House. If you ever get the chance, Gordon, buy the old place because I would love to have you for a neighbour. The fields are rented out to farmer Quinn. So you would always have an income from them. I'm sure from the way that this one looks at you, she would move in with you in a minute."

"Aw, hush Auntie!" Mavis protested.

"You can protest as much as you like, lass, but I know a bit about how a woman looks at a man because, before I got old, I was a woman, too. But, anyway, it's time I was holding my tongue and getting myself gone." So, saying, Nan stood up and made for the door leading to the hall, Gordon following her.

At the outside door, Gordon let his aunt out and watched her walking down the pebble drive. As she reached the white gates, he saw a dark dressed figure pass her and realised when he saw the dog-collar at the man's neck that a priest was coming to visit. Nan and the priest seemed to know each other because they exchanged a friendly greeting as they passed at the gates. Standing on the porch, Gordon took in at a glance a tall, slim figure with a high forehead and an intelligent cast to his sallow, lean face. The priest was wearing a dark coat over a black suit. The only splash of colour or brightness in his apparel was the circle of white at his throat, making him look like a great, dark collared-dove. In one hand, he was carrying a battered black leather briefcase.

"Aiden O'Donnell S.J.," the Jesuit said with a smile, extending his free hand. "You must be Gordon?"

"That I am," Gordon replied and, taking the proffered hand, gave it a convivial shake. "Come on into the house, Father." Then, as the priest stepped up on to the porch, Gordon pushed open the front door of Colonel's Fallow and led the way into the front parlour that he had just been in moments before. "Can I take your coat Father?" Gordon offered. "That way you'll get the benefit of it when you leave because, while its been a fine, bright, sunny day, now that the sun's gone down, there's a bit of a nip in the air."

At that, the priest slipped his coat off and passed it to Gordon who, in a moment, was hanging it on the coat-stand in the hall. Then, slipping back into the parlour as quickly as he had left it, Gordon was puzzling over the fact that, although he was sure he had never met the priest before, somehow the man looked familiar.

"This has sure been an evening for visitors," Gordon went on. "First Nan and now yourself. Was there any particular reason for your visit, Father?"

"No, mostly curiosity," the priest admitted." I met Mike Smart in Tuam earlier and he told me about your visit to Galway, the music festival, and all. So, being a bit intrigued at the thought of an O'Brien back in Colonel's Fallow, I thought I would drop in and make your acquaintance. I had to be in the area on a pastoral visit anyway. So it did not take me at all out of my way. The

O'Donnells and the O'Briens are related and, while I am not one for wrestling out the intricacies of Galway kinship, probably we are distant cousins of some sort."

"Excellent!" Gordon responded smilingly. "First today I met an aunt I did not know I had and now I have gained an extra cousin. In Scotland, the O'Briens have been less than prolific and that has kept us a fairly small family. So it is good to know that the Irish side is still doing well."

"Less birth control over here," the priest responded. "Or maybe it's just that the transplanted plant never does quite so well as the native species in its own native soil. It's interesting that you should turn up in Ireland just at this juncture," the priest continued. "Because, just the other day, I was helping a distant cousin clear the attic of a house that his folks have had for generations. My cousin had inherited the farm but had little interest in it or use for it, having a good university job in London. Anyway, the next-door farmer had bought the land while a holiday cottage letting company was acquiring the house to add to its portfolio of letting properties. Tim, my cousin, has not been well recently. So I was helping him to clear the house. The better furniture and books were going off to auction in Dublin, while the poorer bits and pieces were being sent to some local charities for disposal. One of the things that I have learned from being involved in clearing this house is that things are only things. When you see the important and cherished possessions of one generation becoming valueless to a younger generation, it gives you some insight into the whole nature of so-called possessions. They come to us at a point in time, stay with us for a shorter or longer period of time, and are then dispersed.

"With the clearing of that house and home, I was given the task of clearing the attic, and when I was sorting through generations of bric-a-brac and old family papers, one of the items I unearthed was a notebook journal belonging to my cousin's great, great grandfather, a man who had gone out to Spain to do his bit against Franco and his fascists during the Spanish Civil War. It is an absolutely fascinating document and one that should really be in some museum or public archive, which is where it will be once we can figure out where best to put it. The journal speaks of your own Captain Jamie quite a bit, how the two men met up in Dublin as part of Frank Ryan's contingent and all of the obstacles they had to overcome to get to Marseilles and how, from there, they had to cross the Pyrenees on smugglers' donkey trails to get into Spain at all and then how they had made their way to International Brigades' headquarters for some very brief basic training prior to them being thrown into the thick of the fighting, doing their best despite having very little in the way of food, medical supplies, or even arms and ammunition. You probably didn't know this but, at one point, Captain Jamie was actually captured by the fascists and not many survived that, many of those boys being shot out of hand the moment they were captured. So it seems that these two old Galway stalwarts, at a time just after the fall of Madrid, when the Republican leaders and military council had left Madrid and based themselves at Valencia, these two old soldiers and their volunteer comrades were investing Hill 481, a high point of some strategic importance because of its dominating the Valencia road. Known to the International Brigaders as both The Pimple and The Heights of Hell, when amid all of the noise, smoke and confusion of the battle to take the hill, the two Irishmen suddenly realised that they were surrounded by German field-grey uniforms. One German N.C.O. even told them, in passable English, that, for them, the war was over, when all of a sudden there was a shrieking of bagpipes and a wave of kilted fighters with fixed bayonets came charging up, causing the German and fascist troops to scatter and flee. What I will do, Gordon, is get a copy of that journal made and get it to you in Scotland. There really is a lot in that journal about Jamie O'Brien I think you would find interesting. It seems that your forebear never really considered himself off-duty when he was in Spain and, no matter how long he had been in the line, he was always ready to lead another patrol or go out and bring a prisoner in for questioning. Even when he was behind the lines in rest positions he was often to be found on some eminence with his sniper's rifle, trying to pick off fascist officers and N.C.O.'s. At that time, all International Brigade officers, if captured by the enemy, were shot out of hand by the fascists. Because of that, some of the officers developed the habit of having a particularly good private shadow them and learn as much as possible about how their Officer approached his work, secure in the knowledge that, in dangerous situations when capture looked likely, they could simply take off their badges of rank and disappear, knowing that a good man was covering for them. It seems that Jamie was particularly good in that way and, because of that, he was nicknamed Captain Jamie, a name which followed him both throughout his time in Spain and also through his life as an active Irish Republican."

"Very interesting," Gordon interjected. "When I look back on the history of your family and mine," the priest when on, "the O'Briens were more men of action than we O'Donnels. The O'Donnels produced lots of priests over the years and many of the family were blessed or cursed with The Sight, one of my female forebears even managing to get herself burned as a witch in the 1700s. No doubt she was probably harmless enough, or just said too much about her fore knowledge to the wrong people."

"So you believe that The Sight exists?" Gordon asked, intrigued by what appeared to be an Irish Catholic priest admitting the existence of Second Sight.

At that, the priest looked Gordon up and down for a long moment before replying. "I sure enough do young Gordon, and for the simple reason that I possess it myself. And, for that reason and no other, I would like to make a request of you."

"And what might that be?" Gordon responded. "Well," the priest continued. "I would guess that, with your family background, you would have had some sort of Catholic upbringing? Though, that said, it does not tell anyone anything about your current relationship with the Church of Rome. I find that many of our own young men these days are somewhat anti-Catholic."

"I could not say that I am anti-Catholic," Gordon responded, "but my personal search has taken me away from Christianity and quite far in the direction of Hinduism and Buddhism."

"That became quite a popular route in the 1960s," the priest went on. "Even the popular music of the time was full of it, what with the Beatles and George Harrison's 'My sweet Lord.' So many young people at that time followed the hippy trail to India, though most of those were probably looking for a readily available supply of cheap drugs rather than for Indian spirituality."

"Having been there, I found that many were looking for an amalgam of drugs and spirituality," Gordon continued.

"I can understand that that might be the case," the priest said thoughtfully. "I can also understand that Indian spirituality could be a strong attraction to many Westerners. And despite my bishop's opposition, I have read a few of Thomas Merton's books and like his mixture of near Eastern Christianity and far Eastern Hinduism and Buddhism. I get the feeling that you may just have made a deep study of this area, Gordon O'Brien. I am right?"

"Merton I have dipped into but not to the extent that you could call it a study," Gordon replied. "Hinduism and Buddhism have both been strong influences on me and those I have and do study, as well as practising some of their rituals and approaches to yoga and meditation."

Father Aiden stroked his jaw thoughtfully before asking his next question. "Which is the nearer to your heart, Hinduism or Buddhism?" "Buddhism was a strong and formative influence and that influence is still always with me but, in terms of being close to my heart, I would have to say that Hinduism, or certain schools of Hinduism, is the more important to me," Gordon replied.

The priest nodded thoughtfully, clearly pondering on the implications of what Gordon was saying. Then, after a moment's pause, he made eye contact with Gordon and held his gaze for a long moment. "Well, Master O'Brien, what would you say is the essence of Hinduism?" The priest asked.

Without any hesitation, Gordon began to speak. "For myself, I would have to say that it is 'Athato Brahma-jijnasa.'"

The priest smiled. "What language is that? Where is that quote from and what does it mean?"

Taking that as three questions and not one, Gordon smiled. "Here goes…The language is ancient Indian Sanskrit, which you could say is the equivalent of your priestly Latin. It is taken from a text known as the Vedanta Sutra and it means that now is the time for us to become involved in the human mission, which is to make serious inquiry into the eternal verities, the meaning of life, where we have come from and why and what is the nature of the living entity and his relationship with the Supreme."

"Another question Gordon. What is the significance of the text using the word now, now is the time?"

"An interesting question," Gordon replied. "If we simply take the quotation at face value, we could miss the implied statement that, just as this is the right time to be asking these spiritual questions, there also would have been a wrong time to ask them."

"And what would that wrong time have been?" the priest asked.

"No doubt the compiler of the Vedanta Sutra expects us to be aware of the cycle of samsara, the wheel of birth and death and the cycle of reincarnation," Gordon answered. "Some people who believe in reincarnation maintain that we can only be reborn as humans, but many Hindus and Buddhists maintain that we can also come back as animals. So what the Vedanta Sutra is saying is that, now we are human, it is incumbent upon us to take up the spiritual quest and thus become truly human."

"And this knowledge you found in Hinduism but did not find in our Catholicism?" the priest asked.

"I would not be so rash as to say that it cannot be found in Catholicism, but I did not find it there and that, not finding, caused me to look elsewhere," Gordon explained.

"And are you a better person for making that search?" the priest asked.

"While realising that a quest of this sort is always a work in progress, I do believe that I am a better person than when I was still a disillusioned Catholic," Gordon went on.

The priest looked startled and sat stiffly for a long moment before he began to speak. "Gordon," he began gently, "I would like, with your permission, to ask you two things. One being a question, the other a request."

"Sounds find to me, Father. Just you fire away," Gordon invited.

"I will start with the question, Gordon, which is mostly out of professional curiosity and then I'll get round to my request later," said the priest.

"That sounds reasonable," Gordon began. "So what is your question, Aiden O'Donnell?"

"It's just this Gordon. Could you describe for me the events which took you out of Catholicism and the events that took you into Buddhism and Hinduism?" the priest asked.

"By my late teens," Gordon began, "I had come to realise that you cannot love the thing that is forced on you. Tolerate, yes, but love, no. Catholicism, to repeat an old cliché, was the club that my parents enrolled me in, and it was done without my permission or leave. When my schoolteachers belted me on a Monday morning for not having been at Mass on Sunday, that could not have done other than make me angry and resentful and less than enamoured of Catholicism. On top of that, when we get a little older and start to read up on the history of your church as an organisation, it does not always come up smelling of roses. Then there are the doctrines. A bogey man who will torture me for time beyond memory if I will not live as he wants me to live."

Looking thoughtful, the priest was silent for a moment. "And the steps that took you elsewhere?" he prompted. "At about the time of my late teens, I had been reading a lot of Herman Hesse and, in Hesse, I came across the idea of the Journeyers to the East. That is, individuals who, through either an objective or subjective period of travel to the East, had been changed by and found wisdom through that journey. As a youngster still living at home with my parents in a council flat on a council housing estate on the outskirts of Glasgow, the immediate likelihood of my being able to travel to, say, India, was not a strong one and, in fact, was one that only happened quite a few years later when, on one of our busking/hitch-hiking trips round Europe, Pete and I found ourselves further East than planned and, at that point, decided to push on towards India. Realising in my youth that travel to India was unlikely I began to realise that, since the late nineteenth century, various Indian spiritual teachers, yogis and mystics had been finding their way to the West. And once I realised that I decided to search out any books these individuals might have written and, at the same time as researching where they had gone and what they had done, I began with Vivekananda who had taken his particular slant on Vedanta to the World Parliament of Religions in Chicago in 1893. When Vivekananda began his opening address to the delegates present with the words *'American brothers and sisters,'* he was probably unaware that he was laying the foundation of a relationship between America and Vedanta which would go on for generations. Without Vivekananda, there could not have been the Hollywood Vedanta set of the 1930s and 1940s, a set which drew in W.H. Auden, Christopher Isherwood, Gerald Heard and others. Without Vivekananda there would not have been a previously prepared and fertile American soil waiting for Maharishi, Mahesh Yogi, Sri Chinmoy, Ram Dass and others. After investigating Vivekananda, I next turned my attention to Sri Purohit Swami, a university educated celibate ascetic, who also found his way to the West. When Sri Purohit published his two-volume summary study of the principal Upanishads, it contained an introduction written by W.B. Yeats and, towards the end of Yeats' life, Sri Purohit invited Yeats to retire to his ashram in India to devote his remaining time to the life spiritual an invitation that the poet did not take up. After Sri Purohit, I turned my attention to Paramahamsa Yogananda, whose book, *Autobiography of A Yogi,* many people today would still list as one of the all time spiritual classics. These were only the main individuals and main milestones on my journey. There were a number of others but, without a doubt, the most influential was A.C. Bhaktivedanta Swami, who left India in 1965 at seventy years of age, with only seven dollars worth of rupees in his pocket, setting off by sea for America as a representative of the Gaudiya Math and the mission of Srila Bhakti Siddanta Sarasvati Goswami, a brilliant mathematician, astronomer and influential Hindu scholar and mystic, who was also the son and main student of Srila Bhaktivinode Thakur, an Indian High Court judge and prominent Vaishnava teacher. Bhaktivedanta Swami suffered and survived three heart attacks on board that ship, landing in America with nothing in the way of finances or backing behind him. He went on through the sheer strength of his personality and personal realisations to write over one hundred large hardback translations and commentaries on the Vedic literature. At the same time as setting up scores of temples, ashrams, and spiritual farming communities in America and in other countries. On lecture tours and, at an advanced age and in indifferent health, he circled the globe fourteen times. Of these travellers to the West he was the only one that I actually met, meeting him face to face on a garden path under the trees of Bhaktivedanta Manor, the mock Tudor manor house in Watford near London, gifted to him by George Harrison of the Beatles, to be used as an ashram, temple and training college for Hindu priests. After meeting Bhaktivedanta Swami I approached the I Ching and asked it if Bhaktivedanta Swami was what he seemed to be. After all these years I can no longer recall which hexagram or moving line or lines the I Ching gave me in answer to my question but, to paraphrase the I Ching, basically it was saying '*And then some.*' Just looking at this man's life and achievements would tell most people that this was an empowered soul of almost unbelievable potency. The books and the ashrams and temples still stand as testament to the significance of his mission. And that, Father, is a quick thumbnail sketch of the steps that I took when leaving Catholicism and when making my way first to Buddhism and then on to Vaishnava Hinduism." After that enthusiastic outpouring of words, Gordon finally paused and remained silent. The priest was looking both serious and thoughtful, sitting upright and stock still, and sat that way for long moments before beginning to speak. "And now for the request that I mentioned earlier. What would you say, Gordon," he began after a long silence that neither man seemed to be finding uncomfortable, "if I asked you to humour me and let me hear your holy confession?" At that, Gordon's brow furrowed and he took a long pause before he began to reply. Then, speaking slowly, as if still not sure what his answer was going to be, he slapped his thigh, giving the impression of just having come to a decision. "I do not believe in the so-called Sacrament of Confession and am well aware that many modern Catholics do not believe in it either, or get involved with it, but what the heck! What harm can it do?" At that, the priest, who had been looking tense and worried for a moment, let out a long sigh and smiled to himself with a well-satisfied look. Then, going into the battered black leather briefcase that had been sitting on the floor at his feet, he brought out a long and narrow strip of green and gold vestment, which first he put gently to his lips before draping it round his neck like a minimalistic stole or scarf. t At the sight of the green and gold cloth, Gordon's eyes widened noticeably. The priest folded his hands in his lap and gave the impression that he was contemplating some inward prayer. "I take it that you still remember the form of words Gordon?"

"I do," Gordon replied in a less than enthusiastic tone and then began to say the traditional words of request for Confession and Absolution. "Bless me Father for I have sinned. It is many years since my last confession." Gordon turned inside, trying to remember anything that he had done over those years that he was uncomfortable with. And, then, as an aid to memory, he began to work his way through the Ten Commandments, using each one as a platform for self-scrutiny, before beginning to speak. "Despite a fairly thorough search," he began, "there is very little I can come up with that seems to be greatly serious. Lots of the common or garden misdemeanours, the common sins of omission and commission that you probably hear about on a daily basis. Too much of lust and the flesh no doubt. As a working musician, I am more likely to be tempted by my neighbour's wife than my neighbour's goods. Try as I might, I don't seem to be able to find anything really wicked in my past to tell you about. As a boy, I was an avid collector of birds' eggs and, looking back at it now, it seems unreasonably cruel. I could have done better by my ex-wife Donna and there is an old Tom Paxton song which kind of sums up how I feel about that debacle."

"And how does it go?" the priest asked.

"Could have loved you better didn't mean to be unkind. You know that would be the last thing on my mind." Gordon said in a half-speaking, half-chanting voice that was close to breaking into song." I did less than my best in that relationship and still have lots of regrets and recriminations against myself for that time."

"That is not a bad state to be in," the priest continued. "I wish there were more who could say it."

"Too much drink at times and occasional lapses with stronger and less legal stimulants." Gordon continued. "Sometimes losing sight of my own quest and values."

"With the passing of the years, Gordon, I doubt if you will remember any of the standard Catholic prayers?" the priest asked.

Gordon shook his head. "Nary a one, Father."

"Well, in your own heart and in your own time, Gordon, just express to yourself your sorrow for not doing the best that you could and, that done, just ask whatever concept of Deity that you are comfortable with for forgiveness. And with that and for today, at least, I will feel I have earned my keep as a priest. And just determine that, from this point forward, you are going to be as moral and positive as you can be."

Gordon folded his hands in his lap and gave the impression facially that he was involved somewhere deep inside.

"Whatever happens in the days ahead, I think you will be fine," the priest said, making the Sign of the Cross over Gordon's head.

"Thank you for that, Father," Gordon said, rising to his feet. For a moment, he watched as the priest repacked his briefcase. "I don't think this will have me back at mass as a regular attendee," Gordon said, following the priest in the direction of the coat stand as he began to put his coat back on. "Still, there is no knowing what the future holds for us and it's not always what we expect," Gordon said as the priest extended his hand towards the handle of the front door.

"For sure," the priest responded, a serious look coming to his features. "It's probably best not to know," the priest went on. "Though not knowing is not always a luxury in my possession. The sight is both a blessing and a curse. But a final word on Cousin Tim's notebook before I forget. That journal is an absolutely fascinating document and one which I believe, with just a minimal amount of editing and the hand of a sympathetic editor, could easily be published and turned into an excellent book. The Spanish Civil War was a nasty and complex conflict, and although the world has changed since those days, many of those old battle lines are still drawn and man's inhumanity to man, not forgetting womankind, as seen in Spain of the 1930s, is not something that is completely foreign to our own times. So the old boy's journal could still be a caution and a warning for those with the ears to hear because, as a historian once said, 'A civil war is not a war but a disease.' And we would all like to be able to see a healthy human family on the planet," Father Aiden continued. "It seems that the two old comrades, Captain Jamie and George, my cousin Tim's great, great grandfather, kept up their relationship and their relationship with Spain, taking joint family holidays there, at a time before that became fashionable. Captain Jamie, according to the latter part of the journal, had a friend Miguel from Madrid, usually known to the International Brigaders as Madrid Mike. This man, it seems, was from a family with roots in the Basque region and Mike became one of the founders of a political group that would eventually amalgamate with several others to form ETA, the Basque separatist organisation. According to the journal, the time came when Captain Jamie helped his ETA contacts with arms, ammunition, and explosives—this, of course, being Jamie's area of expertise. In the journal, George quotes Jamie as saying how anyone who had ever fought in any war would have to be a monster of some sort if they could claim to have no regrets from those war experiences. Jamie had been speaking to George about his regrets over comrades maimed and killed, of men he had had to kill but whose deaths he always regretted. The two old soldiers had discussed an incident that had taken place in Spain, a story about what Jamie called 'The One Who Got Away,' a tale about a man who Jamie could have shot but did not and always regretted that omission. From what I remember, George and Jamie, at a place not far from Valencia, were sent out on patrol to bring back a prisoner for questioning, a common enough task. The two snipers had slipped away from their own lines and managed to infiltrate the enemy lines but not coming across a lone enemy in a situation where he could easily be captured and quietly spirited away, they continued to push on deeper into enemy territory until eventually Jamie spotted a group of Fascist officers and N.C.O.s in a huddle around an officer they seemed to be treating with great respect and deference. Jamie had noticed the amount of gold braid that this individual was wearing and concluded that he had to be someone of some importance. Lifting his sniper's rifle to his shoulder, he had drawn a bead on this officer's head and was just beginning to apply a gentle pressure to his trigger when George tapped him silently on the arm. When Jamie looked at his companion to see what he wanted, George was extending the index finger of his left hand, to which he was adding, the circled index finger and thumb of his right hand, forming the letter P and reminding Jamie what their mission was. Jamie then led the way back, retracing their footsteps until they found a lone sentry in an isolated trench. There they managed to capture him without a great deal of struggle and thus were able to complete their mission. Later on, they discovered that Baron von Richtofen, not the World War I fighter ace, but his cousin, the commander of the Condor

Legion, whose Stuka dive bombers had taken such a heavy toll of Republican men and equipment, and who would come to be responsible for the destruction of the town of Guernica, had been in the area at the time and was probably the officer with all the gold braid. Jamie had told George that this was the only man he regretted not having killed."

"But would shooting him have saved the people of Guernica?" Gordon asked.

"That we will never and can never know," the priest replied and seemed ready to be on his way. "Travel safe, Gordon O'Brien," he said, stepping out of the vestibule and on to the porch. "And not too many of the neighbours' wives, young Gordon," he offered as his parting shot, heading off down the drive.

Gordon stood in the doorway, paused for a moment, then threw a half wave, half salute into the darkness where the white gates were just clicking closed. "And read the *Vedanta Sutra* if you should get the opportunity, Aiden O'Donnell, and send that journal copy. Thank you and good night."

As Gordon stepped back into the vestibule, he saw Mavis coming towards him from the direction of the kitchen. "Long-winded, some of these priests," Mavis smiled.

"How did you know I was talking to a priest?" Gordon asked.

"I was looking out of the upstairs window when Nan was leaving and I saw him at the gates. Pete and Sadie are hungry and want to know what we are going to do about eating?"

"That depends on what's in those kitchen cupboards," Gordon replied. Back in the kitchen, he found that Sadie and Pete were both sitting at the kitchen table, a glass of wine in front of each of them and Pete having an open bottle of wine sitting at his elbow on the scarred tabletop.

"Well, the estate agent chap did tell us to help ourselves to whatever we found in the house and actually there's quite a bit of booze here," Pete said with some enthusiasm. "Any thoughts on eating because some of us are getting fair peckish?" "I'll just have a quick rummage through these cupboards and, once I know what we have, I'll have a better idea of what I can make," Gordon replied and started to work his way through the kitchen's storage areas. Soon, he had unearthed and laid out on the work-surface close to the cooker a bottle of good olive oil, a litre of sieved tomatoes, a cauliflower, a bag of potatoes, a carton of cream, and a packet of frozen peas from the freezer in the fridge. In one cupboard, he found a good selection of herbs and spices as well as a kilo of Basmati rice, the latter being an item that he was particularly pleased to see, knowing how adaptable and useful rice can be.

"Looks like we are going to be having something a little Indian in flavour," Pete said, looking over Gordon's shoulder to see what the cupboards had given up.

"Don't pre-empt the cook unless you are prepared to cook the meal," Gordon protested, then continued. "What I think you should do, Pete, is take

Mavis and Sadie through to the front parlour, leaving me here to get on with it, and when dinner's ready I can give you a shout."

"Suits me just fine, Gordon," Pete responded, and was soon leading the two women out of the kitchen, wine glass in one hand, wine bottle in the other.

"Mavis!" Gordon called down the hall after the retreating back of the airhostess. "Before you get too comfortable in the front parlour, why don't you check out upstairs and if there's a bedroom that you like with a double bed, claim that one for us for tonight."

"I did that earlier. My bag, your pack, and your guitar are already up there. It's a nice bright room with yellow walls, the double next to the shower room."

"Okay, you three. Off to the parlour while I get cooking," Gordon continued. "Give me about forty minutes." That said, Gordon retreated back into his kitchen and, lifting a nest of stainless steel pans out of a cupboard where he had noticed them earlier, was soon leaping into culinary action.

On the brown leather suite in the front room, his three companions were enjoying a quiet moment to savour their wine. "Dinner will not be long," Pete announced, speaking in the direction of the two women, one sitting on either side of him on the couch. "Gordon is usually a good and a fast cook. So expect to hear from him sooner rather than later."

Quicker than even Pete was expecting, Gordon was back in the parlour, rounding up his friends and shepherding them back in the direction of the kitchen, whose open door was exuding the smell of herbs and spices frying in olive oil. In the kitchen, they found that four places had been set at the table, in the centre of which were placed two large serving bowls, each with a stainless steel serving spoon placed close at hand. One bowl was brimming with boiled rice, cooked with peas and lemon juice, while the other was filled almost to overflowing with a cauliflower and potato curry in a spicy tomato and cream sauce.

"Ideally," Gordon began, introducing his meal while the others were taking their seats, "I would like to have served chapattis or puris with this meal but, while I can cook both of those, there is no flour of any kind in the kitchen and the olive oil that we have would not be enough for deep frying puris." That said, Gordon began to heap generous helpings of food on everybody's plate. Mavis took a trial taste of the food in front of her and sent a hugely appreciative smile in Gordon's direction. "I must say that this is excellent, Gordon. It's professional chef standard."

"Tuck in everyone," Gordon ordered. "I want to see all of that finished tonight because I, for one, prefer fresh-cooked food to leftovers. I suggest that we all have a fairly early night tonight and, in that way, in the morning we will be ready to explore the area or maybe head up to Sligo to see some Yeats country or maybe the band can hit Galway City and we can do some street busking."

"Whatever," Pete responded, going back to the serving spoons and ladling food on to plates. As the serving bowls were beginning to empty, Pete was watching Sadie and catching the slide-guitarist's eye. He asked her if she was up for an early night and then seeing that she seemed fairly amenable to that idea, he got up from his seat, walked round the table and, catching Sadie by the hand, led her across the room to the stairs that led to the upper floor of the house. The others continued eating until the serving bowls were empty, then the table was cleared and the dishes stacked in the sink for attention later.

"That was Big Pete being his direct and forthright self," Gordon said smiling in Mavis's direction. "And does it usually work?" Mavis asked.

"More often than not," Gordon replied. "Put it this way, I've never known him to go short." Next Gordon and Mavis headed upstairs, Gordon going for a quick shower while Mavis got herself into the four-poster bed in the yellow room. By the time that Gordon got to the bedroom, Mavis was already in bed with only her nose, eyes and shock of blonde hair sticking out of the duvet. She smiled a warm greeting as he approached the bed and slipped under the covers. Immediately he was enveloped in Mavis's arms and legs and held fast. He smiled into her vivid blue eyes and began to sing, "Just Louise and her lover so entwined."

"And what was that?" Mavis asked in a surprised tone. "That, my girl, is the result of free association and is a line from Bob Dylan's song 'Visions of Joanna. It just popped into my head as you wrapped me in your fine and loving hold. But enough talking. I need to be searching again for what I found in the car under the trees."

"Some kinds of confectionary gets finished up quickly, while other kinds come in an inexhaustible supply." Mavis said in a teasing tone, which left Gordon in no doubt about what she meant. "Yes but not always under trees." Gordon laughed and then entered fully into the searching he had just mentioned. When he opened his eyes next morning, at first he did not recognise where he was but, in a moment, he became aware that the yellow room was alive with light as the sun streamed in through a part open window, open just enough to allow a balmy, blossom scented breeze to enter the room. As he lay on his back with his eyes open to the yellow ceiling above him, he was drinking in birdsong from a sweet post dawn chorus. He could make out the call of a song thrush, quickly followed by the challenging scrabble of a blackbird. After that, the theme was taken up by what he thought had to be a mixed group of tits and finches. Then, a serene smile on his face, he drifted off to sleep again, only to be reawakened half an hour later by the insistent, guttural song of crows, most likely rooks. Then, as Mavis started to stir at his side, in a jazzy, bluesy voice, he began to sing. "Wake up baby, get your morning exercise."

"Gordon O'Brien, you seem to have a song or a fragment of a song for just about every conceivable situation," Mavis protested gently. "What was that you were singing just there?"

"It's an old blues and one that is fairly to the point," he replied, searching for her lips with his own. "I can't remember where I got it from. From one of the old masters no doubt. Maybe it was from Blind Boy Fuller but there are a legions of other possibilities. Songs are what I do, writing them and delivering them. So don't be surprised if I quote them a lot. I love the folk-poetry of the blues as well as the poetry of folksong generally." As Gordon lapsed back into silence, it became clear that Mavis was not responding with as much enthusiasm as his own. Outside, there was another sustained burst of guttural crow calls. Kissing Mavis and releasing her so that she could roll over on to her side, Gordon was listening closely to the crow calls. "Bet you don't know what that crow is saying out there?" he said in a teasing tone.

"I speak a few languages but have to admit that crow talk is not one of them," Mavis replied. "Do you know what it's saying?"

"Sure do," Gordon replied. "That is a young crow, probably a recent hatchling, and it's saying something to the effect of 'Help! Help! I fell or was pushed out of the nest, flapped down to the ground and now I'm cold, hungry, and frightened. Come and get me!'"

"And will the parent birds do that?" Mavis asked.

"Right now," Gordon replied, "that young crow is probably hiding in a clump of long grass or under a bush but the parent birds will know where it is and, in time, they'll be down to feed it and generally look after it. The danger is that with all of that squawking, it might just attract the attention of a passing fox or cat and, if that happens, then it's goodbye, crow."

"Can we not bring it into the house or feed it?" Mavis asked.

"If this was my house, Gordon replied, "and I was living here permanently I might bring it indoors but it is a wild creature and turning it into a pet crow living amongst, even kind-hearted humans, is not the best possible outcome for a wild bird. If it was a straight choice between pet life or no life, I might go down the pet route but, so often when humans interfere with nature in situations like this, they end up doing more harm than good. What I think I'll do is this: I'll keep an eye out for the youngster and, if I find out where it is, I can put some bread down where it is likely to find it, making sure that the parent birds do not see me close to the chick and, because of that, come to reject it."

"Sounds like you know what you're doing in this situation," Mavis commented as Gordon slipped out of bed and began to pull on a pair of jeans, a t-shirt, and his trainers.

"Why don't you sleep on for a bit?" he suggested, "because I would like a little quiet time to go downstairs and do some meditation outdoors on this fine morning and, only after that, think about sorting out last night's dishes and getting breakfast on the go." So saying, Gordon picked up his jacket and his guitar case and slipped quietly out of the room. He went downstairs, being careful not to make a sound that would alert Pete and Sadie to the fact that someone was up and about. Noiselessly, he reached the bottom of the open-plan wooden stairs that led to the kitchen. Then, crossing the kitchen to the modern back door, he placed his guitar case just inside the kitchen door and then, silently opening the back door, he let himself out on to the sun-kissed concrete platform that made up the top step. He scanned the farmyard and the clumps of greenery that were growing here and there but, wherever the young crow was, it was well hidden. Going into his jacket pocket, he pulled out what almost any Hindu or Buddhist would have recognised as a pouch for holding a mala, the traditional circlet of wooden beads customarily used to count the number of mantras that a practitioner had meditated on. Slipping the little bag's cloth straps over his head, Gordon allowed the little pouch to dangle down his chest and then, folding up his jacket, he placed it on the warm concrete step as a seat and then sat down on it. After a moment, he re-arranged his legs and feet so that he was sitting in a full lotus position. That done and it being as comfortable as could be reasonably expected in that yoga asana, he inserted his right hand into the recesses of the little bag. With his index finger, the finger that is so often in the ears or nostril, poking out of the hole in the front of the pouch so that, although the right hand was inside the bag, the index finger was customarily kept out. Then, with his right hand thumb and second finger gripping the Tulsi bead closest to the central or 'head bead,' silently, he began to repeat to himself, three times for each one, the three lineage mantras that he used by way of introduction before he began to meditate properly on his main meditational mantra. Rolling each bead gently between his thumb and second finger, he repeated the mantra one hundred and eight times, which was the number of beads on the circlet. That completed, he reversed the direction that he had been travelling in and finally, when that, too, was completed, he went through the journey round the beads again knowing that at the end, he had completed three hundred and twenty four mantras. That done, he glanced at his watch. The meditation had taken him just over twenty minutes.

That exercise completed to his reasonable satisfaction, and leaving the little pouch hanging around his neck, he retrieved his guitar from the case in the kitchen. Deftly, he quickly tuned the instrument and was just sitting back down on his jacket cross legged with the guitar cradled in his lap and starting to pick out a classical sounding melody, when the kitchen door opened and Mavis stepped out into the early morning sun, sitting down on the top step at Gordon's side. With the index finger of her right hand she gently drew a circle round the circumference of the little pouch."What is it?" she gently breathed into Gordon's ear, keeping her voice low in case the young crow or the parent birds were within earshot.

"In there is a mala, probably the yogic prototype of the Catholic rosary. Mala is a Sanskrit word meaning a circle and the mala is made up from one hundred and eight beads carved from the sacred Tulsi plant. It is used to count mantras and also to keep the practitioner's sense of touch involved in their meditation. The common name for Tulsi is Holy Basil and, when prescribed by a herbalist or homoeopath, is usually seen as being a strengtheners' of the urito/genital sphere of the body."

"Which you clearly don't need to take," Mavis commented.

"This particular mala was meditated on by a very powerful Vedic scholar, spiritual teacher and author, whom I consider to be my guru. I wrote a song about him which I think you heard, the one called Acharya. If you like I will be more than happy to sing Acharya for you right now."

"Right now and considering last night.... If you know any, would you please sing me a love song?" Mavis asked.

"One love song coming right up," Gordon said, slipping his capo on to the neck of his guitar. Then, fingering a first position A major chord and hitting his open B string, he immediately hammered into an F note on his open first string to present Mavis with a James Tayloresque introductory riff. That completed, he repeated the riff before launching into a rhythmic picking pattern and beginning to sing:

In the chilly hours and minutes of uncertainty I long to be in the warm hold of your loving mind; To feel you all around me and to take your hand along the sand; Ah but I might as well try and catch the wind."

After that, Gordon allowed his voice to trail off into silence and, as he did so, he went back to his introduction, playing it twice before tacking a short ending phrase on to it to bring the song to a close.

""Was that a Donovan song?" Mavis asked.

"It sure is and a very fine one," Gordon replied. "But for a short time this morning, we have just made it yours. I doubt if, under the circumstances, Donovan would mind."

"It's a song I've always loved," Mavis admitted, "but now it will always remind me of you and our time at Colonel's Fallow."

Gordon then went on to play a bass run flourish which allowed him to finish his song on a folksy sounding ending. When that was completed, with the penultimate note still causing ripples in the air both inside and outside the guitar, Mavis leaned forward to gently kiss him on the lips.

"That was wonderful," she breathed sibilantly. "It's exquisite to have a lover who can both cook and serve up love songs on request like he was a human jukebox. Can I have another one?" "Of course, you can." Gordon replied, sliding his capo to a different fret on his guitar and fingering a C ninth chord to play a catchy introduction similar to the one he reserved for his rendition of Cocaine Blues." That his version of that song owed something to both John Martyn and Davy Graham, he would have been happy to admit. Then introduction completed, he began to sing:- *"Yellow is the colour of my true love's hair in the morning, in the morning when we rise;*

That's the time, that's the time I love the best.

Mavis came in singing quietly on the chorus lines and, although they were both singing with the least possible volume, the combination of the song, the singers, the gently picked guitar, and the night before, felt very special.

"Wonderful," Mavis breathed into his ear huskily as he played a few bars of instrumental to round his singing off. Almost at the same moment as she spoke, Mavis pushed her tongue into Gordon's ear, causing him to laugh.

"Someone once told me that singing and playing the guitar with someone, in the right circumstances, can be better than sex." Gordon commented. "And while I might not go quite that far Mavis, I would have to admit that it comes close and may be just as good in its own way."

"Agreed," Mavis concurred and then said no more, hesitating to go off into more wordy conversation for fear of undermining the gentle, sunny ambience of a spectacular morning.

"So what next, Gordon?" she asked eventually, after they had been silent for a long and closely intimate moment. "Because I have to get back to the ordinary and mundane. If you want to return your guitar to the safety of its case and put it back upstairs, I'll wash up the dishes from last night and start to get breakfast organised."

Gordon was soon upstairs, glad to get his guitar out of the heat and sunshine, while Mavis was starting to put together a meal of scrambled eggs and toast, plus Nan's scones with strawberry jam and the small amount of cream that Gordon had left unused when making his sauce of the night before. Gordon was the last to appear at the table and, ignoring the eggs, which he maintained were no better than liquid meat, made a good breakfast of tea, scones, and toast. That finished, he picked up the last remaining piece of toast and, with that in hand, he went out to the back door steps where he paused to carefully scan the farmyard, looking for any possible crow hiding places that he might have missed on his earlier inspection. Just as Mavis appeared at his back, his gaze fell on a red sandstone drinking trough, sitting close to the low field wall opposite him. As he scrutinised the trough he realised that it was not sitting directly on the cobbles but seemed to be raised up on something that he could not quite make out so that beneath the trough, there was an area of dense shadow, suggesting a space where a young crow might just be hiding. In a moment, Mavis realised what he was staring at and nodded in silent agreement. This was the cue for Gordon to be off down the stairs and into the barnyard where, instead of walking directly to his goal, he strolled in a seemingly purposeless manner, strolling in a half-circle that saw him, a few seconds later, walking parallel to both the field wall and the trough he was passing and acting as if it was of absolutely no interest to him. And when he was all but past the trough, he quickly bent down without breaking stride, darted a swift look under the drinking trough. Sure enough, in the farthest away corner, there was a patch of darkness that was deeper than shadow. In the same instant that he realised the hatchling was there he let the bread he was carrying drop from his hand to land across the line where sunlight and shadow met. He kept on walking but even before he was back on the kitchen steps, he could hear what he assumed were the parent birds shrieking above him.

"Did you see that?" Mavis asked as he climbed the steps towards her. "For a split second, just as you reached the first step, something moved under the trough and pulled the toast in out of sight."

"Good," Gordon responded and, slipping his arm round Mavis's waist, began to sing in a challenging tone

Crowjane, Crowjane, don't hold your head so high;
Because someday Crowjane you're gonna have to lay down and die.

"What was that, Gordon?" Mavis demanded the moment her singer paused to draw breath.

"That," Gordon replied, "is my one and only crow song. It was a Blind Boy Fuller song and I don't sing it too often because some of the words might seem to suggest that male violence towards women is something that the singer might find acceptable or that he might even condone. It expresses a sentiment not unlike Jimi Hendrix's "Hey Joe," if you remember that one."

"And who is Blind Boy Fuller?" Mavis asked.

"Real name, Fulton Allen," Gordon replied. "He had a string of hits in the 1920s and 1930s. He was a guitar student of the Rev. Gary Davis. On Fuller's death Brownie McGee took over part of his repertoire and mantle. Brownie, like Davis, went on to become a New York City guitar teacher. Later on Happy Traum, who would later set up Homespun Tapes, was a student of Gary Davis. Blind Gary was the best of the Carolina school of guitar players and was a man who influenced people like Bob Dylan, Taj Mahal and some of the Grateful Dead, right down to unknowns like myself. I saw Happy himself perform at Glasgow's now defunct Third Eye Centre, and he was excellent, a very fine player indeed. Not only did Happy provide an unrivalled teaching facility, he preserved a lot of traditional music which might otherwise have been lost to posterity."

Mavis smiled at the enthusiastic torrent of words that her question had unleashed. "What are you going to do now?" she asked.

"I'm just going to have a solitary walk round the old place," Gordon replied. "Probably take a stroll round the front garden and over the fields, maybe up to the Grocery Wood and just see if I can get any sense of my forebears from their land. Probably after that, I'll have a word with Pete and see if he is up for some street busking in Galway." So saying, Gordon slung his jacket casually over his shoulder and set off down the steps and across the farmyard, pointedly staying well away from the direction of the drinking trough, heading towards a small gate in the wall that bounded the Nursery Pasture. Then, as first one crow, followed by a second, dive-bombed him and coming within a whisker of his head on both occasions, an idea seemed to come to him and, in mid stride, he turned off to his left and veered away in the direction of the barn, ignoring the parent crows who came at him a second time, even though he was moving away from the drinking trough. As he walked, he felt for his jacket pocket, checking that the keys for the property were still where he had put them. Feeling the bulk of the keys through the rough denim of his jacket, he began to survey the huge double doors of the barn. They had obviously been designed to allow tall horses and high piled wagons in and out. Stopping in front of the great doors, he pulled out the heavy bunch of keys, glanced at the three largest and selecting the biggest and rustiest of those, he slipped it into the lock. Noticing that it slipped straight into the lock like a ship going into its dock, he began to apply pressure until the lock turned over as easily as had the roadside gates and the front door of Colonel's Fallow. Next, he pulled the key back out and dropped keys and key ring into his pocket. Finally turning his attention to the door handle, which seemed to be made from a round bar of brass, gleaming in the sunlight as if it had been polished bright by generations of hard, horny Galway working hands, he took the handle in both of his slim musician's hands and pushed the door away from him expecting it to swing inward. But despite him applying more and more pressure to the task, the door did not budge at all. Then, giving that up, he began trying to pull the door towards him in case it opened out rather than in. That attempt was also unsuccessful and he began to wonder if it might be a sliding door. Looking down at his feet and the bottom of the door, he could see a strip of rusty metal, suggesting that the door might be set in some sort of runner. Then, gripping the brass handle firmly, he began to exert his strength in a two-handed pushing motion and, at that, the door began to slide. At first, there was a gap of about a quarter of an inch and then, as he battled on, it was open an inch and then six inches. Gordon tried to see into the barn but, while there seemed to be light coming from somewhere overhead, it was a dull, diffused light, as if coming from a dirty skylight window. Running his hand over the wall just inside the door, he was trying to find a light switch by feel alone but could not find one. Then his hand brushed what felt like a piece of metal pipe on the wall and he felt hope rise in his heart that this might be a length of electrical conduit. Running his hand down the length of the pipe, he came to a box at its bottom. Finding the switch mechanism, he clicked it on. Immediately the dull light from the unseen skylight was flooded with a harsh, bright, glaring light and Gordon knew in that moment that there had to be fluorescent lights somewhere up above. Turning his attention back to the great door, he struggled on with his task of getting the door open until, eventually, he had made an opening that a small car could have been driven through. The first thing that Gordon did when he stepped into the barn was to look upward and, as he had expected, several large fluorescent light fittings were hanging on rusty chains from the huge dark wooden beams that supported the slate roof above. Gordon looked around him, facing him was an old looking red Massey Ferguson tractor which, while far from being the latest model, still looked to be in good condition. To his right were several well-worn but solid wooden partitions that split that part of the barn into a row of stalls, probably for horses. On the left side of the barn was a large open space with what, if he had known more about old farm equipment, he would have recognised as a horse-drawn reaper, which gave the impression of not having been moved in many years and was now in an advanced stage of disintegration. Against the opposite wall of the barn was a long stone-built workbench built from slabs of red sandstone, which reminded Gordon of the sort of stone benches that he had more than once seen in the basements of large country houses as part of a pantry or wine cellar. Attached to the workbench was a well-maintained vice for woodworking. Also sitting on top of the stone bench was a modern pillar drill that looked to be a recent acquisition. It was plugged into a double electrical socket on the wall. Above the bench were a number of wooden racks holding tools for both joinery and mechanical repair work. Underneath the bench and leaning against the wall was a collection of shovels, spades, pick axes, and crowbars, as well as rakes, hoes, and a pair of riddles. In the stall nearest to where Gordon was standing, there was a modern power washer, already connected to the tap, which was in that stall and plugged into a nearby electrical socket. Gordon stood for a long moment looking around the barn and just drinking in its atmosphere, ambience, and smells, imagining previous generations of his family going about their hard-working farm lives with the barn and its equipment as their nerve centre and work focus. As he looked above the horse stalls to the storage area above, he could imagine that, at one time, hay and oats would have been kept there beside horse harness and the bric-a-brac of farming. Finally, he remembered the last time that he had spoken to his late grandfather, Jimmy the Carter, and how they had discussed the barn he was now standing in. Gordon had known about the Lewis Gun and how it had been captured from the British at the time of the Irish Civil War. His grandfather had told him how he remembered, although still young at the time, the day the weapon had been buried under the barn. The Lewis Gun was something that Gordon had heard stories and tall tales about for most of his life and he knew that Captain Jamie had decided to put the weapon under the barn a long time ago. He knew that the old man had taken some teak boards that he had acquired when the gymnasium attached to a local school was being demolished and its flooring had ended up at Colonel's Fallow. Captain Jamie had built a sturdy box with the teak and then filled the box with grease, a living organism which that was capable of surviving for a long time, even in the ground. Filling the box with grease, he had then pushed the separate parts of the Lewis gun deep down into the yellow gooey stuff and then, putting the teak lid on to the box and nailing it shut, the whole thing had been buried under the barn against the day when it might just be needed again. Gordon thought back to that last conversation he had with Carter Jimmy and how he asked him how he would know where to look if he ever had to dig for it. For any reason and, much to his surprise, that conversation came back to him quickly and in detail. He remembered how his grandfather had told him to think of the words right and left and the letters in the words. Left was for Lewis and right had an H in it. So Captain, the horse was buried on the right beneath his stall. The other thing that Gordon was to remember was the sixteen of nineteen sixteen, the year of the Easter uprising; Gordon was to step out twelve steps up the barn, take two steps to the left and two down, to find the weapon. At that, Gordon went back into the open doorway and placing heel to toes, counted out twelve steps, which took him just beyond the Massey Ferguson tractor, then, turning left to face the wall, he counted out two further paces and came to a halt in the space between the horse drawn reaper and the stone bench on the far wall. To mark the spot where he had stopped, he let the house keys fall to the ground to mark the result of his calculation. That done, he put his jacket aside, hanging it from a nail which was protruding from the wood of the nearest horse stall and then he picked out what was the newest looking of the spades stacked under the stone bench. Embedding the spade forcibly into the earthen floor, just to the side of his marker, he began to dig. Next, he retrieved the keys, dropping them into his jacket Pocket. From outside, he could hear the raised voices of scolding crows and began to wonder if a cat or a fox was about. The challenging aggressive crow talk soon abated and he quickly realised that whatever alarm had been going on outside was now over. At first, Gordon had thought that the barn floor looked densely hard packed and compacted but the digging was easier than he had expected and, within ten minutes, his spade struck something that sounded and felt like wood. Continuing to dig, he followed the shape of whatever was hidden under the barn, until he was sure that he was digging round a large, square object. Enlarging the hole as he went along, finally, he looked back under the stone bench and, laying his spade aside, he selected a pickaxe. Taking the pickaxe back to the site of his excavations and with the smooth wooden shaft securely gripped in both hands and with legs spread securely apart so that his footing was firm, he raised the pick above his head to deal the crate a great two-handed buffet. Immediately there was the sound of wood splintering and, after two or three further blows, he was soon adding pieces of broken timber to the pile of earth he had already raised on the barn floor. Putting the pick aside, he selected a narrow bladed spade of the type that a man would use to dig a trench for a single row tile field drain. Down into the hole he pushed the narrow spade into the space where the shattered timber had been and down into the darkness beyond that. Whatever he was digging into now it was fairly soft and soon he had added several spadefulls of a dark substance that might have been very old grease to his mound of soil. Once a good number of spadefulls of the dark substance had been unearthed and deposited on the heap, his spade hit something hard and metallic sounding. Putting aside his spade, Gordon reached down into the hole and felt about until his right hand had a good grip on something solid and cold. Exerting his strength, he pulled and pulled until whatever was down in the hole had come a little closer to him and he was able to get a two-handed grip on it. Suddenly it came away from its dark bed and Gordon had to step back quickly to prevent himself ending up on his back on the barn floor with, whatever it was, on top of him. Beginning to examine the triangular shaped object, he began to use the spade to shave off as much of the clinging dark substance he could. Eventually, when he had placed the mysterious piece of metal to one side of the hole, he came to the conclusion that he might just be looking at a tripod for a Lewis gun. Then, going back to his task with a will, before too long he had unearthed what was probably the barrel and breech mechanism and two smaller wooden boxes. Cleaning off most of the gooey stuff from the large metallic object, Gordon laid it aside and went on to break open the boxes. One held a round object which he guessed was probably a magazine for a Lewis gun, while the other held a quantity of loose ammunition of two distinctly different types. Beginning to think that he probably had laid out in front of him the main component parts of an Irish Civil War era Lewis gun, he crossed over to where his jacket was hanging and, extracting a notebook and pen from his pocket, opened the notebook at what turned out to be a blank page and began to write down an idea for a song or poem or *'DIALOGUE BETWEEN A LIVE POET AND A DEAD LEWIS GUN,'* followed by *'AH, YOU NASTY, BRUTISH, BRITISH, BUTCHER'S CLEAVER OF A THING. BUILT FOR NO GOOD, POSITIVE OR AUSPI-CIOUS REASON, BUT FOR THE SOLE PURPOSE OF TAKING HUMAN LIFE.'* Then, putting his pen away, he aimed a kick at the weapon, which was more symbolic and rhetorical than anything else. That comment made, and holding his notebook open in two hands in front of him, he imagined himself in the middle of a reading to a group of people, and in a loud and melodramatic voice, he began to declaim what he had just written. As he did so, he felt a presence behind him and turned to see Pete standing in the doorway surrounded by the fiery glow of a fine, bright morning.

"Thought I would find you in here making like a rabbit in the shadows when there is a beautiful last of the summer's fine days going on and being ignored outside."

Still in his reverie, Gordon was wondering about the men who would have built that Lewis gun so many years before, what sort of lives they had , when they had died, and how they had come to meet their end.

"You got it there then?" Pete asked, pushing his question into Gordon's attention, when he was beginning to wonder about the British army armourers who would have cared for the weapon, as well as wondering where the British army would have used it and when and whether his great grandfather had taken it with him when he had lead his column to ambush the Black and Tans outside of Macroom.

"So does it look like a Lewis gun to you Pete?" Gordon asked.

"Maybe," Pete responded, "but look here Gordon. Mavis told me that you were going to have a wander over the old place, walk through the pastures and garden and go up to the wood. So why don't you do just that and enjoy this fine day in the old O'Brien place and leave me to clean up this ancient piece of scrap iron? If it can be cleaned up and put together in anything like a serviceable working order, then I will do just that."

Gordon followed Pete's gaze to where he was looking at the tool racks on the wall above the stone bench. "That hardly seems fair leaving you in here doing all of the unpleasant work," Gordon argued.

"Not unpleasant work at all," Pete argued. "You know what I am like pottering with mechanical things and tools."

"I sure do." Gordon replied. "You have mucky, greasy fun and I'll see you in an hour or so, big man."

"Do you think that power washer might just be in working order, Gordon?" Pete asked.

"In any other barn I would say probably not," Gordon replied, "but, seeing how well this place is maintained generally, I wouldn't be at all surprised if it works." That said, Gordon unscrewed the power washer's hose attachment from the tap in the wall and, helping himself to a handful of Swarfega industrial hand cleanser from a red and white tin sitting on one side of the tap, he began to rub the powerful cleanser into his hands and forearms. soon he had turned the tap on and was observing, with some satisfaction, a rivulet of greasy water which was running down off his hands and arms to disappear gurgling into a slatted metal drain grating set into the floor.

Chapter Ten

The Lewis Gun

Cleaning himself up took no time at all and soon he was picking up his jacket to make for the open doorway.

"If you are ever going to get any sense of your roots, Gordon, then this is the time to do it because you might never be back in Colonel's Fallow again," Pete admonished.

"You sure you don't mind me leaving you here like this?" Gordon asked, as if trying to reassure himself.

"Not at all, man." Pete replied. "You go to it."

"Do you think you still know your way around a Lewis gun, Pete? After all, it's a long time since your Air Training Corp days."

"It wasn't just with the A.T.C.," Pete replied. "Years later, when I was well into working life, I joined the T.A. for a bit. We trained with Lewis guns, the incredibly accurate Bren gun, and with the more up-to-the-minute general purpose machine guns and the armaments sergeant we trained with at Eglinton Toll had us field stripping them in the dark in case we were in a war zone fighting at night and had to dismantle and assemble them without a glimmer of light. Don't worry, Gordon, your smelly old antique is in good and skilled hands. So get out of here now for your walk before I go back on my word and swap roles with you."

Carrying his jacket slung over one shoulder, Gordon paused just outside of the doorway, luxuriating in the heat and sunshine. Then, remembering the crows and their dual attack on him, he scanned the area all around the barn and the back of the house but, as far as he could tell, the coast was clear. Making for the low wall surrounding the Nursery Pasture, he opened the rusty gate to the field and started off up the slight incline. He ignored a green plover that was running on ahead of him, no doubt trying to decoy him away from the area where it was likely to have a scratch of a nest and a cluster of eggs. After several minutes, his leisurely and pleasant climb was blocked by a second low wall and, because the gate set into its dark stonework was some fifty metres away, he simply vaulted the wall to get himself to its far side. Pushing on up the slope a little further, he came to a rutted track running in the direction of the Grocery Wood and Falling into step with it, he allowed the track to lead him towards the trees and their beckoning shade because, by now, he was feeling hot. No sooner out of the sun and into the tree shade than he heard a whirr of wings from several different places in the branches overhead, which he recognised as the distinctive sound of startled Woodpigeons. For a moment, he stopped to watch the birds flying on their individual trajectories until they were clear of the wood, where they united into a flight of seven grey, white-collared forms.

"Perhaps priests in previous lives," Gordon smiled to himself as the birds veered off to the right to cross the road just beyond Nan O'Brien's house, where they passed out of sight. Finding that the rutted track continued through the wood, he was content to let his feet take the line of least resistance and followed the track on and into the heart of the trees. As he walked, he was surprised to hear the sound of a twig snapping somewhere ahead of him and looked up to see the figure of a man coming along the track towards him. It was Mike Smart, wearing a black leather jacket with a black beret on his head and a white shirt with a black tie under his jacket. He looked like a man who had either just been to a funeral, or else, was going to one.

"And hail to you, young Gordon," Smart called out in greeting. "You can probably see from my attire that I have just been to a burial this morning. We lost one of ours yesterday and I have just been visiting Jimmy's widow to see if there is anything our welfare department can do for her or the kids. While it won't bring back the husband and father, or make her changed life circumstances any easier, I was able to leave her with a cheque large enough to ensure that the boys' education will not be as difficult as it could have been. Certainly, she won't be short of the wherewithal to pay for new football boots, or even some piano lessons."

"Do you do much of that kind of work?" Gordon asked.

"More than you might imagine," Smart replied. "Usually, we are only in the press when we have outraged public opinion in some way, blowing up the Household Cavalry or assassinating somebody prominent, but most of the money that comes our way does not go to buying arms and ammunition but goes to helping look after Republican widows and children. It was worse when the British government was using internment and the H-Blocks against us. At that time, with so much of our community behind barbed wire, our whole income was going into welfare, looking after families whose men folk being locked up could neither work nor provide."

"Interesting," Gordon said as Smart continued in the direction that Gordon had just come from.

"Let's walk back a bit to where there is a section of wall we can sit on and talk at our ease." Smart suggested. That said, they retraced Gordon's track back along the path until they were sitting on a stretch of wall where they could see both Colonel's Fallow and Nan O'Brien's house laid out below them.

"So how come you are up here walking in the woods?" Gordon asked, sitting down on the wall and making himself as comfortable as a drystane dyke would allow.

"Well, old Murdo Mcleod, the shepherd on the farm just beyond this wood, does some work for me and it was time that I got him paid. As well as being a bloody good man with sheep, he is an excellent all-round handyman who can turn his hand to just about anything from gardening to electrics and joinery. And for that reason, I get him to keep an eye on the house here. Also, he said something to Nan O'Brien that I needed to check out. Which reminds me that I have an important meeting scheduled to be held in Colonel's Fallow this weekend. So we will need you to be gone by Saturday afternoon when people will be arriving. That okay with you and your friends?"

"Sure is," Gordon replied. "We will be heading for home on Friday, a drive into Dublin and then the Glasgow flight."

"It was handy meeting you here today, Gordon," Smart continued. "Because, if I hadn't bumped into you, then I would have had to come looking for you. Not many people know this, but the whole nature of Irish politics is just about to change. A lot of guys like myself, who some people would call the men of action, are about to hang up our Kalashnikoffs and put on our politicians' suits. One of the people coming to this weekend's meeting will be a senior British politician and we are sure that an offer we have been expecting for some time is about to be made to us. On a practical level, what this might mean for Republicanism is that we may have to stand down our whole armoury at one fell swoop—weapons, ammunition, and explosives. Old Murdo maintains that a British army helicopter landed in one of the Quinn fields last week and, since then, he has been finding fresh tracks in the woods and snares of a type he has never seen before being set for rabbits. He is sure they have not been set by any of our local lads and, me being a suspicious and careful man, I am wondering if some covert British intelligence operation is going down around here. Normally, I would not be too worried about this but the timing of it disturbs me, just before this important meeting. It could just be the British bringing in extra security to provide protection for the two British visitors we are expecting. Also, there will be a couple of guys of ours coming to this meeting that the British government would love to get their hands on. So, as well as checking things out with Murdo, I just wanted to sniff around the place a bit."

"If the British army is in the area, could that not be a bit dangerous, you being up here on your own?" Gordon asked.

"I can look after myself and, anyway, I'm always armed," Smart replied, tapping the breast of his leather jacket. "Just to step up our own security in the area tonight and tomorrow night, I am going to have my brother, Martin, and a couple of our boys camping out in the woods here overnight, just keeping a lookout. It's unlikely that you will see or hear anything of them but if you do have a problem of any kind, then you know that there is good help close at hand. You may not know this, Gordon, but your great grandfather was one of the best collectors of funds that our cause ever had, especially in America. Some of the supporters that he brought on board over there were contributors to their dying day and some of them continue to support us from the grave, having set up bequests and trust funds that fill our coffers to this very day. There was one guy from Memphis, Tennessee, who set up a big chunk of his estate in such a way that we are still drawing on it. He was an O'Brien, too, and twice a year, depending on the vagaries of the stock market, a large sum of money is paid into a Memphis bank in our name. the downside of that arrangement is that we have to arrange for it to be collected in person in cash. During Captain O'Brien's time, he used to collect it himself on his regular American visits and bring the funds back here to Ireland...which leads me, young Gordon, to matters that affect or might affect you. Talking to your Auntie Nan, she gives me the impression that you might like to live in Ireland and, if possible, acquire Colonel's Fallow." "If only pigs could fly," Gordon smiled.

"In Ireland they sometimes do," Smart went on. "My masters have authorised me to make you a job offer and see what you have to say about it. What would you say, Gordon, if I was to tell you that in the inside pocket of this jacket, as well as my Walther automatic pistol, I have an envelope containing a receipt on Terence O'Farrell's letterhead, made out in your name, for three hundred thousand Euros, that being part payment for Colonel's Fallow as well as covering the first five years' payments of a ten-year mortgage plan. There are also other details in there that, either you or a lawyer would have to look at closely, detailing what you would have to start to pay in five years time and all of the other things that you might expect to be told when getting into a mortgage situation."

"So on this day, when it seems that pigs do fly, what would I have to do to be on your masters' payroll?" Gordon asked.

"I know that the MAVIS VALLEY BAND. has a website because I have looked at it and on the website as is usual, there is a section for making contact with the band Smart went on. "I am wondering if, during the time that you have been away from base, if you have managed to keep up with your e-mails?" Gordon shook his head.

"Usually, when away, I leave my laptop with a friend who can deal with most things and ring me on my mobile if anything significant is happening. I have not heard from her, so I guess that no fabulous offers have come in."

"I don't know so much.," Smart disagreed. "You are getting a fabulous offer at the moment and since you have been in Ireland, there is a message on your laptop inviting the band. to take part in the Greater Appalachian Acoustic Music Festival, as well as touring on their home gig circuit, whatever that is?"

"The home gig scene," Gordon explained, "is where a group of enthusiasts get together and invite an artist or band to play a series of gigs in the members' homes. Sometimes they might charge an entrance fee or ask the attendees for donations so that, after expenses have been deducted, there can be something left for the performers."

"In this case and, from what I can remember, Gordon," Smart continued, "they will pay all travel expenses and probably a fee as well. Something that you might not know Gordon is that Frank Sinatra's career only really took off after the Mafia started to take an interest in him. Only with that input did some venues open up for him that had previously been closed. With both your invitation to play here in Galway and with this Appalachian invitation, there was some Republican leverage applied to get you those gigs."

"Yes, but what would your masters expect of me in return and I expect that it will be myself that they will want and not big Pete?" Gordon continued.

"No, not completely," Smart disagreed. "Yes, you would be the main man in the equation but Pete, as well as being a singer/songwriter, was a bit of a boxer at one time and it seems that he was quite good and, it would not be any bad thing for what my bosses have in mind for you to have some muscle travelling with you. Sure, we could provide that in the States, but most of our boys are well known, whereas Pete is an unknown quantity and one with a great cover. Who would ever expect that two Scottish hippy musicians on tour would be a front for an Irish Republican fundraising drive? You see, if this offer we are expecting to be made to us goes down, we will have to be able, if asked, to be in a position to stand down all of our weaponry resources secure in the knowledge that if we were to do that on, say, a Friday afternoon, we could be re-stocked by Monday lunchtime if push came to shove. To do that, and it can be done, would be expensive. At this moment, we have first refusal on a huge quantity of Russian weapons that only require a phone call and a deposit to be ours. After that phone call, the weapons would soon be on board a Russian ship heading for a point off the Irish coast where a number of fishing vessels, loyal to us, would quickly have a military cargo on its way to our storage facilities. Just when the British government and our loyalist counterparts were secure in the knowledge that we had no weapons left, we would be at full strength and operational readiness. And what we would want from you, young Gordon, is to take up the several offers from America that are, or will be coming your way, and while over there, do some simple tasks for us."

"How simple?" Gordon asked.

"Twice a year we would want you to visit a bank in Memphis and withdraw a previously agreed amount in cash and keep it safe until delivering it to one of our agents. Memphis is not so far from Nashville, and if you and Pete wanted to record in either of those places, that could be possible. The Nashville sound and top session men if you wanted. On top of that, we would ask you to do some fundraising talks at a number of Irish clubs and associations but not encroaching on your performing schedule." Gordon frowned. "You would not even have to write your own speeches.," Smart went on. "We have a guy, a lecturer at Belfast University, who is very good in that area. He would write your scripts and you would just have to choose the one or the parts that you liked best. For a performing musician and singer, it would be a breeze. You would be among friendly Irish people, or at least the descendants of them and so, if you want it, Colonel's Fallow plus a generous salary is yours for the taking. The details and small print we would fill in with you later, though much of it is typed out and in my pocket along with your receipt for cash paid or capable of being paid in your name. And while my masters are keen, they are also security minded and will not want our side to say too much until they are at least convinced that you are interested in coming on board with us."

"There is something that I like about you, Mike Smart," Gordon responded. "I saw it back there at the Traveller's Rest Motel but, while I do have some sympathy for your cause, I would not do anything to put a live round into the breech of any weapon anywhere in the world. And while I am not a Hindu or Buddhist in any formal sense, I have been influenced by their concept of Ahimsa or non-violence for most of my adult life. And for that reason, cannot be party to any aspect of political murder. Another fine Buddhist concept is right-livelihood, which means that I won't work at anything that kills or hurts another living entity."

"I hear you and think that I can, at least in part, understand where you are coming from," Smart replied. "Anyway, let's not slam the door and double bolt it as this stage. I will tell my masters that you are thinking about our proposal. If you ever wanted to be a star in the music world, today could be the place where you start to break into the Big Time."

"I am not any sort of Christian," Gordon went on, "but I can remember from my schooldays that there is a part in the New Testament where the Devil takes Jesus up to a high place to show him all of the worldly pleasures that he could have if he would just agree to do the Devil's bidding. His reply was something to the effect of 'Get thee behind me, Satan!'"

"We're not quite that bad, Gordon. Just think of all the harsh injustices that the British and their Irish supporters have dealt out to the Irish people over the centuries. Someone had to and still has to protect them. I am just asking you to fall into line and do your bit as your forebears did and reap a lot of personal benefits for doing no more than your O'Brien duty. If you wanted, you could concentrate on fundraising for our welfare activities. If any part of your coming over here was to find your roots, you have found them. And now, young Gordon, another matter and one not connected to what we have been discussing: Those two apparent doctors that you teamed up with in Dublin and brought to Galway, what would you say if I was to tell you that they are both captains in the British Army? We have caught spies and undercover agents with creative and almost foolproof cover stories before now, but this has to be one of the best yet."

Gordon looked puzzled. "If that is true, it leaves me dumbfounded!" he finally went on. "To me, they come across more as idiots than anything else but I have heard of some medical students who rather than slaving their way through university on the strength of low paid bar jobs and similar work, join the army and do their studies while collecting an army salary. At the end of their studies, they are expected to go into the army and become military medics. So, if they are army captains, as you say, what do you plan to do with them?" Gordon demanded.

"My bosses have ordered me to shoot them," Smart replied.

"You can't do that!" Gordon protested. "If I thought that was going to happen to them," Gordon continued, "I would be forced to find someone in authority and tell them every single iota of what I know about yourself."

"Be careful, Gordon," Smart went on in a subdued and almost sad tone of voice. "I don't want my masters ordering me to shoot you as well and that is what it could come down to."

"Anyway," Gordon went on, "I need to be getting back to the others. Big Pete will be sending out search parties."

"Fine," Smart said, turning away towards the wood. "Think carefully and do nothing before we meet again."

At that, Gordon stood down off his rocky perch and began to walk back down the slope, heading in the direction of the barn. Then, as he neared the little gate that opened into the farmyard, he saw Pete standing on the far side of the gate, looking in his direction with an impatient look on his face. Letting himself out of the field and into the farmyard, he began to describe what had happened with Mike Smart, the offers, and the threats.

"Sounds like a good deal to me," Pete commented. "In fact, it's probably the best offer we've ever had and, for all we know, it may be the best offer that we'd ever get. All we have to do is find a way that will let you square it with your conscience."

"It will be easier to find pigs that fly than it will be for me to find a way to square that *particular* circle. If, as Auntie Nan suggested, one of my grand-father's reasons for leaving Ireland may have been to free himself of the kind of work I have just been offered, then this O'Brien will not be climbing aboard. But enough of this stuff. How did you get on with the Lewis gun?"

"I got on just fine," Pete replied. "As you suspected, that power-washer was working and between that and a lot of kettles of boiling water from the kitchen, it cleaned up without too much difficulty. The biggest problem was finding an appropriately thin oil of any sort. I searched the house and the barn but other than olive oil, which is too thick, I drew a blank. However, Mavis finally saved the day as she had some aromatherapy oils and stuff in her trav-elling toilet bag and, even although I passed on those as probably too sticky, she had some grapeseed oil in her aromatherapy kit and I used that to good avail. Auntie Nan will probably never forgive me because I completely de-stroyed some of her kitchen towels by using them as cleaning rags."

"So can we go into the barn and look at it?" Gordon asked.

"It's not in there. I moved it," Pete went on. "I got fed up working inside a dark and damp old barn on such a fine day. So, once I had got it half cleaned up, I moved the parts round to the porch, which was in full sunshine and I worked on it there."

"So, did you still know your way around a Lewis gun after all these years?" Gordon asked.

"At first, when I broke it down into its smaller component parts on the porch, I had a temporary panic because none of them looked familiar at all. Then, as I continued, it all came back to me and soon, I had it into what I think is working order. I even loaded the magazine for you and, although I haven't tried it, I believe it would fire. The reason for the two types of ammunition is that they used to load them with every sixth round either incendiary or armour piercing. Let's go round to the front and you can have a look at it."

Skirting round the side of the house nearest to Nan O'Brien's place, with Pete leading and Gordon following on, they were soon approaching the porch. At the front door and just to the left of the entrance to the house, a green tarpaulin that Pete had found in the barn was covering and hiding something that Gordon guessed had to be the Lewis gun.

"Good idea," Gordon commented. "With the cover, nobody can see it from the gate or spot it from a passing car. I wonder what the penalty is for being caught in possession of a machine gun over here?" he asked.

"Well, it has to be a bit more serious than being caught in the possession of a flick-knife or a set of brass knuckles," Pete commented wryly. Then, while Gordon was still chuckling at his flick-knife remark, Pete pulled back the tarpaulin just enough so Gordon could see what was under the cover, with no possibility that anyone on the road could see it. "That there is the safety and that is the trigger," Pete explained while pointing out the salient points of the weapon. "Just by flicking off the safety and pulling the trigger, it should fire," Pete went on.

"Damn thing should be in a museum, along with Mike Smart and his merry men," Gordon commented. "They are all relics from a bygone age, genuine civil war era antiques. I once saw Michael Collins's machine pistol in a glass case in Dublin Museum and that's where this beast should be, or back down its hole. I sure don't want to see it falling into the hands of the Mike Smarts. So Mavis saved the day with the grapeseed oil?"

She sure did," Pete replied. "What are your plans for that girl and this relationship?"

"It sure won't be to let Mike Smart underpin it," Gordon replied. "If I can keep it up between here and Glasgow, or between Glasgow and Dublin, then I will. An old friend of mine managed to keep alive a long distance relationship like that for a couple of years. In the long term, she did manage to get two good years out of it."

"What about Sonia in Glasgow?" Pete asked, naming Gordon's second wife.

"There is very little left in that relationship," Gordon admitted. "With me having been ill so much these last few years, I am not much good to her. I am hardly able to really work and, because of that, she has had to become the main earner. And with my left hand not able to do much anymore, I can't even keep up the D.I.Y. side of the house."

"What about 'for better and for worse and in sickness and in health' and all that wedding vows stuff?" Pete asked.

"Yes, it's a thought," Gordon replied. "What it reminds me of is Kafka's *Metamorphosis*."

"Tell me about it," Pete encouraged.

"Well, it's either a short novel or a long short story and in it, overnight, the main character, a human, just turns into an enormous bug. At first, his parents are understanding. That is, as long as he stays in his bedroom and does nothing to embarrass them in front of the neighbours. And then, one night, the great bug just dies in its sleep. After that, the family are faced with what to do with the body and, in the end, they cut it up into pieces and dump the parts on some waste ground at night. So, although you might think that my situation is not too bad and not really analogous to Kafka, I'm the one who can't really work or lead my life the way that I used to. So, I just have to say 'No' to the Mike Smarts of this world, continue on the best that I can with Mavis, and wait for Sonia to fly the coop."

"Just accent the positive and do the best you can, man," Pete advised. "I've known you for a long time and, if anybody can beat this stroke thing, then it's you. I know boxers and people who took too much LSD who are a lot less to-gether than you are. And, on a mundane note, what do you want to do next?" Pete said, pulling the tarpaulin back into place, making sure that the weapon was well concealed.

"I thought we were going to go into Galway for some street busking, seeing that we need to keep our hand in and keep the band practised?" Gordon said.

"Sounds good to me," Pete responded, then threw the car keys to Gordon, who caught them and slipped them into his pocket. "I would like to go and grab a shower and change into some clothes that are as clean as these were before I went into armourer mode," Pete went on. "So, if you could round up Mavis and Sadie and get them and the instruments into the car, I'll meet you there in half an hour.

"See you then," Gordon responded, heading into the house with Pete fol-lowing in his wake, Gordon going off in search of Mavis and Sadie while Pete went to organise a shower and change of clothes.

Thirty minutes later, with the Renault standing in the space between the white gates and the road, Gordon was locking the gates behind the hire car while Pete busied himself with his windscreen washers and wipers and checking his fuel, readying the vehicle for the drive into Galway. Dropping the house keys into his jacket pocket and chuckling to himself because, al-though they only had the Renault for a relatively short time, not only did the group always sit in the same seats in the vehicle, but they had become accus-tomed to describing those seats as 'Gordon's seat, Mavis's seat' or whatever. Gordon was aware that he had two seats, the front passenger seat where he mostly sat, and the rear seat where he had first made love to Mavis. Smiling to himself at that thought, he climbed into his travelling seat and began to make himself comfortable. It being an exceptionally fine day, he was feeling upbeat, relaxed and happily looking forward to some street busking. Busking was something that they did not do in Glasgow, feeling that they were too well known in Scotland to be seen out among the street people and beggars. However, having done several long distance playing and travelling trips in Europe, and even an overland journey to India, it was something they had done a lot of and Gordon always enjoyed its informality, finding it very different from playing a set in a bar or performing in a club. Then, as Pete turned his key in the Renault's ignition, Gordon glanced over his shoulder to where, behind his seated companions, he could see the top of the trunk and the tops of three guitar cases. Between that and the fact that Pete was sitting on his right hand in the driving seat, he was confident that he had everything with him to make for a good day.

"So, Mavis, do you know the way so Sean O'Riordan's bar?" Pete asked, releasing his handbrake.

"Yes, I do. It's down near the quayside in an area that's seen a lot of redevelopment in recent years. Previously, the area was quite run down and was a locale where you would watch your back and your handbag if you were down that way after dark, and, in fact, it was an area that you might avoid at night. So, I'll navigate Pete and, for what is a relatively short drive in my home territory, even I can't get us lost."

"I hope that's right," Pete said, as Gordon pulled a notebook and a pen from his pocket and began to write. "A song?" Pete asked, raising a quizzical eyebrow.

"Who knows," Gordon replied. "Probably too small an idea to translate into any kind of worthwhile song, but worth jotting down nonetheless. I don't know if it's because of being in Ireland or because of being at the old house, or maybe it's just being relaxed and on the road, but something has been good for my creative juices. It's not just what I've seen over here but I can't remember in any similar space of time so many ideas coming to mind as well as old ideas that were never fully developed, that have been coming back to my attention, which is good. What I was jotting down there goes back to a visit to Rhu near Helensburgh in Scotland. A friend has a house on the shore there, close to Loch Gare." "I know that area." Pete responded. "It's well known to the fishing fraternity because of it being just where that sea loch meets the Firth of Clyde. It's well known for good fishing."

"One night, when I was staying over there," Gordon continued, "the full moon that was shining in my bedroom window was so bright that I've never forgotten it and that's what I was reworking. Something for a poem, a very short one, though. Those very short ones can sometimes make a haiku. Not a haiku that any Japanese haiku poet would recognise as such but a short, aphoristic verse that, while not any sort of major idea, is still worth hanging on to.

Anyway, this so-called haiku is called "Full Autumn Moon on Loch Gare and goes as follows:

Moon rise, moon set, you bet.

"Nice one," Pete commented. "Short, sweet, and very much to the poetic point."

Gordon was pleased at his companion's praise for his work and settled back comfortably in his seat. He was relaxed and happy, enjoying the sense of being on holiday and glad to have found Galway, Tuam, and Colonel's Fallow. On top of that, the fact that he had found Mavis, and his muse being so active, was making him feel almost euphoric and, as was often the case when travelling by car, he was soon half asleep, so that he saw no more of the outskirts of Galway than he had the outskirts of Tuam. Then, when he opened his eyes, he realised that he was on a street he knew.

"Are we close to Kenny's secondhand bookshop, Mavis?" he asked, rubbing the sleep from his eyes. "We are but how did you know that?" Mavis asked as Gordon looked out at a narrow-cobbled street with shops at pavement level and what seemed to be apartments above. "I was in Galway one time previously Mavis, and spent an enjoyable hour browsing the shelves in Kenny's."

Knowing that Gordon's conversations about books and bookstores could go on forever if encouraged, Pete ignored what his companion was saying to keep the Renault rolling while Mavis kept up a solid commentary of travel directions until they were driving through an area reminiscent of a public park and, in some sections, it was not too dissimilar to parts of the campus where they had been staying. The road they were on was bordered by Beech hedges, and Pete was catching glimpses of little bays with park-type benches, while over the top of the beech hedges, he could see the tops of taller stands of trees, copper birches, and rowans for the most part. "All of this planting and landscaping is new," Mavis explained. "Part of the upgrading and revamping of the area. Just up ahead where the road passes between those two clumps of yew trees, there is a parking area. So, if you drive on and park where you can, we will be within a short walk of Sean's." Driving as directed, Pete took the Renault past the yews to find himself in a large and mostly empty car park. Like most of the area around, it was surrounded by patches of shrubbery and occasional flowerbeds. "So, where are we going, Mavis?" Pete asked, scowling at a vista of urban regeneration, a look of distaste clear on his face. He was looking for something that looked like a bar or a café but was not finding it.

"See that pavement on our left?" Mavis replied. "Thirty or forty metres walk along it will being you right to the door of Sean's place and I know that there is a popular open area outside where, in good weather, he often puts out tables and chairs. It can be a busy spot, popular with tourists, students, and locals alike."

"I tell you what," Pete responded, "you guys stay here with the car and I'll take a stroll on up there, have a word with Sean, if he's around, check the place out and then we can take it from there." So saying, Pete was out of the car in a second and following the pavement Mavis had pointed out. A little further on, he passed a second clump of yews framing the road and then found himself in an open area ringed with a fence-like semi-circle of conifers. On the benches scattered round about, a few people were sitting, either reading newspapers or talking. Several women with baby buggies were also sitting on the benches, either young mothers out for a stroll or, perhaps, employees from some nearby crèche or nursery. Beyond the open area was a scatter of stainless steel topped tables and red plastic chairs and a long, low, slate-roofed building that reminded Pete of miners and farm workers' rows he had seen all over the British Isles. Whatever it was now, he was sure that its past lay with either miners or farm workers. Observing the building more closely with its white painted walls and slated roof, it made him think of a poorer and more down market adjunct to the old O'Brien place, Colonel's Fallow, being for landowners, the rows being for the usually poor, manual labourers. Staring at the building, he observed that someone had either improved or ruined the building by adding modern windows, each of which was framed by glossy, green painted shutters of a kind quite at odds with the style and age of the building. A modern door, also green painted, had been added. Above which was a large green and Gold painted sign bearing the legend, SEAN O'RIORDAN'S CAFÉ/BAR. Noting that none of the outside tables was occupied, Pete strode on across the open space, past the tables and chairs, and continued up through the open, beckoning doorway and into the empty, shadowy premises beyond. At the far end of a long narrow room, beyond the wooden tables and chairs which framed the walls to his left and right, was a modern bar, constructed from what, at a quick glance, seemed to be a mixture of red plastic and cheap plywood, giving the impression that it had been built both to a price and to a limited budget. On the top of the bar was a huddle of taps for draught beers and stouts, while behind the bar and mounted on the stone wall was a well stocked gantry virtually groaning under the weight of optics holding a selection of whiskies, both blended and single malt, Scottish, Irish, and American. Out of sight, behind the bar, was kept the locally and illicitly distilled tax-exempt whiskey, usually referred to by those of the regulars who knew of its existence as the White Lightning, this being the tipple of choice for several of Sean's regulars and particularly those free thinkers with a dislike of bureaucracy and punitive taxation. None of the regulars, however, were in attendance and, other than Pete, the only other person in the bar was a tall, fair-haired individual behind the bar wearing a white barman's jacket with green collar and cuffs, worn over a long, white bar apron. His shock of unruly hair was combed up in a style that made its owner look almost like an Elvis Presley imitator and, like Elvis, he sported a pair of long, well trimmed sideburns.

"A pint of stout please," Pete requested. And then, as the man picked up a pint measure to position it under one of the draught beer taps, he continued. "Hi, I'm Pete Lafferty of the MAVIS VALLEY BAND We were over in Galway playing at the acoustic music festival and, having some free time today, we thought we would do some street busking. When I was talking to Mike Smart, he suggested that we try the open area just outside of your premises. He also suggested that if we were in the area we might pop in here. Are you Sean?" "Yes, that's me right enough." The blonde barman replied. "It's good to meet you and if you are friends of Big Mike that must make you friends of mine, too."

"We usually find if we play outside a bar or café, that place generally gets a turn because we do draw a crowd."

"And we could sure do with one of those," Sean said, taking a step backwards so that he could watch the dark liquid drop into the pint glass and start to form a thick and creamy head.

"If I was you," Pete continued, "I would put a few extra tables and chairs outside, if you have any."

"Sounds like reasonable advice to me," Sean responded, "and I could easily do that."

"One favour, if you would," Pete said, scanning a price list on the wall and laying some coins down on the bar. "Could we plug our extension cable into one of your sockets so that we can power up two amps.? They don't use much juice and shouldn't cost you any more than a few cents. And, before you ask, we won't be too loud and we won't draw the attention of the Guards to you through excessive noise." At that, Pete drank deep from his glass and then stopped for a moment to wipe the foam from the stout off his face with the back of his hand. "So, in a minute," Pete said while savouring the dark brew, "I'll get back to my guitar buddies. We'll bring our gear in and get it set up and in thirty minutes from now, you'll have some live music going on just outside your door. Hopefully, it'll be good for business." "It can't make it any worse," Sean said, looking around the empty room.

"That's not because of any problem with what you sell," Pete said appreciatively. "That was excellent, but I better get back to the others and, as soon as we can get set up here, we can get into it."

"Great," Sean said with some enthusiasm as Pete made for the door. "There are electrical sockets just inside the door, one on either side," Sean shouted after Pete's retreating back. Pete did not stop or slacken pace but brought a hand up to shoulder height in a backward wave, letting Sean know that he had heard him. "I'm looking forward to hearing you, guys!" Sean continued. "Played in a band once myself. Used to kid myself I was Galway's answer to Chuck Berry. Then I played in a showband for a while. I still take the old guitar out of its case once in a while. It relaxes the mind after a difficult day."

Outside, Pete rejoined the pavement that had led him to Sean's and began to retrace his steps. Back in the car, he quickly described his talk with Sean to the others.

"So how shall we do this?" Gordon asked.

"Like this," Pete replied. "I'll get the trunk out of the car on my own and just trundle it on up there. Then I'll start to get us set up. If you just wait here with the others for five minutes or so to give me a start and then, bringing the instruments with you, take a slow walk up to Sean's. By the time you get to me, I'll be just about set up. When you arrive, Gordon, just get the instruments in tune and then we'll take it from there. We can do a fairly middle of the road set, light on our own material as far as possible, sticking to songs that anybody hanging around might have heard before."

"I'm looking forward to some music in the sunshine and open air," Gordon said, catching the keys that Pete had just slipped out of the ignition and thrown in his direction.

"That was with your left hand you caught those keys," Pete commented. "That has to be a good sign because a few weeks ago, you couldn't have managed that catch."

"It's improving slowly," Gordon commented.

"Great, man!" Pete enthused, getting out of the Renault and making for the rear of the vehicle. In a moment, the trunk was on the pavement and Pete was setting off with a will, pushing the trunk up the slight incline, the metal wheels putting out a throaty rumble as they were set in motion over the rough concrete.

As soon as Pete and his burden reached the open space outside the bar Pete saw that Sean had filled the area with some extra tables and chairs. Then, as soon as he had the trunk open, he was turning himself into a one-man whirlwind of a road crew. He pulled out his trusty extension cable and, plugging one end into a socket just inside the bar, he then began to play out more cable as he made for the spot where he thought the multi-plug end would be most useful. That done, he began to unpack the two amplifiers, mikes, and mike stands. Finally satisfied that the first part of his setting-up was completed, he selected a table close to the entrance and positioned two chairs beside it where he and Gordon could sit with their backs to the door, facing out into the ring of tables, where he hoped an audience would gather. Then he added a third chair in case Sadie wanted to play sitting, rather than in her usual standing posture. A moment later, Gordon arrived, carrying his own instrument as well as Pete's. Quickly scanning the equipment to determine what stage Pete was at, he got Big Red out of its case and, sitting down, began to tune the guitar. Just then, Pete appeared at his elbow and, seizing the empty guitar case, he poured all of the coins that he had in his pockets into it and laid it on the ground in front of the spot where they would be playing. Gordon also searched his pockets and threw a handful of coins into the case. Pete had noticed that, as soon as he started to get set up, his activity had caught the attention of several passers-by who had hung around the area of the circling bushes and were now waiting to see what was going to develop. Tuning his own instrument, Gordon could see that Pete was about ready to begin. So, switching his mike on, he tapped it three times with a guitar toughened fingernail and was gratified to hear the sound coming back at him from his amplifier.

"Testing, one, two, three,." he spoke the legend into his mike and almost immediately people began to come forward and make their way to seats.

Fingering a G major chord while hunched over his guitar and began to play the introduction to a Mance Lipscomb instrumental, a rag that Mance had named simply "G Rag." Without breaking stride, Gordon went seamlessly from that piece to two other Mance Lipscomb instrumentals in the same key, using the medley to get his fingers limbered and loosened up, at the same time as entertaining the few people who were around and also alerting anyone who was within earshot, that something was happening While he was playing those tunes, he began to concentrate on certain one and two bar phrases within the pieces that he particularly liked, mixing and matching and repeating them to his heart's content, juggling his favourite riffs. He was playing in a way that was very similar to how Mance and other Texas guitarists commonly played, with the palm of his right hand lying on his strings at the bridge of his in-strument. This allowed him to concentrate on getting a solid beat and tone without having to bother playing cleanly or getting perfect notes. It was a powerful and effective technique and one that had all eyes on him, as well as Sean's, who was hovering around the tables, equally keen on taking orders and seeing what the band was doing. As he was working and observing the steadily growing crowd his head was nodding in time to the M.V.C.B., particularly now that Sadie and Pete had brought their instruments into the mix. By the time that Sean was starting to deliver orders to tables his outdoor space was beginning to fill up and, while there were still some empty seats, there were no longer any completely empty tables. Concluding his Mance Lipscomb medley with a flurry of high Octane and high speed single string blues runs, Gordon had come to the conclusion that it was high time he was getting into some spoken communication with his audience who, drawn in initially by his fiery guitar playing, were now relaxing, thinking about getting a drink and wondering about what further entertainment might be in store for them. Concluding his introductory pieces with a fast treble string run, Gordon took that into what even non-guitar players could see was the end of something. Then, taking his capo off and dropping it into a handy pocket, Gordon smiled and looked out and around a circle of faces that were all looking at him ex-pectantly.

"Hi," he began. "I'm Gordon O'Brien, and when playing with these good people you see here with me, we are the Mavis Valley Band over in Galway from our base in Scotland to take part in your well-known acoustic music fes-tival. And, with a day off before going back to Glasgow, we are here to play for you at the excellent Sean's bar and listening to music being the thirsty work that it is. That gentleman over there in the white jacket is Sean himself, and he will be only too pleased to take a drinks order from you. After those instru-mental tunes that were my pleasure to play for you, it is time for me to sing you a song and I would like to start with a song written by Woody Guthrie. It is called 'Deportees,' although sometimes you will come across it titled Plane Wreck at Los Gatos.' Actually, at the time of Woody's death, this song was found as an unfinished piece or poem among his papers. It was later set to music by Richard Farina who, before his untimely death, was married to Joan

Baez's sister. Julie Felix recorded it on one of her early albums and The Byrds included it on their *Ballad of Easy Rider* album, and I'm sure some of you will have heard it before. As a band the M.V.C.B. is not a very political outfit. though sometimes we like to let our audiences know our feelings on man's in-humanity to man. 'Deportees is a song about poor Mexican workers illegally in America and, most likely, poor Mexicans are not too much different from poor Irish or poor Scots. So the next time we are faced with poor Eastern Europeans begging on our streets, this song will be a useful reminder about how not to react to them. After all, it is not all that long ago in the U.K., when houses were being advertised for rent, to see the words 'No Irish.' Similarly, with ads for work opportunities they would commonly add, 'No Irish need apply.'" That said, Gordon adjusted his tuning, arranged his capo and, with his left hand holding down a C major chord, he began to sing as Pete and Sadie's guitars fell into place behind him. At the same time as he as was executing some fast pinkie moves on his first and second strings:- he began to sing;:

Your crops are all in and your peaches are rotting, oranges stacked in their cre-osote dumps; You're flying them back to that Mexican border to spend all their money to wade back again; Goodbye to my Juan, goodbye Rosalita, adios mes amigos Jesus y Maria; You won't have a name when you ride the big airplane;

All they will call you will be Deportees;

The sky-plane caught fire over Los Gatos Canyon, a fireball of lightning it shook all of our hills; Who are these friends who are scattered like dry leaves, the radio says 'they were just deportees" Some of us are illegal and others unwanted, our work con-tracts out and we have to move on It's six hundred miles to that Mexican border, they hunt us like outlaws, like rustlers, like thieves; Goodbye to my Juan, goodbye Rosalita, you won't have a name when you ride the big airplane;

All they will call you will be deportees.

At that, Gordon went back to his peripatetic pinkie fingering and added a handful of Spanish guitar sounding bars to play his song out on an appro-priate note. Pete added his guitar's voice to the ending and together the two M.V.C.B. main men played the song to a close with some excellent country picking. Then, as the last notes of their combined ending were fading away, Gordon thought back to what they had discussed earlier about not doing too much of their self-penned material and decided to go on with one of his own songs anyway. "Thank you, friends." He breathed into his mike. "Brought up in Scotland from good Irish stock, sometimes I'm not sure if I'm Scottish or Irish. But this next song is a self-penned number that is a Scots/Irish mon-grel's take on certain aspects of Scottish life and culture." So saying, Gordon fingered a D major chord and began to play an introduction which took him to a G major chord, which he continued to hold down while he began to sing:

The shipyards are dead and gone; Never again will you hear the caulkers or the riveters song; The Kailyard it never existed;

No mythical golden age, or time when nobody died, hungered or thirsted;

The Clyde needs no more steel nor warships on the slips;

The shipyards are dead and gone;

Let them go for all their great show because never again will you hear the caulkers or the riveters song;"

Without them we're getting along. Real life is moving on.'

Then, as Gordon's voice trailed off towards an ending, he wondered if an Irish audience could pick up on his digs at Scottish social stereotyping. But he need not have worried as a brisk applause came his way and coins rained down into Pete's open guitar case. Here and there among the coins, folded up small so that they could.

More easily be thrown, were several notes. Pete had become aware that Sadie, standing at his left side, had moved closer to him and was staring fixedly at him in a way that suggested that she was trying to communicate something to him. For a moment, Pete was puzzled and then he concluded that Sadie wanted to sing. Pete then pointed at his mike and the slide guitarist responded with a grin.

"Take the mike, babe Pete said, moving the mike stand closer to Sadie, who started to adjust it to suit her height. "As my friends here with me all know," Sadie began to speak, "I pretty much only like to sing blues and this old guitar here rarely sounds good if I try to play anything other than blues on it. So, after this next song, which is Gulfcoast Blues" by Clarence Williams, I'm hoping that you, me, and my guitar are all going to be happy with the song that I've chosen for us."

Sadie next fretted a G major chord and, slipping her steel slide along her treble strings, pushed out a dramatic sounding introduction that served to focus the audience's full attention on her. That achieved, she began to sing in a hard-edged voice:

I've been blue all day, my man's gone away; He's left his baby cold for another gal I'm told.'

At the end of each line of her song, Sadie would sway back from the mike a little and then concentrate all of her energy into pumping out a guitar lick she had lifted from McKinlay Morganfield, a guitarist better known under his stage name of Muddy Waters.

I tried to treat him kind, thought he would be mine;

If it keeps on snowin' baby's gonna be lower than down, I'll be Gulf Coast bound;

That man I hate to lose; That's why baby has the blues.

Then, as her line trailed off into silence, Sadie repeated her Muddy Waters lick and used it to take her into a spirited slide guitar solo that owed more than a little to Elmore James. This had the effect of getting the audience clapping along, which they did with gusto. At that, Sadie motioned to Pete to take his mike back, which he did and was soon adjusting it to match his greater height.

"Glad to see that you're all still here," he quipped as he adjusted his tuning. "This next song that I'm going to do is called "Stagolee" and just about every bluesman or folksinger known seems to have a version of it. It is based on an episode that took place in 1896, a fact that reminds us that folksong can have a long memory and even a lot of years after the event, can still be accurate in the details. My version of this song is mostly based on the versions of Leadbelly and Mississippi John Hurt. The instrumental that I usually finish this song on is based on Duck Baker's piece, "Still Staggering, which is Duck's tribute to a lot of different versions of this song." Next, Pete played a dramatic introduction based around several slides into an A major chord and began to sing:

> Stagolee was a bad man, everybody knows,
> Spent five hundred dollars just to buy himself a suit of clothes,
> He was a bad man, that mean old Stagolee,
> Stagolee shot Billy de Lyons, what do you think of that?
> Shot him down in cold blood over a ten dollar Stetson hat,
> Billy de Lyons said, 'Stagolee please don't take my life,'
> I've got two little babes and a darling, loving wife,
> Stagolee said 'You stole my Stetson hat and Im bound to take your life
> He was a bad bad man, that mean old Stagolee
> Stagolee said, 'What do I care about
> Your two little babes or your darling, loving wife, you
> Stole my hat and I mean to take your life,'
> A bad man, that mean old Stagolee.

His singing section completed, Pete went straight into his version of Duck Baker's instrumental and played his song out. His audience were by now applauding enthusiastically with lots of coins finding their way into Pete's ever-hungry guitar case. Pete and Gordon seemed to realise in the same moment that with so many people round about them eating lunch and drinking beers and coffees, that this might be a good time for the band. To grab something to eat.

With a mostly liquid lunch inside them the M.V.C.B. were soon ready to continue. Adjusting his mike stand, Gordon began to speak.

"A little earlier, we did that Woody Guthrie song for you. So, next, we would like to do a song by a great bluesman, singer and guitarist, and one time friend of Woody Guthrie, Huddie Leadbeater, famously known as Leadbelly. For those of you who are thinking that you've never heard of him, he is the man who wrote Goodnight Irene...Amongst guitarists his he is still called 'The King of the Twelve String Guitar.' That said, unfortunately on this trip, we don't have a twelve-string with us because Lead's music always sounds better on a twelve-string. Though, in some ways, it's better that we don't have one with us because they are a bitch to tune and equally difficult to keep in tune. In fact, a lot of twelve-string players will tell you that if you are going to play one regularly, then you are just going to have to accept that a lot of the time you are going to be playing out of tune. This well-known Leadbelly song we are just about to do for you is called 'Good Morning Blues' and we hope that you like it."

With that, Gordon grabbed hold of a D major chord and began to pick out the melody of the song on the bass strings of his guitar, playing in such a way that, after every melody note, he would strum up across all of his strings with his right hand index finger, so that he was simultaneously playing the melody and a backing rhythm. Pete was watching him closely and, as soon as Gordon had completed his melodic introduction, came in with a flurry or rolls before settling down to play a complementary arpeggio. Sadie and her steely tones followed Pete into the mix, helping to build up the band's full and bright sound, as. Gordon began to sing:-"

Good morning blues, blues how do you do? I'm doin' all right, good morning, how are you?

I lay down last night turnin' from side to side, I was not sick, just dissatisfied;
I got up this morning blues walkin' round my bed;
Went to eat my breakfast, blues was all in my bread.

Periodically, and at strategic moments, Gordon would repeat his melodic section on his guitar much to the appreciation of the audience. Then, he played it one last time as an ending that he augmented with two high-speed bars played with a flourish, letting the audience know that the song was delivered. Then, almost ignoring the loud and sustained burst of applause greeting his offering, he went on to talk his next introduction.

"This next song we are going to do for you is an old jazz and blues standard that seems to have been around forever and, although I can't tell you who wrote it, I can think of many memorable versions of it. It's called "St. James Infirmary." When I was younger, I could sing it almost without hearing the words and certainly without dwelling on them. But as we get older, with a bit more life experience behind us, it becomes a song to make you think. I take care when performing this one, to only do it among friends and to stay away from it if I'm feeling a bit down or melancholic. Sometimes if I sing it without all of my defences in place it can be a little too much. I've seen strapping men in audiences before now with tears streaming down their faces. Jorma Kaukonen does a great version of this one on his *Country Heartbeat* album. As does Champion Jack Dupree on his old folkway album, *Women Blues*. If you prefer piano to guitar, check that one out. Actually, I saw the late Jack Dupree in Glasgow's Club Maryland a while ago. Some idiot tried to heckle him that night and Jack just said 'Why don't we reverse roles. You come up here, sing and play piano and I'll come down there and act the fool.' Which sure put that chump in his place."

So saying, Gordon slid into an A minor chord and began to sing:-

It was down in Old Joe's bar room on the cornerby the square;
The drinks were served as usual and the usual crowd was there;
On my left stood Big Joe McKennedy and his eyes were bloodshot red;
As he looked at the crowd around him, these were the words he said;
I went down to the Saint James Infirmary, I saw my baby there;
She was stretched out on a long white table, so pale, so cold, so fair;
Let her go, let her go, God bless her;

She can ramble this wide world over, never find another man like me;
Now when I die please bury me in my high top Stetson hat;
Put a twenty dollar gold piece on my watch chain
so the boys will know I'm standing pat;
I want six guitar players for my pall-bearers;
A blues singer to sing me a song;
Put a jazz band on my hearse wagon to raise hell as we go rolling along;
And now that you've heard my story, I'll take another shot of booze;
I've got the guitar-picker's blues.

Then, with his left hand fingers dancing over his first and second strings, Gordon threw in an E7 chord before going back to an A minor and using it as a springboard to launch himself into what he liked to call his John Renbourn run, always remembering who he had borrowed it from and used that run as an outro. Looking around the onlookers, he was checking to see if his song had brought any sadness or introspection to any of his audience. At a table off to his right, he saw one elderly man put a finger to the corner of his eye while seemingly adjusting his spectacles. The Mavis Valley Band, in a laidback mood.

Chapter Eleven

Busking and feeling themselves to be among friends, played a relaxed, low key set that reminded Gordon of many similar sets they had delivered in friends' apartments where they could be friendly and intimate, close to their audiences. Sticking mainly to blues, jazz, and folk standards that the crowd at Sean's seemed to both know and enjoy, the band was having fun. At the end of their set, Pete was just transferring their collection of coins and notes out of his guitar case and into his pockets, when Sean approached them from the direction of the bar.

"Thanks, guys," he breezed. Pulling a chair over towards them and sitting down, he said, "That was a great set and one that I really enjoyed. Live music breathes some life into this old place and I think I'll stay with it. Takings wise, it's been excellent. One of the best shifts ever and some of my regulars are suggesting that I turn the bar into a live music venue and take it forward that way. It's something I'm going to think about seriously and listening to you guys play has made me decide to get my old Harmony Sovereign out of its case in the spare bedroom where I keep it, and get back into practising. If I can get back into regular practice then, in six months or a year, maybe I'll be ready to start playing here in my own residency. It's just a pity you guys are not based over here because, between this bar and all of the people I know in the trade, you could have a gig every night in the week if you wanted it," Sean pointed out. "How about if I was to offer you a paid gig in the bar tonight?"

"How much pay?" Pete asked in his usual blunt, almost aggressive tones.

"Well, trade has not been brilliant recently," Sean dissembled. "How about if I gave the four of you ten Euros each with dinner thrown in and I'd pass the hat for you, too?"

"We don't have anything else on tonight and we did come over here to play." Gordon replied. "What time would you want us to start?" Pete asked.

"Say, about seven," Sean replied.

"What I would like to do, if it's all right with you, Sean," Pete continued, "is take our guitars with us when we leave but leave our gear in the bar. That way, we can get set up quickly and easily when we come back."

"There's an alcove just inside the bar to the right of the door; if you leave your gear there, I can see into that alcove from behind the bar, so I can keep an eye on your equipment for you."

"It's my turn to move the gear this time," Gordon pointed out. So, while Pete sat on chatting to Sean, he began to disconnect cables and move their amps and mike stands into the alcove that Sean had described. Gordon had just finished moving the equipment when he realised that Don had appeared at his side.

"How did you know we were here?"Gordon asked, .

"The radio was playing in the campus café where we had our lunch today and the DJ announced your gig on the air."

Gordon was looking serious. "I want you to listen closely to what I'm going to tell you, Don," he began. "Don't ask me any questions about what I am going to say but do act on it and act fast." Don was looking puzzled as he waited to hear what was coming next. "A little green bird has just given me the whisper that you and Phil are both captains in the British Army and because of that, you are in danger here. If the two of you have got any way of getting out of Ireland in a hurry, I suggest you do just that."

As Don spun on his heel and went off at a fast walk, Sean came over to check and see what stage Gordon was at with the equipment. "Good." The bar owner commented. "For tonight's sake," Sean said, "I'm going to get my skates on, get into my office and start phoning to let a few people know we've got live music on tonight." Next, Sean looked around the room at his customers and began to address them. "Folks, if you've enjoyed the band, they will be back with us at seven for another session. So, come back later and spread the word to your friends." Pete slipped Big Red back into its plush lined case, snapped the safety catches shut and, that done, he was bidding farewell to several new-found friends, while around them, their erstwhile audience was breaking up and beginning to drift away. "Thank you, folks!" Sean was shouting after their retreating backs. "If you enjoyed that, the band will be back in the bar at seven tonight. Tell your friends if you can."

Shortly, Gordon and Sadie, instrument cases in hand, were following Pete and Mavis back towards the car park and the waiting Renault. On the return drive to Colonel's Fallow, Pete realised from the fact that only once did he have to ask Mavis for directions that he was starting to be able to find his way around Galway.

Back at the house, Pete quickly got the hire car in off the road and on to the driveway. Then, with Mavis and Sadie on either side of him, Gordon was leading the way up the drive with Pete following just a little behind. Gordon was listening to the sound of his feet crunching on the pebbles, luxuriating in the hot sunshine and drinking in the garden's flower scents and colours when a Scottish-sounding voice with a definite rough, Glaswegian accent rang out in a threatening and verbally aggressive challenge.

"Halt! Armed SAS patrol! Freeze and do it now!"

In the same instant that the "Freeze!" command was hurled spear-like at them, two vicious cracks shredded the idyllic ambience of the garden. In that moment, Pete recognised the sounds for what they were and Gordon realised that the intangible something whose slipstream had passed within a hair's breadth of his head, must have been a bullet. As that first round so narrowly missed Gordon, its companion hit Pete in the right thigh, cleanly passing through the fleshy part of the limb without coming into contact with bone. Then, as the searing pain burned into his leg and brain, and neither knowing where their attack was coming from, nor the further intentions of their attackers, Pete roared out the single word "Scatter!" and immediately threw himself into the fuchsia thicket on his left. Landing heavily on his side and using his elbows and knees for leverage, at a fast crawl he got himself as far into the heart of the bush as he could get. Realising, after a moment, that their attackers were in the fuchsia thicket between himself and the house, Pete pulled off the green bandanna he was wearing around his neck and, hurriedly folding it into a pad, he applied it to the front of his thigh where the bullet had exited and began to apply pressure in an attempt to staunch the flow of blood which had already turned his trouser leg from his knee to the top of his blue leather boot into a blood-soaked rag. Next, he pulled off the pink and white Sanskrit scarf, a souvenir of his overland trip to India a few years before, and used it to hold the green pad in place, being careful not to turn the scarf into a tourniquet because, in the Territorial Army and in the Air Training Corp, he had been warned on almost countless occasions of the dangers of battlefield applied tourniquets. Just then, another round passed close to him, not close enough to be a worry but close enough to be a warning that someone knew where he was. Across the driveway in the rhododendron patch, first one and then a second round passed uncomfortably close to Gordon, who was staring at the green tarpaulin on the porch and wondering about the open ground between his bush and the porch.

"GORDON!" Pete roared out, coming to the same conclusion as Gordon and at almost the same moment. "Get to the Lewis! It's our only hope. Go on, do it, man! If it jams, I'll get to you. They're in the fuchsia at the house end."

Hesitating only for as long as it took to get to his feet, Gordon, bent double and crouching low, sprinted up the garden path as fast as his awkward position would let him. Reaching the porch in a handful of strides, he was soon tearing the tarpaulin aside and throwing it away from him into the garden. As he slipped down into the space between the breech end of the Lewis gun and the house wall, two bullets aimed at head height hit the stone at his back and sent slivers of sandstone flying in all directions. Sitting down cross-legged on the porch, he braced his trainers against two of the Lewis gun's metal feet and ran his eye over the safety catch that Pete had pointed out to him earlier.

This is ridiculous, Gordon thought to himself, *here I am, almost a life-long vegetarian, a pacifist, a guy who rescues spiders trapped in the bath to release them and moves slaters to where the dog can neither stand on them or eat them and I'm being called upon to unleash this piece of military diabolism.* Later Gordon would say that it was almost as if he was in a state of shock when he had been sitting behind the Lewis gun wrestling with his conscience. Certainly, his face was pale enough for a state of shock, except that is for the place on his forehead where a sliver of stone from the house wall had hit him and opened up a slight wound where blood was now seeping and threatening to get into his eye. He flicked the safety to the off position and, for no explicable or logical reason, began to think of Liam O'Flaherty's novel *The Assassin* and how the main character, having been sent out to kill a man, rehearses all of the reasons why the man should die and then, after examining all of his counter-arguments and reasons why the victim should be allowed to live, decides to go ahead and kill him anyway. No sooner was that line of thought banished than Gordon was reminded of Mathieu in John Paul Sartre's trilogy *Roads to Freedom* and how at the time of the Fall of France in nineteen hundred and forty when Mathieu, along with most of the French army, had been retreating in front of a successful and overpowering German blitzkrieg. Eventually, Mathieu, having met up with a group of demoralised French soldiers and throwing in his lot with them, shares some wine with them and then, coming down off his intellectual's ivory tower, decides to help them defend their position against the roller-coaster that was the advancing German army. That moment and decision seemed to be a moment of self-realisation for Mathieu and a critical moment in Sartre's novel.

"Come on Gordon! For God's sake, get that Lewis going!" Pete roared out across the garden. "Get it going or else we're done for! Come on, man, rise up and do the needful! You've got the blood of ancient Fenian warriors running in your veins. Pull the trigger. If it jams, I'll get to you."

At that, Gordon swivelled the Lewis gun until its muzzle was pointing at the nearest section of the fuchsia patch. Then, wondering if the ancient weapon with its equally ancient ammunition was capable of firing, he pulled the trigger. Immediately the weapon burst into shuddering life and, at the same moment as he saw the fuchsia in front of him being scythed down, he was enveloped in a thick cloud of cordite smoke. Looking at the fuchsias he was reminded of what Pete had said about some of the ammunition being incendiary rounds and realised the smell of cordite that was coming to him was mingling with the tang of smouldering vegetation. Bracing his feet against the tripod's legs he held on to the breech end to make sure that the Lewis gun did not vibrate itself off the porch. *Just like in a band.* Gordon thought to himself. "The bass drum needs to be anchored to keep it out of the first row of the audience." Then, as he wondered about what had happened among the fuchsia, he realised that Pete had hobbled to the porch and was lowering his bulk down to sit at his side. "It had to be done." Pete commented, knowing Gordon well enough to understand something of his likely thoughts connected with what they had just gone through. "We didn't start this violence. All we did was defend ourselves and our friends; surely everybody has a right to be able to do that? What do we do next, Gordy?"

"Next I think I get my mobile phone out, ring Mike Smart, tell him what's happened here and see what he can do to help us." That said, Gordon pulled his mobile phone out of his pocket, switched it on and, clicking on menu, was soon scrolling his was through a long list of numbers until he found the one he was looking for. *"Please, let there be somebody at the other end* he thought to himself as the phone began to ring out.

"Hi, Gordon, what can I do for you?" Mike Smart's voice came on and asked. "I've just got a report of gunfire coming from your neck of the woods. You got problems there?"

Gordon quickly explained what had just happened at Colonel's Fallow.

"Okay Gordon, here's what we're going to do," Mike Smart responded. "I think I told you about my security trio camping out in the Grocery Wood. I'll get right on to them now and the minute I make contact, they'll be on their way to you. If Martin has his Triumph motorcycle with him, he should reach you first. Just relax and be aware that the cavalry is coming. Martin, although young, is a good man and very capable. I'll get some medical help organised for you, too."

In the moment Gordon clicked his phone off and dropped it back into his pocket, he heard the high-pitched aggressive whine of a powerful motorcycle somewhere in the distance and realised that Martin was already on his way. Passing that information on to Pete, he stood up just in time to see a red, yellow and white motorcycle with a racing number on its side burst through the open white gates and come hurtling up the drive and screech to a halt just short of the porch. The helmeted and goggled rider was wearing a leather jacket and leather trousers, whose colours matched those of his highly charged machine. Dismounting, he pulled the bike back on to its stand and, cutting its engine, he pulled off his white gauntlets before taking off his helmet to reveal features that could only belong to a close relative of Mike Smart.

"Hiya fellas." He began breezily. "Mike tells me that you guys have had a bit of trouble and that I need to help you out."

Gordon nodded and went on to describe the events that had just transpired.

"And you must be Gordon?" Martin said, half making a statement and half asking a question, recognising Gordon from his brother's description.

"Dead right and no pun intended," Gordon responded sharply, being in no mood for social pleasantries.

"So where are the bad guys?" Martin asked.

"There's four of them over there in the bushes," Pete said, pointing. "Soldiers of some sort, according to their kit. I think they're dead."

"I'll make sure," Martin said, snapping open the map pocket on the thigh of his leather trousers and pulling out what Pete recognised as a Walther automatic pistol.

"That, you won't!" Gordon snapped back tersely, swivelling the Lewis gun threateningly until its muzzle was pointing directly at the motorcyclist. "If they're alive, we will get them help," Gordon continued.

"Four of them right enough and all very dead," Martin was saying a moment later back on the porch. Just then, a battered red Transit van swung through the open white gates and pulled up behind the parked Renault. "That's Dougie and Liam and they're with me," Martin explained when a moment later the driver and passenger from the van and both with red hair and freckled faces, clearly brothers, jogged away from the Transit and came to a halt in front of the huddle on the porch.

"What now, boss?" the smaller of the two asked.

"Now, guys, we get tidied up here," Martin responded. "What you find in the bushes there to the right go into the van to be dropped off where their masters will find them and, after that and using our usual code, we will contact the local radio station to let them know that we ambushed a covert army patrol in the field. It would not be the first time and, by us admitting responsibility for the action, it should break any connections to you guys and, hopefully as far as you are concerned, that should be the end of it."

"So how are you feeling, fella?" Martin asked, jabbing a thumb in Pete's direction.

"It's bearable," Pete replied. "And what do you want done with that thing?" Martin asked, scowling in the direction of the Lewis gun, which was still pointing at him.

"I would like to see it in a glass case in a museum it being a genuine Civil War era relic," Gordon replied. Failing that, it can go back down the hole under the barn where it came out of and where it should have remained. It's just amazing what can be attached to your family roots when you dig them up," Gordon continued.

"Bullet wounds are a bitch." Martin said feelingly, looking in Pete's direction.

"I am in a bit of pain," Pete admitted. "But nothing that I can't handle. The nausea is probably worse than the hurt."

"Just thole it for a bit," Martin advised. "I've already contacted our Doctor Jack who, on the quiet, is a really good man and an expert on bullet wounds. He's been patching up our wounded for years. He's good, careful, and very discreet. I stopped two bullets on the day of the Bloody Sunday debacle when the Parachute Regiment opened fire on our demonstrators. The army knew that one of us was hit twice and no doubt were searching for a wounded man. Doctor Jack was brilliant. He got me into an army uniform and, using lost or stolen papers, he smuggled me into a military hospital where nobody knew who or what I was all of the time they had me in that private room. And after that, Doctor Jack had me back at work in no time at all. And back then, with two young kids, that was important. As soon as Mike called me today, I rang Doctor Jack and although his secretary told me that he was already out on his calls, she assured me that we would have absolute priority. So, Liam and

Dougie, help us to get this wounded man into the house and, once we've done that, you two get what you find in the bushes there into the van and that includes the weapons that are there. This ancient machine gun here goes into the van and gets kept discreetly safe until Big Mike decides what's to happen to it."

"Careful," Gordon warned, pushing the safety catch to the on position, when Martin stretched out a hand to touch the muzzle of the Lewis gun. A moment later the two newcomers positioned themselves one on either side of Pete, gently getting him up so that he was standing on his uninjured leg. Then they clasped their hands together so that Pete could sit on their improvised human seat/stretcher, and with Gordon going in front of them to open both the house and front parlour doors, in a matter of moments they had Pete lying outstretched on the leather sofa in the front room, Mavis going off to take a tartan travel-type rug off one of the beds to keep him warm. "I guess the M.V.C.B. won't be playing Sean's tonight," Pete said with a tired, pale attempt at a smile.

"You won't be but I might," Gordon said, tucking the travel rug around his clearly shocked and shaken friend. "Some bands might let people down but our tradition has always been that, if it's humanly possible, the Mavis Valley Band. Always makes its gigs."

"Are you well enough to do the gig and do the drive to Sean's?" Pete asked. "You know you haven't been driving since that illness." "I know I haven't been driving but I'm sure I can, especially with the Renault being an automatic. I can take Mavis and Sadie with me. Every time Mavis sings with us, the better she gets. With Sadie, she's versatile, being able to sing lead or harmony and with her guitar, she can add picking or slide. So it will be okay."

"Sounds fine in theory," Pete said doubtfully. "But you know that after the gig, we need to be heading straight to Dublin for our flight."

Gordon thought for a moment before continuing. "What we'll do is this, man. Mavis, Sadie, and I will get to Sean's for seven, do a set, then load our gear into the car, getting some help at Sean's end if necessary. We'll then get back here to pick you up for a fairly leisurely drive to the airport and then it's back to Glasgow and a different reality. Me to get down to some work on a few ideas that came to me during this trip and you to stay away from work until that leg's properly mended."

"Unless we just stay here and work for Mike Smart?" Pete said in a half-joking, half-serious tone. Then, as Mavis came back from the direction of the kitchen, the motorcyclist's mobile began to ring.

"Looks like Auntie Nan has been here while we were out," Mavis commented. "From what she's left behind, those of us who are fit to eat won't go short of dinner." Martin clicked shut a slimline mobile phone and slipped it back into his pocket. "That was our Doctor Jack," Martin explained. "He's finished his calls and we are next on his list."

"Martin" the readheaded liam began. "That's the doc on his way and if you don't need us any longer, I'll go outside with Dougie and get the van loaded.

Even for the doc., there are things that it's better not to see or even know about."

"Very true," Martin responded. "You go and get cleared up outside and, as soon as you have, on your way. Don't bother coming back to me here because I'll phone you later."

Obeying orders, Liam, Dougie, and the red Transit van were gone as quickly as they had come, as was the motorcycle and its rider, Martin overtaking the van the moment that both vehicles were beyond the white gates and leading the way in the direction of Galway.

Inside the parlour, Pete, Mavis, Sadie, and Gordon heard what sounded like a small car pulling up outside and, a moment later, they heard the unlocked front door opening. When the small and portly Doctor Jack came into the parlour, he was carrying not the small leather doctor's bag beloved of stage and screen, but something more akin to a large black rucksack, no doubt containing all of the equipment a busy country doctor might need in a variety of medical situations. As soon as Mavis had introduced Doctor Jack to the band he asked her to go to the kitchen and boil him a kettle of water. When that was ready, except for Pete, he ejected everyone from the room. That done, he explained to Pete that he was going to give him a shot of painkillers that would make him more comfortable and make the cleaning and dressing of his wound less traumatic. Continuing to keep Pete informed, he explained that he was going to clean the wound thoroughly, pack it and bandage it, telling Pete how packing the wound with gauze would help it to granulate from the inside with less likelihood that it would fill up with pus later.

"I'll give you the name of a good doctor for you to see when you get home. Do you know the Southern Hospital in Glasgow?" Doctor Jack asked.

"That's probably the Southern General." Pete responded. "Yes, that's the one," the doctor went on. "My brother works there. A good and discreet man. So you can safely take a bullet wound to him." That said, the doctor took a printed card from his pocket and handed it to Pete. Next, he prepared an injection and administered it, before going on to pour some of Mavis's boiled water into a stainless steel dish that he had produced from the black rucksack. After which, he proceeded to carefully and meticulously clean the wound, before packing and bandaging it. "Just keep off that leg as near to completely as you can, for as long as possible. If the pain becomes a problem, use paracetamol as necessary and get to my brother sooner rather than later. When I was coming here, I was sure that my house calls were all done but there is one patient I want to double check on before I sign off and call it a day. So, on that note, I'll leave you to be looked after by your friends and get back to my car."

Once the Doctor had gone, Mavis retrieved her kettle and, heading back to the kitchen, began to turn the baking potatoes and salad that Nan had dropped off earlier into a meal. Also on the worktop beside the produce from her garden that the old lady had left was one of her home-baked loaves and a bag of her scones. As Mavis busied herself around the kitchen, she noticed what looked like fresh bed linen and towels lying close to the food. Picking up an envelope that was lying on top of the towels, she saw that it had her name on it and proceeded to open it. Scanning the contents of the note Nan had written to her, she saw that Nan, being concerned about Mike Smart's scheduled meeting, and because of that, was asking if Mavis and Sadie would do her a huge favour and change the beds before leaving. Having been a nurse before working for airline companies, Mavis considered herself an expert at changing beds. So that request would be no problem at all. Reading on, she saw that Nan was wishing them all well, especially her "favourite" Gordon, and hoped that they would all come back some day. Or better still, just stay for good. Then, remembering Doctor Jack's comment about paracetamol, she made a mental note to check and see if there was some in the little monthly first-aid kit that she always travelled with. Mostly, it was filled with her favourite homoeopathic and herbal remedies but the paracetamol was usually there just in case she was experiencing bad pain. Her crew knew that when her first-aid kit was in evidence, she was likely to be difficult and cranky, and mostly tried to keep out of her way. Going upstairs to the yellow room, she quickly found the tablets and then, returning to the kitchen, she placed them on the tin tray where she planned to put Pete's meal so that he could eat it sitting up in the couch in the front room. She intended that Pete would eat on his own while Gordon, herself, and Sadie would eat at the big kitchen table. Just then, the microwave beeped, letting her know that her jacket potatoes were ready and all that was left for her to do was to grate some cheese from the fridge to fill them, wash the salad, and get everything spread on plates. She was confident that Sadie would soon appear and offer to help her but, if not, Mavis would go and get her from her room where she was probably sleeping. No sooner had that thought come to her than the door at her back opened and Sadie stepped into the kitchen.

"If you'll just finish getting this lot together and set the table for you, me, and Gordon, I'll take this tray along to Pete and see if he is able to eat anything." So saying, she picked up Pete's tray and headed for the hallway.

"How are you feeling, Pete?" she asked the moment she reached the parlour.

"Not too bad," Pete replied. "There is a bit of pain but nothing too serious. Mostly I'm just feeling weak and queasy."

"You'll feel stronger after you've eaten something," Mavis said confidently. "There's paracetamol on your tray as Doctor Jack suggested. Use them sparingly and only when you need to because, in my nursing days before I took to the skies, I saw big guys like you die from a paracetamol overdose."

"If I have to go out on an overdose," Pete smiled, "I'd like it to be on something that was more fun than painkillers. What do you think of Doctor Jack, Mavis?"

"The local para-militarys all think the world of him," Mavis replied. "He's always been great at quickly patching them up. At one time, he was an abortionist in Dublin. The backstreet kind. Some people say he will do anything for money. Others will tell you that he has a serious drug problem and that is why he needs so much of it. It doesn't seem to matter where it comes from. It could be some little girl in trouble or some married man she has gotten in tow with. Or it could be Republican euros, pounds, or dollars. I believe he set up one of the first methadone clinics in Ireland and, apparently, that was a nice little earner."

"That one seems to be as much part of the problem as it is part of the solution," Pete commented, paraphrasing the saying made famous by Eldridge Cleaver, the one-time Black Panther leader. "Hope he wasn't on dope when he treated me," Pete went on. "Though it depends what sort of dope he uses. Keith Richards once famously reported that he had learned to ski on heroin and that is probably more difficult than a doctor patching up a kind of wound that he has dealt with many times before. Has Gordon said much about the band gig tonight?"

"Not much," Mavis replied. "Other than that, along with Sadie and myself, he is definitely doing it. The idea seems to be to leave you here when we head to Sean's and come back here for you after the gig. We'll then take a fairly leisurely drive into Dublin and get the two of you onto your flight to Glasgow. Right now, I should probably get back to the others and see about eating. I guess Gordon will pop along soon to see how you are."

With that, Mavis headed back towards the kitchen, having set Pete's tray across his lap where he was sitting on the couch.

Back in the kitchen, Gordon and Sadie were waiting for her, clearly ready to eat the meal they had prepared. After finishing his meal, Gordon, being the kind of person who hated to be late for anything, began to prepare for the evening's gig long before he really needed to. Nobody watching him would have known what he was doing but slowly and in a relaxed, leisurely fashion, he began to tidy up in Colonel's Fallow so that Nan would have as little to do as possible when they were gone. First, he cleaned the table, washing and dried the dishes, remembering, in passing, that Pete had destroyed several of the dishtowels working on the Lewis gun. Then, picking up a heavy galvanised metal bucket of a type he had not seen in Scotland for twenty years, he took it with him into the front parlour where, sitting the bucket in front of the fireplace, he turned his attention to the little old fireplace set of brush, shovel, and poker all hanging on a neat brass stand sitting on the hearth. Soon, he had the fireplace swept out until it was ready for a fire to be laid in the grate. If he had known where the coal and kindling was kept he would have set the fire but, despite searching, he did not find what he was looking for. Next, he took the bucket through to the kitchen and sat it out in the yard. Then, checking he still had the keys in his pocket, he crossed the farmyard to the barn where the great door was still standing open. With the merest glance into the barn, and speaking out loud in a theatrical tone, looking down at his hands and parodying Lady MacBeth after the death of Duncan, began to declaim. "Out foul Lewis gun that has put blood on to the hands of more than one generation of O'Briens." Shaking his head as if to clear it of dark and gloomy thoughts, he pulled the heavy door shut and locked it before taking himself back indoors where he wrote a note for Nan O'Brien. After leaving it in a spot where the old lady could not fail to find it, he went back upstairs to the yellow room to return all of his bits and pieces to his pack. That done, he slipped into the room Sadie and Pete had shared, where he put everything, he recognised as being Pete's into the battered, green rucksack that was an exact copy of his own. Then, with that self-imposed task completed, he got the two packs and two guitar cases downstairs, where he sat them on the porch. Next, he put his head around the kitchen door, only pausing long enough to tell Sadie and Mavis they were leaving in five minutes time. That done, he popped into the front parlour to see how Pete was doing.

"Just about ready to get going," he greeted Pete.

"Good," Pete responded. "Hope it's a great gig. Bring me a pizza or something because by the time you all get back here, I'll most likely be getting hungry. Get back as soon as you can because there's only so much sleeping I can do."

"We'll probably do a fairly short set, eat our free meal as fast as we can, and be right back here to collect you. How's the leg?"

"About as well as can be expected," Pete replied. "It reminds me of the time I broke this same leg playing football. A grudge match against the Royal Marines. It healed quite fast that time. So here's hoping it does the same this time round and it does sound as if Doctor Jack has treated his share of bullet wounds. So, if he has done his job, it's up to me and my immune system to play our part. Right, Gordon man, out of here because I think I feel another snooze coming on."

Accepting that he had been dismissed, Gordon was soon out of the parlour and out of the front door, where he moved packs and guitar cases until he had laid them on the ground at the rear of the Renault prior to getting them on board.

A minute later, Mavis appeared, slung her case in the back and got into the car on Gordon's left. Not having driven for a while, Gordon was feeling a bit nervous, but, by the time he had run his eye over the controls and knew where everything was, he was feeling a lot more relaxed about the drive ahead. He quickly got the hire car moving towards the house where he had room to get it turned and pointing towards the road. Then, as Sadie appeared with her luggage and guitar case in hand and started to make a space for them in the back of the Renault, Mavis was out of the car and opening the white gates. Finally, with everybody aboard, Gordon signalled for a left turn and, carefully, while feeling a bit rusty in his driving, he drove them out of the house driveway and on to a quiet, in fact, all but deserted road and on in the direction of Galway City.

As Gordon scanned the road signs, he tried to remember where Pete had piloted them and, between that and occasional directions from Mavis, they made good time back to the exact spot in the car park where they had stopped earlier. As Gordon was pulling on his handbrake and switching off his engine, he was convinced that his driving was coming back to him. Getting out of the vehicle, he walked round it, examining each tyre in turn, also giving them an exploratory kick to determine if they were solid or not. During the drive, he had the feeling that the Renault was pulling to the left and found himself wondering if there was a puncture to be dealt with. Discovering there was no puncture was puzzling and he was concerned by the fact that the car was pulling to the left, the side of his body affected by his illness. He began to wonder if it was his brain in some way pulling to the left and not the car. He made a mental note to watch out for that in the future. He was aware that this was so typical of the human condition, trying to make sense of the mind through the mind, the brain with the brain. Just then, Sadie got out of the car and, without wasting any time and guitar case in hand, was off up the sloping pavement, Mavis following in her wake. Knowing how paranoid Pete was about leaving Big Red in unattended parked vehicles, Gordon arranged the Gibson guitar case between the seats with his jacket draped over it by way of camouflage, preventing anyone looking into the vehicle being able to see that there was an instrument inside. Gordon got his own guitar case out of the car until, looking ahead on the pavement for Mavis, realised that she was already out of sight. The first thing Gordon noticed when he arrived in the area where they had busked earlier was that the outside tables and chairs were gone, having been moved inside and what appeared to be a small queue of people waiting to get into the bar was already forming. Some of the faces Gordon recognised from previously. A few feet away from the queue, Mavis and Sadie were waiting for him, already engaged in conversation with what would be a large part of their evening audience.

Greeting the queue with a cheery "Hi!" Gordon walked on into the bar, noticing that the tables and chairs from outside had been moved into the bar proper and were now taking up most of the bar's main space in the middle of the room. There was not enough space to add another single table and most tables were already occupied.

"Evening, Gordon," Sean said, walking towards the open doorway where Gordon was standing. "I made a few phone calls earlier, including one that got your gig a mention on local radio. I think that's where a lot of these folk have come from. I suggest you use the area just in front of the bar as your performing area. There are a couple of chairs sitting beside your band. trunk. So you can use them. Better get started as soon as you can because the place is really filling up and I don't want them wandering off elsewhere."

Leaving his guitar case with Sadie, Gordon approached the two tables just to the left and right of the bar and asked the seven or eight people sitting there if they would mind moving their tables and chairs a couple of feet back in the direction of the side walls to open up the area where Sean wanted them to play.

That accomplished, he began to move the band's. equipment out of the alcove where it had been left earlier, and was just starting to think about what he would place where, when he spotted Mike Smart sitting at a table to his right. With Smart were two older looking, heavyset men, as well as Joey Cassidy, the sound technician.

"Hi, Gordon." Joey hailed the singer/songwriter. "Big Pete not with you?"

"No, he's hurt his leg and can't make the gig," Gordon replied.

"Want me to set up for you while you get tuned and get your head ready to perform?" Joey offered. "I've got a pretty good idea of what gear you guys are travelling with and how you like to play and sound. Without a mixing board of some sort, I won't be able to do a lot for your sound but even an experienced ear doing your amp settings should make some difference."

"I'm sure that it will," Gordon responded as Joey positioned two AER amplifiers and began to set up a singing mike in its stand. "If I'd known you were going to be short handed, I'd have thrown my old guitar into the car and could have sat in with you," Joey commented, straightening out guitar leads.

"Thanks, but I'll be fine," Gordon responded. "With two good singers with me and Sadie being able to add both her finger-picking and her diesel-powered slide playing, that should be adequate."

"I'm sure you're right," Joey agreed, while continuing to set up the M.V.C.B. equipment. Just at that point, Mike smart caught Gordon's eye and waved him over. As Gordon drew close to their table, the Republican and his two companions all rose to their feet as one.

"Gordon O'Brien, Michael and Patrick, my bosses," Mike Smart said briefly, presenting the introductions but keeping them as anonymous as circumstances would allow. Gordon accepted one horny hand and then another, exchanging vigorous and cordial handshakes with the two strangers.

"Both pleased and proud to meet you," the man identified as Patrick said breezily. "One of these Michaels, as I think you know, is Smart Michael, our intelligence officer, this other Michael is defence staff, while I am welfare. Should you decide to come on board with us, after due thought of course, it is myself you would be working with, helping me to look after lots of orphans, widows, and sundry other deserving causes. But you take your time with your decision, Gordon. I am a patient man and, to get the right co-workers, I will go a long way, including the so-called extra mile. I'm sure you would enjoy an American tour."

"I'm also sure that we would," Gordon responded.

"Time will tell." At that point, Gordon realised that something was moving at the corner of his vision and looked up to see Joey Cassidy waving to catch his attention.

"Excuse me, gentlemen," Gordon apologised and crossed over to where the sound tech was waiting for him.

"Glad to see that your kneecaps are still intact," Joey quipped. "Three real heavy dudes you were talking to there. Not guys to ever cross or turn into enemies. You're pretty much set up here. Once you start to play, I'll make any adjustments to your amps that I think will help."

"Thanks, man. I really appreciate your input." Gordon responded.

"Just glad to be able to help, especially after what happened to Big Pete. I was talking to Red Liam earlier and he told me about it. But you can relax, anybody who knows me would tell you how tight-lipped and generally circumspect I am about what I say. So not a single word about what I know will pass my lips."

"I'm grateful for that reassurance," Gordon commented, while extending a hand in Sadie's direction for his guitar case. The slide guitarist passed it over and, in a moment, Gordon had produced his Yamaha and a tuning fork and was starting to tighten his High E string. By the time Gordon had finished tuning to his satisfaction, Mavis had appeared at his side to stand in her usual spot, while Sadie had her instrument out and was starting to tune to Gordon's guitar. After a moment, Gordon began to strum a G chord, Sadie doing the same on her instrument, the smiles that the two guitarists exchanged, testifying to the fact that both were pleased with their sound. Joey was less convinced and hunched over the amplifiers was making small changes. Gordon adjusted his mike stand slightly and then, clicking his mike on, turned his attention to the audience.

"Good evening, folks. It's great to see so many of you turning out for a gig that was very much a last minute affair. This time yesterday, we didn't know we were going to be here tonight but I see that some of you were here with us earlier. But, anyway, just relax, enjoy a drink and the band will do its best to entertain you and make this a pleasant evening for all of us."

With that, Gordon took up a D major chord and, while holding the chord down, used his pinky to play a lively bluegrass flavoured bass run introduction and at the end of his flurry of catchy notes, he settled down into playing a bass heavy picking pattern and began singing:

In the early morning rain, with a dollar in my hand;
With an aching in my heart and my pockets full of sand;
I'm a long way from home and I miss my loved ones so;
In the early morning rain, with no place to go;
Out on runway number nine; Big seven four seven set to go but I'm stuck here
on the grass; Where the cold winds blow;
Where the liquor tasted good and the women all were fast;
There she goes my friend, she's rolling down at last;
Hear the mighty engines roar, see the silver bird on high;
She's away and westward bound;
Far above the clouds she'll fly, where the morning rain don't fall;
And the sun always shines;
She'll by flying over my home in about three hours time;
But this old airport's got me down, it's no earthly use to me;
Because I'm stuck here on the ground, cold and drunk as I can be;
You can't jump a jet plane like you can an old freight train;
So I'd best be on my way in the early morning rain."

Gordon sang the last line three times in all, Mavis singing harmony with him on all of the repeated lines. Then, with Sadie picking along with him, Gordon played a slight variation on his introduction as an ending and stopped to a huge roar of applause, suggesting that the audience knew this fine and evocative Gordon Lightfoot song and liked what Gordon and friends had done with it.

"Thank you, folks." Gordon continued. "I always enjoy doing that one. You know, I've been singing that song for most of my adult life and never get tired of it. Any of you who are singers will know that no matter how many times you have sung a particular song before, you can always find something fresh in it, because no two renderings of it are ever exactly the same. When we first push out the boat that is the start of the first line, we never know exactly in advance just where that boat is going to take us. This next song is also by Gordon Lightfoot and it's called "Sundown." I don't know about over here in Ireland but in the U.K. some years ago, it was a huge hit for Gordon. I used to love the electric guitar solo on that record but you can't do that justice on an acoustic. So for those of you who know the original well, we'll just have to dispense with that fine electric solo." With that, Gordon fingered an E major chord and began to lay down a hard driving rhythmic figure and, as he played a little riff around alternating E major and E 7th chords, began to sing:

See her standing there in her faded jeans, she's a hard lovin' woman;Got me feelin' mean Sundown you better beware if I find you've been sneakin' round my backstairs;
Sundown you better beware if I find you've been sneakin' round my backstairs.

Mavis, who liked Gordon Lightfoot and had a couple of his CD's, came in on the chorus, as did Sadie, the band's sweet three-part harmony filling the bar for a moment. Then Gordon continued:

"See her standing there in her satin dress in a room
where you do what you don't confess;
Sundown you better beware if I find you been sneakin' round my backstairs."

Staying with an E major chord, Gordon played an ending which sounded like a fairly standard blues turnaround. "At one time," he went on, "I used to know a lot more Gordon Lightfoot material including his *Canadian Railroad* trilogy but a repertoire is a bit like a colander just as you are always putting new stuff in at the top, a lot of your older songs are draining away through the holes. If I get the chance to play here again, I'll brush up on my Gordon Lightfoot songs, seeing that you seem to like them." Looking at Sadie, Gordon realised that the slide-guitarist was staring at him and had a look on her face as if thinking of something along the lines of "I wonder what he's going to play next and will it be something I can usefully play along with?" For himself, Gordon had decided not to use up his songs too quickly and had decided to play some instrumentals next. So, fingering a C9th chord, he began to play an instrumental version of "Cocaine Blues, knowing that later on if he wanted to or needed to, he could come back and do the vocal version also. When he was coming towards the end of his Cocaine Blues" instrumental, he began to work around several blues riffs and runs in the key of C, before using them as a springboard to take him into another instrumental, Blind Blake's "Westcoast Blues," also in C. Although Blind Blake had probably been thinking about the American west coast when he had written the piece, having grown up on the West coast of Scotland and with forebears from the West of Ireland had always given the piece extra meaning for Gordon, making it a personal favourite. Gordon ran through the piece at a fast pace before returning to the piece's last eight bars, a bluesy sounding section with lots of note bending and vibrato and repeated that section several times. Just then, as if on cue, Sadie slipped her bottleneck on to the little finger of her left hand and was soon adding her fiery blues runs to Gordon's slick finger picking. Next and without breaking stride or changing key, Gordon went straight into a third instrumental, Gary Davis's "Candyman." This being another one that he could come back to later to do a vocal version of later if his set needed it. With the "Candyman" piece, Sadie pocketed her slide and began to add some more appropriate arpeggios to what Gordon was playing.

By now, the audience seemed to realise that they were witnessing some excellent acoustic guitar playing and broke into enthusiastic ripples of clapping. For his part, Gordon was pleased with the applause but longed for an audience who could applaud in time to the music rather than trying to capture his music in their timing.

"Thank you to both Blind Blake and Gary Davis for those two standard tunes. Tunes that so many guitarists seem to have a version of in their repertoire" Gordon smiled, then went on to announce the band's next number. "For our next song, we would like to do Kris Kristoffersen's Me and Bobby McGee." As he was speaking he grabbed an A major chord and began to pick. Almost at the same moment Sadie went for what guitarists call a long A chord, the sound coming from a metal constructed and a timber built instrument, both playing the same chord though in different inversions. seemed to be pleasing to everybody in the room, including Mike Smart and Joey Cassidy, both of whom were clapping along enthusiastically Gordon went on to play a tricky treble string run by way of introduction, then began to sing:

Busted flat in Baton Rouge and heading for the trains,
feeling nearly as faded as my jeans;
Bobby thumbed a diesel down just before it rained,
took us all the way to New Orleans,
Took my harpoon out of my dirty red bandana
and was blowin' sad while Bobby sang the blues, With them windshield
wipers slapping time and Bobby clapping hands;
Finally sung up every song that driver knew."

As that line came to an end, Gordon repeated his treble string run. And When he was getting into his instrumental stride, Sean had come round from his serving side of the bar and had taken up position a foot or two from where Gordon was sitting, first watching Gordon's hands and then Sadie's, looking as if he was trying to commit to memory what the two guitarists were doing. Thank you, good people," Gordon said to the audience who were still applauding in the background. "Before we did Me and Bobby McGee...."

"That was a little medley of three well-known blues and rag time tunes, which, when put together, I consider to be my party piece. For our next number, I would like to do for you Jesse Fuller's "San Francisco Bay Blues," a song and a singer that are both great favourites of mine. Although Jesse is no longer with us, I was lucky enough to see him when he did a concert in Glasgow's Woodside Halls, a scruffy venue in a run-down and rough part of Glasgow, it also being the hall where I was fortunate enough to be have been able to attend a lecture given by A. C. Bhaktivedanta Swami, two formidable events though so very different." That said, Gordon fingered a bass run that took him into a C Major chord and he began to sing:

> *Walking with my baby, down by the San Francisco Bay,*
> *An ocean liner took her so far away.*
> *Didnt mean to treat you so bad, best gal I ever had,*
> *And if you come back to stay*
> *Gonna be a brand new day, Walking with my baby down by the*
> *San Francisco Bay;*
> *Stayed a while in another city, just about to go insane;*
> *Thought I heard my baby call, the way she used to call my name;*
> *If you ever come back to stay, it's gonna be a brand new day*
> *Walking with my baby down by the San Francisco Bay.*"

Mavis sang a close harmony on that final line, a harmony which brought a smile of pleasure to Gordon's face as he repeated his introductory bass run and used it to take his playing into an ending phrase.

After the harmony that both Gordon and the audience seem to have appreciated, Mavis was content to rest her vocal chords. Lapsing into silence, it was obvious, as Mavis stood at Gordon's side, not singing but swaying her hips to the beat of his guitar, that she was getting more and more confident about being on stage. From time to time, she would dance a few steps, moving away from Gordon and his guitar, to then dance back to her original position. Watching her and liking what he saw, Gordon spoke on. "For our next song we would like to do one written by a man well known for the sombreness of his writing. Ladies and gentlemen, a song by one of popular music's few real poets, Leonard Cohen's 'Suzanne.'" With that, Gordon adjusted his capo, fingered a G major chord, and began to play a syncopated arpeggio.

Sadie had slid her long A chord to her twelfth fret to pick up her G chord in a different voicing and fall in behind Gordon's playing as Gordon began to sing Leonard Cohen's timeless, haunting and atmospheric classic:

> *Suzanne takes you down to her place near the river,*
> *you can hear the boats go by;*
> *You can spend the night beside her and you know that she's half crazy;*
> *But that's why you want to be there*

and she feeds you tea and oranges that come all the way from China;
And just when you mean to tell her that you have no love to give her;
She gets you on her wavelength
and she lets the river answer that you've always been her lover
And you want to travel with her and you want to travel blind;
And you know that she will trust you;
For you've touched her perfect body with your mind;
Now Suzanne takes your hand and leads you to the river;
She is wearing rags and feathers from Salvation Army counters;
And the sun pours down like honey on Our Lady of the Harbour;
And she shows you where to look among the garbage and the flowers;
There are heroes in the seaweed; There are children in the morning;
They are leaning out for love and will lean that way for ever.

Then, as the song went into its intense chorus, Mavis was focused on a restrained, slow, yet very sexy dance sequence. Gordon played an elongated ending built around a cluster of jazzy sounding minor chords then went into a medley of fairly standard and well known Scottish folk songs.

"Thank you, folks," he said, smiling. "You are too kind. That's us finished as we have a drive to Dublin tonight and then a flight to catch."

"Don't tell the whole world what your movements are," Joey Cassidy said, coming over from where he had been sitting talking to Mike Smart. "Or so Big Mike told me to tell you and he's as cautious as they come. That's probably one of the reasons he's still alive because he sure has plenty of enemies, many of whom would be more than happy to put a bullet into him. That was an enjoyable set and some first class guitar. Both Sean and Mike were telling me there's hope that you might move over here with your band and base yourselves in Galway. You've certainly got Sean keen to get back into his own guitar playing again. I think a move over here would be good for your band and no doubt it would be good for our local music scene also. So is there a chance you might move over here Gordon?"

"As they say, the Devil is in the detail," Gordon replied.

"I know a lot of people in the Irish music scene and between that and with both Sean and Big Mike looking out for you, you could hardly go wrong here," Joey enthused. "You should certainly give it some serious consideration. If I was in your shoes, I would."

"There are big and serious issues involved and it's not something that can be rushed into. So despite anybody else's enthusiasm, I can't see any way to make it happen," Gordon replied.

"Anyway, you'll know your own heart and mind or you wouldn't be a Galway O'Brien," Joey commented.

Just then, Sean crossed the bar from Mike Smart's table and, pulling up a seat, sat down at Gordon's elbow. Then, going into his jacket pocket, he laid a pile of euros on Gordon's guitar.

"There's ten each for the two girls, ten each for you and Pete, plus another thirty because I said I would pass the hat for you and I clean forgot. And there was dinner, too. I promised to feed you. This has been just about our busiest night ever with the kitchen running out of food, so feeding you here is no longer an option. My apologies, but it just can't be done. So that said, I've thrown in an extra twenty so you can eat at the airport."

"Eating at the airport will be fine," Gordon said, accepting the money, and was just slipping it into his jacket pocket as Joey Cassidy pushed the M.V.C.B. trunk across the floor beginning to simultaneously dismantle the band's equipment and get it neatly and securely packed into the black trunk. By the time Gordon had retrieved his guitar case and found a yellow duster to wipe down his strings and fingerboard, Joey was just finishing his self-imposed task."

"Where is your van parked Gordon?" he asked next.

"It's just down the slope in the parking area.," Gordon answered. "Not far at all."

"Good," Joey responded. "If you round up the girls and lead the way, I'll bring your trunk along and give you a hand to load it when we get to the car."

Motioning for Mavis and Sadie to follow him, Gordon led the way. The steel wheels on the band's trunk evoked some protesting squawks from the shrubbery round about where several blackbirds seemed to have been ensconced.

"Sorry boys and girls!" Gordon said in the direction of where the blackbirds had been. At the Renault, he opened the back door and, with Joey's help, just managed to get the trunk on board.

"You can never find a Pete when you need one," Gordon quipped.

"Yes, he's a strong lad," Sadie said feelingly.

Then, with a final flurry of waves to Joey from inside the hire car, the Renault was soon moving and slipping away from the parking area. With traffic very light on the road, it was not long before Gordon had them on the last and, by now, familiar stretch of road leading to Colonel's Fallow. Then, as the white gates were sliding into view, Gordon realised that not only had he enjoyed his drive back from the gig, he had found his way back to instrumental pieces he had thought were lost and gone forever. He recalled how, during the gig, pieces which he believed to be lost, completely obliterated by his illness, had come back to him. He had no idea what the process had been but for some time he had suspected that a lot of his music was locked up in a part of his brain that he could no longer access but somehow, during his performance, he had stumbled into that room and, sure enough, his instrumental material was just as he had left it. Watching the black strip of tarmac ahead of him and the stand of conifers growing just short of his destination, he realised his health was improving and that things were falling back into place.

This has been a good day for me, he thought to himself. *What with getting both music and driving back on the same day. The brain must have been reconnecting and rerouting those circuits, just as the experts say that it does.*

Bringing the Renault to a halt just short of the double gates, he waited while Mavis hopped out to open them. In the driveway. He parked the hire car as close to the porch as he could get it so that Pete would only have to cover a few feet to get from the house to the Renault.

"This is going to be a quick turnaround, girls," he announced, leaving the car's engine running. "We're only here to collect Pete. So no disappearing for quick showers or anything else. Mavis, you're a bit taller than Sadie and closer to my height. Can you give me a hand with Pete? With one of us on either side of him it shouldn't be too difficult for us to get Pete from the parlour into the car."

Just at that the front door of the house opened and they could see Pete standing framed in the doorway, leaning on a metal walking stick. As the girls passed him in the doorway, Pete demanded to know how the gig had gone.

"Good, good to great," Mavis threw over her shoulder as she rushed into the house.

"Where did you get that walking stick?" Gordon threw in Pete's direction.

"Your Auntie Nan came round when you were away. She brought the stick that apparently she has had from the time a couple of years ago when she fell and injured herself. She made me a scone and a sandwich and generally fussed over me. She can sure talk and her company helped to pass the time for me. Mike Smart popped in just before you got here. He didn't stay long and I think he was just checking that we would be away by the time his people begin to arrive tonight. When Nan was here, she had three young women with her. The daughters of farmer Quinn from beyond the Wood. It seems that Mike Smart sometimes employs them to give Nan a hand with the house, especially when they have a few guests staying or if a meeting is scheduled. Anyway, they brought their hoovers and dusters and cleaning paraphernalia with them.

Chapter Twelve

Homeward Bound

So the old house is sparkling. What I thought was going to be a long and quiet evening has seen this place a hive of activity. So what is the plan? Are we pretty much just heading off for the airport?"

"Pretty much," Gordon responded. "But what we'll do is this: We'll swing past Tuam on the way there so that I can drop off the keys for this place through the estate agent's letterbox."

"I don't think you need to do that, man," Pete protested. "From what I've seen, both Nan and Mike Smart have keys for the house. So if we just lock up when we're leaving, putting the keys back through this letterbox, no doubt they will find their way to Tuam in time."

"I guess we could do it that way," Gordon responded, his tone saying quite clearly that Pete's reasoning had left him unconvinced. "It's just that Terry O'Farrell was generous with us," Gordon continued. "Generous with his time and with information, as well as letting us visit and stay here. So I want to do the right thing by him and return the keys like I said I would."

"I reckon it was Mike Smart and nobody else who got us the keys to this place," Pete argued. "In fact, where the paramilitaries are concerned, I suspect that there isn't much in these parts where he doesn't have the final say or at least a substantial part of it. I've met heavies before now and he's a heavy for sure. But if you don't mind the extra driving for a Tuam detour, then it's all right by me."

"I enjoyed the driving earlier," Gordon responded. "And who knows, it may be the last time I get to see Tuam. But, more importantly, how's the leg?"

"I'm feeling okay," Pete replied. "The leg is a little bit sore but Mavis's painkillers seem to have it well under control. Not much of a high from them but, as painkillers go, they do their job. The next hurdle will be when I have to get from here to the car and then from the car to the aircraft. Anyway, by this time tomorrow, I'll be home and, after that, it's just a matter of taking things easy and letting nature take its course. I'm confident that Doctor Jack did his part well and soon I'll be seeing his brother."

"Are you ready for the ordeal?" Gordon asked, taking up position on Pete's uninjured side. Mavis moved to Pete's other side and, taking the walking stick away from him, slipped her arm around his waist while Pete steadied himself with an arm around her shoulder. On his side, Gordon took up an identical position and then very, very slowly, like partners in some three-legged race, they started to make their way out of the door and across the porch.

At first, Gordon thought that the step down from the porch to the driveway would be difficult but they passed that obstacle without too much trouble and made their way to the car where Sadie already had the door open so that Pete could just slide inside and lie across two of the seats. Once Pete was on board, Sadie took off her jacket and, rolling it up, placed it as a pillow behind Pete's head. When Pete was settled and seemed to be comfortable enough, Gordon locked up Colonel's Fallow and, mentally thanking the house for its supportive hospitality, he then sent up a little inward prayer, expressing his regret for what had happened to the Army patrol. Next, Sadie slipped into the back of the Renault where she was able to sit on the floor facing Pete. It did not look as if she was going to have a comfortable journey but she was close to Pete and near enough to be useful if he needed help.

"Everyone comfortable, or at least close to it?" Gordon finally asked.

The murmur of comments which greeted that question suggested that the occupants of the hire car, if not exactly comfortable, were satisfied with how and where they were. Gordon took one last fleeting look in his rear view mirror, being careful to keep his gaze clear of that part of the garden where the fuchsia bush had its place. Then as the Renault rolled down the driveway and Gordon switched on his indicator for a turn into the road, he was wondering if life would ever bring him that way again and, if so, under what circumstances. As he found his way and place in the light and sparse traffic flow, he realised that the hot and sunny day was going to extend its bounty into a bright and sunny evening, a circumstance that should make for a pleasant drive to Tuam and then on into Dublin. Retrieving the one tape that they had with them from the Renault's glove compartment, Gordon slipped it into the tape machine and, at the same time, settled back into a relaxed, comfortable, interior place. With Gram Parsons singing "We'll Sweep Out the Ashes in the Morning" filling the vehicle, Gordon decided to concentrate on the happy music being made by the Grievous Angels, rather than allowing himself to become fixated on Gram's pathos and pain. Wishing he had sunglasses with him to help with the glare of the sun filling the car, he was surprised to hear Mavis announce that, "The first outskirts of Tuam should not be all that far ahead. Although Gordon had only been to Tuam once before and that for only a few hours, it was as if his brain had understood and memorised the salient points of the town's street plan.

Ignoring their previous route to Terry O'Farrell's office, he unerringly piloted the Renault and its occupants to the sloping street where the estate Agent's office was situated, pulling the vehicle close to the kerb. At almost the same moment that Gordon had pulled on the handbrake and switched off the engine, he was reaching for the notebook and pen in the breast pocket of his jacket, having decided to write a note for the estate agent so that he could post it through the letterbox of the closed door along with the keys. Realising that it had gotten very hot inside the Renault, he slid his window down to let some air into the vehicle.

"Although we are only going to be here for as long as it takes to write a note and post it with the keys through yonder letterbox, anyone who wants to get out, stretch the legs, and catch a breath of air can do it now," Gordon began, "Excluding Pete who is exempt. Unless, after all, you really want to get out, man, then we will help you."

"No. I ain't goin' nowhere," Pete responded. "I was just dozing off when we got here. So, probably, I will sleep all of the way to the airport."

Just then, Mavis and Sadie climbed out of the car, glad of the welcoming coolness and glad to snatch a quick girls' moment, lounging on the pavement away from the boys.

"So what are you going to do when we get to Dublin, Sadie?" Mavis asked.

"I've got a friend in Dublin," Sadie replied. "She lives not far from the airport, and with her being a singer and an actress, she had arranged some solo gigs for me around the area to coincide with the end of the acoustic festival. So, I will stay with her for a bit, do whatever gigs I can and, when I feel like it, I'll organise a flight home. When we get to the airport today I'll see the band and its equipment on their way and then I'll either jump a cab or I'll ring Polly and see if she wants to collect me from the airport. What about you?"

"I've got a long haul flight coming up in a couple of days time," Mavis replied. "So, like you, I'll see the boys off then probably ring my sister. She's recently bought a big house in Clontarf. So I may connect with her, get a family report while I'm at it." "And where will you be flying to this trip?" Sadie asked. "New York, and then onward to Paris," Mavis replied.

"Are you going to be keeping in touch with Gordon?" Sadie asked.

"I sure mean to," Mavis replied.

Inside the car, Gordon was finishing his note while Pete was doing his best to read it over Gordon's shoulder.

"Dear Terry," Pete read, "With this scrawl, I'm just returning the keys to the old O'Brien place and wanted to thank you for letting me visit the house and have the use of it. I guess Mike Smart and his superiors must have played a part in us being allowed to stay there. It was a wonderful opportunity to see just where the old folks came from and I even got to meet a couple of relatives whose existence I had known nothing about. So, my sincere thanks for everything you did to make my Tuam visit so memorable. You will no doubt know this already, but I have recently had an offer which may make it possible for me to be able to buy Colonel's Fallow but you can ask Mike Smart about that and, if you would, tell him I will ring him once I get home."

"And I for one will be very, very interested to see what the outcome of that call will be," Pete commented. "Gordon O'Brien, guitarist, singer-song-writer and welfare officer. That is the outcome I am hoping to see because I really fancy an American tour and I suspect that a move to Galway would really get my juices flowing. What about you, Sadie?" Pete continued. "Would you and your slide guitar fancy a U.S. tour with the M.V.C.B.?"

"Just with the M.V.C.B. or with you, too?" Sadie asked, climbing into the back of the car and slipping down close to Pete.

"Both," Pete replied.

Just, at which point, Gordon got out of the car and, in a moment, keys and note were deposited through the estate agent's letterbox. Back in his seat in the hire car and ready to get going, Gordon was thinking back to when the band. had first arrived in Galway and how he had asked Pete to commit to memory the configuration of some of the local roads. Casting his mind back to that part of their journey in light of what he had seen of Galway since then, he was confident that he could pilot them to Dublin. Finding his way to Dublin airport might be something else, but he fully expected they would pick up signs for the airport once they got close to Dublin.

Come on, Gordon, it's time to get going, he admonished himself then, leaning his head out of his open window, trying to get a breath of cool air that was just not available. No sooner had he refocused himself back into driving mode and got the Renault settled into a comfortable cruising speed than an orange warning light lit his dashboard and he began to keep a lookout for a petrol station. Almost immediately he spotted a Shell sign and pulled the Renault onto a busy, sun-scorched forecourt, where, in a moment, he was filling up with petrol.

Wish I was in my shorts, he was thinking to himself as he headed towards the garage office to pay. A minute later when he was climbing back into his driver's seat, Pete noticed that Gordon was carrying a white plastic bag.

"What's in there?" Pete immediately demanded, looking at the bag.

"Mivvis," Gordon replied.

"Mivvis?" Pete said as if making a statement and asking a question at the same time. "I haven't seen a Mivvi in years."

"And what's a Mivvi?" Mavis asked in a puzzled tone.

"A Mivvi," Gordon went on, "is something straight out of my childhood because, like Pete, I haven't seen one in years. And, for anyone who has never been initiated into the arcane mysteries of Mivvis, a Mivvi is a strawberry flavoured ice-cream, an ice lolly."

That said, Gordon pulled a handful of ices out of his plastic bag and passed them around until everybody had one and was doing their best to finish it off before the heat in the Renault caused them to melt. Gordon was trying to juggle driving, navigating, and Mivvi eating and, despite having problems with melting ice-cream, soon had them well on their way towards their destination.

As the road seemed to improve and his confidence and driving skills were returning, Mavis produced some wet wipes from her shoulder bag and Gordon, using one to free his hands and steering wheel of sticky pink goo, used a second one to deal with the perspiration from his brow that was threatening to run into his eyes. Glancing into his rear view mirror, it looked as if Pete was asleep, a contented half smile on his face. As Sadie reached over to freshen up Pete's face with one of Mavis' wipes, Gordon was looking beyond the drystane dykes at the sides of the road to the open fields beyond, mostly full of cattle and sheep rather than standing crops.

Lazy farming! he thought to himself.*"Instead of working the land to grow produce that people can eat, they simply fatten up animals before sending them off to be slaughtered, so that carnivores can eat them and later get bowel cancer.Does the world need any more killing or cruelty?* he asked himself rhetorically, secure in the knowledge that it definitely did not. "These Mivvis take me back to when I was a boy of nine or ten." He commented. "It was at a time when few of our family, friends, or neighbours had as yet acquired cars. Anyway, one of my friend's dads, who had a better job than most of the people where we lived, had this little green Morris Oxford Shooting Brake that came with his job. So, one day when I was just a lad, my pal, myself, and my pal's brother—little creep that he was!—You know, the kind of kid who never shares any of his toys with you but always manages to lose or break yours.... It was a hot day, just like this in Scotland, absolutely baking hot, when the man with the Shooting Brake took a bunch of us kids out for a drive in the country. In a garage just like the one behind us, when the dad returned from paying for fuel, he brought back a clutch of Mivvis with him. That was a huge treat for us boys because we were your typical Glasgow street urchins and our drives in the country were few and far between, as were Mivvis. We were usually noisy, grubby, and impecunious, and while we knew every piece of cheap confectionary invented by man and loved by children, including its exact price down to the last farthing, the scant pocket money that we boys got never extended to Mivvis unless, that is, they were bought for us by some extravagant adult. We were clean when we went to bed at night and also in the early morning but during a day of street and back court play we were usually mucky."

In his rear view mirror, Gordon could see that, unless he was intending to eat the stick, Pete had finished his Mivvi. Mavis pulled another wet wipe from her bag and proceeded to dab at her face and forehead.

"Even thinking about those two boys, the neighbours' kids, has reminded me about lots of stuff from that era." Gordon commented with a half laugh, as if amused by his memories. "Where I was growing up back then, it was a four-storey tenement building in a council housing estate. There were eight families in our close, ten kids plus sixteen adults, as well as sundry cats and dogs. In our back green, what Americans would call a yard, there was a little cement structure that we called the midden, because it housed the eight rubbish bins, one for each family in the close. We kids were always under dire threats to prevent us playing in or with those bins, though the midden was something else. In our imaginative play, that little concrete edifice could be one of a thousand things. If it was a day when we were playing with the girls, it could be a shop or, in boys' war games, its flat roof could become the deck of an aircraft carrier or a British ship of the line. The little unglazed windows in the concrete could, with a minimal amount of imagination, become the gun ports where canon would be rolled out on a Spanish galleon. And on those few days when we were playing with the girls, when we stretched a tarpaulin from its roof to the ground to make a makeshift lean-to tent, it could become a clinic or hospital where we played doctors and nurses. There always seemed to be a couple of little girls who wanted to lie you down on their make-believe bed and get your snake belt and shorts off you to play with your willy. Then there was June, the "bad girl," who lived over at my gran's place. She was just a little kid but was always asking me if I wanted to go behind the air raid shelter with her. When I asked her 'What for?' she said I could look at her bits if she could look at mine. 'Only looking, no touching, honest!' was how she put it. The air raid shelter was the place. These were Anderson shelters, usually half-buried in the ground during the war years but after the close of hostilities, they were brought up and turned into garden sheds. Behind the one at my gran's was a secluded spot where precocious little girls liked to hang out."

Just then, Mavis and Sadie were asking Pete how he was feeling, a question he answered with a smile. That in itself suggested that he was doing all right. Inside the car and even with the windows open and cold air blowing, the temperature was still stifling.

Still wish I had put my shorts on, Gordon was thinking to himself as he kept the nose of the Renault pointing in the direction of their destination. As he drove, he was singing a snatch of song to himself,

> *Where are all of my boyhood friends?*
> *Is it too late to say sorry or try to make amends,*
> *All scattered, does it really matter?*
> *Are you still in Glasgow, or is it*
> *Buffalo, Idaho, or Chicago?*

Pete was trying to make out what his band partner was singing, aware that Gordon's conversation about his boyhood, seemed to have put him into song-writing mode.

"Think we'll reach Dublin in the daylight, Gordon?" Pete asked, laying a hand on Sadie's shoulder and giving her neck a friendly squeeze.

"What's up, Pete?" Sadie asked in a bantering tone. "All that talk of doctors and nurses too much for you?"

"I don't know about the daylight, Pete," Gordon replied. "Are we in a hurry?"

"I don't think we need to rush," Pete responded, "but, equally, we don't want to dawdle either. With me being a bit slower and less mobile than usual, getting ourselves and the gear on board the plane might take longer than it did on the way here."

"When we get to the airport, Gordon and I can get the trunk checked in and then I'll get a wheelchair and come back for you, Pete." Mavis suggested.

"And while I'm going on to my friend's place," Sadie explained, "I'll stick around at the airport until I see that the M.V.C.B. are organised and on their way," Sadie volunteered.

Although the temperature was still high, Gordon could see that the sky was not as bright as it had been earlier and could judge that the shadows were lengthening. Then, as Gordon was piloting the Renault round a long shallow curve and starting to accelerate out of it, a movement at the side of the road caught his eye. Almost imperceptibly at first, he began to brake and then, when the hire car was starting to slow, he realised that what seemed to be a British soldier had stepped out of a gate in the field wall on his left and was signalling for him to stop.

Remembering what Pete had said about not wasting time, he felt irritated at the stop command. Then, as the Renault continued to slow down, he could see from the soldier's expression and body language that the man was convinced the vehicle was stopping. The Renault continued to slow until Gordon simultaneously trod down hard on the accelerator and spun the wheel.

As Gordon was swerving round the man, he remembered the incident soon after their arrival in Ireland and, in the moment that the vehicle began to pull away, his gaze swept the grass verge at his inside, convincing himself that no other soldiers were hiding there. Then, just as had happened previously, he was no sooner past the soldier at the gate than camouflage netting was thrown aside and an observer would have seen that two camouflage suited men and a general purpose machine gun set up on a tripod had appeared to view as if by magic. The first burst of fire not only shredded the Renault's rear tyres but shredded the metal of the Renault's wheels as well. When Gordon heard the roar of the machine gun and felt the vehicle suddenly become difficult to control, he realised what had happened and accelerated as hard and fast as he could. Even without tyres on the road the hire car answered his urgent demand for more speed as best it could under the circumstances. Then, as the gunner kept his finger on the trigger of his weapon, he must have leaned down on the Breech end of the machine gun, bringing its deadly muzzle higher, so that the burst of fire that had began at road level came through the rear window of the hirecar at head height. Just prior to the commencement of firing, Mavis, Sadie, and Pete had leaned their heads together in conversation so that when the incoming rounds of machine gun fire pierced the passenger capsule of the Renault, all three were hit in the head and killed instantly. Several of the incoming rounds continued forward to slam into and pierce the back of Gordon's driver's seat and, just at that moment, the army gunner swivelled his weapon so that it swathed from left to right, effectively cutting Gordon in two at the waist. With the last remaining life and strength left in him, Gordon struggled to control the Renault as it veered off the road to smash into the field wall to his left hand side. Then, in the instant that the petrol from the hirecar's ruptured fuel tank burst out and reached the hot exhaust pipe, the

Renault exploded into a seething fireball of flame that rebounded off the field wall, to be catapulted back into the middle of the road and directly into the path of an oncoming cement lorry travelling at speed. In the ensuing collision, the cement truck threw what remained of the Renault and its passengers hard to the right of the road and beyond the right-hand drystane dyke, where it continued to burn in the field where it had come to rest. The road from one side to the other was strewn with burning oil and debris, the heat from the flames adding their own fierce heat to that of the still warm day. In the field where the remnants of the Renault had ended up, a herd of Jersey cows was taking itself as far away from the fiery wreckage as fast as a panicked trot would take it.

Initially, Gordon was feeling confused and disorientated but, despite that, he fought to hold on to consciousness. For some moments, he was not sure who he was or where he was from but, as he struggled to bring memory into some sort of focus, he remembered the name Gordon O'Brien and that recollection brought back to him the fact that he was a musician and singer-songwriter. From there, he was able to recall his friends and his trip to Ireland and that moment was the point where he seemed to be able to unlock the detailed door to his past. He remembered driving the hired car and how it had apparently come under machine gun fire. In the moment he recovered that particular memory, he began to wonder if he had been killed but, because he could see fields, a road and cattle in front of him, he discounted that idea as quickly as it had come to him. In an attempt to settle that question with certitude, he began to struggle with his memory to see what recollections he could summon up of his last moments in the Renault. The last picture he could come up with of the interior of the hire car seemed to be a view of it as if he was looking down into the vehicle's interior from a vantage point close to the inner roof of the car. Looking down at a smashed and shattered interior, littered with body parts and drenched in blood, he was convinced by that split second glimpse that what he had seen must have been part of some near death or close to death experience. *But how can I be dead?* Gordon thought to himself, realising that what he was experiencing was totally at odds with everything he had been taught as a boyhood Christian. If that view had been correct, he should have reached the Christian Heaven, there to be judged and, either kept there or sent elsewhere. Regardless of his old parish priest's enthusiasm for that scenario, that did not seem to be happening. Next, he began to wrack his brains, trying to recall everything he could about the Hindu and Buddhist teachings on reincarnation. But beyond the broad principle that he would be born again, either in a good or a bad situation according to how he had lived his life and previous lives, he could not come up with much. He could not remember if Hinduism or Buddhism contained any concept of a halfway house, anything similar to the Christian concept of Limbo. But if they did, he was unable to recall it. That line of thought reminded him of the *Tibetan Book of the Dead*, which he remembered describing states between life and death on the so-called Bardo Plane and that thought got him to wondering if he had ended up in or was destined for some Bardo-like plane of existence where he would be more or less a ghost. That thought he found somewhat frightening because in various Buddhist sutras he had come across references to "hungry ghosts," these being living entities who had not gone on to their next birth after dying but were earthbound, having no corporeal form while still retaining a range of urges and drives which require a body to be satisfied. He began to wonder what it would feel like to experience the need for food, drink, heat or cold, and sexual consummation but not have a body capable of satisfying those desires. That took him to pondering the situation of the incubus and succubus, subtle entities with powerful sexual drives who can only gratify them by hovering close to the beds of living men and women, trying to feed on the subtle energies of copulating couples, or trying to affect their dreams when sleeping so that, through dreaming, they would give out energies that a hungry ghost could batten onto. As he thought about how it would be a miserable fate, he began to think about a fragment from a poem by Allen Ginsberg. He knew that he was paraphrasing but, as far as he could remember, it was something to the effect of, *Feel sorry for the person who calls to you from a crack in the pavement because he has no body.* He went on to try to remember anything he could recall about hungry ghosts, particularly wondering how long they might survive and seemed to recall that eventually they would fade away and just disperse, the subtle elements breaking down and decomposing, just as a physical body does. Gordon tried to look down at his legs and arms but, while he could see the road and fields, he could not see his own limbs and this convinced him that he had become some sort of disembodied spirit. Although puzzling, his condition did not seem to be unpleasant or painful but then, that might come later. He began to speculate about what the birth experience might be like for a newborn child and began to wonder if it took time to get used to having passed from womb life to something quite different, where air was breathed through mouth or nose, where breast or bottle milk was drunk and nappies were either changed or not. He could understand that, more than likely, it might take some time for a newborn to get used to and make sense of its new situation with dying being something similar

Time will tell, he thought to himself, at the same moment as it struck him that wherever those last moments in the Renault had left him, he seemed to be living in his mind pretty much as he always had. "I am because I think I am." He repeated to himself, taking some pleasure in the fact that he could still remember Rene Descartes' famous words. Then, realising that the day was almost over and dark was not far away, he heard the siren of some sort of emergency vehicle and looked on as a fire-engine appeared on the far side of the incident site, the driver parking it partially on the grass verge, no doubt in an attempt to ensure that the narrow road was not blocked, nor the protruding rear of the appliance becoming a hazard to traffic. Just then, two uniformed men stepped down from the fire engine and began to walk up the stretch of tarmac. The foremost was Willy Mulrine, Tuam master butcher, taxi-cab owner and volunteer fire officer. As Mulrine walked he pulled out a notebook and pen and began to make notes, also drawing a sketch of the site, sure in his mind that his superiors would want to see the notes he had made on the spot and not just a formal report written up after the event. As he walked and continued with his writing, he heard a car at his back and turned to see a black Volkswagen Passat Estate car pull in and park behind the fire engine. As he looked on, he saw the driver's door open and the figure of a priest get out. Crossing the road, the dark clothed figure climbed the field wall and drew closer to Mulrine.

"So what happened here, Willy?" Aiden O'Donnell asked, white-faced. The fire officer paused as if preparing to deal with something that was going to be difficult to even express and then launched into a torrent of words describing what he believed had happened on the road. "Okay, Willy if I just walk up this piece of road and say a prayer or two while I'm at it?" the priest asked.

"Sure it is, Father," Mulrine replied. "But just watch where you put your feet because there are body parts all over this stretch of road." "I'll be very careful where I walk." The priest assured the fire officer. As the hand in his coat pocket closed over the shape of a solid silver *semper gilleum* full of holy water that he always carried when he was in his priest's working clothes, never knowing just what sort of situation he might be called on to help with. The antique holy water holder that he was running his hand over was probably of some value, a gift from an old and retiring priest whom he had worked with in his first parish in Scotland, a parish he had gone to as a much younger man. Finally, turning his back on the fireman, slowly and carefully and squinting at the road surface as he went, he traversed the incident site, offering up prayers, some in English, some in Irish, and others in Latin, as he went. From time to time, he would pause and, wielding the *semper gilleum* much as he would have done at a funerary mass in his chapel, he would send flurries of water out into the shadows, some of it hissing and spluttering where the flames got to it but burned no less brightly.

Just as I saw in the sight, he thought to himself, before going on to speak out loud.

"I told you that you would be all right, Gordon O'Brien," he said in a voice that would have been just audible if someone had been standing very close to him. "By now, lad, you will either be ready for the judgement at our Pearly Gates or ready for your next rebirth. But wherever you are, Gordon, I am convinced you will be fine. Or, as Roy Rogers and Dale Evans used to say, 'So long, good luck, and may the Lord take a liking to you.'" Walking along in heavy silence, the priest was alone in his thoughts until he suddenly swore out loud. "Jesus, Mary, and Joseph for fuck sake!" This was said in a tone of anger, indignation, and exasperation as if the priest was blaming the powers he had just invoked for not having done something to prevent the tragedy that had so recently been enacted on that stretch of road.

Willy Mulrine, now having recorded all of the information he thought he was likely to need, replaced his notebook and pen in his pocket but decided to take one last walk around the vicinity just in case there was something he had missed. As he walked, he was rehearsing in his head the start of the report he would write later.

At the same time, Gordon was still struggling to make sense of his changed circumstances. He had watched the priest walk up the road and then retrace his steps. It was clear from Aiden O'Donnell's demeanour and actions that he was doing something related to the earlier events on the road. Gordon continued to look on as the priest headed back towards his parked car. No sooner had the man reached the car and got back inside the vehicle than the mobile phone in his pocket began to ring and he took a call summoning him to the home of a parishioner coming towards the end of a long and painful illness and, according to his son, very close to the end and in need of the priest and his Last Rites. Gordon watched as the Volkswagen's headlights came on and the priest began to follow them, pulling away at speed from behind the parked fire engine.

Internally, Gordon was attempting to take stock after his sudden and unexpected death. At first, he had experienced a period of confusion followed by a time of insight and apparent understanding when he had more or less decided just to remain as cool as his new circumstances would allow, while waiting to see how things would develop. Now with the priest and his car gone from the scene, except for a few stubborn and lingering flames, the area around him was quite dark. In the darkness some of the clarity that he had been experiencing seemed to have dissipated and he was feeling, not only alone and suddenly lonely, but again was struggling with a sense of puzzlement. Becoming aware of this frame of mind, he started to search his memory, trying to remember every book he had ever read that touched on death or after-death states. In his mind's eye, he could see a long row of volumes in cheap library bindings that he remembered as being the *Proceedings of the Society for Psychical Research* but, while he could remember what those books looked like, very little of their contents would come back to him. After that, he remembered books by Sir Oliver Lodge, C.W. Leadbeater, Harry Edwards, Harry Price, H.P. Blavatsky, T.C. Lethbridge, and Rudolph Steiner. These works reminded him of *The Tibetan Book of the Dead* and, out of all of the books he could recollect, he felt that this one, with its account of the Bardo Plane and accounts of various intermediate states between life and death, was the one most likely to throw light on his situation. Although he had read the Tibetan classic on more than one occasion he could not recall it in any great detail but could remember enough to be aware that, according to Tibetan Buddhism, there are various states between life and death, and decided to keep an open mind on that subject while accepting the strong possibility that that might just be where he was. The more he thought about this and what had happened to him in the Renault, the more convinced he became that he had been killed and was now existing in some sort of ghostly or Bardo -like state. This took him to wondering about how long ghostly life might last for and he recalled some of his reading, maintaining that ghostly life can last for a very long time.

"Long or short, pleasant or not," he told himself, "I'll deal with whatever comes my way and, as always, just do my best in whatever circumstances I find myself in. From there, Gordon began to think about the writing of two authors whose work he had been quite familiar with at one time. H.P. Blavatsky, the Pioneer Theosophist and Max Heindel, the Point Loma Rosicrucian. Both of these thinkers and writers had taught that humans were creatures who existed on various planes of consciousness, an idea that Gordon had also been familiar with from his Vedantic studies. Blavatsky, Heindel, and various commentators on the Vedas, both ancient and modern, had all pointed out that just as humans have a gross physical body, they also have a subtle body consisting of mind, emotions, and intelligence and, just as at death, the physical body begins to break down and rot, so at death when the soul goes on to reincarnate, the subtle body would continue to exist for some time, perhaps for a very long time, although, eventually, the elements of the subtle body would begin to break down and eventually disperse, it being the subtle body that would, in common parlance, come to be known as a ghost. Turning all of this over in his mind, Gordon began to wonder what had happened to his companions in the Renault's final moments, feeling a wave of sadness wash over him at the thought that he might never see any of those friends again.

By now, it was quite dark and with the priest and his vehicle gone and the two firemen having passed out of sight, probably on the far side of the fire engine, Gordon was wondering if his friends were dead and perhaps in the area in a situation something like his own.

Standing in a patch of shadow at the rear of the fire engine that was denser than the darkness round about, Willy Mulrine was lounging close to the fireman who had gotten out of the vehicle with him. Although the two men were standing close to one another, neither man was speaking. Mulrine had seen the priest reach his car and head off into the night. Beginning to think about the incident, whose aftermath he had examined, he realised that, with the loss of life, this event would probably see him involved in almost endless reports, meetings and, in time, formal inquiries. With that prospect in front of him, he decided to inspect the site one final time.

"George," he said to his companion, "I'm going to inspect this whole area again. I would like you to ignore what I am doing and inspect the area for yourself. Make sketches and notes because eventually that way we will have two separate accounts of what took place here."

"Got you, Skip!" the second fireman responded and both men began to separately walk over the area. Mulrine had just reached the point on the road nearest to where Gordon was standing in the field when he heard the sound of a vehicle at his back and turned to see a white Thames van with a blue flashing light on its roof coming to a halt. Mulrine swore silently to himself, recognising the vehicle usually driven by his boss, Dick Durkan, County Fire Officer. Mulrine's heart sank at the prospect of having to deal with such a high-ranking officer and an awkward individual to boot. Just then, Mulrine looked up to see a man in the camouflage tunic of a British Army Corporal coming towards him.

"This mess your work?" Mulrine barked at the soldier, "and what happened here anyway?"

"A car failed to stop for two of my guys and it was a car whose number was on our army list of suspect vehicles," the soldier replied.

"And your guys were as trigger-happy as ever?" Mulrine grimaced.

"They are under strict orders that when a vehicle fails to stop when challenged, they must stop it by firing on it. They have very clear rules of engagement and, as far as I can see, Sir, they stuck to them. It will all come out in the inquiry."

"I can tell you without a shadow of a doubt that the people who were involved here were not paramilitaries and, in fact, were not even Irish but a group of musicians from Scotland, over here for a cultural event," Mulrine went on angrily." That being the case, I don't see how they could have been on anybody's list. I went to the concert they gave at the University on Saturday and also to the masterclass that one of them gave on the Sunday morning."

"That the acoustic festival?" the soldier asked, "because we had reports of some very doubtful people at that event. Mind if I round up my guys and get them and their equipment back to base, Sir?" the soldier asked, beginning to worry in case any of the local Republicans might be planning to set up an ambush in the area for them.

"I would have liked to have seen the back of the whole damn lot of you about seven hundred years ago," Durkan growled, thrusting his notebook and pen in the soldier's direction. "I want the names, ranks, and Army numbers of you and your men.

"So, yes, get yourselves out of my sight and back to base as fast as you can."

As the soldier jotted down the required information and returned the notebook to its owner, he went off to round up his men. Just then, Mulrine heard the door of the Thames van slam shut and looked round to see the corpulent figure of his boss bearing down on him, an angry look on his florid face.

"Surprised to see you here this evening, Sir," Mulrine greeted his superior.

"I was just cruising with the radio on when details of this one started to come through," Durkan replied. "And being close by, I decided to take a look. So, just tell me what happened here, what you've done, and what you plan to do next?"

"I've inspected the area, made notes and diagrams, as well as getting the soldiers' details. Guess I'll see you at the big meeting in the morning? When we've finished here, I'm going to pop into Colonel's Fallow and report this one in. It will be one less report to be given in the morning and, believe me, having seen the agenda for this weekend, it's going to be a heavy session."

"Fine," Durkan responded and, with a wave of his hand, he went striding off in the direction of his vehicle. Mulrine waited until the tail lights of the white van were fully gone before examining his notebook by the light of his pocket torch, the scene had no sooner returned to darkness and quiet with the Thames van gone than the mobile phone in Mulrine's pocket began to vibrate against his side. Half suspecting that it would be his wife calling him at an inappropriate moment and most likely about some minor domestic crisis, he saw that the incoming call was from the County Fire Officer who had just driven away.

"Make sure you have got all, and I mean ALL, of the army details that we will need and, with that done, you can damp the whole place down with foam and then get on your way," Durkan barked in his usual pushy tones.

"You want everything damped down with foam?" Mulrine asked, pushing a guitar case with his foot to move it away from a patch of oily flames. " It's just that where I am standing right now there is a case lying on the ground in front of me that I happen to know contains a valuable musical instrument."

"Put it in your vehicle and take it to the station with you. Eventually, it will find its way back to the next-of-kin. Didn't you use to play guitar or banjo at one time, Willy?"

"Banjo. I used to play banjo way back," Mulrine replied. "And as the big Scots lad said, *They would have to go some to get his guitar.*"

"Didn't catch that last bit," Durkan said in a puzzled tone. "But one last thing from this end. Mike Smart has just passed me, heading in your direction. I told him what had happened down there and that it would be all right for him to stop by and say his farewells to the O'Brien lad. The rescue boys are also heading towards you. They will give the site a good clean up for you. And on that note, after that's done, you can get back to base. Good night, Willy."

"Good night, Sir," Mulrine responded, bending down to pick up the Gibson guitar case.

No sooner had he stowed Big Red on his fire appliance than he saw a green Land Rover Discovery nosing its way towards him. Then, as the driver's door opened, Mike Smart climbed out and began pulling on a black beret as he walked.

"A bad business, Willy," he greeted the fireman. "I had a report of gunfire in the area and was hot-footing it down to take a look when I met your boss, Durkan. A bad business right enough. Although Durkan briefed me on what happened, I would like to hear your version of events, seeing that you were first on the scene and it was you who spoke to the Brits."

"A very bad business.," Mulrine said with feeling, and went on to describe how the band had met its fate. Smart listened to what Mulrine was saying, growing visibly pale. he warned the fireman not to be late for the morning meeting and crossed the road to climb the low wall into the field where some of the fiery wreckage was still smouldering. Approaching the fiery debris, he stopped just short of it and, slipping an automatic pistol our of his jacket pocket, pulled himself stiffly erect and, with the weapon held in both hands, arms extended above his head, he let off three shots into the dark night sky and, through gritted teeth, murmured, "Transvaal Cell salute their own. To fallen friends and comrades!" Inwardly, he began to recite the Lord's Prayer to himself, struggling with the wave of sadness that threatened to engulf him.

"See you at the meeting Willy." He threw over his shoulder and headed for his car. "Got to drop the bosses off at Colonel's Fallow next."

Gordon watched these events unfold and listened to what was being said. He did not know how ghosts did or did not travel but the thought came to him that if he could get back to the old house, he might be able to take up ghostly residence there. He began to wonder if there would be O'Brien family ghosts around the old house and, if so, would he be able to communicate with them? He was beginning to think that this ghostly business might be a long drawn-out affair. So it might be good to have some company along.

While Gordon was still thinking along these lines, Mike Smart reached his car and set off, driving into a sombre Irish night.

"I, too, might drop into the old place later," Mulrine said to nobody in particular, though Gordon heard what he had said. Standing in the cow pasture, Gordon was still feeling shocked, confused, and disorientated but, as time went by, he was becoming more used to his sudden change in circumstances. Always having been a resilient personality, he was sure that he was capable of giving this ghost thing his best shot. For the moment, his two main concerns were the loss of his companions and how he had been severed from just about everything he considered to have been his life, plus wondering just how long his unexpected new circumstances might last. He began to try to remember the mantras he customarily used in meditation and realised when discovering them intact in his memory that he could meditate his way through eternity if need be. Then, because he had remembered only some fairly short mantras, he next turned his attention to the Bhagavad Gita, a Hindu and Vedantic text that he had studied in some depth, even previously committing some of its key verses to memory. Trying to summon one of these up, he discovered that, while the Sanskrit original of the verse he was focussing on was lost to him, the English translation still seemed to be accessible. The verse in question occurs when Arjuna, the hero of the ancient Mahabharata, is put into a situation where he is the wronged party in a fratricidal civil war where he is expected to fight like the wronged champion that he is. On the field of battle when he views so many of his relatives gathered in front of him, relatives whom he is duty bound to offer battle to but is equally duty bound not to harm. In his quandary and perplexity, he turns to Sri Krishna and asks him to explain his true duty to him. Sri Krishna, answering from the standpoint of the soul, which the Gita says, unlike the body, cannot be slain, gives an answer which contains the verse Gordon was trying to remember. *"Never was there a time when I did not exist, nor you, nor all of these kings, nor in the future, shall any of us cease to be."* Gordon began to examine this quotation in his mind's eye and, while buoyed up by the positivity of the verse, he is even more convinced that he might have to exist as a ghost for a very long time. Bearing that thought in mind, he began to look about him, searching the area for his lost companions, just in case they were in the field and in a predicament similar to his own. He recalled how

Michelangelo did not have any friends and did not want any and, in fact, did not speak to anyone, and that scary thought had him examining the field for any sign of his friends. At first he saw nothing, but then he thought he had seen Mavis at the side of the fire engine, staring off into the darkness beyond the appliance's headlight beams. Not sure if he was walking or doing some sort of ghostly floating, he was able to move himself across the twenty or thirty metres to where he thought he had seen Mavis. When he got there, it was Mavis, looking less corporeal than usual and, in fact, looking fairly insubstantial but, nonetheless, it was Mavis. Although Gordon was standing quite close to her, she seemed to be unaware of his presence. When Gordon tried to speak to her, he could not make out his own words, though Mavis's changed facial expression suggested that she had understood him and, from the fact that he understood her, he began to wonder if they were communicating by some sort of ghostly telepathy. Gordon concluded that this must be the case and then as he explained what had happened to them, at least as far as he understood it, he also explained he was going to try to slip inside the fire engine and steal a lift back to Colonel's Fallow.

Chapter Thirteen

Maelstrom

Having concluded that it might be better to be a house rather than a field ghost, Gordon next attempted to take Mavis's hand, but it was as if there was no substance to either of them. A moment later, the closed door of the fire engine opened and he slipped inside, Mavis close behind him. As she moved, she brushed his side with what, at another time, would have been her breast and, Gordon realising that and the fact he did not feel any of the normal stirring in his loins he would normally have experienced in that situation, he began to wonder if the old Buddhist texts were wrong because, although he had become a ghost, he did not seem to have become a hungry ghost.

Just as well, he thought to himself, *saves a lot of frustration*." Gordon became aware that Mulrine was speaking.

"It's suddenly got freezing cold in here, guys. So the sooner we get going and get the heaters working, the sooner we are going to get comfortable."

Hearing that, Gordon moved away from the knot of firemen in the cab in case it was his ghostly presence that was affecting the men. Mavis realised what he was doing and also moved away from the firemen. A moment later, the fire engine's powerful diesel engine burst into life and the appliance was underway, its width almost filling the narrow road as the vehicle's powerful headlights picked out echoing lights in the field, which must have been reflections from the eyes of the cattle. Gordon was feeling exhausted but not being sure whether ghosts slept or not, nor what might happen if he completely relaxed, he concluded that it would be wiser to stay awake and keep his wits about him

At least until he got used to ghostliness.

Back at Colonel's Fallow, Mulrine led the way up to the front door. Gordon was looking around for any possibly angry and unfriendly ghosts who might be hanging around the area of the fuchsia patch, but saw nothing. As he reached the porch, the door was just being opened and he saw Mike Smart standing in the little vestibule.

"I think we should just slip inside," he said to Mavis.

"The yellow room again?" Mavis responded.

"I don't see why not," Gordon continued. "Though this might just be for a longer visit. You go up to the room. I'm going to check out this meeting to see who is taking part and if anything is said which throws light on what happened to us."

That said, both Mavis and Gordon moved into the back kitchen, Mavis settling close to the stairs leading up to the bedrooms, while Gordon took up position to observe proceedings.

Around the table were sitting Mike Smart, the two heavy-set men from Sean's, Willy Mulrine, and another fireman, father Aiden O'Donnell, Dick Durkan, Terence O'Farrell, and three men who Gordon had not seen before were with Joey Cassidy over by the sink, clearly making a pot of tea. On the kitchen table was a collection of bottles and glasses, mostly beer and wine, although there were one or two containing spirits. What I would like to know," Willy Mulrine was saying angrily, "is how come that hired Renault's number was on the Army's suspicious list?"

"If indeed it was," the older Michael objected. "For all we know, we may just be dealing here with an over-zealous soldier now trying to talk himself out of trouble."

"When it gets to the inquiry stage, it will all come out in the wash," Mike Smart interjected.

"But if the number was on that list," Willy Mulrine continued doggedly. "I want to know who put it there and why, because I was the guy who had to go and deal with parts of people. I want to know who put it there and if it was done by their side or ours?"

"It would have to have been done by the enemy or else someone who is at this table would know about it and, until I see hard evidence to that effect, I for one am going to believe that this is not the case," the older Michael said thoughtfully. "Anyone here have anything they want to say or own up to?"

"What puzzles me in all of this," Mike Smart began, "is what could that band. individually or collectively have done to warrant a death sentence because that is what this is beginning to look like. I believe our handling of the S.A.S. patrol incident effectively drew a line under that event. A line which took the musicians out of the frame." There was a long and heavy moment of silence before Smart continued. "I have been wondering about those two fake doctors who managed to vanish so quickly and completely. Do we have any information on that?"

"Well, it seems that when they checked out of their University accommodation, they handed their room keys in at the security office," Joey Cassidy replied. "There they got one of the security fellas to call them a cab and the cabby, one of ours, was asked to drive them post haste to Belfast, where they transferred to a local cab and, again, the driver was one of our lads. Anyway, he was asked to drive them to the nearest police station, which he did. We do know that an army Chinook flew up from South Armagh around that time before flying on to Scotland. And there is some evidence suggesting that our two doctors may have been on board."

"Now, if that was in any way connected with these musicians or if somebody had concluded they were somehow guilty by association, then that might have got them onto somebody's list," The older Michael suggested.

Mike Smart was silent, thinking back to his conversation with Gordon at the wall bordering the Grocery Wood, a conversation he had reported in outline rather than in detail, a fact which underlined for him that Gordon's more dangerous comments were not known to any of the others in the group. For himself, he was content to see the whole thing written off as just a regrettable incident, an unfortunate accident and just one more tragedy among countless others. Nonetheless, there was still a definite feeling of unease in the room.

Mulrine looked decidedly unhappy and the determined thrust of his jaw suggested he was more than ready to debate the issue further.

"I, for one, hope that our hands are completely clean in this one," The older Michael commented. "Because I was really hoping that the O'Brien lad was going to work with us."

"Me, too," Mike Smart responded, "but Gordon thought with little real enthusiasm." If he had become a fundraiser for us, I suspect he could have turned out to be every bit as good as what Captain Jamie was in his day."

"Quite possibly," Mike Smart put in as Gordon noticed that Mavis had gone, drifting up the stairs towards the room that, in years to come, would always be called The Haunted Room, the room where a ghostly couple were often seen and where some people reported hearing snatches of singing and what sounded like a distant guitar being played. Gordon took a long hard look at Mike Smart before leaving the kitchen. Then, with a ghostly shrug of his shoulder and no wiser on the question of who might or might not have plotted his demise, he was gone after Mavis. It was looking as if he was going to be seeing a lot of her.

THE END